Praise for *Wit...*

"Unwinding like a bandage from an old wound, *Withered* explores the cost of living with ourselves and our fragile histories. Wilmot deconstructs the haunted house and finds a home worth saving."

—Andrew F. Sullivan, author of
The Marigold and *The Handyman Method*

"*Withered* is a slow-burn psychological horror that will consume its readers through its exploration of the toxicity and timelessness of grief and the way it chokes all those it touches. Wilmot elegantly illuminates the power of art and its impact on identity and memory, while painting a vivid definition of a ghost town with their prose."

—Ai Jiang, Nebula finalist and author of
Linghun and *I Am AI*

"*Withered* is a compassionate exploration of mental health, hauntings, and the way grief can pull, stretch, or erode our sense of self. Told with wit and warmth, it is a triumph of love in the face of heartache and death."

—Suzan Palumbo, Nebula and
World Fantasy Award finalist

"In this clever mix of *The Haunting of Hill House*, *Stranger Things*, and *Death with Interruptions*, A.G.A. Wilmot has created a narrative that digs beyond the abyss and provides something entirely new, merely by asking a simple question: What if we just said 'no' to Death? It's a beautiful examination not just of grief, but of the will to live — something we sorely need."

—Adam Pottle, award-winning author of *Apparitions*

"*Withered* is the very best kind of horror novel, a book that makes visible the challenges of mental illness and grief and gives them a story that deeply acknowledges that pain and trauma. Beautiful, sad, and scary, and I couldn't have asked for anything more."

—Jen Sookfong Lee, author of *Superfan*

Praise for *The Death Scene Artist*

"From the jaw-dropping opening pages when we meet a protagonist perusing their remarkable inventory of 'outfits,' up to the very last page, this novel kept me riveted. This is a wonderful book, surreal, disturbing and liberating in the very best way."

—Suzette Mayr, author of *Monoceros*

"Wilmot brings a sensually complete sense of reality to the unreal worlds of on- and off-screen Hollywood. Wilmot's serious play with language and with form makes *The Death Scene Artist* a hypnotic, surprising novel that doesn't sacrifice emotion for irony."

—Nathan Ripley, author of *Find You in the Dark*

WITHERED

A.G.A. WILMOT

Published by ECW Press
665 Gerrard Street East
Toronto, Ontario, Canada M4M 1Y2
416-694-3348 / info@ecwpress.com

Editor for the Press: Jen R. Albert
Copy-editor: Rachel Ironstone
Cover design: Ian Sullivan
Cover art: Ian Sullivan
Author photo: Jaime Patterson / Hidden Exposure Photography

LIBRARY AND ARCHIVES CANADA CATALOGUING IN PUBLICATION

Title: Withered / A.G.A. Wilmot.

Names: Wilmot, A. G. A., author.

Identifiers: Canadiana (print) 20230580769 | Canadiana (ebook) 20230580998

ISBN 978-1-77041-703-8 (softcover)
ISBN 978-1-77852-310-6 (ePub)
ISBN 978-1-77852-311-3 (PDF)

Subjects: LCGFT: Queer fiction. | LCGFT: Paranormal fiction. | LCGFT: Horror fiction. | LCGFT: Novels.

Classification: LCC PS8645.I4571 W58 2024 | DDC C813'.6—dc23

This book is funded in part by the Government of Canada. *Ce livre est financé en partie par le gouvernement du Canada.* We acknowledge the support of the Canada Council for the Arts. *Nous remercions le Conseil des arts du Canada de son soutien.* We acknowledge the funding support of the Ontario Arts Council (OAC), an agency of the Government of Ontario. We also acknowledge the support of the Government of Ontario through the Ontario Book Publishing Tax Credit, and through Ontario Creates.

PRINTED AND BOUND IN CANADA

PRINTING: MARQUIS   5 4 3 2 1

For Jaime
Thank you for being my Quinn

"She herself is a haunted house."

—ANGELA CARTER,
"The Lady of the House of Love"

"The dead have no choice but to listen."

—V.H. LESLIE,
"The Quiet Room"

PROLOGUE

FIFTEEN-YEAR-OLD TESSA SWEET STOOD IN FRONT OF THE house at the end of Cherry Lane, ready to destroy it. In her left hand, she clutched a dirty orange canister of gasoline taken from the trunk of her father's car; in her right, a handful of stained, grease-covered rags she'd found in the shed, draped over the handle of the lawn mower he'd promised to repair every summer for five years now. She moved her eyes up from the space between her feet; from the polished black shoes her mother had spit-shined for her that morning, before the funeral—scuffed now, caked in mud from where she'd traipsed through the ravine at the edge of town rather than come home for dinner like she should have. It was preferable to having to sit there with her parents and pretend, somehow, like saying nothing was better than crying; screaming; throwing crap against the wall while a bucket of fried chicken a neighbour had brought over—"Because you need to keep your strength up"—sat cooling in the centre of the kitchen table, uneaten.

Not destroy; kill. Destroy was what you did to an object or a thing.

Killing was for the living. And she would kill this house—*their* house—by any means necessary.

1

She looked up then, at the front of the house, windows dark, front door closed. The porch light flickered. "A short in the electrical," her dad said the day they moved in.

"It's time," whispered a voice in her ear. A voice that shouldn't be—that *couldn't* be, if not for how he'd been taken from her.

It's time, Tessa's mother said earlier that morning, before they piled in the car to head to the cemetery.

It's time, her father said when on the third day following *it*—the *incident*—she had still not gotten out of bed. *You need to eat something; do something; say something.*

"It's time," she echoed, and glanced to her left. To the boy her exact age and height, with an alabaster complexion—an image that she knew was, in fact, out of time. A betrayal of time, really. Because how could—

No. She shook her head.

"It's time," he said again, standing at her side.

She inhaled sharply. "I know." The longer she stood there, the heavier the canister became.

"Tessa, you promised. I would do it myself if I could, but—"

"I know, it's just—"

"You swore to me, you promised you'd do this."

"They're still in there!"

"They'll get out. They'll have time. But they'll try to stop you if you warn them."

"But what if—"

"They're not safe here." His voice swelled, tinged with venom. "You can't protect them."

Tears streaked her face. "Reece, I don't . . . I don't know about this."

"You can't save them! But I can. I can. I swear it."

The porch light continued to flicker, quicker and quicker flashes, as if short-circuiting.

"It's hungry, Tessa. The house wants them, like it wanted me."

"But we—"

Reece stepped forward; the flickering intensified—a startling arrhythmia, like a heart attack in Morse code. "Do it now! While you still can!"

Tessa shut her eyes, items still in hand, and marched up the front steps to the porch and opened the door, which her parents had left unlocked every night that week, every night since—

Inside, it was as warm and thick as it always seemed to be, no matter the season or how many fans her mother set up in each room. It was as humid and sticky as the night outside. She touched the wall with her shoulder as she made her way forward. Felt how hot to the touch it was—like the throat of a living creature. In the kitchen, she unscrewed the cap from the gasoline canister, poured it out all over the floor. She placed the empty container down on the tile floor, accidentally kicking it over as she crossed to the counter. It made a hollow clanging noise; the house sighed then, a drawn-out sound like wood settling. She stopped and stared down the hallway, aghast at what she was seeing: the walls flexing outward as if an artery constricting. Reece, her brother, watched from the porch, staring at her through the open door.

"Don't stop!" he shouted.

"Tessa? Is that you?"

She looked up to see her parents coming downstairs. Quickly, she went over to the oven and cranked every dial to its maximum. She threw several rags atop the slowly heating elements and dropped the last two to the ground, using her foot to thoroughly soak them in gasoline before picking them up and shoving them in the toaster, unsure if it would work but willing to try anything. Reece had told her: she had to try. She had to do what she could to save them. She had to kill the house.

"It's a menace," he'd said when he first appeared to her. She was walking home alone from the library the day after he'd died. She hadn't believed what she was seeing, not at first, but he'd known everything about her. Everything there was to know, from their earliest days together up until their very last. "It's a threat. It wants to devour you whole. The house . . . *our* house . . . it's alive, Tessa. You know this. You've heard it—you've heard *them*. It's alive, and it's dangerous."

You're dangerous, she thought then, watching as the walls heaved; breathed. *And you won't take any more of us.*

She'd known something was wrong with their house from the very beginning. The way people in town talked about it, the whispers-like-song they'd both heard at night—her and Reece—inexplicable hushed tones as if the air itself were attempting to communicate. It's why Reece had followed her to the clearing that night, the one deep in the woods behind their house, where they'd met up with her friends and performed the seance from the book that Eleanor had stolen from her mother's collection.

She'd known there was something more to it, to their house, and now she knew what. It had taken her brother from them, and it would take the rest of them, too, unless she put a stop to it.

"I see you!" she cried, terrified at the sight of the undulating walls. Her heart was beating in time with what looked like ridges, a harp of veins suddenly pushing up through the drywall, like creases in wallpaper, too many to count. They pulsed then, as if in tandem with her insides, her fears. "I see you for what you are."

Her father came up from behind her then and wrapped his arms all the way around her torso, pulled her out of the kitchen and into the hallway as she kicked and screamed and threw her head side to side in a panic.

Her mother came over to them, still dressed in her night-gown. "Oh my god," she said, staring at the kitchen floor awash in gasoline. She ran over to the stove and started switching dials off, used an oven mitt from a nearby drawer to sweep the smoking rags into the sink.

"Stop!" Tessa screamed as her mother unplugged the toaster. "I need to save us!" She wrestled free of her father's grip and darted over to her mother. Grabbed the toaster and threw it and the rags to the ground, but what little flames there'd been were already extinguished.

Her parents took hold of her and hugged her tight, bringing her to her knees—all their knees—coughing and crying amid the gasoline.

"I need to do it." Tessa turned her head, buried it in her mother's chest and started to weep. "He told me to. He told me ..."

And they held her, and cried, and the house shook just enough for Tessa to feel it. She watched, pleadingly, over their shoulders and down the hall, as Reece, her brother, her twin, turned from the door, from the house, and vanished into the night.

PART ONE:

FRESH STARTS

CHAPTER
ONE

TWENTY-FIVE YEARS LATER

OPTIMISM, THE SIGN READ IN LARGE BLOCK LETTERS OVERTOP *population* and a number too small to make out as they drove past. Ellis Lang scoffed as if the word itself were a bad joke—as a concept, it was a difficult enough pill to swallow, but as the name for an entire town? Yeah, that was just too much.

And that was before they—Ellis and their mother—had passed the first of the town's cemeteries, a sprawling once-was-a-meadow that stretched across the horizon outside the passenger window. A rusted wrought iron gate arched above the main entrance. Probably said something like *Shady Acres* or *Restful Gardens*—or it had, once, long ago, before the archway had been taken out by time, or, perhaps, vandals. Time, Ellis assumed, from the brown, rigid-looking grass pockmarking the landscape in scraggly tufts like a teenager's poor attempt at growing a beard.

The two of them drove on. Another minute or so passed, and Ellis wasn't sure if they'd come across another cemetery or if it was still the same one, stretching on and on. There were houses—two in the distance—a couple of stores, and cheap motels dotting the landscape as it hurtled by. Robyn was eager to make it to Black Stone before the movers.

"You'll love it," she assured them that morning, coaxing Ellis out of their asphalt-firm motel bed with a gas station muffin and an Americano. It's where Robyn had grown up, though she hadn't been back in over twenty years, not since she left town to attend university in Cypress. There, she'd met Michael. Eventually, they got married and had Ellis, and Robyn simply never returned. Her parents had both moved away by that point—and had since died—and she hadn't done much to keep in touch with any high school friends. And then Michael, he . . . And then, and then.

There'd always been another "and then"—a reason to not go. "It's not that I don't like the place," Robyn said during dinner a few years back, when Michael once more brought up the idea of a summer road trip to Black Stone, so Ellis could see it for themself. "It's just . . . It's so small, you know? I always felt trapped there. Going back, I . . ." She'd trailed off then, and nothing more about it was said.

And now here they were, on their way to a new life in an old town, minus one part of their previously well-oiled machine.

Ellis knew their mother did not want to be there now, driving toward a place they'd once overheard her describe while on the phone with a friend as "the last stop on the road to fuck-all." They didn't say anything, though. They couldn't; Ellis knew they were only moving there because they didn't have a better option. Their mom couldn't afford their old apartment anymore. And then there was Ellis's "problem"—because life hadn't been difficult enough already.

"I want to stop you right there: Why did you use that word?"

That was the question posed by Ellis's therapist, Dr. Bianca Webb, during their last official appointment the week prior.

Ellis had shifted uncomfortably in their seat, crossing one leg over the other and back again. They folded their arms over their chest, gripping their upper arms as if to create a shield. Their nails were painted a greyish purple, chipped where they'd bitten them almost bloody. Dr. Webb did this every time they used the *P*-word.

"Because that's what it is," Ellis had replied. "I mean, am I wrong?"

Dr. Webb put down her pen and leaned forward. Several braids fell across her face, and she quickly tucked them back behind her ear. "There's so much more to this, Ellis, than simply defining what is or isn't a problem. Our brains and bodies don't adhere to strict binaries like that, no matter what some out there would have you believe. You know that as well as anyone."

Ellis placed one hand on their thigh while the other rested protectively across their belly—a very slight paunch on their otherwise narrow, almost brittle-looking frame. They were still fighting the instinct to visually carve their body into discrete parcels, as if pieces to be cut free. They forced their hand from their midsection, exhaled, and looked up to see Dr. Webb staring intently.

"Don't say it," Ellis said. "I'm trying. I really am."

"I know you are, and it shows. You've made impressive strides over the past six months—"

"—but there's still so far to go."

She smiled warmly. "Therapy isn't a race, Ellis."

They nodded. "I know. It's just . . . Sometimes I wish I could see the shape of . . . whatever it is I'm moving toward."

"Health and self-acceptance, if not love."

Ellis let out a short laugh. "Those start to sound a little less made up the more you mention them." They sighed. "Some days I think humans are just perfectly good monkeys that god fucked up with anxiety and self-criticism."

Dr. Webb sat back. "Not only are those things real," she said, "they're things to which all of us are entitled. Even the fucked-up and anxious among us."

"You jest."

She raised one hand by her head and placed the other on an invisible Bible in her lap. "It's true, I swear it. And here's another truth for you. Are you ready? It's a doozy: you're also entitled to—get this—*hope*."

"Now you're just messing with me."

"I'd never." They both laughed. "In all seriousness, Ellis, you do deserve these things, same as anyone else. You're worthy of them and so much more. You just have to believe it for yourself. Your body is not a problem to be solved. It's important you keep telling yourself this."

"What is it then? What I did to myself?"

She'd called it a piece of them. An aspect of their personality, their entire being, and that looking at it—at anorexia—on its own, as a problem, meant they would always be looking for a way to "solve" it. In reality, she'd said, it was a thing to understand; neither enemy nor obstacle but a piece of their self-puzzle. And that like with their body, they couldn't take it on its own, divorced from the rest of who they were, are, or might one day be. Maybe it was a keystone of sorts, at least for the moment—a thing around which they felt constructed—but it was not separate from or more important to who they were or desired to be than any other piece of them.

Ellis told her she was right. Maybe they even believed it too. But several days later, sitting there in the car watching the town of Optimism pass by, it was still difficult to accept. They felt at once scared, concerned, and a bit like a fraud.

Scared that they weren't as well as they needed to be to deal with the challenges of a whole new town, even if only for a short time before, hopefully, they headed off to university.

Concerned about the role their illness had played in getting them to this place—this "fresh start" that neither of them really wanted but both definitely needed.

Fraudulent in how they smiled and nodded and promised that everything was all right when all they could think of, in that moment, was the sharp tug of the seatbelt digging into their gut, reminding them that it was there.

It wasn't reality, Robyn had said repeatedly during a year's worth of tears and trips to various doctors to see if there was something, anything, apart from the glaringly obvious, that might explain Ellis's threatening and very sudden weight loss. ("It wasn't sudden," they'd shouted one night, a week before finally agreeing to speak to a professional. "You just didn't notice!") They weren't what they saw in the mirror, she'd cried. Couldn't they see that? Couldn't they see what they were doing to themself?

They did, finally, that night. Briefly. As their mother broke down and cried in the other room, they stepped in front of the bathroom mirror and were able to see, plainly, the whole of them, not just isolated pieces as if errors on a test. They saw then the narrowness of their silhouette, their profile, and were suddenly, profoundly, afraid. Afraid of what they saw in the mirror, yes, but also in the realization that their brain had been lying to them. Was continuing to, even now, in the car—trying to convince them of dangerous untruths about their appearance.

Regardless of how they felt, though, they would continue to smile, and nod, and say that everything was all right until they managed to convince themself that it was. Dr. Webb had cautioned them against this—they couldn't bullshit their way to good health. But Ellis didn't know where else to begin. Maybe under different circumstances—maybe if Dad hadn't gotten sick and died, maybe if the fight against his illness hadn't left them with barely enough money to make rent—they could have taken a stronger, healthier approach to getting better.

Right now, though, they just needed to keep their feet on the ground. For Mom's sake, if nothing else. She needed them to be well, they knew that. So, like all great artists, they decided they'd fake it until they made it.

"We're here," Robyn stated cheerfully, breaking Ellis from their thoughts. Together they looked out at the road ahead and the large fir trees lining it on either side. Ellis watched then, through sudden brush and distinctly lush and healthy-looking green grass, as they drove past the sign for Black Stone and left Optimism behind.

Population: whatever, plus two.

It was a little past one in the afternoon on the first day of June when they turned down a small tree-lined street and Ellis saw, for the first time, their new house. It was two storeys with a wide front porch and a plain white fence in desperate need of a new coat of paint. A few of the upstairs windows had been broken, slats teetering on loose, damaged hinges, and the eavestroughs were clogged with leaves and, probably, at least a squirrel carcass or five, but—

It was theirs.

Ellis recalled how scary it had been two months prior when their mom revealed she'd lost her job at the hospital. "Cutbacks," Robyn said matter-of-factly, as if to try and hide her total exhaustion. "The new budget came in and . . ." She awkwardly cleared her throat. "It's okay. We'll make it work. I've already got a new job lined up—working in an ER this time. It's better pay. I even found us someplace to live."

"Someplace . . . else?" Ellis had said, slowly realizing the truth: they were leaving their apartment in the city. *Their* apartment, where all of them had lived. Together.

She nodded. "It'll be all right. It will. I mean I haven't seen it in . . . It's not an apartment this time; it's a *house*. Isn't that great?"

Sure, they supposed. It sounded good, anyway. Just . . . different. *And a lot*, they thought as they stepped out of the car and took in their new house in all its . . . glory. Robyn hadn't been certain they needed so much space, especially with Ellis hopefully going off to school at some point soon, but the price simply couldn't be beat. And as it happened, it was a place she knew—had known. She'd played there with friends when she was a kid and had always loved it. Felt a pull toward it she couldn't quite

14

explain. But no one had lived in that house on Cherry Lane in over twenty years. And the last family that had . . . All Robyn said when Ellis asked was that there had been "an incident." Nothing more.

And now it was theirs. Michael's life insurance policy had left them sufficient funds to cover any remaining bills from his illness, with just enough left over to make a down payment on this house. Yes, it was more space than they needed, but when Robyn saw the listing for it, she just knew: she'd found their new home.

Ellis pulled out their phone to take a pic of the house and paused, realizing they didn't have anyone to share it with—not since they'd nuked all their social media accounts in a last-ditch attempt to curb at least some of their anxieties. They went and stood by the fence to face the house head on.

Right then, the porch light flickered—just once, like a spark from a frayed wire. "Huh," Ellis said. "Someone left a light on for us."

"That's weird." Robyn came over and stood next to them.

They smiled at her. "At least we know something in this place works, right?"

She wrapped her hands around their arm and leaned her head on their shoulder; she was softer than they were, in every respect, though Ellis was slightly taller. "See?" she said. "It's not so bad. We can make this work, right?"

Ellis nodded. "I think so." And they caught themself in an unexpected realization: they meant it. They *believed* it, if only just. They even felt a light flutter in their chest—as if to prove it to themself.

"We'll make this work," she said again, as if to convince herself this time. She looked back then and saw the moving truck as it turned onto the lane.

Robyn waved to the truck with both hands as if she were an air traffic controller. Ellis took her distraction as an opportunity to take a quick walk around the house. To better see what they'd gotten themselves into. The grounds were surprisingly well kept in ways the house wasn't—the grass appeared to have been recently cut despite no one having lived there in many years. Tall, thick trees surrounded them on all sides. The closest house to them was at least thirty yards down the long, narrow tree-lined road that stopped at their front door.

Total privacy, they thought to themself—something of a relief given all the ways their lives had been blown open and picked apart, for better and worse, over the past few years.

"Death has a way of doing that," Dr. Webb said near the end of their time together, as Ellis relayed to her their fears about moving away—how tired and exposed they felt—and at the prospect of starting over somewhere new, especially somewhere as small and out of the way as Black Stone.

Now, seeing how closed off they were from the rest of the community, indeed the entire town (much of which they'd seen on the drive in), Ellis felt a pang of hope. That everything would be okay. That they could make this work.

They continued their tour around the property, pausing briefly to pull out a mound of leaves clogging one of the storm drains out back. Job done, they leaned against the side of the house and sighed—paused, pulled away, turned around, and stared, confused. Reached out and put their hand to the wall.

It was warm.

Not just warm; it was hot to the touch.

Must be where the heater is, they thought before continuing on, making their way back to the front lawn where their mom was helping the movers unload the first round of boxes. She led them up the front steps and unlocked the door.

Ellis was about to ask if there was anything they could do to help, but they stopped when they saw, out beyond the moving truck, a small collection of teens around their age and younger, all staring, watching curiously as the Langs moved in to their new house.

16

Ellis waved. The unexpected crowd hesitated, remaining in place a few seconds more before dispersing without a word between them.

"El?" Ellis turned to see their mom striding over. "What's up?" Robyn asked, staring down the street as the last of the teens disappeared from sight.

They shrugged. "Neighbourhood un-welcoming committee, I guess."

She patted their shoulder. "Give it time," she said. "We were all new kids once."

"Sure." They stayed put as Robyn went back to helping the movers. They'd head into the house in a minute, see what their new life looked like on the inside. For now, though, they simply stood there, watching to see if any of the onlookers would come back, to say hi or ask if they needed any help.

Hope, they thought to themself. *Right*. They turned around then and jogged up the porch steps to the front door of their new house.

Their new home.

CHAPTER TWO

THE TOWN OF BLACK STONE STRETCHED APPROXIMATELY TEN kilometres from one end to the other. The outskirts were undeveloped farmland to the east and a pair of quiet beachfront communities to the south and west. The "downtown," if it could be called that, was a single sad-looking strip mall a mere fifteen-minute hike from Black Stone High, a large red brick building circling a grass courtyard, where Ellis's mom had been a student some two decades prior.

Two days after they arrived, while Ellis was busy stripping wallpaper in the living room, their mom appeared in the doorway dressed in a plaid shirt covered in several shades of paint she'd selected as possible candidates. Her long black hair was tied into a ponytail, and she held a roller dripping wheat—or was it beige? khaki?—onto the dark brown hardwood.

"You know," she said, "the town's also got a fantastic library. It was pretty expansive back when I was there. I bet it's even better now."

Ellis nodded and thanked her, and then returned to stripping wallpaper that looked—and felt—older than they were. They knew what she was doing; she'd been at it for days now, dropping subtle hints and tips about the town as if to sweeten the pot. She wanted them to go out, meet people, get a summer job. More than anything, she wanted them to feel like this could be home. That even if they did go away for school, like she did, they would have someplace to return to.

This went on for the better part of their first week there, during which time Ellis remained focused on helping with repairs and organizing their bedroom at the top of the stairs and just down the hall from Robyn's room. They only left the house once, at the end of the week, to go get some Thai food.

"There's a Thai place in town?" Ellis said as they drove up to a fairly nondescript box of a building, dirty white stucco with a blue overhang that read *TAKEOUT – CHINESE – JAPANESE – THAI*.

"Well, sort of," Robyn said.

"Ah, the three food groups."

"I hear it's pretty good."

Ellis shrugged. "Long as they know how not to fuck up a red curry, I think we'll be okay."

The restaurant itself wasn't so bad—and the food was decently spicy, and fast. The two of them ate mostly in silence. Eventually, Robyn spoke up: "You haven't gone out much this week."

Ellis finished their water. "Yeah, well, things have been a bit chaotic, you know?" They adjusted the napkin in their lap, using it as an excuse to gently touch their stomach, to pinch it as if expecting to find it ballooning outward.

Robyn sighed; Ellis quickly moved their hand. "You're okay," she said.

They nodded. "I know."

She reached across the table, touched their forearm. Squeezed lovingly. "You're okay," she said again, and Ellis nodded. That's just how it was sometimes. Recovery isn't a one-and-done sort of thing; it's a long, often difficult process, and occasionally one takes a step back. The key to surviving, though, to making it through, is in knowing that a step backward is not the same as *falling* backward. Some days, Ellis was able to keep these thoughts at the forefront of their memory; they spent other days still trapped in a bargaining cycle with their mind and body—attempting to quiet one while feeding the other. On the days they felt in control, they saw what they put in their body as fuel: necessary, life-giving. The rest of the time, however, they perceived every bite that passed their lips to be only mass *added* to their body that never worked *with* it.

Robyn cleared her throat. She motioned for the bill. "You wanna get out of here, kiddo?"

"Yeah, sure."

"Maybe this weekend we'll head into town, make a day of it? That way you can see what there is to see."

Ellis didn't know what more there was to see in a town this size. Probably a few shops owned by people who'd lived there their entire lives, a cemetery filled with their ancestors, but not much else. Nothing they could imagine really taking their breath away.

That weekend arrived, and, reluctantly (and with some urging from their mother, who decided to stay behind to get started on a few repairs), Ellis crawled out of bed and got dressed to meet the day. They took a glance in the mirror to see what damage they'd done: long, near-black hair that went down their back, parchment-like complexion, rectangular glasses, nails painted bright purple with silver and black rings on most of their fingers, and a pair of skinny black jeggings and a navy blue T-shirt for an indie band they loved—a yellow graffiti'd face screaming the words *The Go! Team*.

There was some nervousness attached to going out into the world as they were. They'd said as much to Robyn while in the car their very first day in town—that they were worried about drawing too much attention to themself—and she all but slammed on the brakes right then and there.

"I don't want you to ever care about that," she'd said, gripping the steering wheel vice-tight. "You're perfect as you are. Shine your damn light."

"But I—"

"Your father thought so, and so do I. Two against one— we win."

"So mature you are."

But in that moment, getting ready to head out and do some exploring, her words resonated. Ten minutes later, a piece of toast in hand, they'd made it outside and started walking. They were barely at the end of their street, silently praying that they would be able to slide through town without drawing any undue attention, when—

"Hey! New kid!"

Shit.

Ellis took a deep breath and looked to the left. A brown girl their age was walking toward them along the side of the road, beneath a canopy of trees. She had straight black hair to the small of her back, long nails painted black, and an ankh on a chain around her neck. Her eyes were deep set and ringed with heavy black eyeshadow, and her body was rail thin—so thin that the long black skirt she wore billowed as if fitted around a single narrow pole and not two legs pressed together.

Ellis felt a tug of envy at her appearance—at how effortlessly the whole of her came together. "H-hi," they stammered.

"School's that way, if you're looking to register." The girl gave a nod to indicate behind her.

"Thanks, but I'm not— How did you know I was new?"

She rolled her eyes. "Seriously? There isn't a person alive here who didn't see the moving truck roll through town. So, where're you from?"

"Cypress. It's about an hour northwest of—"

"I know where Cypress is. What brings you to town?"

"Stuff," Ellis said, feeling suddenly defensive. They weren't expecting to leave the house to a barrage of questions. "Personal shit."

She smiled with half her mouth. "All shit's personal shit, and in a place like this everyone's personal shit is *everyone's* personal shit. You'll see," she added, and then resumed walking.

"Ellis," they called after her.

She turned. "Come again?"

"My name, it's Ellis."

"Amara." She glanced down. "I like your nails, Ellis. Welcome to Black Stone." And with that, she turned back around and continued on.

"Amara," they repeated. They let out a strained breath, steeled themself, and continued their trek toward downtown.

At the centre of town was a mall—a term, Ellis thought to themself, which seemed extremely generous. It was a squat, dilapidated-looking place, with a defunct department store at one end, a grocery store at the other, and a handful of shops in between—mostly clothing and consignment stores. And a small food court that appeared to be the meeting place for Black Stone's elderly, sporting an A&W, a sandwich place called Nibblers, and an Orange Julius, which Ellis was shocked to discover still existed.

They had just about walked the entire length of the Sandcastle Shopping Centre and were somewhat lost in thought, cataloguing the different shops—wondering if they should come back and drop off a resumé at any one of them—when they almost collided with a girl exiting what looked like an electronics repair shop with a backpack in one hand and a camera bag slung around her neck. She was taller than Ellis, with wide hips, a noticeable belly, and soft upper arms. Black with wavy black hair to her shoulders, she wore a drapey dark blue dress that fell off one shoulder, and gladiator sandals.

Ellis was immediately taken by how striking she was.

Both Ellis and the girl looked up in time to avoid running into one another. "Oh!" Ellis said. "Sorry, I didn't— I never— I wasn't—"

The girl avoided eye contact, lowered her head again, and hurried away, disappearing in the direction opposite Ellis's trajectory.

Ellis sighed and muttered, "Well that could've gone better." *It could've gone worse too*, they thought.

Such was the theme of the day.

Exiting the mall only a few minutes later, Ellis went to see what else they could find that was of interest. Up the street a bit, right next to a bank, they spotted a bustling café called Twitch, the *i* in the logo a cartoon tornado. Immediately their stomach began to rumble—turns out, a single piece of dry toast wasn't enough to carry them through the day. They decided to head inside.

The walls were filled with paintings of the ocean from what they assumed was a local artist. Smooth jazz echoed throughout. They remembered something their dad said once, that coffee shop music was designed to lull people into a relaxed state. This place didn't seem relaxed, though. Nearly every table in the narrow establishment was full, mostly with people around Ellis's age.

They went up to the counter. A gentle-looking woman in her late thirties with light brown hair in a tight bun greeted them. "What can I get for you?"

Ellis perused the snacks on display. "I'll take an Americano, please, and one of those yoghurt-granola thingies." The woman reached over, grabbed one of the parfaits, plopped it down on the counter, and got to work making Ellis's drink. Ellis looked around casually then blurted out, "So, uh, are you, I don't know, looking for help?"

23

The woman came back a moment later and handed Ellis their drink. "Are you asking me for a job?"

"I . . . yes?"

She side-eyed them a moment. "This your first?"

"Is it that obvious?"

"Painfully. You're new in town, right? Yes, that, too, is painfully obvious."

Ellis blushed and held out their hand. "Ellis Lang."

"Patricia Thomas. Ms. Thomas, if you're going to be in my classroom next year."

"Oh, I'm not— I'm done. I just graduated." They paused. "Wait, you're a teacher?"

She nodded as she started wiping down the counter. "Twelfth-grade English. This is just my summer gig. It's my sister's place—I manage it for her."

"Times are tough all over."

"Tell me about— Hey! Mr. Hillcox! That's enough!"

Ellis spun around, spotted a tall, muscular boy with blonde windswept hair. He'd turned his chair to the side and perched his feet atop another chair in front of him, lightly prodding the head of a boy sporting a mop of brown hair cut short above his ears.

Hillcox sat up abruptly, swivelled his seat, and placed both hands firmly on the table in front of him, to the amusement of the girl he was seated with. "Yes, Ms. Thomas. Right away, Ms. Thomas."

"One of yours?" Ellis said.

"Former student, thankfully. Some years, I tell ya, graduation is sweeter than others. Those two over there"—she pointed to the boy again and the girl with him, rose-blush skin and long brown hair to her waist—"Travis Hillcox and Adrian Lavoie . . ."

"Headaches?"

"Migraines. The head-splitting type. So, why do you want to work here, Mr. Lang?" She regarded Ellis again. "Or is it—"

"Mx. works. Or just Ellis."

24

"Okay, Ellis—why this place?"

"Is loving coffee a good enough answer?"

"Close."

"I'm also super punctual and much less of a dick than that guy over there." They thumbed over their shoulder.

Patricia laughed. "Tell you what, we could use some help with bussing, washing dishes, some basic food prep. It's not glamorous work, but—"

"I'll take it!"

"Great! You start next week. Now go, get outta my sight. Enjoy your yoghurt-granola thingie." She smirked. Ellis turned to walk away. "One more thing," she added. Ellis faced her again. "I'm sure I don't have to tell you this, but Black Stone is very small. And the thing about small places, they're that much more difficult to wiggle your way into."

"Uh . . ."

"I'm trying to say . . . look, being new is never easy. Especially not in a town like this."

"What do you mean 'like this'?"

"Oh, it's nothing to worry about. But, well, most of us grew up here. For better or worse, it's a pretty close-knit community. I'm not trying to alarm you, just . . . People are tight here. But they're friendly. Mostly. And if you have any questions, or you just need to talk . . ."

"Thank you, Ms. Thomas."

"Patricia."

Ellis nodded, collected their things, and hustled over to an empty seat. They took a deep breath; they honestly hadn't expected to land a job on their first attempt. It wasn't anything special, but they needed something of a routine—Dr. Webb's suggestion—and this would go a long way toward establishing that. They couldn't wait to tell Robyn.

They'd been seated only a few seconds when someone plopped down in the chair across from them. Ellis looked up—

it was the kid whose chair Travis had used as a footstool only moments prior. He was sweaty and red-faced, and clutching a loose-leaf notebook in one hand—bursting with what looked like Post-its and newspaper clippings—and a mostly empty tea in the other. They recognized him from their first day in town— he had been part of the group standing at the end of the street, watching as they moved in. Before Ellis could speak, the boy thrust his hand out across the table.

"Hey, you're the new kid, right? I'm Dominik."

Ellis started to get up, not wanting to be impolite but feeling drained and in need of some space. They didn't make it far; a hand appeared at their shoulder, gently pushing them back down. Ellis glanced left and right as three more kids their age—two boys, one girl, all of whom they'd seen that first day hovering at the end of the street—sat down at Ellis's table. Ellis sighed. "Can I help you?"

The girl to their right—her hand still on their shoulder— stared at them and said, "You . . . you live there, right? The house?"

Ellis stared at her, confused. "Yes, we live in 'the house.' It's a nice house. It's got walls and a roof and everything."

"No," Dominik said. "We're not talking about *any* house; it's *the* house. The one down at the end of Cherry Lane. That one's yours, right, new kid?"

"Name's Ellis. And . . . yeah, so?"

The collective leaned in all at once.

Ellis looked at each of them. The other's faces showed a mixture of awe and . . . was that suspicion? Ellis felt suddenly hot all over. Overwhelmed. Like they were under a microscope. Like they had been for fucking long enough already. "Okay, so, like, is this a cult thing?"

"We're part of a very exclusive club here in town," Dominik explained. "We're mystery solvers. We embrace the strange, the unknown, the paranormal. All that can't be explained by—"

"Scoobies. Got it."

Dominik looked confused. "What?"

"The Goonies, version two-point-oh. Wannabe Ghostbusters. The Party . . . ?" They caught a circle of bewildered faces. "Not even fucking *Stranger Things*? Christ, don't any of you have Netflix?"

"As I was saying," Dominik continued, "this is a very exclusive club."

"Not interested."

"Wait— Why not?"

Ellis stood up, drink and yoghurt in hand. "Listen up, Junior Crime Stoppers, or whatever you are, I'm not really looking for a new thing to belong to. So, I'm just gonna leave now and—"

"Your house belongs to the devil!" Dominik shouted, palms flat on the table. Snickers, then, from Travis and Adrian's table. Ellis caught them staring at what was quickly turning into a sideshow attraction.

Ellis hesitated. They had to admit it: they weren't expecting that level of intensity. "Come again?"

Dominik grinned. "Ah, now you're interested."

"You just said we've signed a mortgage with Satan. Yes, I'm interested in hearing more about how you're clearly out of your mind."

The others scoffed, incredulous at Ellis's dismissiveness. Dominik glared. "You came here through Optimism, right?"

"Yeah, you . . . kind of have to." There had been other ways into town, once, Robyn had said on the drive in. From the north. But that route had been washed away by a freak storm that hit part of the highway there twenty-five years earlier, carving a new ravine north of town in the process. Several bridges had been proposed over the years, to cross the gap, but so far nothing had made it past the bureaucratic handwringing stage. So, the only way into Black Stone from any of the northern cities was to head southeast and loop back around to the west. "Seemed like a great place to up and die."

"You don't know the half of it. Black Stone borders a handful of small towns just like Optimism. You know what they all have in common?"

"Motel 6s?"

"They've got more cemeteries than they have land on which to build. Rumours were, a few years back they just started cremating everyone—they were running out of space. That town, others like it, they're killing fields. They've got the highest death rates in North America."

"Well that's . . . optimistic." Ellis glanced around. "Get it, Wikipedia Brown? Because the town's called . . . Okay, not sensing a lot of humour in this crowd."

"Black Stone's different," Dominik continued. "Our death rate is lower than the national average. In fact, it's the lowest on the continent. Maybe even in the world. Go ahead, ask around, find out for yourself."

"Sure won't."

Dominik went on, unfazed. "Been that way for decades, as long as anyone can recall. No one knows for sure—town records only go back so far."

"But I'm sure you've got photocopies of them pinned to a murder board in your bedroom, right?"

"Will you stop interrupting me?"

"I will when you start making sense."

"The house down Cherry Lane—your house—is responsible. It's haunted. Everyone here knows it—everyone!"

Ellis cleared their throat, experiencing a twinge of second-hand embarrassment. "So what?"

Dominik was shocked. "What do you mean 'so what'?"

"You're saying my house is haunted and that, what, people here are living abnormally long, healthy lives as a result? You really need to work on your sales pitch if you want me to think that's somehow a negative."

"Your house, it—it's not normal. We've seen things, all of us."

"What kinds of things?"

One of the other boys spoke up: "Well, my mom told me she thought she saw a friend of hers just walking down Marine Drive one day, except it couldn't—"

"It's evil, okay?" Dominik's face was growing red. "Whatever's in there, it's feeding on this town. It's keeping people around. Unnaturally. And until we know why—"

"And you expect me to do something about it?"

"We expect you to be vigilant!" Dominik was shouting again.

Ellis smirked. "Okay, look, I get it. I'm new here, and you're trying to screw with me. But I gotta tell you, this story of yours needs some workshopping. If this house is so bad, why haven't *you* done anything about it?"

"People have tried. But the house . . . it won't let us."

Ellis shook their head. "All right. Look, my coffee is cold, and my yoghurt is warm, so if we're done here, I'm going to go home now to my scary ghost house. But hey, if you want to come over and hang out, just let me know. Me and my Beelzebuddies will whip you up some snacks."

"Beelze-who?"

Ellis blinked twice. "Aaaaaand I'm done. See you around, *Unsolved Mysteries*. Good luck with your satanic panic revival."

Not wanting to risk any further odd encounters, Ellis took a different, slightly circuitous route home after leaving Twitch, cutting through the high school's athletic field and the small forest beyond. By the time they emerged on the other side, Cherry Lane was only half a block away. The sky had grown overcast and grey. They thought back to their run-in with what seemed to be the town's most vociferous junior conspiracy theorist.

Bullshit, they thought as their house came into view. *None of it makes any sense.* As they approached, however, they noticed someone standing at the foot of their gravel driveway.

Getting closer, they recognized the girl they'd almost run into back at the mall. She was holding something up to her face while staring directly at the darkened porch of Ellis's house.

A distinctive sound then—the mechanical snap of a camera shutter—and a flash, followed by a gasp. The girl lowered the camera, letting it hang around her neck. She dropped her hands to her sides and continued to stare.

Ellis walked over quietly. From only a few feet away, they said, "I was going to say take a picture, it'd last longer, but you beat me to it."

She turned and stared at them. Ellis was taken aback. The girl's mouth hung open and her wide, kind eyes were wet, cheeks streaked with tears.

"Jesus," Ellis said, "are you—"

She didn't let them finish. She shoved her camera in the bag slung across her shoulders and walked away at a fast clip. She was a good distance already before Ellis even thought to call after her, to see if she was all right, practically at the corner by the time they saw their mom turn onto the street. They watched as Robyn drove past the girl, the two of them travelling in opposite directions.

Ellis continued to watch as the mysterious girl turned right at the end of Cherry Lane and vanished from sight. Robyn parked and got out of her car. Ellis glanced at her—she was still dressed in her baby blue nurse's scrubs with a maroon hoodie overtop.

"Who was that?" Robyn asked, looking to the far end of the street, searching for the girl who was no longer there.

"Not sure," Ellis said.

"There's something familiar about her . . ." She shook her head clear of the thought. "Here—" She leaned into the backseat of the car and pulled out a bag of groceries, which she passed to Ellis. "Make yourself useful."

"Yeah, sure thing." Ellis was distracted, though, and wondered if the girl was okay. Wondered who she was.

Wondered why their heart was beating just that little bit harder than usual.

Two streets over, the girl unlocked the door to her house and ran upstairs without a word. She didn't even reply when her mother called out, "Quinn, honey, is that you?"

Upstairs, she hurried into her bedroom and shut the door. Slumped hard against it.

A few seconds later, there was a knock. "Quinn? Is everything okay?"

Quinn wiped her eyes and sniffed, hoping it wasn't loud enough to hear through the wood. Hoping her mom wouldn't notice the crevasses in her voice. "I'm fine, Mom," she said at last. "I just . . . I'm getting changed."

From the other side of the door: "Okay . . . well, dinner's in ten."

"I'll be right down." Quinn waited until she heard the sound of footsteps returning downstairs. When she was certain the coast was clear, she pulled the bag from around her neck and took out her camera. She turned it on and started scrolling through photos until she found what she was looking for.

A single shot, clear as day, of the face of the house at the end of Cherry Lane. Black Stone's very own haunted house. She'd never believed any of it, not really, not before today. Now, she didn't know what to believe: her own eyes or the image in front of her, absent the very thing that had led her there in the first place. The reason she'd taken a picture at all.

No, not a thing.

A person.

CHAPTER
THREE

IT WAS TWO IN THE MORNING WHEN ELLIS'S STOMACH, KEENLY aware that they were still awake, decided to announce its presence—as if to say "Hey, jerk face, I thought we had an agreement."

And they did . . . sort of. Ellis had promised some months ago to start feeding it again consistently, and to try and do so intuitively—paying less attention to whether something was "good" or "bad" and more to whether or not it was actually something they wanted to eat. It wasn't always easy, and they still found themself more often than not trapped in a bargaining posture—knowing they needed to feed their body, but still quite aware of just how much they'd taken in already during a given day.

"It's normal to not want the same amount every day," Robyn said on their first night in the house, when she noticed Ellis staring vacantly at the last slice of pizza in the box, knowing they were struggling with whether or not to go for it, knowing something inside them was probably telling them they would feel better if they left just a little bit untouched, showing they still had control. "Your stomach is growing again. That's a good thing—that's what you *want* to happen."

She said, too, that she knew it wouldn't be a simple thing for them to process, that there would be "off" days here and there. Such days were still difficult to get through; they brought up harsh memories that Robyn wished she could eradicate: the image of her child, having poked extra holes in their belt to keep their pants from falling down, standing shirtless in front of a bathroom mirror and thinking they were fat while their ribs—all of them—were plainly visible; a xylophone with pale, slightly yellowed skin stretched over top.

Ellis knew such thoughts had run through their mom's head again earlier that night, at dinner, when she fell silent in the middle of telling them about her first day at work at the nearby hospital. They'd looked up from their plate, where they'd been moving around a couple of roasted potato wedges as if expecting them to up and vanish and caught their mother staring at them, fear in her eyes.

"I'm not restricting," Ellis was quick to say. "I'm just not that hungry right now. Honest."

Robyn breathed out her nose. "Did something happen today?"

Ellis continued to prod at their food. "Not really. Some awkward run-ins with the locals. You know how it is—water, wet."

She folded her arms on the table. "Lots of 'hey, new kid' and ultra-personal questions from a bunch of people you've never met?"

"That, and learning that we live in a haunted house."

"Huh." She shifted in her seat. "That's a new one."

"So, kids didn't talk about this place back when you lived here?"

She shrugged, but Ellis thought they caught sight of a slight tremor, like a shiver. "Kids said all kinds of stupid stuff back then. Much as they do now, I imagine. Every small town has ghost stories of its very own. I—I never paid much attention."

"Yeah, but . . . they seemed *really* certain." Ellis proceeded to tell their mother about what had happened at the café.

Robyn sat back and chuckled to herself. Ellis couldn't be sure, but something about it sounded forced. "Back in school," she began, "I remember there was this club that met every day at lunch. I forget what they called themselves; all I remember is walking in on them and seeing this corkboard covered with poorly printed images and index cards overflowing with notes and these ... ridiculous scribblings. They'd even gone so far as to run brightly coloured lengths of string between each photo and fact like they were detectives solving some great mystery."

"What was it?" Ellis asked.

"An episode-by-episode breakdown of *Murder, She Wrote*—all two hundred–plus episodes laid out with, frankly, alarming detail."

Ellis snorted. "For real?"

Robyn nodded. "They were trying to prove a hypothesis— that Jessica Fletcher was actually television's greatest mass murderer. I mean, all those murders in such a small town, and somehow she was always involved ..." She shook her head. "I won't say they were *wrong*—Jessica Fletcher might in fact be history's greatest fictional monster—but what they were doing ... it was the kind of absurdity that stops being funny when you hit eighteen, especially in a place like this, where there's only so much trouble you can get into."

"Aha, so you admit you've dragged me to a vacuous black hole of boredom."

"Back when I was in ... I can't remember which grade ... something happened to one of those kids. A boy from that group died one night while practising witchcraft or something. Freak heart attack, they said. The doctors, the news. He lived here, in this house, but it didn't happen here. I remember, we were—I mean, we had been ..." She cleared her throat. "The point is, El, people in small towns will find whatever they can to obsess over, no matter how ludicrous. And if they can't find something, they'll make it up instead."

"In other words, they're full of shit."

"Language, kiddo. Honestly, they were probably just messing with you."

Ellis paused, recalling the girl they'd spotted outside their house, the one who'd been crying. They wondered if she was a part of this—if she'd been messing with them as well. It didn't seem so, not in the moment. No, she struck them as being hurt . . . or scared. Of what, they didn't know. They didn't even know her name. Robyn said she'd looked familiar, but when pressed on it, she couldn't say why.

Ellis hadn't finished dinner. They'd remained at the table until their mom went to do the dishes, then got up and discreetly tossed their last few potato wedges in the trash.

And now, in the middle of the night, their stomach was protesting this short-sighted decision. They tried to fall back asleep, but it was no use. Reluctantly, they crawled out of bed and made their way downstairs, careful to keep to the edges of the aged wooden steps so as not to alert the entire neighbourhood to their presence. They placed their left hand on the wall as they descended, noting how oddly warm it was—like the outside of the house had been their first day in town.

They rounded the banister at the bottom of the stairs and went down the hall to the kitchen, where they stood in front of the fridge for several minutes debating between leftovers from the night before or a simple spoonful of peanut butter that they hoped would be enough to shut their stomach up at least until morning.

They sighed and shut the fridge door, then went to the sink to fill a glass with water. Standing there, holding the glass under the tap, they heard something new: a whine—like a tea kettle going off, but . . .

They turned off the tap and listened. They heard:

Wind rustling the trees outside.

Water travelling through pipes.

A fan whirring in the living room down the hall, which Robyn had set up to help dry the freshly painted walls.

Nothing more. No whine. They drank half the glass of water and headed back. They'd just placed their hand on the banister when they heard it again: a plaintive cry that seemed to grow.

It sounded almost musical, like a single note held far too long. Not at all like a part of the house settling, creaking. It continued, getting louder and louder until they were able to make out something behind the din.

A syllable.

A word.

From outside, through the tall windows on either side of the front door, they saw a flash—several of them in quick succession. The porch light flickering. They peered out through one of the sidelights. Seeing nothing out of the ordinary, they opened the door. As they did, the sound cut off suddenly, as if a throat had been slashed midsentence. There was only darkness out past the edge of their driveway, a porch light or two glowed in the distance like fallen stars. The wind kicked up, and Ellis shivered, catching a gust far too cold for June.

The porch light continued to flicker. Ellis tapped its black metal frame until its light was steady again. They took one last look out past the driveway—halted suddenly at what they spotted. A fold, a crease in the dark, like swishing black fabric. It briefly severed the night and then disappeared. "Hello?" Ellis said, quietly, timidly. But there was no response, and whatever they'd seen was gone. Slowly, peering out until the very last moment, they shut the door and locked it. Rested their right hand on the wall next to the door, and jumped a second later when the surface grew hot—almost scalding. They stared at the spot on the wall, searching for . . . something. Evidence of maybe an outlet behind the wallpaper there, or some faulty wiring that they needed to address. Maybe a source for the porch light—the switch for it, which they still had not found.

They heard it once more then, that sound—that whined *word*, tapering, like a plane passing overhead—and shivered. Not from the chill but from the simple, upsetting clarity of it:

No.

O ver years, as a mattress takes on weight from dead skin and oils, so does a house grow dense with the memories of all who've dwelled within. Their experiences seep into the walls, the plumbing, even the foundation; their fingerprints along surfaces and banisters are musical notes, scattered and unstaffed.

"It's like a scale," Samir said, smiling as he passed his wife on the stairs. His face was round and tan, a large sand dollar with short black hair. He pointed to the several small tomato-red stains on the painted white banister of their house—their forever house, he called it—as Analiese scrubbed hard at them with a soapy rag. "Do, re, mi . . ."

Analiese wiped her brow, heat splotching her pale, pinkish skin. Her long hair was in a tight rust-coloured bun tucked beneath a plaid kerchief. She offered her husband the damp rag and bucket. "You're more than welcome to take over, smart guy."

Samir held up his hands. "No-ho-ho thank you, love." He glanced left and right. "Where is your little artist anyway?"

"Oh, so she's mine when she's making a mess, is that it?" she asked. Samir tapped the side of his nose accordingly. Analiese shook her head. "She's in the kitchen. I left her at the table with her colouring book, god help us all."

"I like it," Samir said, staring at the "art" on the walls. "It gives this place character. Who knows—maybe she'll be famous someday. This house will skyrocket in value." He put out his hand, as if giving a presentation. "Behold, the earliest known works of Isabelle, artist extraordinaire."

"Just Isabelle?" Analiese said, looking up. "No last name?"

Samir mock-scoffed. "The best artists are all mononymous. Everyone knows that—it's practically a law."

"Uh-huh."

Samir smiled wide like an excited child and jogged the rest of the way downstairs, leaving Analiese to continue scrubbing furiously at their four-year-old's handiwork, wondering as she did how a child so short had managed to reach high enough to leave such a mess in the first place. Samir reached the bottom of the stairs and his sock feet slid out from under him, sending him careening into the front door, just missing the cardboard boxes stacked to either side.

"You're adorable when you're an idiot," Analiese said, without glancing up. Samir clicked his heels together and bowed before disappearing down the hall into the kitchen.

Our forever house, Analiese thought as she continued to scrub. Swell. Maybe that'll be long enough for me to get this gunk off the walls. Despite her frustration, though, she couldn't keep from smiling. It wasn't finished yet, and they had some things left over from the move that still needed putting away, but already it was everything they'd hoped it would be—everything they'd dreamed it to be those long nights they stayed up discussing all the things they would do, the life they would build for themselves if only they could get out of their one-bedroom Lakefield apartment, which was too tiny for a couple let alone a young family—Isabelle's crib at that point still crammed into a corner of their bedroom.

Or it would be. In time, once they'd settled in.

This forever house. The home they'd scrimped and saved to build for themselves. The one they'd risked everything for. Uprooted themselves for. It would be okay, Samir promised her when she came upon the perfect listing, one they could afford. She could continue to work on her novel, and he could commute. Or, who knew—maybe Black Stone needed an accounting firm, something he could build for himself, brick by brick. He would figure it out, he said—they would figure it out.

They'd dreamed of this. They'd make it work, no matter what.

Minutes later, Analiese was broken from her reveries by Isabelle shrieking wildly from the kitchen. She dropped her rag and accidentally upset the bucket, sending soapy water cascading down the steps. She raced downstairs, careful not to slip on the newly created waterfall.

In the kitchen, she saw Isabelle standing atop her chair, clutching the back of it, screaming at the sight of her father sprawled on his back on the floor. Analiese caught the look of terror in her husband's stunned eyes before she noticed the rigid claw of his left hand, twisting the fabric of his shirt into a distorted pinwheel. Analiese dropped to her knees and put her hand over his. She could feel his fingers, stiff as steel pins in a shattered limb, as he breathed bullets from his nose, jaw clenched. Between tears she told him it would be okay, he'd be fine, really, she swore it, he just had to hold on. For her.

For them.

But by the time she'd made it to the phone on the wall by the kitchen's entrance, he was gone.

That was the first time Death visited the house at the end of Cherry Lane.

CHAPTER
FOUR

ELLIS WOKE TO A TIGHTNESS IN THEIR STOMACH, AS IF THEIR insides had knotted while they slept. It took them only a moment to remember why—and what they'd heard in the night. Or thought they'd heard.

They sat up in bed, remembering the voice—a soft voice, from what little they'd been able to discern. Gentle, a little ethereal. Or it could've been exhaustion or hunger, plain and simple, screwing with their head.

Slowly, unamused at the prospect of facing another day under a very weird small-town microscope, they pushed the memory of the voice from their head and dragged themself out of bed, almost tripping over a pile of dirty clothes next to a short stack of canvases at the foot of the mattress.

Downstairs, they were almost run over by their mom rushing around with half a bagel sticking out of her mouth. Ellis stood aside as she searched for her keys, digging through her purse, which was hanging on the coat rack by the front door. They stared past her.

"Hey, did you ever find the switch . . . ?" they asked.

"Huh?" Robyn looked up and saw Ellis pointing to the window.

"The porch light. I came down for a glass of water last night and saw it flickering, like it had a short."

"I haven't found it yet," she said between bites, chewing only twice before swallowing. "But— Aha!" She pulled out her keys, clenched them in her fist. She went and kissed Ellis on the cheek. "Honey, I'd love to help you sort out the porch light, but I've gotta run—I'm already late for my shift. We'll look for that switch when I get home tonight, all right?"

Before Ellis could respond, Robyn was out the door, waving at them from the driveway. They stood in the open doorway and waved back, watching as she pulled out and drove away.

Their gaze drifted to the right, to the spot on the wall that had almost burned their hand. It had happened, they were sure of it. They reached out, carefully, and put their hand to the spot—just a finger at first, then two, then their whole palm flat against the surface. They felt nothing—no hidden light switch buried beneath the wallpaper, no loose wiring that might have given them a shock. The wall was flat and cool.

They sighed and shut the door.

It was a good thing they hadn't said anything more that morning, Ellis thought on the way into town; they'd decided they didn't want to stay at home alone. Their mom seemed frazzled enough as it was—she didn't need to hear about how Ellis was maybe hearing voices now, on top of everything else.

One major life crisis-slash-adjustment at a time.

Ellis turned off Cherry Lane and onto Main Street, from which it was more or less a straight shot to Black Stone's downtown, and their thoughts shifted to a new concern: whether they would face a similar gauntlet today. The last thing they wanted was to have another run-in with that group of conspiracy-theory fools. No, scratch that—the actual last thing they wanted was to have to consider that maybe those weirdos were right about their house being haunted.

They sighed and started rooting through the pocket of their long black cardigan until they found their headphones, scrolled through a playlist on their phone, and hit play. They sighed and walked on, Frightened Rabbit's "Escape Route" like a balm to quiet their thoughts.

Reality slipped through again a few minutes later when, about ten or fifteen feet ahead, they spotted her—the girl they'd found standing outside their house yesterday afternoon. She turned out of a neighbouring subdivision, head down, both hands clasping the straps of her backpack. She had on black stretch jeans and a red-and-white kimono-style top that ruffled in the morning breeze.

Ellis, a fist of nerves clenching their insides, slipped their headphones down around their neck and jogged up to her. "Hey!" they called when only a few feet away.

The girl jumped and spun around. Her face—a little frightened, a little ready for a fight—slackened when she saw Ellis approaching her. "Jesus!" she said. "Give a girl some warning before you come running up like that."

Ellis slowed to a stop, leaving a small gap between them. "Right. Sorry." They blushed. "I—I recognized you, and I just wanted to say hi, but . . ." They pointed back over their shoulder. "I should probably go and leave you alone forever now."

She sighed. "Are you always this awkward?"

"Only on days that end in *y*."

"Come on." She turned, continuing down the street, not toward downtown but toward the school. Ellis hesitated briefly, then jogged to catch up with her.

"You're heading to the high school? Are you taking summer courses or something?"

"Mrs. Kroeker, the art teacher there, she gave me a key. She lets me use the darkroom when I need it."

"You're a photographer?"

"Wow, your powers of deduction both marvel and astound."

"I'm so good I even picked up on your sarcasm just now."

They walked in silence for another minute or so before Ellis spoke again. "I, uh, guess we saw each other yesterday. I don't know if you remem—"

"You almost ran into me at the mall." She looked straight ahead as she spoke.

"Okay, sure, but you almost ran into me too."

She cast them a quick not-buying-it glance. "How do you figure?"

"There's never just one person involved in a run-in, right?"

"That's some expert-level blame shifting."

Ellis opened their mouth to speak but couldn't think of an effective counter.

"I mean at least I knew where I was going, new kid."

"So, you know who I am."

"Kid—"

"Ellis. Ellis Lang."

"Ellis, everyone here knows who you are."

"Well that's . . ." They exhaled loudly. "Swell."

She shrugged. "It's not like anything stays secret in this place. Half the town saw you and your mom drive through your first day here."

"Is that why you were at my house yesterday? To welcome fresh meat to the grinder?"

She opened her mouth, readying a counter of her own, but could not find the words.

They continued on for another silent, mostly uncomfortable minute. "So, speaking of yesterday . . ." Ellis began.

She hesitated.

"Hey, you two!"

The girl jumped and swung her head to the left. A light wisp of a boy dressed in a maroon vest and jeans was sprint-flailing over to them from an adjacent laneway.

"What is it with white boys trying to scare the crap out of me today?" she said.

"Shit," Ellis muttered, loud enough for only her to hear.

"You know him?"

"Not really. I met him yesterday, at the coffee shop across from the mall. Seems like a clown."

She laughed. "Dominik O'Brien. Black Stone's very own Ed Warren, minus the charm."

"Ed who?"

She stared at them, aghast. "Any self-respecting horror junkie should know the Warrens."

"And what makes you think I like horror?"

She grinned knowingly. "Who else would move into a haunted house?" She started forward again.

"Wait—"

But she sped up as the high school came into view. Dominik called Ellis's name, but Ellis wasn't paying attention; they watched as the girl crossed the street, heading for the main entrance.

"Hey, what's your name?" they shouted.

She turned, cupped both hands around her mouth. "Quinn!" she shouted before turning back around and heading inside.

Ellis stopped in place. "Quinn." They smiled to themself.

Dominik ran up behind them and slowed to a stop. "Ellis, hey, didn't you hear me?"

Ellis continued to stare at the school, for any sign she might reappear.

"Ellis?"

"Huh? Oh, yeah, sure did." They turned and started walking again, back toward downtown, leaving Dominik panting with his palms on both thighs.

Quinn took one final glance back through the doors as Ellis disappeared down the street, Dominik trailing slowly behind them like a lost puppy. Ordinarily, she cringed at the sight of the obnoxious wannabe spirit hunter who, she imagined, had watched *Poltergeist* way too many times as a child and now fancied himself a reimagined version of the Tangina character, only without Zelda Rubenstein's flare for the dramatic. Today, however, she was relieved. Relieved she didn't have to answer any more of the new kid's questions. Relieved, too, she didn't have to listen to any more of Dominik's nonsense. His mother and those who thought like she did . . . they were dangerous. Quinn knew, though. She *knew* the house wasn't evil. She didn't subscribe to their fears.

Still, she wasn't ready to explain, to Ellis or anyone, why she was there yesterday afternoon, outside their house. Having followed something she knew couldn't be. It just utterly could-fucking-not.

Except it was.

The camera hadn't caught it, but it had been there, she was positive. Like she had been the other three times she'd seen it.

She felt it then, same as she had the day before: a mess of emotions welling suddenly, filling her, making it hard to—

She hurried down the empty hall to the school's south wing and ducked into the art room, turned right immediately, and entered the small darkroom off to the side. No one used it anymore—not since Mrs. Kroeker announced two years earlier that they were going all digital (to the relief of a misinformed PTA convinced their kids were getting high off the developing chemicals).

She wanted more than anything to be left alone.

It was all the more disconcerting then, when she went into the empty darkroom of the even more empty school, sat down against the wall facing the entrance with her head in her hands, and looked up a moment later and saw a child's face staring back at her.

CHAPTER
FIVE

ELLIS'S SECOND DAY SPENT WANDERING THE TOWN HAD GONE considerably better than the first, with fewer sets of eyes focused on them like they were some walking, talking car accident. Black Stone was like an alchemical mixture, they found themself thinking as they walked: a perfectly balanced concoction, predictable in every way; but throw a little something extra in there and it all goes to shit. And Ellis and their mother, they were that something extra.

Robyn had grown up there, but she'd been gone so long that no one Ellis encountered seemed to remember her. Not even when they dropped her surname before marriage, Ridley. It made sense: since she'd been gone, she'd finished a degree, fallen in love, started a family . . . and lost part of it too. She'd returned to Black Stone a different person, while by all accounts life here hadn't changed much at all. That whole first week she'd remarked to Ellis how the place seemed "stuck in time."

"But not in a bad way, I suppose," she'd said on their third night in town. "It's like coming back to a book you once loved and finding a bookmark still there, right where you left off, but you can't really remember the plot or the characters or anything."

"Yeah," Ellis replied, while eating takeout on the floor in the downstairs hallway. "But you know what else is great? Reading a new book."

Robyn sighed. "Ellis, you know we didn't have a choice. Black Stone's affordable, and my friend Cynthia was able to put me in touch with the HR director at the hospital here."

Cynthia, whom Ellis had heard about but never met. They were childhood friends, Cynthia and Robyn. Both had left town around the same time, to attend university. After, while Robyn had stayed in Cypress, Cynthia had returned and raised a family in town. The two had kept in contact, though *contact* in this case mostly meant phone calls at Christmas, the occasional email—nothing deeper. Ellis wondered why, since their return, Robyn hadn't reached out to Cynthia. Maybe she just needed some time.

Gradually, they wound their way back to the school and walked its perimeter. They didn't try to go in; they knew, even if the girl from that morning—Quinn—was still in there, she'd probably locked the doors out of safety. They hadn't even realized it, but they'd thought about her on and off all day—how quickly she'd used Dominik's arrival to make a break for it, and in the process managed to not answer Ellis's question.

Not seeing anyone, they decided, finally, to make their way back home. They were fewer than five steps away when—

"Ellis."

They turned and— It wasn't Quinn they saw leaning up against the side of the school but Amara, arms crossed, head down, peering up at them through a gap in her long black hair.

She gave a sly grin and stepped away from the wall. She looked left and right, but the two of them were alone. "Good to see you again," she said. Her voice had a noticeable rasp to it.

"Yeah, it's been a minute."

"Well, from what I hear, you've had an eventful time thus far."

Ellis groaned. "Great. Is that just it then? Am I 'that person who lives in a haunted house' for as long as I'm stuck in this town?"

Amara's left eyebrow shot up. "'Stuck'? Why do you say that?"

Ellis shrugged. "Sorry, I know this is your home and all, but ... I dunno, I feel like this sort of place is geographical quicksand—like, once you're in it, you're in it, and the more you try and fight it the more you just keep sinking." They paused. "It feels small, I guess. Can't say I like that. It's ..."

"Suffocating?"

"In a word."

"You don't have to dance around things, Ellis. It's not like there aren't people here who feel the same."

"Right, of course, I just—"

"But you *are* trapped."

"Uh, what?"

"I said you're trapped," Amara repeated. "This town isn't suffocating; it's cursed. I'm cursed, you're cursed, we're all cursed."

"Oh shit, you're another of Dominik's misfit supernatural conspiracy theorists? Do y'all have a podcast or something?"

Amara scowled. "That fool doesn't have a clue."

Ellis was taken aback by a sudden tremor in her voice, a bass note that caught them by surprise. "Tell me about it. He's the one who tried to convince me that my house is actually haunted."

"He's not wrong: your house *is* haunted." She moved closer, a shadow crossing her eyes. "It's devouring us. That place, your house—it's feasting on this entire town. It has been for generations, and it will continue to do so long after you're gone. No one here understands that. Not fully."

"And you do?"

"Enough to know that you should be terrified. Your house *will* take your life. Yours and your mother's. It's only a matter of time."

Ellis let the moment swell uncomfortably before they clapped their hands together and said, "Well, it's been great talking with you, Amara, but I think I need to run. Far away from here, possibly very fast." They turned and started walking away.

"That home is a threat, Ellis, not just to you but to this entire town. It's already taken more than one person's mind—don't let it take yours."

Ellis ignored her and kept walking. They looked back only once, but Amara was gone—she'd disappeared around the rear of the building, they suspected. Either way, they weren't sticking around.

Ellis was halfway home, listening to a playlist on their phone, when a figure appeared to their left as if out of the blue. Ellis took off their headphones, put them around their neck.

"You probably shouldn't walk down the middle of the street with headphones on," Quinn said. "Someone might think you're reckless."

Ellis glanced over their shoulder to the empty street behind the two of them. "Well, when I finally do see a car around here, I'll give it some thought."

"People here have cars, you know. They just don't use them all that much."

"Because you can walk from one end of town to the other in about an hour?"

"More or less." She paused. "Listen, about earlier, I want to apologize for bailing on you."

"It's fine," Ellis said. "I mean you *did* leave me with a legit weirdo who thinks my house is a danger to us all." They exhaled, recalling their run-in with Amara. "Everyone seems to think it, in fact. Even you."

"What's that?"

"This morning when I saw you, you said you knew my house was haunted."

"Well, yes, but that's not news. Some of us are just more worked up about it than others. There are . . . differing schools of thought on the matter."

Ellis shook their head. "Has everyone in this town lost their minds?"

"Your first mistake is in assuming Dominik had much of a mind to begin with."

"Valid point. What's his deal anyway?"

Quinn shrugged. "Watched a few too many horror films as a kid?"

"Said the girl who name-dropped the Warrens just this morning."

"Pfft, that's beginner-level ghost story shit. Amityville, dude."

Ellis shook their head, lost.

"Okay, I might need to give you a horror education."

"Oh yeah? What makes you think I want that?"

She eyed them up and down: the long black cardigan, dark nail polish, black jeggings, and distressed T-shirt. "Just a hunch, really."

"Well now you're jumping to conclusions. I might just love black, you know. It goes with everything." The two of them continued on, walking slower and slower, Ellis realized, as if they both wanted to take their time. "So, everyone in town thinks my house is haunted then."

"Knows," she corrected them.

"Fine. Everyone knows it. How is that exactly?"

Quinn hesitated, as if selecting her words with the utmost care. "Most people in town say they've seen things," she said at last.

Ellis stopped, faced her. "Seen things? What kinds of things?"

She shook her head. "Let's drop it, okay? You'll just think I'm crazy."

"First: already kinda do, and I'm here for it."

She tried—and failed—to hide her grin.

"Second, I've been here a little over a week and have already been told on multiple occasions that I need to fear my own house, so either this whole town has gone off the deep end or there's something to all this." They thought back to the previous night—the sounds, the heat emanating from the wall near the front door. "Maybe. Potentially."

"Well," Quinn started, "maybe, *potentially*, I can tell you that a lot of the residents here, especially those who've lived here the longest, they've . . . seen people."

"People."

"Yeah."

"As in, dead people?"

She nodded.

"Okay, are we talking zombies or ghosts or—"

"Ghosts," she said plainly, as if it were the most obvious thing in the world. "At least I think that's what they are."

"And you've seen one too," Ellis said. "That's why you were there yesterday, at my house—you saw someone you knew. Who was it?"

"Not who—what," Quinn quickly said. "My . . . pet chinchilla, Chinzilla."

"Really? You called it—"

"I thought I saw him crossing the street," Quinn said, continuing on. "I—I followed him to your home. I tried to take a picture, but as soon as I did, he . . . disappeared."

Ellis watched Quinn as she spoke. They saw the shift as it happened—saw her face scrunch up as she tried to keep from crying.

"Hey, it's okay," they said. "I mean Chinzilla is a terrible pun of a name, but—"

Quinn shook her head, stepped back when Ellis tried to touch her arm. She wiped her eyes. "I should go," she said. "I'm sorry, I'm not usually like this." And she turned down a nearby street—the same one she'd exited that morning.

Ellis's heart started to race as they watched her walk away. "Prove it," they blurted out.

She stopped. "Say again?"

Their stomach erupted into a whirlwind of nerves. "Give me a chance to see that for myself."

"O-okay, but I don't—"

"What are you doing this weekend?"

She paused. Cocked her head to one side. "I'm crying in front of you, for the second day in a row, and you . . . want to go out with me?"

Ellis grinned, blushing so hard they feared they were turning crimson. "I just wanna know for sure that you're okay."

She sniffled, chuckling to herself. "Are you always this bad at pickup lines?"

"I don't really know—this is a first for me. And I really could use that horror education you promised."

She smiled wider, and with a warmth that had been missing only seconds prior. "You're cute," she said. "But I gotta say no."

Ellis nodded. "Right. Okay."

"But," she quickly added, "no doesn't mean never. I just . . ."

"Yeah. Bad timing. The worst. I get it."

"Yeah."

They stood there awkwardly, the two of them staring at one another. Finally, Ellis hooked their thumb down the road. "I should probably get going."

Quinn nodded. "Yeah, totally."

"So . . . I'll see you tomorrow maybe?"

She smiled. "Potentially."

Ellis returned the smile. They waved and continued down the street.

"Hey."

They turned. Quinn was staring at them.

"If you really want to know more," she said, "there's a place in town. A curiosities shop. It's run by a couple of . . . I'm not sure, witches maybe, but, you know, cool ones. They might be able to tell you more. Also . . ."

"Yeah?"

She swallowed hard. "Just because a house is haunted, doesn't mean it's bad." She turned then and walked away, head down.

Ellis remained in place, watching until Quinn was out of sight before turning back around and heading home.

CHAPTER
SIX

THE REST OF THE WEEK PASSED WITH LITTLE FANFARE. ELLIS managed to avoid any further run-ins with Dominik or any other of the town's eccentrics, opting to mostly stay at home and continue slowly unpacking, setting up their room. They were finally feeling like they might start a new painting again after a long dry spell during which they had no desire for it. Both Robyn and Dr. Webb had been encouraging it for weeks, suggesting that doing something normal again, something that they loved, would help with their recovery. But every time Ellis had picked up a brush during the last six months, they'd found themself just staring at a blank canvas, unable to go any further.

Things were starting to shift, though. They could feel it— their focus was coming back to them, bit by agonizing bit.

Dr. Webb explained that it was natural for their creative well to have run dry. "The anorexia, it's starving your mind as well as your body, overwhelming it with calculations and bargains. The disease is a greedy one: it feeds on you—it wants to have all of you and leave nothing for anyone or anything else."

That idea had stayed with Ellis, along with an awareness of the disease's uncompromising reach—like a maelstrom that would, at its full strength, wipe a location off a map entirely.

They still didn't know if it was a thing to be beaten or one you simply learned to live with, but they were hopeful—when they allowed themself the luxury of hope, that is.

They'd not seen Amara again since that day. Part of them hoped to; they wanted to ask her more about their house, but then again they weren't entirely sure that was a topic they wanted to explore any further. Whenever the nature of their house had come up, when either stopped by people in town or when Ellis had decided to do the asking, the response was either a disconcerting silence (which led Ellis to believe people knew more than they were letting on) or an over-the-top fear-laden rant about how dangerous it was, though without ever actually giving any specifics. It was like political factions on a supernatural playing field; Ellis was starting to get a strange sense that they lived in a town divided. Like a battleground of ideas, where everything seemed idyllic on the surface, but take a quick scratch at the skin and oh, looky, there's that unwarranted fear and animosity just itching below the surface.

Best they could tell from store clerks, random passersby, and even from the postal worker whom they'd met on Friday and who seemed to want to deliver their mail and get off their property as quickly as possible, no one had lived in the house for almost twenty-five years, when a young girl, on the night of her twin brother's funeral, tried to burn it down with her and her parents still inside. Rumour was, it was the house's doing—it wanted that girl to kill herself and her entire family. And for those who feared the house, it was, they claimed, only a matter of time before it struck again. Before it convinced someone else to do its nefarious bidding. Some had since tried to burn it down themselves, to put an end to its perceived influence, but the fires never caught. Vandals had broken in year after year, smashing walls and breaking windows and light fixtures, but when they'd returned, everything was as it had been originally. Or so it was said. Ellis wondered how it was that with so many stories of vandalism and attempted arson, the house remained in such good shape. Liveable. They'd imagined ghost houses as being run down and falling apart, with broken floorboards, cobwebs in every corner, rat colonies in the walls. But when they walked in that first day in town, other than a thick layer of dust coating every visible surface, it seemed like the house had been empty for weeks, months perhaps. Not years. Which meant, Ellis realized, that if there was any truth to what they'd heard, to such fantastical tales, then someone or something was maintaining the house.

As they listened to these stories and more, they understood that the young boy's death must have been what their mom had alluded to. But his death didn't explain why people in town thought it was haunted. And from what Ellis had heard, such suspicions went even further back in time. Talk of certain elderly residents wandering the town on overcast days or at night—people who'd somehow been in their late eighties or nineties for ten, twenty, thirty years still out and about, still greeting their neighbours and fellow townspeople, seemingly healthy and without care.

These stories made it difficult for Ellis to sleep at night. Every creek, every gust of wind outside—every time the house settled or the pipes rattled or the porchlight below their bedroom window sparked in the dark of night, they sat up, wondering if it was the voice. If it had returned.

If they'd heard it at all or just imagined it.

They thought of revealing some of this to their mom, but she'd been gone most afternoons and evenings. Ellis hated it when she was on a late-shift rotation. When their dad was alive, it wasn't so bad; there was still someone around to talk to. But ever since . . . the late shifts seemed just that much more unbearable.

Solitary.

It wouldn't be so bad if they had someone else to hang out with, but they hadn't made very many inroads yet, and the one person their age who'd seemed kind to them without there being some sort of catch was nowhere to be found.

For days, Quinn's last words to them had rolled around in Ellis's head—that a haunted house wasn't necessarily a bad thing. What she'd said had been so much the opposite of what they'd heard around town, and they had to know more.

Waking up late on Saturday, the first thing they did was open their bedroom door and look to the end of the hall. Robyn's door was closed and the lights were off. They sighed and went downstairs. At the bottom, they touched the wall by the door, as they had every day since the night it almost burned their palm. But like every other time since, the wall was cool to the touch. Other spots on other walls sometimes felt warmer than what would have been considered normal, but it seemed, to Ellis, like this warmth spread from space to space without rhyme or reason. A trick of an old house.

In the kitchen, there was an empty mug on the counter with a twenty-dollar bill pinned beneath and a note in Robyn's barely legible scrawl: *Go. Get in trouble. I'll see you at dinner—M.* They pocketed the cash and opened the fridge to find something for breakfast. Among cartons of eggs and almond milk were several containers of a meal replacement shake that tasted like Pepto Bismol with a shitload of chalk added to it.

"I don't care if it's gross," Robyn had said some months prior, when she'd handed Ellis their first container of the stuff. "You need to not be a skeleton anymore."

So Ellis stood there, on a beautiful Saturday morning with twenty dollars burning a hole in their pocket and a disgusting half-drunk meal-replacement shake in their hand. They finished what they could and dumped the rest of it down the sink, grabbed their phone and shoes, and headed out.

Standing on the porch and staring down Cherry Lane, they remembered what Quinn had said about the curiosities shop.

That the owners might know something about their house. They decided then that today, finally, was the perfect day to see what more they could uncover about their house and its history. Because at this point, true or not, their curiosity was piqued.

Outside was cool and bright. Ellis was glad to have brought their cardigan with them. A downside, their mother had warned, of having gone from a landlocked part of the region to something more coastal; the southwest corner of Black Stone sat along the edge of the Pacific Ocean.

"It's gorgeous," she'd said, "living right down by the water, but it has its drawbacks too. Summer dies a quicker-than-expected death. And winter? Winter is just . . . damp."

It sounded great, Ellis lied. But now that they'd experienced it, there was a crispness to the air they found unexpectedly satisfying. And on quieter days, when the wind kicked up just enough, they could hear the ocean from their front porch.

Downtown, as they had learned, wasn't much to write home about, to use a phrase their father had employed with great frequency—write home to whom, and why?—but it was large enough that it had taken them several days to see it all. Today they hit the town's main intersection, where everything seemed to be clustered, and headed in the opposite direction of the mall. They passed a large grocery store with a pharmacy next to it on one side of the street, a row of antique shops and restaurants on the other. Half a block farther was a two-screen movie theatre called the Rialto, with an art deco marquee that some poor teen making less than minimum wage had to change by hand from atop what was likely a very rickety ladder. Riding Memorial, the hospital where Ellis's mom worked, was another fifteen minutes' walk in the same direction. It wasn't a large hospital, though it was more than Black Stone needed. It served Optimism as well—apparently, back when the hospital was built the neighbouring town was still somewhat thriving.

Despite the nice afternoon, things seemed pretty dead. There were a handful of people milling about the grocery store, and one gangly, acne-ridden teen flaked out in the Rialto's ticket booth, but otherwise Black Stone was still asleep.

And then there was the small park they passed. Quiet enough, serene enough . . . except for the curious elderly couple they spotted standing under a maple tree and staring up, as if waiting for the rain to clear—but on the sunniest day Ellis had yet experienced in Black Stone. Ellis waved to them, but rather than wave back the couple stepped away slowly, receding from view beneath the canopy.

Ellis walked a little longer, until finally a strange sign caught their eye, just a short distance from the movie theatre and across the street from a delicatessen advertising the best sandwiches in town. It was a black wooden shield hanging off a horizontal post, gently swaying in the breeze. On it was a carving of a cauldron in white below the words *W & S Conundrums and Curiosities*. The building itself was a squat structure, dark brown crossbeams over off-white walls giving the store a look somewhere between "West Coast countryside" and "small town Scottish pub."

The bell above the door chimed as Ellis stepped inside. Right away they noticed how dark it was—the blinds were drawn, and the only light source was the assortment of candles spread about the space, on the various shelves and over by the register. Then there was the smell: like someone had stumbled across an entire hay bale's worth of incense, tossed a lit match into it, and walked away.

The shelves, they noted, were filled with selections of candles, crystals, candles, books on witchcraft and divination, candles, more incense—oh, and some candles too.

They chuckled to themself. *Everything a suburban occult shop needs. All that's missing are some demonic-looking bookends and a skull or two.* And then they turned and saw, on a shelf between a few candles and some candle holders, a tall onyx winged demon cradling a human skull in its palm, poor Yorick–style—because someone, somewhere, needed that for a coffee table centrepiece.

"Oh," came a voice from behind them.

Ellis turned and saw a woman, frost-white skin, late teens or early twenties, medium height, with heavy, long black hair, a slight torso beneath a black dress with a keyhole cutout, and a dark grey shawl draped across her shoulders. Her arms and what Ellis could see of her torso were heavily, beautifully tattooed. The woman stepped out from behind the counter at the far end of the tiny store.

Ellis swallowed. "Uh, hi." The woman didn't respond yet continued to glare, as if looking somewhere far beyond—or perhaps through—them. Ellis pointed to the door. "Are you closed? I can come back."

"Don't mind her," came another voice, causing Ellis to jump. They spun and found themself facing a second woman, quite a few years older, white, similar height and build, dressed in jeans, a plaid shirt, and a toque. She had a takeaway coffee cup in one hand with the Twitch logo stamped across it.

"Sorry?" Ellis said.

The second woman nodded to the first. "Andrea likes to mess with first-timers. Pay her no mind."

Ellis regarded the first woman again—Andrea—as she laughed.

"You looked ready to piss yourself, kid," she said, and moved back behind the counter, where it was darker.

"Andrea," said the second woman, "do me a favour and try not to frighten *all* our potential customers, okay? I'd like to not have to live on instant noodles again this month, if it can be avoided."

Andrea shot her a grin and gave the finger. "Killjoy."

"I know, I ruin all your fun." The second woman had made her way over to the counter to put her coffee down and remove her jacket, draping it across the surface. Andrea stared at it as if it were too much trouble to bother moving. The other woman turned back to face Ellis again. "Now, how can I help you?"

Ellis shuffled in place. "I, uh, I'm not sure. I didn't really come in here for anything. I'm new in town and kind of just exploring. I saw your shop and thought it looked . . . I don't know, interesting, I guess."

She raised an eyebrow. "Interesting?"

"Yeah, you know, cool."

"We don't have any weed here, sorry."

"Wait—what?"

"Whatever your friends told you, it's just incense. This is a legitimate business, and we don't—"

"Alex . . ."

The second woman—Alex—turned to Andrea.

"It's him," Andrea said simply.

"Them, actually."

Andrea nodded. "Apologies."

Alex eyed them curiously. "You said you're new here?"

Ellis nodded.

"And where do you—"

"The house down at the end of Cherry Lane. And I already know what you're going to say."

"Oh?" Alex said. "What's that?"

"That it's haunted. And . . . I was told you might know something about it."

Andrea snort-laughed. Alex grinned and leaned back against the counter. She shook her head. "Kid, your house isn't haunted."

Ellis sighed with relief. "Thank Christ, I was worried everyone in this town had lost their damn minds."

Alex continued: "Haunting implies malevolence, or some sort of nefarious behaviour at play. Usually, in a haunting, a ghost or poltergeist is seeking something greedily—your life or your help. No, your house isn't haunted; it's occupied. There's a difference."

Ellis paused. "O-okay . . ." They pointed over their shoulder to the exit. "I should probably just—"

"Don't go!" Andrea shouted. Everyone fell suddenly silent. She shrank back. "Please."

Alex sighed. "Let's try this again, in a less-creeptacular sort of way, shall we? I'm Alex," she said, hand to her chest, which she then stretched out behind her. "And this is my friend, Andrea. This is our shop. And you are?"

"Ellis. Lang. My mom and I moved here a couple of weeks ago, from Cypress."

"And already you're regretting it because half the people in this town have told you your house is haunted."

"Don't you mean occupied?" They smirked.

Andrea grinned. "You'll have to forgive us. Black Stone has a bit of a history. We're a part of it as much as it's a part of us. We forget that sometimes. It can be a bit of a wall for anyone new to town."

"It's not the wall I'm worried about; it's the weird. And so far, it seems like everyone here's got a case of it. Even—" They stopped themself.

"Even who?" Andrea asked.

Ellis hesitated. "There's . . . I met this girl. She's tall and Black and a photographer—"

"Quinn Simkins," Alex supplied. "And you might want to take a breath—you've gone a little red in the cheeks."

As if on cue, Ellis blushed harder, their face now practically a shade of violet. "Yeah . . . she's the one who told me about this place. You know her?"

"Everyone knows Quinn. Her family's been here for some time now. And when she . . ." Alex fell silent.

Ellis cleared their throat. "Anyway, I thought maybe she was normal, but . . ." They shook their head.

"Normal is relative around these parts, Ellis," Alex said.

"And a little ableist," Andrea called out from behind her.

"My point is," Alex continued, "try not to judge anyone in Black Stone too harshly. A lot of people here have lost something or someone over the years. And almost everyone here has . . . seen something they can't fully explain."

"You mean like ghosts," Ellis said.

"I mean like something they can't explain." She sighed. "If you're looking for answers, you're going to have to dig deeper than just gossip and hearsay. Black Stone isn't like other towns."

"Are you talking about the people-not-dying thing?"

Alex and Andrea seemed confused. "What's that?" Alex asked.

"I heard from some kid, Dominik"—both women groaned in unison—"that people don't die here, I guess? And then this other girl I met, she said the house was feasting off this town and everyone in it."

"Dominik's full of shit—better you learn that now. And the house isn't feasting off anyone," Andrea said. "It's feeding us."

Alex glanced back at Andrea. "Do we tell them?" Andrea nodded; Alex faced Ellis again. She exhaled. "What makes Black Stone different isn't just what's here, it's what surrounds us. You saw it, didn't you? When you were driving into town? The cemeteries in Optimism . . . It's less that death rates here are abnormal and more that it's, let's say, far above normal just outside our borders."

"What are you trying to say—Black Stone is like the eye of a death hurricane or something?"

"I'm trying to tell you that over the past forty or fifty years, the towns that surround ours have been decimated by death, so much so that people look to this place and think it's us that are abnormal and not the other way around. I'm trying to tell you that Black Stone . . . that this town is the one bit of fertile land in a plot of irradiated earth, and that your house is the reason why. It's our protection, not our condemnation." Alex paced between

Ellis and the counter. She continued: "Have you ever heard the story about Death's day off?"

It was Ellis's turn to cock an eyebrow. "Are you talking about that classic Brad Pitt film?"

Andrea almost exploded out from behind the counter. "First," she said, finger in the air like a knife, "*Meet Joe Black* is not a goddamn 'classic,' and it never will be. Second"—another finger, straight up—"I'm offended on behalf of Mitchell Leisen. *Death Takes a Holiday*, now that's a classic. *Meet Joe Black*? Jesus tap dancing—"

Alex put up a hand. "Can I continue, please?" She faced Ellis again. "It's an old story and does not involve Brad Pitt in any way. I heard it first from my dad. It went like this: Death arrives at a small town it has been to many times before. It roams the same streets, visits the same houses, and takes members of the same families that have lived there since time immemorial. One day, a woman sees Death sitting on her doorstep looking forlorn. She knows Death is there for her, but something's different. Something is just . . . off. She asks what's wrong, and Death tells her It's tired, that It doesn't want to just keep doing the same thing anymore, to the same people It's come to know and maybe even understand. But It can't stop—It's a force of nature, and if It doesn't do Its job, who will? So, the young woman says, 'I can help you, if you spare my life.' Death considers the woman's offer, and in a spurt of unexpected relief, agrees to her terms for one week. Death then bestows upon her all Its powers—of sight, of omniscience, of the natural order of things. It says to her, 'Existence is a balance. The scales must always be level.'

"The woman accepts the title of Death's apprentice and sets out, travelling the world, folding in and out of space as if it were second nature. Meanwhile, Death, not mortal but no longer tethered to Its obligation, ventures out into the woman's town, on foot, to see what life has to offer.

"The week passes, and Death returns to the woman's front porch to wait for her. When finally she appears, she tells Death she has been forever changed by the experience. She understands Death now, and how essential It is to the fabric of our reality. Death thanks her for her efforts and invites her to now follow It into oblivion. But the woman does not want to go. She tells Death there's so much more they can do if they work together. They can get to know people, see their worth, their merit. They could save the world by assuming control over who lives and who dies, and not merely following the call. 'That's not the way of things,' Death tells her. She is defiant, though. She says *they* impose the natural order of things; that life answers to them, and not the other way around. They could balance the scales themselves. But Death, knowing Its true purpose, ignores the woman's pleas. It tries once more to convince her to come with It, but she refuses. 'I will not give in,' she tells Death, and when It tries to take her by force, she roots herself to Earth and refuses to be torn from it. She tells Death she can protect the world better than It ever could; that there's more to existence than balance. Death, enraged, tells her she's wrong, and that she will see so for herself. It will teach her a lesson if It must. But the woman holds her ground. Death leaves her there, removed from time and life, to wither in solitude. She is left unable to change a world she no longer belongs to."

"And Death belongs?" said Ellis.

"Death understands what it means to exist, but that doesn't mean Death understands why we *want* to exist."

Ellis pinched the bridge of their nose. "Okay, I'm gonna need the CliffsNotes here. What the hell is the moral of this story?"

"There is no moral to it." Andrea swept out and around the edge of the counter, still half in darkness. "There's just a reason. This town isn't some fountain of life; it's ground zero for a decades-long stalemate."

"Between Death—actual, literal Death—and my house."

Andrea nodded. "What you saw in Optimism, that's Death's balance. It takes from what surrounds us what It can't take from us directly."

"But I mean, people still die here, right? You said Dominik's claims were bogus."

Alex nodded. "They die," she said, "but they don't leave."

"All right . . ." Ellis heaved a deep sigh. "I think I've had enough for one day. My mom and I, we've been through enough, okay? We're only here because—" They choked back a sob. "So, whoever's in charge of this little town-wide hazing ritual, you can tell them to cut it the hell out, got it? We're not leaving."

"We're not trying to scare you," Alex said. "We just want you to understand. For your own protection."

"I get it, okay? I understand. Death is an asshole with an accountant's obsessive need to keep everything balanced, and my house is haunted, and everyone here knows it."

"Your house isn't haunted," Andrea said.

"Right, occupied, whatever, I just—"

"But it is being hunted."

CHAPTER
SEVEN

A TALL, SIXTY-TWO-YEAR-OLD WOMAN WITH A STERN, PALE FACE cracked like rough asphalt and short black hair streaked through with wide tracts of grey, stood outside the police barricade blocking off access to the Jackson-King Mental Health Facility. It was the middle of the night, and she was smoking her seventh cigarette inside of thirty minutes. She'd been so good too; she'd managed to stick to gum for three months this time. Stephen had told her there was no way she'd last; she didn't have the willpower. "Why not?" she'd asked pointedly the last time they carried out a full conversation without either of their attorneys present. "I've done it before. Back when we first met. I was clean of this crap then." He'd shaken his head, but she'd read the subtext in his dismissal as clearly as if he'd written it across the sky in neon: *That was the before-time, you fool. Before we went to shit. Before we had to leave our home and our lives. Before we lost everything.*

She'd been good, though. She'd been great, even, until about an hour ago when she received a panicked phone call from Dr. Lee. "You need to come," she'd said. "You need to get here as quickly as you can."

"Is it an emergency?" Helen had asked, but the doctor only repeated her words. She sounded shaken. Frightened.

So Helen got in the car she'd bought only a few weeks earlier, to get to her new job, and drove thirty minutes to the facility—they didn't like it when you called it a hospital; too many connotations, too much stigma—stopping off at the first gas station she saw along the way to pick up a pack of whatever-the-brand, unfiltered.

And she'd been standing there ever since, chain smoking amid the strobing lights from six police cars, shuffling foot to foot, waiting for—

A decades-old hatchback turned down the long, winding driveway and drove as close to the barricade as possible. The engine shut off, and a man emerged: average height but with a hunch on one end and a paunch on the other; weathered skin that looked dry to the point of flaking away; thin light brown hair swept messily over the bald spot atop his head.

"Took you long enough." Helen dropped her cigarette and stubbed it out with her toe. "I've been here for a half hour already."

"And you didn't go inside? Why, so you could be here to scold me when I arrived?" He came around the car and, noticing the graveyard of crushed butts at Helen's feet, sighed disapprovingly. "Good to see you've kicked the habit."

She stared past him. "You're in a fire lane, Stephen," she said. "They'll tow you."

"Maybe I'll get lucky and they'll take the last bit of dignity you couldn't pilfer for yourself." He walked past her and up to the line of bright yellow police tape. "Let's get this over with. Hey, hello?" he called. An officer came over and was about to tell them to vacate the premises when a slight woman with fine black hair to her shoulders and dressed in a bloodied no-longer-white lab coat, came jogging over.

Helen swallowed hard. "Stephen, did . . . did they tell you what happened? Why they called?" Stephen silently shook his head as Dr. Lee explained something to the officer, who proceeded to raise the tape so Helen and Stephen could slip under it. Dr. Lee motioned for them to follow, and they did.

Inside, they were met by a half-dozen officers milling about the lobby, and a lone paramedic tending to a security guard with his bloodied arm in a makeshift brace. Dr. Lee led Helen and Stephen past the front desk and through the first security checkpoint—a sturdy white fence and grate that locked in three places. "For added protection," she'd said ten years ago—their first visit to the facility after the transfer from up north. They couldn't take any risks with their patients, not one.

Helen looked around as they walked. She heard faint screaming in the distance but couldn't quite place it, directionally speaking. "Dr. Lee, what's this all about?"

"This way, just a little farther." Dr. Lee didn't turn back to address them.

Helen looked to her right. "Steve, what's—"

But Stephen's face had gone slack; he stared straight ahead. Helen followed his gaze and saw immediately what had snatched her ex-husband's attention.

Beyond the next security gate, about fifty or sixty feet ahead, was chaos: debris strewn across the ground; light fixtures sparking, dangling from the ceiling by only their wires; two men—security guards—on their backs being treated by some of the nursing staff.

"What in the hell . . ." Stephen said.

To their right was an open door. Dr. Lee stepped to one side of it and motioned for them to enter. "This way, please."

Helen and Stephen entered the room; Helen fumbled for Stephen's hand, which he accepted, gripping hers tightly.

"Doctor," Stephen said, "what's happened? Where's our daughter?"

Helen glanced around the room: a conference table in the centre and a small security station to the left, complete with monitors showing real-time visuals from several spots around the facility—the chaos, it seemed, was everywhere. A young woman sat waiting at the security station.

"Mr. and Ms. Sweet," Dr. Lee began, "let me first assure you, we're doing everything we can to—"

"Where's our daughter?" Helen shouted, frightened. "Where's Tessa?"

Dr. Lee's shoulders fell. "We don't know."

Stephen paused. "You don't— What do you mean you don't know?"

"Rest assured, we're doing—"

"—everything you can to locate our daughter. Is that it?" Stephen stepped forward, but caught himself just as the woman at the station rose from her chair to intervene.

Dr. Lee exhaled deeply. "There was an . . . incident here tonight."

"An incident," Helen repeated blankly. "Involving Tessa?"

Dr. Lee nodded. "I should say so, yes." She paused. "When you . . . that is, when the incident with your daughter occurred—"

"Which incident, Doc?" said Stephen. "We seem to have our pick of them. Those officers out there—did she hurt anybody? Is she—"

"When she tried to burn down your house . . ."

"Yes?" asked Helen.

Dr. Lee cleared her throat. "Did Tessa ever exhibit any uncharacteristic strength or abilities?"

Helen stepped forward. "Dr. Lee, what are you trying to tell us?"

By way of an answer, Dr. Lee nodded to the young woman at the security station who, with a click, put up a single video across every screen arched around the station. The Sweets crept forward, one cautious, disbelieving step at a time as they watched their forty-year-old daughter, sinewy thin, shouting at seemingly no one—a darkness just off screen, cast in shadows—before raising both hands in the air, above her head, and then bringing them down and—

Static. On every screen.

"The feeds go dark then. Things don't come back online again for several minutes," said Dr. Lee. "In that time, Tessa managed to break out of her room—she knocked the door right off its hinges. She moved effortlessly through every person who tried to stop her—"

"My god," Helen gasped.

"—before bursting through the south wall and disappearing into the night."

Stephen hesitated. "When you say 'bursting through'..."

Dr. Lee regarded him directly. "I mean *straight through*, Mr. Sweet, as if she were a human wrecking ball." She paused. "Some among the wounded said they thought they saw a shadow behind her, smoke like a pair of hands atop her shoulders."

Stephen forced a laugh. Stepped back, shaking his head. "I mean, how much can you trust what anyone here says, right, Doc? With all the meds you have these people on—"

"It is not our patients who saw this . . . this apparition, Mr. Sweet. It is my own staff."

Helen walked right up to Dr. Lee. "Doctor, please, tell us what you know."

Dr. Lee stared straight into Helen Sweet's eyes and said, plainly, "Your daughter is gone. We don't know where or why." Her breath hitched, and she returned her gaze to the monitors. "And we have no idea what she's capable of."

CHAPTER
EIGHT

FOR A FULL WEEK, THE OCCULT STORE WORKERS' FINAL, DIRE words had made a nest of their very own in the recesses of Ellis's mind. There they festered, like tiny insects buzzing around their head as they continued to unpack, as they worked their first few shifts at Twitch, as they attempted to paint.

"But it is being hunted," the one named Andrea had said, plainly and without emotion.

Ellis had stared at her a moment. "Come again?" they said at last.

"Your house—"

"—my 'occupied'"—they made air quotes with their fingers—"house—"

"—is being hunted."

Ellis sighed. "All right, I'll bite: Hunted by whom?"

"By forces beyond your imagination."

They scoffed audibly. "I don't know about that. See, I was working on this sketch a while back. It was of this enormous ogre just oozing from every conceivable orifice and— Never mind. Point is, I can imagine a lot."

"Not this," Andrea said firmly. "You're not ready."

"Not ready for what?"

"To believe."

"Okaaaaay . . ." Ellis crossed their arms. "So, let's run this down. My house is both hunted and occupied by supernatural forces. And according to you, it's not the ghosts inside the house I need to worry about but some otherworldly boogeyman pretending to be Death? Cool. I think I understand: you're completely fucking insane. You, the other kids around here, even—" They stopped themself. They thought of Quinn. Of what she'd said—that not all hauntings were bad. They knew: they had to ask her what she meant.

"We're not crazy." Alex stepped forward. "There's a lot you don't know."

"Tell me then," said Ellis. Alex was about to speak when Ellis put a hand up to stop her. "No, you know what, I'm good. In fact, I'm gonna bail. This is all . . . it's too much. You keep your weird-ass small-town superstitions. I'm not interested."

Alex tried half-heartedly to stop them, but Ellis was outside the store and walking away before she could get a word out.

Ellis had thought, at the time, about going back inside, telling the two of them what they'd heard that night, what they'd felt beneath the wall. But they'd quickly shoved the idea aside. It was ludicrous—there was no point even entertaining the notion.

Over the days that followed, Ellis did what they could to avoid Dominik and his friends, who'd started hanging out in the café more—conveniently whenever Ellis had a shift. Dominik had tried seven times to start another conversation with Ellis, but each time Patricia had called them away. Ellis made a mental note to thank her for exercising her experience running interference with troublesome teens. Ellis still didn't know if they were being courted for Dominik's weird little after-school mystery team or if he wanted something more from them.

Their more pressing concern was Quinn. Given what she'd said, what Alex and Andrea had revealed . . . they didn't know what they would do if they ran into her again. What they would say. They had questions, for sure, but how to phrase them in a way that didn't sound like they thought she was not in her right mind . . . Fortunately, for now, Quinn was nowhere to be found, and Ellis didn't know where she lived, not exactly. So, they kept their head down and focused on establishing a routine. On becoming invisible all over again.

But it was still there. The thought—the idea they'd been implanted with by too many different voices now, like a needle behind their eye, driving itself into their brain: that their house was something more, and not entirely theirs.

Ellis woke the following Saturday with a jolt—a loud crack, wood splintered aggressively. The sound repeated itself another two times.

"Mom?" They slid out of bed and pulled on a dirty-but-not-too-gross tunic they'd worn the day before and had left draped over the foot of their bed.

Another crack then, followed by a few smaller ones—boards being loosened somewhere.

"Mom?" They went to the top of the stairs.

"Down here!"

Ellis bounded downstairs and was about to round the corner when something caught their eye through the glass to the left of the door. A pair of somethings, actually, blurs at the edge of their property. Ellis approached the window and peered out. Standing at the foot of the gravel driveway was an elderly couple holding one another—clutching each other, their faces streaked with tears. Ellis opened the door, went out onto the porch, and asked, "Can I help you?" The two women just shook their heads gently and continued to stare—not at Ellis but at the house itself. At the porch light to Ellis's right, shining, albeit dimly, even in broad daylight.

The couple turned then and started walking away, shoulder to shoulder, as if to keep each other upright. Ellis watched them leave, then slowly closed and locked the front door. Checked the lock again, just to be sure, when something inside caught their eye. Ellis let out a sharp gasp. Blinked twice to be sure they saw what they just thought they saw.

"El? Everything okay?"

They pivoted. Robyn was standing in the hallway dressed in a paint-stained T-shirt and cut-off jean shorts, a dust mask down around her neck. On the floor by her feet, propped up by her left hand on its handle, was a ten-pound sledgehammer.

Ellis swallowed dryly, nodded at the front door. "I—I think so. I just saw . . ." They paused. "I hate to break it to you, Mom, but your hometown is populated by a bunch of weirdos."

She smiled. "Takes one to know one, kiddo."

Ellis put a hand to their chest, feigning injury. "Ouch."

"I call it like I see it."

Ellis shifted their gaze to the sledgehammer. "I see we've moved on to the 'blunt force' phase of remodelling?"

"Ha ha." She heaved the tool up over her shoulder like a lumberjack would an axe. "I think I found something. A false wall in the cupboard under the stairs. I was in there putting some boxes away when I felt a breeze coming through some rotted wood slats. I think we've got ourselves a cellar."

"So, did you try prying them off first, or did you go straight to smashy-smashy town?"

Robyn stuck out her tongue. "Sometimes you have to make your own fun. So, what's on the agenda for today? Got a shift?"

Ellis shook their head. "Actually, I think I'm going to stay in today. Might try and pick up a brush again, start something new."

Robyn's eyes ignited. "Really? That's fantastic!"

Ellis rubbed their upper arms nervously. "Yeah, I'm starting to feel like . . . I'm wanting to feel like myself again," they said, hoping the words sounded more convincing out loud than they did in their head.

Robyn's smile faded slightly. "You sure you're okay? You look like you just saw a ghost."

Ellis laughed, a higher pitch than intended. "Heh, that'd be something."

Robyn went back to work then. Ellis turned, stood in the entryway to the living room.

Wondered silently at what they thought they saw. Or who.

A woman. Standing in their living room, staring out the window there. Daylight like a spear straight through her.

And then she was gone.

Upstairs again with a glass filled with what was left of a smoothie their mom had made and left to sit in the blender—some fruit and something green, probably spinach—Ellis sat down on the floor next to their bed and, trying their best to push out what they *thought* they saw but couldn't have, opened the large brown cardboard box they'd been using as a makeshift nightstand. It was the last box they'd still not unpacked. They set their drink down on the floor and, using a palette knife snatched from an old tackle box they'd used as an art supply chest for years, stabbed and cut along the packing tape sealing the box.

Inside were books, hardbound and spiral. Sketchbooks going back years, to when Ellis was just a child picking up a pencil for the very first time. Their mother had held on to every one of them, from their earliest drawings, tracing over comic panels, to more original designs and self-portraits that they had started around the time they hit middle school and were starting to see themself for the first time—and then when they'd started to see what wasn't necessarily there but felt all too visible. They flipped through the first book, noting the changes in style over time, the idealization that had started to take shape as they learned more who they really were and what labels fit and which ones didn't.

They stuck their hands in deeper and rooted around inside the box, pulling out the bottom-most sketchbook, fat with loose-leaf drawings and photographs crammed between the covers. They took a deep, hesitant breath and opened it up at the midpoint. Several photographs fell out—Polaroids taken more than a year ago with an old point-and-shoot they'd found among their dad's things. The images were of their torso, taken at different angles and over the course of months. In sequence, the images showed a body rapidly shrinking, deteriorating from malnourishment and too much exercise. Ellis flinched upon seeing them again, recalling how for weeks—months, even—they'd tried to convince their mother it was nothing to worry about, that they were fine; they were still eating, they'd started working out, that's all, that's what it was, there was nothing to worry about.

There had been, though. It had very much been something to worry about, but Ellis stuck to their denial until it was almost too late. They'd spent months taking new photos and sketching them, trying desperately to illustrate the divide between what was documented and what they saw in their head—how they imagined they appeared to others. The distortion in their shape.

This was body dysmorphia at its core, Dr. Webb stated during their initial session. It was the first time Ellis had ever heard the term. She'd called it the gulf between what was real and what was seen, your mind trying to convince you of an alternate reality. Ellis had to understand that, she'd said, before they could approach the "why" of it all: undiagnosed depression and anxiety on one hand; social pressures and oppressive, anti-queer cultural norms on the other.

It had taken weeks of tearful, painful unpacking of these issues before Ellis began to comprehend just how deeply entrenched in their psyche so much of it had become. And weeks still before they were able to discuss it, with both Dr. Webb and their mother, without feeling like they were some naïve fool who'd fallen into the most obvious of traps. Dr. Webb assured them it wasn't like that at all.

"This kind of thinking, this illness . . . it isn't just some door you opened despite it being locked with a big sign on it that said *keep out*; it's more like wandering into a minefield without a map. The land mines are already there. They're a part of you. You're incredibly lucky if you can make it to the other side without anything going off, but it's also not your fault if you take a wrong step and lose . . . I'm sorry, I probably should have given more thought to this metaphor."

Ellis had laughed it off at the time, but increasingly what Dr. Webb had said seemed true to life. That's how things had felt for some time now—not just the anorexia but also losing Dad, moving to this place . . . It was like they were hobbling around or crawling through a minefield having lost multiple limbs and being forced to carry them through to the other side.

Now, though, they were tired of the illusion. Tired of other people's tall tales. Tired of letting shit get to them. Imagining things that weren't there. Black Stone was a chance to actually get their head in a better space. This town . . . this strange place full of superstitious, possibly deranged people was their do-over. They just had to learn to play the hand they'd been dealt.

Ellis stood up then, the final sketchbook in hand, photographs and assorted graphite and charcoal drawings spilling out from inside. They dropped it into the trash bin next to their bed. They stared at it there, alone in the bin and very visible, and quickly grabbed a handful of tissues from a box atop a nearby bookshelf and tossed those in, too, loosely covering the sketchbook. They hadn't ever shown that book to Robyn, and they didn't want her to see it. Not ever.

They breathed a sigh of relief, looked up again, and paused. Just stared at the wall in front of them. At a . . . a lump, or something, a series of them close together, causing the wallpaper to bubble up like a tree root. Slowly, they reached out and poked the protrusion with their index finger. It was solid, but there was give to it. They pulled their finger back and it left a slight indentation. They watched as the dip in the wall slowly filled back out again like a piece of memory foam returning to its original shape.

Ellis jumped back suddenly—the root, the vein, it seemed, expanded for a moment and released, growing and then slowly, contentedly, sliding back to its original state as if . . . as if . . .

As if something behind the wall had just fucking exhaled.

"The hell . . . ?" Ellis continued to stare at the wall. The more they focused, the clearer it became: an almost imperceptible rise and fall, a gentle rhythm . . .

Like a pulse.

Quickly, Ellis turned around, bent over and picked up the palette knife. They faced the wall once more and the protrusion, that vein-like thing, was no longer there—the wallpaper was flat again, save for a thin ripple in the material where it had bunched up in the absence of whatever had pushed it out in the first place.

Cautiously, Ellis approached the place where the vein-thing had been only moments prior and touched the spot again. Feeling nothing there, they took the palette knife and scratched at the ripple of taupe amid vertical faded maroon stripes. They managed to create a small tear in the wallpaper and work their fingers inside, started to claw at it. They dropped the painting tool. Using both hands now, they peeled back a cantaloupe-sized piece, revealing the aged drywall beneath.

A brownish red streak, as if burned into the wood surface, extended far above and below the hole they'd made. Arced and jagged, it resembled lightning—or a drawing of lightning.

They touched it, rubbed their fingers together; it was moist and semi-congealed.

Like mud or clay.

Like blood.

*I*n the years following Samir's heart attack, Analiese did what she could to try and make their house, fractured as it was, into a home—to make her and Samir's dream a reality. It wasn't easy, not at first and not once in the seven years that followed. But she tried. She arranged the funeral herself; she didn't have much of a choice—Samir had no family of his own, and she had not spoken to her siblings since her parents' deaths more than a decade prior. The funeral itself was a small affair; they hadn't been in Black Stone long enough to make any significant connections. Acquaintances, yes. Friendly passersby who'd seen the moving truck, said hello, welcomed them to the neighbourhood. But nothing more than that. No one to whom she thought to extend an invitation. No one she could ask to come with her to pick out an urn, to hold her hand, to step in and say "I'll handle this," when she, clearly, could not. Yet she managed.

She took Isabelle to see a grief counsellor. Enrolled her in school at Rosemary Shepherd Elementary, not far from the house, and walked her there every day from kindergarten to third grade. Found a job in town working as a librarian.

She hadn't written a word of fiction since that day seven years prior.

But they'd survived. They'd weathered the storm. Picked up the pieces. Moved on.

Together.

When Isabelle came to Analiese in the middle of the night, it was mere days following her tenth birthday. By then, Isabelle had been unwell for a couple of weeks. She was paler than usual and complained of feeling tired all the time. "It's just the flu," Analiese was told when she took Isabelle to the clinic after several days of worrying. "Make sure she gets plenty of rest and fluids." But Analiese wasn't convinced.

Analiese heard a shuffling in the dark, floorboards creaking. She turned on the lamp on the nightstand next to her bed and was surprised to see Isabelle there, standing at her mother's bedside looking sheepish and holding out a palm speckled with crimson.

"Mommy?"

Analiese sat up straight and grabbed her daughter's wrist, with more force, more panic than intended, and investigated the blood splatter on her palm. She looked up then and spotted red streaks around Isabelle's lips like poorly applied lipstick, and the girl's eyes wider than Analiese had ever seen them. Like perfect dinner plates, she would tell the emergency room doctor later that night, half listening as he pulled her entire world—what was left of it—out from under her with little more than a suspicion.

Analiese took her daughter to the washroom to clean up. She pulled at Isabelle's lips, had her open her mouth; Isabelle's gums were bleeding. Then, the two of them put on their shoes and coats and got in the car to head to Riding Memorial, a small hospital on the east side of town.

It was an hour and a half before they were seen and led into the emergency room. Another four to run some tests, discuss possibilities, probabilities—all equally difficult and heart-wrenching to contemplate.

More testing, then, in the days that followed. Days spent waiting for anything definitive, to rule out what could be ruled out.

And then: a confirmed diagnosis. A single word that devoured a part of Analiese's mind, her future, as if she felt hope slipping past the event horizon of an emotional singularity.

Leukemia.

Not to worry, the specialists said, they would start Isabelle on treatment immediately. She would have the best care. She would be looked after. She would get the best care available. One by one they gave Analiese their word.

Analiese spent days, weeks with her mind turning a cyclone, sitting in various medical offices in Black Stone and even as far north as the city of Ellison, where a litany of professionals explained the disease to her in great detail—its markers, treatment milestones, what to expect. She sat and listened to all of it but was not sure how much of anything she actually heard. How much of anything beyond a slow tick-ticking of a clock in her mind—something ethereal, like a voice whispering to her everywhere she went: it's time. Like knowledge she had acquired against her will.

And no matter the optimism of the professionals attempting to comfort her, no matter the charts they showed breaking down symptoms and survival rates, assuring her they'd caught it early, that they'd do what they could, a part of Analiese knew: someday, sooner than either of them would have, could have anticipated, her Izzy's time would run out.

Not long after the whirlwind had passed and their "new normal" had been established, Analiese lay in bed one night with a hollow feeling in her gut that wouldn't leave and the creeping dreamlike sensation of talons gently caressing her shoulder.

CHAPTER
NINE

ELLIS TOLD THEIR MOTHER ABOUT THE BLOOD-STAINED WALL—
or what they *thought* was a blood stain—but she was skeptical.
When she followed them upstairs, still dressed for destruction
and covered in sawdust and drywall, and saw what they'd done to
their bedroom—what had been a small hole in the wallpaper now
an entire section of wall stripped bare—Robyn was incandescent.

"El, what in the— *What* have you done to your room?" She
craned her head toward the ceiling, to the loose strip of paper
still left, too high for either of them to reach. "How did you
even—" and then she glanced over and saw the mussed sheets
and two foot-shaped impressions in the mattress where Ellis had
stood to continue tearing the wallpaper as high as they could go.

Ellis went red in the face; they'd been so lost in the moment
they hadn't considered how fucked they would be for taking
apart their room. They could even feel their being-fucked-ness
grow by the second. "I—I wanted to see how far it went," they
said, sheepishly. They nodded to the brownish-red veins that
looked more like ancient cave drawings of a spider's web and
seemingly ran across every inch of available wall space, hidden
just beneath the rather hideous 1970s wallpaper.

"Good lord." Robyn sighed. "If you wanted to remodel your room so bad, you should have said so."

"Okay, I know I messed up. I should've asked before I went and stripped my wallpaper—"

"You think?"

"—but can we put aside the fire and brimstone for just one second and check out this bloody zigzag mess all over my wall? I mean, this is far from normal, right?"

Robyn inched down it with her eyes. "Yeah, I'd say it's a state or two over from normal. It's not blood, though."

"It is. Touch it—it's wet."

She rubbed the substance between her fingers. Sniffed it. "I don't know what this is, but it's not blood. It can't be."

"Why not?"

"For one thing, there's no smell. It's probably just, I don't know, old wallpaper glue that didn't dry right. Or maybe grease or something."

"Grease smells."

"Kiddo, it ain't blood. Trust me on this—I see my share of it literally every day."

"Yeah . . . you're probably right," Ellis said while thinking to themself, *It's totally blood.* "Mom . . ."

"Hmm?"

"The kid who died here."

"Not here. Close by, but not—"

"Fine. Whatever. The kid who died, who lived here . . . were you friends?"

Robyn sighed. "I knew him, yeah. I knew them both. Tessa and Reece."

"Did they ever, you know, talk about this place? Did anyone?"

"Kiddo . . ."

"Mom, please."

Robyn wiped the substance off on her pant leg. She hesitated. "People talked, but it was all nonsense. Rumours. Ghosts rattling chains, tossing appliances around, stacking chairs in the kitchen. Real kid stuff. And the adults who believed it . . . well, no one thought much of them. I grew up on the other side of town, but I played here sometimes, with Reece. Tessa and I . . . she was one of the popular girls. She had her own clique. But Reece was always nice to me. Just a sweet, nerdy kid who liked his comics and horror movies. And this one time when we were playing at his house, I was in an upstairs closet, and I swear I—" She blinked and cut herself off. "Look, it's not important. Whatever did or didn't happen here, this is our house now. And we're not sharing it with anyone else, alive or dead. I promise."

"But there's got to be some sort of explanation for—"

"That's enough!"

Ellis was taken aback by Robyn's outburst.

"I need this to work, okay? *We* need this to work, Ellis. This house. This town. And it won't, not if you waste your time listening to every half-cocked . . ." She sighed. Glimpsed a corner of the sketchbook in the trash bin but continued without mentioning it. "Tell you what: I'll finish up downstairs and make us some lunch, and then how 'bout we go to the hardware store and get some new wallpaper and glue, and you can spend some time un-fucking your room, okay?"

"Yeah," Ellis said. "Sure." They watched her leave then returned their attention to the wall. To the stains that were absolutely blood, no matter what she said. Because grease didn't pump through a vein. "Sounds like a plan."

By their Monday afternoon shift at Twitch, Ellis was still digging bits of wallpaper and dried glue out from under their nails, the paint on each now chipped and in desperate need of a refresh. They absently picked at a clump of paper wedged under their thumbnail while clearing mugs and plates from a table. As they did, they couldn't help but reflect on the last conversation they'd had with their mom. On the way to the hardware store to buy new wallpaper, they'd tried once more to broach the possibility that something out of the ordinary was indeed going on with their house. But Robyn wasn't interested.

"I know this town can be a bit strange," she said.

"This town and everyone in it." Ellis recalled the elderly couple they'd seen at the foot of their property, clutching one another and crying. They almost mentioned the couple to Robyn, but then they remembered what else they'd seen—thought, *what else you thought you saw, you idiot*—in the living room and decided against it.

"And I know you'd rather be back home—*home*-home," she added, as if it weren't already clear. "But I really need you to try and make this work, okay?"

"Okay, Mom."

"We don't have a lot of other options, you know, and—"

"I said okay! Christ, I get it." They recoiled then. Noticed Robyn gripping the steering wheel a little bit tighter. They hadn't meant to snap at her like that. They hadn't meant for a lot of things, really.

They didn't bring it up again—the weirdness, the blood-but-not in the walls that, secretly, Ellis now suspected would be found elsewhere in the house if they only looked. If they only peeled back the outer layer of any room, they assumed they'd find more of the same. But they kept their suspicions to themself.

Suddenly, there was a hand on their shoulder. They jumped, turned, and saw Quinn standing there, smiling radiantly and carrying a navy blue polo shirt over one shoulder. Of everyone they'd met who suspected something was up with their house—or apparently knew for a fact something was up—Quinn seemed the most level-headed. She definitely believed the house was haunted, but when compared to Dominik and the occult store owners, and even Amara, she was so much less afraid of . . . well, whatever was going on.

And right now, that was a relief.

"Oh, hey. Sorry," she said. "I really did not mean to startle you like that." She cocked her head to one side. "You okay? You look like you've seen a ghost."

They sighed. "I don't know what I've seen, to be perfectly honest with you."

"Come again?"

Ellis hesitated. "Never mind, it's . . . never mind." They finished putting the dishes in a grey bin and carried it back behind the counter. Quinn followed, keeping to the other side of the counter.

"Right," she said. "Okay. So . . . I want to say sorry."

"For what?"

"The last time we talked. For bailing on you without an explanation."

"I wasn't aware you owed me one."

"I mean I don't, but . . . Look, I've lived here all my life, but a friend of mine growing up, she . . . She was new here, and I remember it being really hard for her to make friends. It didn't help that she was sick all the time, but . . . I'm just trying to say, it's never easy being new, especially in a town this small."

"Or when said town informs you, repeatedly, that you've moved into a haunted house."

She shifted in place nervously. "Yeah. About that. Can we just file that away under 'things I probably should'nt've said out loud'? Last thing I need is to be known as the town basket case."

"What if I told you you're not the only one?" They watched as Quinn seemed to fold inward slightly, gripping the end of the shirt hanging over her shoulder. They quickly added, "I don't mean— You're not a basket case. You're just not the only person in this town who thinks my house is haunted. But you already knew that. I'm just saying . . . Look, you're not alone."

She smiled half-heartedly. "Oh, I know I'm not, but I'm not sure if that makes things better or worse."

"Better, I think."

"How do you figure?"

"Well, if you *were* losing your mind, wouldn't it be better to have a little company?"

She eyed them curiously. "Is that your idea of trying to make me feel better? Because I have to tell you . . . it's pretty shit, really."

Ellis blushed. "Yeah, well, I've never been all that great around pretty girls . . . I mean, people I want to get to know better. That is to say . . . crap."

It was Quinn's turn to blush. "I bet you say that to every girl you find crying outside your house."

"You know, you might actually be surprised by how high that number is." They paused. "What . . . what was it you really saw that day?"

"Nothing," she said abruptly, then shook her head. "I thought I saw . . . It wasn't anything, I was just having one of those really good days that's, you know, not, and I thought I saw . . . Forget it." She cleared her throat, wiped her eyes. "It doesn't matter."

"Right . . . So, listen, uh, I don't . . . I mean . . ." They shuffled nervously in place. "The other day, I'm so sorry I—"

"What are you listening to?" she said very suddenly.

"Huh?"

"Current music—faves, interests, whatever—*go*. And don't say, 'Oh, I don't really like music'—that's sociopath-talk, and you know it."

"Gee, that's not painting with a broad brush or anything."

"Just . . . come on. Let's hear 'em. And don't think too hard about it."

Ellis hesitated. "It's a weird mix of new and old, mostly indie shit you probably haven't heard of."

"Assume much? Come on, try me. I bet I know more than you think."

Ellis pulled out their phone, opened the music app, and quickly rattled off some names. "The Go! Team, Murder by Death, the

Mountain Goats, Frightened Rabbit . . . I'm getting into Sault right now."

"That it?"

Ellis shrugged. "I mean . . . no, there's more, it's just I don't really know what's big right now. I've always been a little behind the times. I've also got a soft spot for Springsteen, Tom Petty—a lot of what my dad liked."

"You're close with him?"

"I was."

Quinn paused. She appeared pensive for a moment. Then: "Yeah, I can work with this."

"Huh?"

"Music taste is one of the most critical things to know about a person. If we're gonna go out, I have to know I won't spend our time together with my fingers in my ears."

"I guess that's fair, but— Hey, wait, did . . . did you just say you wanted to go out with me? Like, on a date?"

She grinned slyly. "Took you a second. You in?"

"I—well—I mean—"

"A simple yes or no will—"

"Yes!" They cleared their throat. "I mean, I would be delighted."

Quinn reached across the counter then, snatched Ellis's phone from their hands, and started typing before they could object. "Movie this weekend? There's only one theatre in town, and they almost never show anything new, but they play a lot of old-school horror. Of which you're clearly in need of further education."

"And I suppose you're gonna teach me?"

She passed back the phone. Stared Ellis right in the eyes. "Yes," she said confidently. Definitively. "I am. Plus,"—she held up the polo shirt, and Ellis saw, stitched on its breast, Rialto, the name of the theatre—"I get a discount."

Ellis turned almost as red as a stop light. "Oh . . . okay."

Quinn grinned and started backing away. "Saturday then. Meet here, six o'clock?"

"Yeah . . . yeah, that absolutely works."

"Great! See you later, Ellis Lang. And take a breath before that grin breaks your face in two." She turned then and walked—almost sort of skipped—away. Ellis watched until she'd vanished from sight. They felt their legs start to buckle then and wondered just how long their knees had been like that—rendered to a state of near-jelly.

They looked down at the open contacts list on their phone and a brand-new entry there.

And then it hit.

Holy shit.

They had a date.

CHAPTER
TEN

THAT AFTERNOON'S SHIFT FLEW BY SO QUICKLY ELLIS HAD TO triple-check their phone to make sure the time was right. They were still buzzing from their encounter with Quinn. No, encounter wasn't right—the holy-shit-what-just-happened with Quinn. Turning down their street again, they were surprised to see a large grey truck parked in the driveway, behind their mom's car. They caught a glimpse of several men in jeans and orange construction vests walking around the sides of the house and disappearing around the back, observing, it appeared, the ground surrounding the structure itself.

Ellis jogged the rest of the way, through the wide-open front door. "Mom?" They skidded to a stop at the sight of a burly looking guy with a steel wool beard standing in the hallway, next to the entrance to the cellar under the stairs. Burly dude glanced at Ellis and nodded once in the direction of the open cellar door.

Ellis climbed down the short wooden staircase there, watching the steps beneath their feet for any loose nails poking through the aged wood. The space itself was small, barely more than a closet, and filled with cobwebs, dust, and probably entire colonies of insects that Ellis couldn't see and was more than happy to pretend didn't exist. At the other end of the small space, however, was a hole where Robyn had smashed straight through a makeshift wall of weathered two-by-four slats.

"Mom?" They approached the hole in the wall, careful not to brush up against any jagged edges. It was barely large enough for a person to squeeze through; they had to crouch slightly to slip through to the other side.

"In here, honey!" Robyn called. Ellis followed the sound of her voice to a darker, mustier area—where the air was so thick it almost had a taste to it, like old socks and mildew. Like this space hadn't seen light of any kind in decades, if ever. They pulled out their phone and tapped the flashlight app to help navigate through a maze of narrow passageways that stretched beneath the entirety of their house.

"So, you're saying you can't do anything." It was Robyn, off in the distance—or possibly right next to them, on the other side of one of the corridor walls. It was impossible to tell.

"I'm saying we can't do anything right now," came a man's voice. "Whatever this is, it goes down pretty far. We're gonna need some special equipment, and right now, what we need is tied up in other projects. City projects."

"But six months?"

"At the earliest."

"That's an awful long time, Mr. Reynolds."

"I'm sorry, Ms. Lang, but that's the way of it. You could always try to find someone in Lakefield or West Pine, but they're going charge you extra to come all the way out here."

Robyn sighed.

Ellis continued to trace the makeshift maze beneath the house, wondering if its walls were load-bearing. They turned left at a fork and stopped in place. Ahead of them they caught what they thought was a shadow standing up against the wall, the shape and size of a small boy. Between its feet, a small red rubber kickball.

"Ellis?"

They turned their head. Their mother was down at the other end, past the fork, alongside a tall man hunched over in the narrow, low space, holding a clipboard in one hand and his hardhat in the other. Ellis quickly turned back around, but the silhouette was gone—only the ball remained. They ignored it, thinking the shadow nothing more than a trick of the eye, and went over to their mother and, presumably, Mr. Reynolds. They were standing in what appeared to be the end—or the centre?—of the strange maze, next to a mound of dug-up earth around a steel door, a hatch inserted flat into the ground.

The hatch's surface was flat, marked by numerous strike marks where, they assumed, an object had been used to try and force entry. There were even some light burn marks around the edges—from a fire long ago, perhaps, or someone attempting to blow their way inside. And off to one side, a simple slot for a key.

"What in the hell?" Ellis said, surprised.

"Exactly what I said, kiddo." Robyn turned to Mr. Reynolds. "This is my child, Ellis. Ellis, this is Mr. Reynolds."

Mr. Reynolds tucked the clipboard under one arm and shook Ellis's hand.

"Ellis, Mr. Reynolds is here to help us figure out what secrets our new home holds."

Ellis stared at the lock. "I don't suppose anyone tried to—"

"I already tried picking the lock," Robyn said.

Ellis stared at the mysterious hatch. "What do you think it is?"

Mr. Reynolds tore a page from his clipboard and passed it to Robyn. "Here's our assessment. We'll be in touch."

Robyn thanked Mr. Reynolds and followed him out of the cellar. Alone again, Ellis crouched down, put their hand to the hatch. They gently moved their palm over its unexpectedly warm surface, feeling every divot, every scratch from where someone had tried desperately to gain entry.

How long had this been here? Had Robyn known this was right beneath their feet?

She came up behind them a moment later. As if reading their mind, she said, "I found this the other day, when I was down here, exploring."

"Exploring—with a sledgehammer," Ellis said, not turning from the hatch.

"Hey, if you can tell me a better way to get shit done, I'm all ears." She put a hand on their shoulder. "Everything okay?"

"Yeah, it's just . . ."

"What?"

"It's warm. Right here. Try it: put your hand where mine is." Ellis shifted out of the way and watched as Robyn placed her palm right where theirs had been.

"Do you feel it?"

She hesitated, then shook her head. "Sorry, kiddo, just feels like cold metal to me." She put her hand to their forehead. "You're not coming down with something, are you?"

"What? No." They ducked out of her touch. "I swear to you, it felt warm. Almost hot. Like . . . like when I touched the wall by the front door."

Robyn sighed. "That was probably a glitch in the electrical, nothing more."

"But for what? There are no switches nearby."

"I don't know, maybe there used to be one there—maybe that's what's responsible for the porch light always being on. I'll tell you what, we'll call the electrician next, have them come by and see if they can help solve a few of our mysteries."

Ellis looked to the hatch again. "Right."

Robyn started back through the maze. Ellis turned as she disappeared down the adjacent corridor.

"Mom?"

She poked her head back around the corner. "What's up?"

"I . . . have a date. Saturday, with a girl I met in town."

Robyn's eyes lit up—even in the next-to-zero light, Ellis could see her grin stretching all the way across her face. "That's

94

fantastic!" she said. "I'm just . . . I'm so thrilled you're making friends again."

"Thanks, Mom." They watched as she disappeared again. They knew there was more she wanted to say—that she was excited they were getting out into the world again, that maybe they'd find some reason to hate their new living arrangement a little less.

Ellis hadn't planned on telling her, though, not like that, but it was the only thing they could think to say that wouldn't worry her. They couldn't mention, again, the heat they felt coming from the hatch. They couldn't say that they'd not only felt that same heat in the wall by the front door but also beneath every strip of wallpaper they'd pulled from their bedroom wall.

And they definitely could not say that they'd just seen a shadow with no body to cast it. They wanted to, but they couldn't.

They couldn't tell her that they thought they'd just seen a ghost. And that it wasn't their first.

CHAPTER
ELEVEN

THE REST OF THE WEEK PASSED WITH LITTLE FANFARE. EACH night, Ellis and their mother ruminated about what might be inside their cellar hatch, who might've put it there in the first place, and, most importantly, the possible location of the key.

"I definitely haven't seen it," Robyn said Wednesday at dinner—tacos from a Mexican place in town that also sold fried chicken and was next to a butcher's that doubled as an ice cream parlour in the summer. Because you didn't get places that specialized in only one thing here like you did in a city; you got hodgepodges, shops and restaurants that doubled- or tripled-up to fill whatever need they could.

Ellis scooped a handful of cheese from their plate and dumped it on their taco. "But how would you know? You might've missed it."

Robyn scoffed. "A mysterious metal door at the centre of a DIY maze hidden behind a false wall that I had to sledge-hammer my way through? Kiddo, please, that key is probably the most ornate, ostentatious thing you've ever seen. Like, an *actual* skeleton key or something."

"With diamonds fitted into its eye holes!"

"Exactly."

"What about your friend who still lives here? Think she'd know anything about it?"

"Cynthia? I doubt it. She wasn't close to the family that lived in our house back then. Besides, I don't want to bother her with this."

"Have you even told her you're back? She'd probably want to see you!"

Robyn quickly averted her eyes. "I don't think I . . . She doesn't want to hear from me."

"But you said you've kept in touch. You said she put you in contact with—"

"Drop it, El. Please. It's not . . . Look, we've kept in touch, but that doesn't mean . . ."

"Are you scared to see her again?" It wasn't what Ellis had really wanted to ask. They'd wanted to say, *Are you ashamed to be back here? In the town you worked so hard to escape?*

When Robyn didn't respond, they changed tactics: "What about the real estate agent who sold you the house?"

Robyn almost choked on her food. "Betany O'Brien? Oh god, no. She was a nightmare back in high school. You remember *Mean Girls*? Regina George?"

"Oh . . . oh, no . . ."

"Yeah. If this hadn't been her listing . . . I swear, she spent half the time we spoke on the phone ranting about her shitty ex-husband and the other half telling me what a disappointment her kid is. Crap, what was his name again. It starts with a *D*. Dino, David, Daniel . . ."

"Dominik?"

"That's it."

Ellis had to restrain their laughter. "I don't think she's wrong. He comes into the café at least once a day to try and discuss our haunting."

Robyn wiped her mouth with a piece of paper towel. "Okay, so, are you going to tell me about your date this weekend, or am I going to have to guess?"

Ellis didn't answer right away. Partly because they were still trying to process what had happened, that Quinn was even interested in them in the first place. And partly because, even more than the hatch and the whereabouts of the key, they were still wondering who would've gone to the trouble of building a ramshackle maze in their cellar—and perhaps even more critically, *why.*

And then there was . . . *that.* That whatever-the-hell-it-was they'd seen down there, in the cellar. The shadow that hadn't reappeared in the days since, when they'd ventured down to check. Hoping it wasn't just a trick of their mind. And also that it was.

They knew better than to tell their mom, or anyone else for that matter, what they were starting to actually fear: that maybe there really was something to what Dominik and Quinn and so many others had suggested. Maybe their house really was haunted.

"For now," they said, smiling out one side of their mouth, "you'll just have to guess."

Throughout the next several days, Ellis kept their thoughts locked away, not wanting to call any unwelcome attention to themself. They spotted Quinn only twice that week. Once while on their way to work; she was in the park snapping photos of passersby. Then again on Friday afternoon—they caught sight of her while she was walking back from the high school. They couldn't be sure, but from what little they glimpsed, it looked as if she'd been crying. She hadn't seen them; she was, it seemed, lost in thought. They wanted to call out to her, to see what was the matter, but she turned down her street before they could act.

They thought of texting her every night that week but couldn't find the courage—or anything interesting to say.

And then it was Saturday. Date night. Ellis, being nervous (i.e., a wreck), had shown up at Twitch more than an hour and one large Americano early. *Probably not the best idea,* they conceded, *ingesting a large amount of caffeine when already keyed up,* but what was done was done. They justified it to themself—they needed to be alert and ready for anything.

Patricia had just patted Ellis on the hand and told them to chill out, it would be okay. She had taught Quinn in her senior year—she knew Ellis was in good hands. Ellis, wanting to talk about anything but their impending date, had tried to shift topics. They asked her if she knew anything about the house ("Nothing more than you've already heard.") or if she had any idea who might, to which she made an uncouth joke about Dominik and went back to cleaning the counter. Then Ellis asked if she'd known their mom.

"Robyn Ridley? Yeah, I remember her. We weren't friends or anything. Oh, it's nothing bad. I was just a few years behind her, is all. And when you're a kid, a gap of a few years might as well be a few decades. Besides, she was always off hanging out with Reece Sweet."

Right then, before they could ask anything about Reece or their mother's friendship with him, Quinn walked into the café and Ellis's mind went blank—they barely noticed Patricia grinning and walking away. Quinn wore a mesh-type asymmetrical black dress over shiny black leggings, and she had on dark red lipstick and a bright silver bracelet with a chain running from it to a wide three-part ring on her left hand.

She approached Ellis's table, smiling her own mixture of excitement and unease as she pulled out her earbuds and pressed pause on her phone. "Hey," she said, breathlessly, as if she'd planned on saying a whole lot more but had lost the words somewhere along the way.

"H-hey," Ellis said, equally flustered. They nodded to the phone in her hand. "What are you listening to?"

"Anderson .Paak. Unlike you, I listen to new shit from time to time," she teased.

"I'll have you know most of my faves are all still putting out new music."

She grinned devilishly. "I'm just messing with you. Besides, most of the time it's Björk or Sigur Rós." She slipped her phone and earbuds into a small zippered wallet with a camera stitched to its face, its lens a heart. "Have you been waiting long?"

Ellis raised their now-empty coffee cup. "Long enough to give myself an arrhythmia."

"Well, that's . . . probably not great."

"It's fine. I mean, if I didn't keel over the moment you—" They stopped themself midsentence, suddenly flushed with embarrassment. Out of the corner of their eye, they caught Patricia chuckling to herself.

Quinn caught every bit of it. "You don't say," she said, offering a sly, knowing grin that only seemed to deepen the red in Ellis's cheeks. She noticed their fingernails, a bright purple gripping the empty coffee cup. "I like your nails—they pop. I bet if you found a similar colour of lipstick, it'd really work for you."

"You think?"

She nodded. "So, you ready to get out of here?"

And just like that, Ellis felt their heart ascending the back of their throat as if to make a break for it. "Yeah, I am." They stood, taking Quinn's hand. Together, they left.

They walked silently for two blocks, hand in hand, before either one of them found the courage to speak. Ellis, finally, broke the silence.

"We're heading to the theatre?"

She nodded. "We don't get a lot of first-run stuff here, but it's still pretty great. Art deco vibes, real butter on the popcorn, and uncomfortable-as-hell seats with arm rests I would pay good money to rip out with my bare hands."

"Because they're gross?"

"Because they're made for hips like yours, not mine. Best thing about this place, though, is that on weekends twice a month they screen classic horror films. A thing that I may or may not have had a hand in establishing."

"Most of which I've probably not seen."

"Which is why this is gonna be so much fun."

They continued on a little farther, once more drifting into awkward silence.

"So . . ." Ellis started, "is this something you do often?"

"What's that?"

"Take the new kid out on a date."

"I dunno," she said. "You try and date every fat girl you see?"

"I mean . . . no, but I haven't dated anyone, really."

"How come?"

Ellis shrugged. "It just never . . . I never felt like . . . And there were other things too."

"So cryptic. Other things like what?"

They looked at her. "You really want to deep dive into TMI territory on our first date?"

"You say 'first' like you assume there's going to be a second." She smirked.

"Not assuming, just hopeful."

Her smile widened. "Then yes, I'm sure."

"In for a penny, in for a pound?"

"You got it."

"All right," they said, "but you first: Why'd you ask that?"

"That thing about dating a fat girl?"

"Yeah."

It was her turn to shrug. "Honestly? Because I'm kind of nervous right now."

"How come?"

She spoke bluntly. "I've encountered far too many assholes who want to treat me like a joke or an object. There are a lot of people out there that want to be with a larger person, but they'll never admit it publicly. They'll never take them home, introduce them to their friends. I had to make sure you were different."

They squeezed her hand tighter.

"I'm less worried now, but that's not the same as being sure. Certainty takes time."

"I get that. Not sure if it helps at all, but I was attracted to you the very first time I laid eyes on you. You know, when you almost ran into me at the mall."

"When I almost ran into— What kind of revisionist bullshit are you trying to pull?"

"I thought you were stunning. I haven't felt that way before. About anyone." They paused. "I don't really know what more to say. I just wanted to get to know you better. And then we talked and you seemed . . ."

"What?"

"Cool, I guess. Funny. Kind too. Those things go a long way with me. Everything else is a bonus."

She sighed. "You know, you're doing a decent job selling me on the whole you-not-being-a-creep thing."

"I'm glad."

She looked ahead. "So, what was it *you* were going to say?"

"The 'other things'?"

"Yeah. That."

They sighed. "The last couple of years have been . . . rough, I guess. My dad died—cancer—and that took . . . it's both longer than you think it's gonna be and shorter than you expect. Anyway, during that time I was—I mean I had—" They took a deep breath. "I had some health stuff that needed addressing."

She regarded them intensely. "You mean like—"

"Anxiety, mostly, and depression. But also . . ." They stared straight ahead. "Fuck it: I'm a recovering anorexic."

"I . . . wow. I did not expect that."

"Yeah, well, takes all kinds."

She hesitated, choosing her words carefully. "Is that something . . . had it been going on for a long time?"

"The actual anorexia and losing weight, no. Maybe a year. But the body dysmorphia, and some gender shit, too . . . yeah, that's been there as far back as I can remember. I've never been comfortable with the skin I'm in. I've just never felt . . . solid, I guess. Real."

"I bet there are a lot of people who can relate to that."

"Sure, but that doesn't make it any easier to talk about."

"Thanks for deciding to tell me. For trusting me."

"What can I say—you seem like the trustworthy type."

"In for a penny . . ."

"You know it."

They kept walking, past the grocery store, the pharmacy. Quinn pointed down a street Ellis hadn't yet explored, noting Centennial Park and the skating rink there, which she off-handedly stated hadn't been used in years, "Not since the peewee hockey coach got drunk one night and drove the Zamboni straight through a wall."

They arrived at the Rialto a short time later. "Here we are," said Quinn.

Ellis glanced up at the marquee. In large block letters, surrounded by stage lights: *SATURDAY HORROR THROWBACK—HELLO MARY LOU: PROM NIGHT II.*

"*Prom Night II*," Ellis said. They turned to Quinn, who was busy cackling to herself. "Do you hate me or something?"

"I thought you hadn't seen a lot of horror." A devious smile stretched ear to ear.

"I haven't, but even I've heard of this dreck. It's notoriously awful."

"No, it's notoriously great, but in a really awful way."

"What's the difference?"

"Well, there's good horror, there's bad horror, and then there's so-bad-it's-actually-amazing horror."

"This is the latter then?"

"Oh yes." She lightly shoulder-checked them. "Still hoping for that second date?"

"Depends."

"On what?"

"Whether or not you share your popcorn."

"Only if you don't huck it at the screen."

"Pfft, fucking fun police over here."

"I know, I'm the literal worst. How will you ever survive this ordeal?"

Ellis pointed to the marquee. "This I can deal with. It's the rest of the night I'm worried about. I mean, what if I hate this film? That might put a damper on the whole thing. Who knows, I might not even want a goodnight kiss."

"Well maybe we should do something about that right now."

Ellis felt their insides start to quiver. Their throat was suddenly desert-dry. "J-just to be on the safe side, right?"

She leaned in. "Absolutely." Locked her eyes on theirs, mouthed, "Okay?"

Ellis nodded, moved in, and—

They kissed.

And everything was quiet.

Perfect.

Quinn pulled away after a few seconds, put her forehead to Ellis's. "That was . . ."

"Yeah," they breathed.

"You still want to head inside?"

"Do we have to?" Ellis asked playfully.

"No, but I promise all sorts of inappropriate laughter and terrible low-budget special effects."

Ellis took her hand again. "Lead on."

———

Two hours later, they exited the theatre among a small hand-ful of others—some Ellis recalled having seen in the café and around town.

Quinn waved to someone she recognized, then returned her attention to Ellis. "Okay, so you haven't said a word. But I've seen your mouth open and close a few times like you've got something you're just dying to—"

"What. The. Hell. Was. That?"

Quinn started to laugh.

"You told me this was supposed to be great."

"I told you it was so terrible that it was actually kind of good."

"What's the difference?" they asked, somewhat incredulously.

"You're kidding, right? Have you never seen a film so bad that you actually had fun watching it?"

"Like, in a glorious-train-wreck sort-of way?"

"Exactly!"

"Does *Rocky Horror* count?"

"No, because that is genuinely great and I won't hear other-wise."

"Fine. *The Room*."

"Okay, yes, that totally applies. See also: most slasher fran-chises, every *Paranormal Activity* film, and *Jupiter Ascending*."

"Hey, that last one isn't so bad."

She stopped and stared at Ellis as if they'd grown a second head. "Eddie Redmayne's pillar-to-post performance. The zero-G orgy. The bees."

"Right, but—"

"*The bees!*"

Ellis shrugged. "Still not that bad."

"Next you're going to tell me *Speed Racer* was actually good."

"That film is art."

"Or that the *Matrix* sequels weren't total shit."

"They could have been great! The story is all there; the problem is, the Wachowskis tried this whole transmedia thing and it splintered the story's focus and—"

"Oh GODDDDD!" Quinn said, half shouting, half sighing as she threw her head back. "You have the absolute worst taste in movies, you know that?"

"*Prom. Night. II.* You did this to me. This is all on you."

She gave Ellis a shove. "You're lucky you're cute, you know."

"You're not so bad yourself." They stopped and faced her.

"So, did it ruin the mood, or do you think you might still want that goodnight kiss for real?" she asked.

"I mean, it was touch-and-go there for a while, what with all the truly terrible acting and godawful writing and—"

"Just shut up and kiss me."

And Ellis did exactly that.

They parted again. Quinn put a hand to Ellis's chest. Sighed. "You're getting awfully good at that."

Ellis smiled slyly. "I'm a fast study."

"Who likes terrible films."

They stayed like that for several long seconds, neither of them wanting the moment to—

A loud, growing rumble from above that sounded like a fleet of trucks barrelling down a highway. They looked up at the same time.

Under the blanket of night, Ellis could barely make out the storm clouds high above. They held out their hand but felt no rain, and little wind. But when lightning flashed across the sky, they were able to see, clearly, the shape of the storm: large ribbed-looking clouds circling the entire town. Lightning flashed again, sliding on the backs of the clouds but not striking the ground. From where they were, the black, almost intestinal-looking loops of cloud, nestled in one another like concentric rings, looked to Ellis like a hurricane.

They pointed skyward. "Um . . . is this normal?"

"Nope. This is decidedly weird." She paused. "I can't even remember the last time it stormed here."

"Well, looks like it's about to start any second. That, or it's the apocalypse."

She stuck out her tongue. "Well, aren't you a bucket of sunshi—"

A bright, violent flash just then—a ragged canyon of lightning that suddenly carved the sky in two, followed by a clap of near-instantaneous thunder, loud enough that it rattled every window on the street. And then the marquee behind them, and all of Black Stone, went dark.

"Come on." Quinn started forward.

"Wait, where are we going?"

"To get inside before we get electrocuted." She held out her hand. "Do you trust me?"

Ellis pointed to the darkened marquee behind them. "After that? Man, I don't—"

"Ellis . . ." She stared at them, warmth in her eyes like a campfire. "Do you trust me?"

Ellis thought about everything the two of them had experienced in their short time together. Everything they'd revealed to one another. And took her hand.

"I do."

CHAPTER
TWELVE

TESSA SWEET HADN'T HAD SUCH A WARM, RELAXING SHOWER IN a very long time. She wore a stiff white towel wrapped around her torso while she wrung out her long dirty blonde hair over the motel room carpet. She'd draped a second towel over the mirror there, tucking it behind the top edge. It was easier than looking away. She didn't like to see her own reflection—she hadn't seen it in anything but glass covered by wire mesh for many years. There had been only so many mirrors at the facility—they were a risk, security told her parents when they abandoned her there. Too many patients had shattered them over the years—to use as weapons, to attempt suicide, or simply because they no longer recognized the person reflected back at them. Tessa wanted to break this mirror herself but held back. She took a few deep breaths and remembered what Dr. Lee had tried to teach her about controlling her anger.

Her brother's death wasn't her fault, Dr. Lee had said. She needed to not bottle up, not hide her rage, but also not point it so entirely inward, lest she try to burn some other home to the ground. For years, Tessa had tried to convince the good doctor, and indeed anyone who would listen to her, that it wasn't rage that caused her to try to set fire to their home; it was survival.

It was desperation, to ensure her home, *their* home, didn't take from them any more than it already had. That it had devoured its last soul. She'd tried to convince them that it was Reece who'd warned her. Then why didn't he come back and warn their parents, too, they asked. Why did he only speak to her? She never had answers for this or any follow-up questions, and the longer she stuck so emphatically to her story, the fewer visitations she received; the less time she got to spend in the facility's common room or outside on the grounds; the smaller her room became, and the heavier and more reinforced the locks on the door. And when she tried to change her tune, when she presented herself as a model patient who had learned from her mistakes and only wanted to do right, to maybe see some of her privileges reinstated, she was met with further resistance, masked in the guise of sincere mistrust: they did not believe in her redemption, in her claims that she wanted to move on and leave her brother and that house—that entire town—behind. They saw only machinations in her words, her willingness to do or say anything if it meant release or even a lessening of the chains.

What they didn't know was that, for a time, she'd meant it. She'd truly wanted nothing more than to start a new life, somewhere far from Black Stone, perhaps even far from her family, where no one would know the first thing about her or her past. But still they denied her, kept her locked away and separated from the outside world.

Which is why when Reece visited her there one night a couple of weeks back and offered her a chance to take her revenge, she said yes without hesitation. Even when she reached out to touch him and her hand passed through his still-teenage self as if he were vapour. Even when he showed her that he could still act, still affect the world around him, still threaten those who needed threatening, she said yes.

And when Reece, dead but there with her, undulated and grew, expanding to fill the tiny room that the doctors and nurses swore to her and her parents was not a cell but was absolutely a cell, she still said yes. She repeated it to herself over and over again as the mass of Reece-but-not smashed its way out of her room. Blew the steel door off its hinges and took out part of the surrounding walls. As the penumbra assuming the shape of an enormous dark minotaur, Reece led her out of the labyrinthine facility. Crashed through walls, barriers, security checkpoints, and guards—anything and everything in its way, and without hesitation.

Wearing only a pair of grey sweatpants and a loose-fitting white T-shirt, Tessa had stepped over the bodies of those who'd tried to stand in her brother's way, who'd tried to stop them both—who'd spent years telling her there was no way she could have seen and heard what she absolutely knew she'd seen and heard—and escaped through a fresh hole in the building's north wall. She followed her shade of a guide, and together they disappeared into the night.

She'd hated everything about those clothes—from the way they looked to how, no matter how new, old, freshly washed, or worn, they remained stiff and itchy, crosshatching her skin with waffle-like scratch marks every time she moved. But they'd been hers, and these new ones ... She finished getting dressed, tugging the looser-than-expected sweater she'd found in one of the suitcases on the motel's queen-sized bed over her body. The person she'd taken it from had been rather slight, which made Tessa realize just how frail she'd gotten during her stay at the facility. Still, it was better than wearing the same thing she'd worn for—god, what was it, ten years? Twenty? More? She couldn't even remember, by that point, how many facilities she'd been in or for how long at each. In what brief glimpses she'd had of her parents over the years, she'd certainly witnessed the passage of time—in the greying of their hair, the weathering of their skin, the increasingly dark recesses beneath their eyes. But it wasn't until she'd seen the calendar at the gas station convenience store she'd stopped at a week ago, for something to eat and drink and to grab a road map of nearby towns and cities, that she realized it had in fact been twenty-five years.

When she asked Reece why it had taken him so long to come back to her, he'd said she wasn't ready. He had tried other tactics during her incarceration, whispering to other people in town, working hard to convince—or try to convince—anyone he could of the house's true threat, but to no avail. The town had largely accepted the house without realizing the Faustian bargain in which they were active participants. And those who knew the depths of its evil couldn't do anything to stop it—they'd tried several times over the years, unsuccessfully, mostly petty vandalism and attempts at arson, and had through their failures grown complacent. But where they had failed, she would succeed. She knew something the others either didn't know themselves or simply hadn't believed: to kill the house, you had to strike at its foundation. You had to find where it was most vulnerable.

You had to stab it in its heart.

Reece explained this to her while at the motel. He'd learned much in their time apart, she realized. More importantly, he had a plan.

If they were going to save Black Stone, Reece said to Tessa, they needed someone who knew how things really were. Someone strong enough to cleave through the town's collective apathy.

They needed vengeance on their side if they were going to win.

Tessa exited the bathroom, careful when stepping over the bodies of the young couple who'd stopped over at the motel for a night or two on their way from nowhere to someplace else. They lay on their backs, eyes wide and mouths permanently slack, in shock or fear or confusion—it didn't matter. They'd not had time to react when Reece burst through their door, oblivion incarnate, and swept into them—*through* them, whisking life from them as if flour through a sieve. They'd dropped in place, leaving Tessa with time enough to clean up and gather her bearings after so many days spent travelling under cover of night, to avoid detection on their way back to their hometown—hers and Reece's. She'd placed the bag of supplies she'd lifted from the gas station convenience store on the edge of one of the beds, taken some clothes from one of the two suitcases there, and gone into the bathroom, where she cried for a full forty-five minutes before finally undressing and turning on the shower.

Now, she opened the bag and pulled out a map of the region, which she unfolded and placed flat on the end of the bed. She put her finger to the map and drew a line south, stopping at Black Stone. From there, she traced the streets and subdivisions until she found it: a lone, long, fir-lined street that dead-ended. She took a pen from the bag and stabbed it through the spot where the house remained. From there, she carefully drew a series of rings around the house, keeping it at the centre, until she'd drawn far enough out to have cordoned off the entire town.

"There are a number of sewage outflows," Reece had told her, "at the north end of town, in the ravine that runs through there. That's where you'll find it."

"What?" Tessa asked. "What will I find?"

"The limits of its reach. That's where you'll strike. That's where we'll wage our war. She can't keep me out forever."

Tessa didn't ask who "she" was, or what Reece meant by being kept out. She only knew she had a mission, and that she would fulfill it no matter what.

The house needed to be destroyed. Of this she was certain.

"When you're ready," Reece said before she got in the shower. He left to give her the space she needed.

And she was ready now. She'd been waiting for this moment for a quarter of a century. She opened up a small black carry-on bag with a shoulder strap and dumped the dead man's clothing and toiletries to the motel room floor before filling it again with the rest of the things she'd picked up along the way: canisters and bags of random cleaning solutions and kitchen supplies she'd stolen from various stores while on their journey—the ingredients required, Reece claimed, for making explosives.

To be safe, and to avoid arousing too much suspicion, Tessa took a few more articles of clothing from the woman's suitcase and placed them gently overtop the pilfered items, to hide the do-it-yourself weaponry. She reached into the man's pockets then, took his wallet and car keys, and exited the room.

Outside, she tiptoed over and around several more bodies strewn about the parking lot in front of the motel. All of them—housekeeping, other guests, two small children who'd been playing nearby—had slumped to their deaths, without blood, without violence, without even the slightest awareness of what was happening. They were soaked from the rain. But Tessa ignored the downpour as she stood there, searching for the right car. She found it a moment later—a nice-looking two-door sedan, the sort of car newlyweds would have—and got inside. She hadn't had much real-world experience behind the wheel of a car, having driven her parents' car only once—and without a licence or their permission.

Nervous but very aware of herself, of what she was about to do—about what she needed to do—she started the car and backed out of the parking spot, careful not to drive over any of the bodies.

"They can't help us," Reece had told her, sworn to her as she watched him take one life after another like a creature starved. "They'll only be in our way. I promise you. I love you. We need to do this. We need to save them, all of them—we need to take away the house's power before it's too late. Together, we will save Black Stone."

She listened. She believed him, even as she saw him outside the car, the shape he took as they moved—a swift blade of absolute void, like the inverse of lightning, slashing through what people, what fools had the poor luck or temerity to live on the outskirts of a cursed town above which a maelstrom now raged. A warning shot, Reece said. A promise, to let the house know: they were coming. While the skies roiled, those on the ground were safe—or thought they were. But Black Stone was not safe and never would be so long as the house at the end of Cherry Lane remained standing.

PART TWO:

A SHADOW
COMES TO TOWN

*I*t was twelve years after its first appearance there that Death returned to the house down Cherry Lane. The middle of the night. A Tuesday at 3:07 a.m., to be precise.

Analiese remembered the time to the minute. Had Death's presence woken her from a deep slumber she would have been more inclined to discount her powers of recollection—the End of All Things might've been a dream brought on by a bit of food poisoning, or an errant hallucination resulting from the two sleeping pills she'd had at bedtime, and the two more she'd taken three hours later when another of Isabelle's coughing fits jolted her awake.

Analiese had woken, as she so often did, with her right hand already clutching her chest. She breathed deeply three, four times before clambering out of bed and hurrying to her daughter's room, just down the hall.

When Analiese arrived, Isabelle was already sitting upright with her face in her hands. She lifted her head when her mother switched on the porcelain pink-and-white elephant-shaped lamp on the dresser by the door.

"Mom." Isabelle's voice quavered, a dial trapped between two radio stations.

Analiese stared at her teenage daughter's hands and the mess of white tissues in them, all painted red. She looked up again, followed a spotted trail like a baby chick's footprints up Isabelle's nightshirt, her chin, to her lips, pale and cracked with a smear of bright crimson drawing down from the centre.

Analiese went and sat at the edge of her daughter's bed. The eggshell walls a sketchpad, with illustrations and signatures and messages from friends revealed beneath and between larger drawings and charcoal rubbings pinned haphazardly and leaving little empty space to be found.

"Oh, Izzy." Analiese reached into the box of tissues on the nightstand next to the bed. Finding it empty, she licked the cuff of her torn black sweater and proceeded to wipe clean the red staining her daughter's lips. She re-wet her sleeve, ignoring its now metallic taste, and cleaned away the last of the blood.

Isabelle pinched the sleeve of her mom's sweater. "It's July," she scratched out. Her words gargled as if her lungs were filled with fluid. "Aren't you hot?"

"That sounded like a bad one," Analiese said, ignoring the question. Isabelle hesitated, then nodded reluctantly; Analiese noted how her body shook. "What do you think, Izzy? Hospital?"

Isabelle coughed again and spat a bloody globule into the tissues, the trail of which dangled from her lip, stretched like olive oil from the tip of a spoon. "I'm okay," she managed at last.

"It's no problem, you know that. We'll go tonight, right now if we have to. Won't be long before they give us our own parking space," she joked.

"Really, I'm fine." It was Isabelle's turn to gaze upon her mother with concern. The shadows on Analiese's face, cast by the lamp near the door, blacker than they'd been—hollowed caverns like punctures in the side of a mountain. Staring at her mother's hunched-over torso, Isabelle noticed just how loosely that ratty black sweater hung across Analiese's frame. "What about you?"

"Don't worry about me."

"Mom, come on."

"I mean it. I'm all right."

Isabelle stared, wanting to say something but knowing it was useless. No sense in pushing her mother to reveal something she didn't want to, especially if it meant admitting weakness. Analiese wouldn't have it—wouldn't think of asking for help. She hadn't always been this way; Isabelle could remember when, before her father's death, her mother would readily admit to her limits. When she closed her eyes at night and tried, often pointlessly, to sleep, she could see snapshots of their lives before: of her father coaxing her mother into rest, trying to convince her to take care of herself. But following her father's sudden demise, Isabelle had watched her mother change. It was as if the colour palette of their lives had been swapped for a muted set; a sun coming up over a field that set the Earth to gold, but its rays, instead of warming, cooled everything they touched.

Analiese stared at her daughter, silent agreement passing between them, for the night at least, not to call the other on their lies.

When Analiese returned to her room, convinced Isabelle was stable at least for the moment, she popped a handful of sleeping pills—more than what had been prescribed, but it was, she told herself, necessary—and another Tylenol for the pain blooming in the space between her eyes. Then she lay back in bed, still wearing her too-large sweater, shivering, cocooned in her blankets. As she waited—hoped—for sleep, she listened for her heart. Curious if she could hear it thumping within its frail cage.

So it was at 3:07, a mere five minutes after returning from her daughter's bedside, when the shadow at the far end of Analiese's room unfolded silently like a deconstructed origami. And Death Itself appeared from within the unfurled abyss.

The Entity emerged from the darkness as silently as the universe itself had torn; the aged wood panels along the floor not so much as creaking as It billowed forward. What Analiese thought at first to be two hollows of a shadow curtain parting along the centre of Its torso were instead two condor-like wings. They swept out, raised upwards in solid wisps of ash that touched the walls to either side of the room. Death's limbs were smoke, constrained by what looked like thin veins of concertina wire too numerous to count; Its genderless torso was crossed corner to corner in a ribboned cloak as black and formless at its edges.

But it was the Entity's face to which Analiese found herself most drawn. Where Its eyes should have been were instead faint spirals of light, spinning slowly, the tendrils of twin galaxies heretofore undiscovered. Between and below those vortices of light were solid planks of black. As if It wore a mask over Its nose and mouth. If indeed It had such things.

When It spoke, Its voice resounded inside Analiese's head, grating: steel wool against the strings of a harp.

It is time.

The sound was tremorous. Analiese sat up straight in bed, hand over her heart to keep it from escaping. "Who—what are you?"

It is time, Death repeated.

Analiese could feel her brain overwhelmed with Death's presence. In an instant she saw bodies filling the streets of cities and worlds she did not and could never recognize, was privy to the function and history of the End of All Things. She'd thought Death at first a drop of rain, a singular Entity, when in truth It was the storm, Its precipitation spread over vast distances and times and dimensions, all to the same idea, the same end. She knew then Its appearance was no simple hallucination.

"No, please," Analiese begged. "She's only sixteen."

Death did not answer her.

"I said no!" Analiese stood. Her legs began to buckle, and with one hand she clutched the bedpost for support. The other went directly to her chest. "You can't. I won't let you take her."

Death reached out Its left hand, and Analiese saw concretely the malformed appendage: five smoke contrails given shape by tight reams of razor wire. In their hypnotic whirring, aimed at her heart—which she now realized, beneath her touch, had stopped entirely—she saw what a fool she'd been.

"No. Please, you don't understand. She won't survive without me. I won't!"

Analiese hadn't realized that she'd taken several steps forward and was now within only two feet of what she so dearly wished was an apparition. Something told her, though, were she to extend a hand into the abyss before her that it would suddenly cease to be, the limb gone and cauterized as if it had never been. She scuttled in reverse, never once taking her eyes from Death, not until she felt the presence of the wall behind her and realized she had nowhere left to go.

Death glided forward, Its lower half a whirling maelstrom of wire and dark. It stopped within inches of Analiese, close enough that she could stare into Its galaxies and imagine the billions upon billions of lives imprisoned within those manifold stars. Were Death to breathe, she would have felt Its icy chill. An emptiness like space. Like void.

Death repeated Itself one final time—the notes of a single octave unmoored by reverb or overlay. One final time, Analiese refused.

The Entity swept back then, and for a moment Analiese thought, impossibly, that she'd won.

Then—

So quick she'd not realized what was happening until it was already done, Death pressed into Analiese's chest with a single razored finger spiraling infinitum. It bore a hole straight through her skin, her sternum, down deep. It rooted around Analiese's innards for an eternity of agony, before yanking back again. It extended from within Analiese a single grey and red and viscous strand not unlike a taut thread of fabric or a guitar string. As It tugged on the strand, Analiese felt her heart—beating again, albeit slower and intermittent— begin to unravel, an apple's thin peel. She watched as Death carried the end of the strand to a corner of the bedroom where two walls met the ceiling, to the right of her bed. The strand grew to reach the top of the room, and Death placed the thin strip of muscle against the waiting surface. The strand immediately took root, conjoined now with the wall. With the house.

Analiese's body sagged as her insides swelled with unfamiliar architecture. She pulled once on the strand and winced, a sharp flare firing through her like an electroshock—like rattling foundations. Though it strained, it would not, could not, be pulled free. She thought to sever the cord but knew, instinctively, that she would collapse if she did, a house tumbling in on itself.

When she again regarded the Entity, It had returned to Its prior, smaller stature. Its galaxies now narrow and pointed. She had challenged Death and found It willing to spar with her. Its long, ethereal wings folded over Itself, and the Entity bled back into the shadows from whence It came.

Analiese remained in place, terrified to move. Her heart raced as much as it could in its now-reserved state, functioning on, she felt, limited power; she saw it as well as felt it: the strand of muscle that connected her to the wall pulsed and throbbed in time with the rest of her. When she stepped forward, the floorboards beneath her creaked and the house sent a signal of its own through the strand—a growing stiffness of her arms and legs, an ache of her chest, her neck, her head.

When Isabelle started coughing again, Analiese took another step, this one hurried. She felt a tug, sharp and spiteful. Then, as *she took another step, and another, she felt her heart unravel further. Yet she kept going, out of her room, down the hall, and into her daughter's room as her heart continued, terrifyingly, to unwind like fishing wire from a reel.*

CHAPTER
THIRTEEN

ELLIS'S ANXIETY WAS SPIKING. IT HAD COME ON SUDDEN AND swift, and seemingly without cause or provocation. They were anxious in a way they hadn't been since before the move. They were anxious the other night when Quinn saw them home. They were still anxious Monday morning at work, and even more anxious later that same afternoon as they sat in front of an open laptop, waiting for Dr. Webb to answer the video call for their agreed-upon monthly check in.

It was obvious enough, present enough that when partway through their session, Dr. Webb announced, "You seem anxious, Ellis," they had to stop themself from snidely responding, "Oh, do I? What tipped you off?" And then they glanced down at the sheet of paper they'd brought with them to take notes and saw that they'd torn it into small strips without even realizing. They let the strips flutter to the kitchen floor and folded their hands beneath the table.

"Oh, yeah," they said. "I guess. Maybe a little."

"Maybe?"

"... Definitely."

She smiled, leaned forward. "Do you want to talk about it?"

They shrugged. "I'm not sure how much there is to say. The

move went okay, work's fine. I'm content soaring mostly under the radar."

"Mostly?"

"Yeah. There've been a few things, I guess. A lot of people in town seem to think our house is haunted." They paused; they weren't sure they wanted to even broach the next topic, not until they knew if it was something worth broaching. Something real. But of all the things that had happened to them recently, they still weren't sure which they should be more taken aback by: the possible ghost they'd seen or—

"And I met someone. A friend. A girl. A . . ."

"Girlfriend?"

Oh god, Ellis thought. *There it is. That word.* They'd been almost terrified to use it, to say, definitively, that she's their partner, but the more they rolled it around in their mind, the more it seemed to just . . . fit. Because it did, right? She was absolutely what they wanted, wasn't she? I mean, sure she had questionable taste in films, but—

"Ellis?"

"Huh?"

"You're doing it again."

"What?"

"That thing where you have an entire conversation inside your head. I can see it in your eyes, you know."

"Wait—you can?"

She nodded. "So, do you want to talk about her?"

"I don't know what there is to say. She's funny, nice, beautiful . . ."

"Well, you could start with what's making you so anxious. Or maybe you just like tearing sheets of paper into tinier and tinier strips?"

Ellis looked down again and, sure enough, they were already hard at work on a second sheet. They put it down on the desk, atop the rest of the small stack there, and shoved it all aside.

"It's not her," Ellis was quick to say. "It's just . . . things are good right now. I've not been restricting, Mom's got a new job, I managed to find a job too. I'm even making art again. And then she—Quinn—comes along, and she likes me and it's just . . ."

"Good."

"Yeah."

"And you don't think you deserve it. Life going your way."

Ellis paused. "It's not . . . I'm not used to it. Also, I've never really dated before, and . . . there's still so much to work through and so much I don't know, and I don't know if I'm ready."

"So much to work through, you mean with—"

"Who I am," they supplied. "She already knows about the body stuff. The short version, anyway. But we haven't really talked about identity stuff. Not yet."

"And how long have you been seeing one another?"

"We've had one date so far, just this past weekend. But it went really well. I think we both want a second."

"And from the sounds of it, you've already touched upon a number of things. Really personal things. That's impressive for a first date."

"Yeah, the way I figured it, I'd put all my crap out there right away and see if she can stand the smell."

Dr. Webb frowned slightly. "Why would you make that analogy?"

"I don't know, it just came to me."

"But why that, specifically? You've just compared what you've been working through—diligently, I might add—to shit."

"It feels like that sometimes."

"And that's a problem, Ellis. What you've gone through, what you're still going through, it's normal. All of it."

"You wanna throw some scare quotes around that word, Doc?"

"I mean it. You're no different than so many others who've fought and beaten this disease. You weren't just airing out your dirty laundry with this . . . Quinn, you said? You were showing her a tremendous amount of trust. You opened yourself up to her, and she didn't run away."

"No . . . she didn't."

"What does that tell you?"

"That some people have *terrible* judgment."

"Ellis . . ."

"Aaaaaaannnnnd that maybe I need to do a better job of trusting others."

"And yourself."

"And myself."

Dr. Webb sat back in her chair and sighed. "I know this is still somewhat difficult for you to believe, Ellis, but you are, in fact, a good person, and you do deserve happiness."

"There are easier pills to swallow. Hell, there are easier suppositories . . ."

"I know, but it's true. And it's something I'd like you to work on."

"What, standing in front of a mirror and giving myself some daily affirmations?"

"Eventually. Right now, I'd like you to start by simply trusting yourself and those closest to you. Trusting that they care for you and *want* to be around you. You're worth the time, Ellis. Remember that. You deserve the same love as anyone else."

Dr. Webb's words resounded in Ellis's mind—the notion that they deserved the same love and happiness as others. The very concept still felt foreign to them. Like something out of a fantasy novel. They also knew that Dr. Webb would never say the opposite, even if it were true; she had a job to do, and that job was to keep Ellis moving forward, and to make sure they were honest with themself.

"That's the problem with being honest," Robyn said to them early on, when Ellis had become dejected over their ability to see so clearly what Dr. Webb was doing—how she was saying all the right things because she had a job to do, a purpose. "When you're able to think critically about something, it becomes difficult to give yourself over to it. It's like advertising: once you see how it works, how they go straight for the emotional jugular, it's hard to ever be swayed again."

"And if you are swayed, you still know it's happening."

"Exactly. And that's the thing. You're smart, kiddo. You know what she's trying to do and why. But you still need to let her in. Just because you can see the lines in the sand doesn't mean you shouldn't still follow them."

Ellis had been trying to do just that, but some days were easier than others. What they found so interesting, though, was that even though their brain was currently flooding the rest of their body with doubt, they also didn't care.

The mind was often a battlefield of competing wants, desires, and fears, Dr. Webb said during their first session together; the trick was being aware of which side you were on—or wanted to be on—and which side your brain was on, and recognizing that at any given moment they might not be one and the same.

Following the call, Ellis headed upstairs. They had to step around the easel they'd set up in the centre of their room, atop a bunch of old T-shirts they'd been using as a makeshift tarp. There was a canvas on the easel; it depicted, in process, a roiling black and grey and purple mass of clouds—the storm they'd seen upon leaving the movie theatre the other night, which had knocked out power to the entire town for several hours. They couldn't say why, but Ellis couldn't stop thinking about it.

"It's like a hurricane," they'd said to Quinn as they walked home that night. "Except we're in the wrong part of the country for that. And there was no landfall or anything—it just appeared."

Quinn hadn't much to say. She'd agreed that it seemed weird but also that weird was relative. "There's already so much strange in this town," she'd said. "A funky-looking storm cloud barely registers."

"Did you just say 'funky-looking'? What are you, forty?" When they looked over at her, she'd appeared lost in thought. Ellis wanted to take the moment to ask her again what she'd seen that afternoon, at their house, and whether that factored into the "so much strange" she'd mentioned, but they thought better of it in the end.

That was a conversation for another time.

They stared at the painting. By this point they didn't know what more—if anything—to change or add. It felt both finished and very far from finished at the same time.

They heard the front door slam shut, followed by, "Kiddo, you home?"

Ellis tore themself away from the painting and went to the top of the stairs. Thanks to a pair of last-minute night shifts at the hospital, Ellis hadn't seen their mom since before the weekend. They spotted her taking off her coat and draping it over the knob at the bottom of the banister.

"You know we have hooks for that." They nodded to the coat rack by the door as they came downstairs. "A whole rack and everything. Tall, wooden, slightly phallic—can't miss it."

"Oh yeah? And I'll bet you put your shoes under your nightstand instead of kicking them across your room like I've asked you not to do, oh, I don't know, about a billion times."

"Look, we could stand here asking ourselves who said what and when but what good would that do?"

"Uh-huh." Robyn pulled Ellis in for a hug. "Love you, smartass."

"Love you too. How was work?"

"Oh, you know: blood, needles, various tests. Better question: How was your date?"

"The same: blood, needles, various tests."

She gave them a light shove and walked down the hall to the kitchen. "I'm going to ruin my dinner. Want to join me?"

Ellis followed her into the kitchen, watched as she grabbed a bag of tortilla chips off the counter and a jar of spicy guacamole from the fridge. Ellis sat across from her as she tore into the bag and started shovelling chips into her mouth. Ellis, very mindfully, grabbed a small handful, which they placed on the table in front of them. They were still working on the whole "snacking" thing— eating when hungry but not feeling like they had to make a full meal of it, or calculating whether it impacted the timing or size of their next meal. That was a thing most people didn't seem to know or understand about an eating disorder: that it was, in essence, a form of obsessive-compulsive disorder. At Ellis's worst, they were planning out meals days in advance, to the hour, obsessively trying to manage their existence in a way that very nearly killed them.

Keenly aware of this fact, Robyn watched them carefully as they ate each chip one at a time, as if rationing them out. "Helluva storm we had the other night, wasn't it?"

"Yeah, it really was—everything okay at work?"

"Oh yeah, we were out for only a minute or two before our backup generators kicked into gear. What about around here? Anything spoil?"

"Nah. Power wasn't out long enough to do any real damage."

There was a pause. Robyn continued to eat and stare, waiting for Ellis to speak. "Soooo . . ." she started, smiling, "are you gonna tell me about it, or am I going to have to pry?"

"About what?" Ellis feigned innocence.

"So coy. About your date, silly. I want it all—every lurid detail."

"You say that now . . ."

"I mean it too. Unless there's . . . nakedity? Nakedness? Nudity—that's the word I was looking for. I swear to god, there isn't enough coffee in the world to kickstart my brain right now."

"You should probably go straight to bed, then, and not ask any further—"

"El." She glared. "Spill."

Ellis sighed. "There was no nakedness, I promise. We just talked, really. For most of the night. It was . . . it was pretty amazing, actually."

"Was all this talking before or after the making out?" she asked, followed immediately by, "I'm kidding!" when she saw Ellis turn violet on the spot. "Geez, you're sensitive."

"Yeah, yeah. Also: while talking, but before going to the movies . . . And then *after* the movie too. Which was . . . god, just a truly horrible movie."

Robyn couldn't hide her smile—not saying a word, just sitting there, grinning. Wide.

"Okay," Ellis said, "starting to get a liiiiiiiittle weird."

She reached across the table, put her hand on top of theirs. "I know, and I'm sorry. I'm just so happy to see you happy."

Ellis felt a sudden pang of guilt. Their health and well-being had weighed quite heavily on Robyn—they knew this. While she'd never confirmed or denied anything, Ellis had long suspected that their finances were only part of the reason for the move to Black Stone—a city as large as Cypress was an inherently stressful place, and stress wasn't ideal for anyone in recovery.

"I know," they said. "I'm working on it. I really am. And Quinn . . . she makes me happy."

Robyn's eyes widened sharply at Quinn's name—so quickly Ellis almost didn't catch it. "And when might I meet this Quinn?"

"Oh, no, you gotta give me time to prep her for the gauntlet."

"How dare." Robyn put a hand to her chest, feigning offense. "I promise to not interrogate her . . . much."

"Sure."

"But there's just one thing I have to know first."

"Okay . . ."

"When you say the movie was horrible, do you mean horrible-bad or horrible-good?"

Ellis dropped their face into their palms. "God, not you too."

"I'm just saying, there's a wide spectrum of bad out there."

"*Prom Night II.*"

She hesitated. "Okay, that's actually just bad."

"*Thank* you!" Ellis said and stood up from the table.

"Where are you going?"

"I started a new piece over the weekend. I want to go stare at it for a bit and pretend like I'm a thoughtful artist filled with deep and intense purpose."

Robyn stretched and groaned, hands pressed to her lower back. "Well, as long as you're quiet about it. I'm going to go have one of those power naps I hear are all the rage."

"Scout's honour. I promise only the quietest of existential crises."

"You were never a scout."

"And you've never napped for fewer than five hours. Know what that's called? A good night's sleep."

Robyn stood and patted Ellis on the shoulder as she made her way past. "Only when you're a teenager. Those of us with joint pain and mortgages need a little more. Oh," she added, halfway upstairs, "I need you to come straight home after your shift tomorrow. I've got a locksmith coming in to take a look at our cellar secret, and I need you here to let him in if I don't make it home in time."

"No problem. If we find any treasure, I promise to divide it equally and in no way hoard it beneath my bed."

"Goodnight, kiddo. Wallet's in my coat if you want to order something for dinner."

"The coat that's still hanging over the end of the banister and *not* on the coat rack like we discussed?"

"*Good night!*"

Ellis chuckled to themself as Robyn disappeared into her bedroom and shut the door. There had been a period when this sort of back-and-forth between them wasn't possible, when things had become a little too real for both of them. Maybe that was the beautiful thing about the move: when all was said and done, it had given them the thing they needed most of all—a second chance.

Their smile faded, though, when once more their thoughts turned to the painting in their room and what to do about it. How unsettled they still felt when they thought about the storm. There was indeed a lot that was strange here—of that, there was no denying. What Ellis was starting to wonder, though, was how much of it, if any, was connected, and whether or not the locked door in their cellar had anything to do with it.

CHAPTER
FOURTEEN

ELLIS HAD JUST LEFT WORK AT THE END OF THEIR SHIFT ON Tuesday and pulled out their phone to text Quinn when they looked up and saw her sitting on a concrete barrier on the other side of the café's parking lot. She saw them and grinned.

"Hey!" she exclaimed.

"Hey yourself." Ellis hurried over to her, reached out and pulled her into an embrace. They kissed.

Quinn turned her head and blushed. "You know, I wasn't sure how comfortable you were being public about, you know, *us*."

"As public as you want to be. And if anyone has a problem with that, they suck. Like, as a person. Because we're awesome."

"Well, you didn't go to school with Travis Hillcox. If there's a fat joke to be made, he'll make it."

"I met him. Sorta. He was here when I applied. Seemed like a dick."

"If he could still make gay and trans jokes, he would, but the school's LGBTQ alliance came down hard on him last year. Principal threatened to expel him if he didn't shape up. Fat jokes are all he has left."

"Well, he seems positively charming."

"As charismatic as food poisoning and about as much fun."

She gripped their hand. "So, you want to try for that second date right now?"

"I'd love to, but I can't today. Mom's got a locksmith coming over. I need to be there in case she doesn't make it home from the hospital in time."

Suddenly, as if in reflex, Quinn squeezed Ellis's hand so hard they winced. "Sorry," she said, loosening her grip.

"It's okay. I didn't need that hand anyway." They paused. "Are you okay?"

"Yeah, it's just . . . it's . . ." She cleared her throat. "Your mom's a doctor?"

"A nurse. In the ER."

"Ah."

Both of them fell silent; Ellis caught moisture in Quinn's eyes, which she quickly wiped away. They wanted to ask what was wrong but held their tongue.

"So," she started, changing the topic, "someone's coming over to change the locks?"

"Not exactly. Mom found this door or hatch or something in the cellar under the house. There's something inside it—there's gotta be—but we can't find the key. The locksmith is coming over to help us break in."

"Are . . . are you sure you should?"

Ellis shrugged. "It's our home. We should know what's down there, don't you think?"

"Normally, yeah, that would be a swell idea."

"There's a 'but' coming, I can feel it."

"A huge one. And you already know what it is."

Ellis wanted to shoot down what she was about to say but couldn't. Not after what they'd witnessed themself, in the cellar, in the walls of their very own bedroom.

"I do, but see, I have this flaw where I need to know the answers to things."

"Mental note: no David Lynch films."

"And if that means deep-diving into whatever crypt or cat-acombs or—"

"Sex dungeon."

"—lies beneath our home, then I want to know." They moved in closer. "So . . . you in?"

"Pardon?"

"Do you want to come over and wait for the locksmith with me? Maybe we could even look for that key a little—in case the locksmith is a bust. You know, checking loose floorboards, dig-ging into heating ducts—the usual."

She thought about it a moment. "Yeah," she said. Then, more confidently, "Let's do it."

It sounded to Ellis—though they didn't say so out loud—like she was having to almost psych herself up for it. "But if it's too much . . ."

"No, I'm in." She stopped then. "Turn your head just a sec—there," she said, reaching behind their ear and swiping close to their neck. When she brought her hand back around to the front, Ellis saw it smeared with blue paint they'd had no idea was even there.

"All right," Quinn said, exhaling. "Let's go."

It was a twenty-minute walk to the house. Ellis paid close atten-tion to Quinn every step of the way, noting how her pace slowed; how they could feel, through grip alone, her body tensing up like she was a walking knot. They knew there was still something she wasn't telling them.

"So . . . do you like working at the theatre?" they asked, hoping to ease the tension a little.

She shrugged. "I mean, I love movies, but it's just a job. I come home smelling like buttered popcorn most nights. But the discount is worth it. Besides, it's just to help pay for school."

"Where are you headed?"

"Haraway. It's an art school, up in Red Marsh."

"No way! Man, I'd love to go there."

"Did you apply?"

Ellis shook their head, feeling suddenly self-conscious. "Gonna try for the winter semester. With everything we've had going on . . ."

"No, I get it. It'll be there when you're ready. So . . . drawing, painting—"

"Painting. Oils, acrylic—if I can make a mess of things, I will."

Arriving at the house, Ellis felt Quinn's hand slip free of theirs. They were relieved the two of them had made it there before either Ellis's mom or the locksmith and bounded up the porch steps. They turned to face Quinn. "You okay?"

Quinn started nervously gripping and re-gripping her palms as if kneading dough. "Yeah, it's just . . . I'm not feeling too great all of a sudden."

The porch light flickered; Quinn jumped, pointed. "Is that normal?"

Ellis glanced over their shoulder. "Yeah, there's a short in it or something. We haven't found the switch for it yet."

She raised an eyebrow. "You haven't found the switch for it, and nobody's lived here for over two decades, but the light is just . . . on? Doesn't that strike you as a little—"

"Odd?"

"I was going to say haunted, but sure, odd."

"Didn't you once tell me that not all hauntings were bad?" They held out their hand.

She sighed and accepted the gesture, taking Ellis's hand again at the top of the steps. The two of them stood next to one another then, staring at the door.

"Ready?" Ellis asked.

"Is 'no' an acceptable answer?"

"Always."

She shook her head. "It's okay. I'm okay." She took a deep breath. "I'm ready, I think."

Ellis nodded and unlocked the front door. Together, they entered.

Standing in the foyer, Ellis said, "So . . . yeah, this is us."

Quinn surveyed the interior. The house still looked in shambles, with open paint cans and tarps covering the furniture in the living room to the left, a rolling hillside of wallpaper rolls and swatches on the desk in the den to the right, and framed pictures resting on most of the stairs directly in front of them.

Ellis cleared their throat. "We, uh, still need to hang those. They haven't just fallen off the wall like—"

"In *The Conjuring*," Quinn finished. "You're doing your homework."

Ellis glanced around, embarrassed. "We're not the fastest at moving in."

"That makes sense—it's only the two of you." She placed a hand on Ellis's forearm. "Shit, I'm so sorry, I didn't mean to—"

They gently, reassuringly, touched her hand. "It's all right. I promise," they added upon seeing the look of oh-I-shouldn't-have-said-that on Quinn's face. "It's been long enough—it doesn't hurt like it used to."

She nodded. "I know what you mean."

Ellis was about to ask what she meant by that when she started up the stairs. "Where are you going?" they asked.

Quinn turned and grinned, though Ellis could still see slight worry in her eyes. "Where do you think?"

Ellis pointed. "If you're looking for a bathroom, there's one here too. Just down the hall."

She rested both forearms on the banister and glared. Sighed. "Let me get this straight: you have, in front of you, a smiling, vivacious, rather incredible person—"

"Don't forget humble."

"—to whom you're attracted, and a completely empty house at your disposal, for at least a little while, and all you can think of when you saw me heading upstairs is to tell me where the bathroom is?"

Elis paused, confused. Then: "Oh. *Oh.*"

She winked at them. "*There* it is." She continued upstairs, glancing back at Ellis, still standing where she'd left them—like they'd taken root. "You coming?"

Ellis was about to follow her up when there was a knock at the door. They both stopped and stared. Quinn came back downstairs as Ellis went for the door.

She leaned forward and whispered, "Some other time."

Ellis didn't say so out loud, but they were almost relieved by the interruption. They really liked Quinn, but the thought of being alone with her filled them with the kind of dread usually reserved for pop quizzes and university admission portfolios. They weren't ready. Not yet.

They opened the front door to a tall East Asian man with white hair, a trimmed white beard, and black Coke-bottle glasses. In his right hand was a black zippered satchel. Ellis peered past the man to a blue pickup truck parked in the driveway, the words *Majima Locksmith and Home Security* stencilled in gold down the side.

The man stared at his phone, peering over the top of his thick glasses and moving the screen closer to his face and then farther away. "This is the Lang residence?" he said.

Ellis stepped aside to let him in. He nodded politely at Quinn as he glanced around.

"My mom should be home soon," Ellis said. "It's in the cellar. The locked door."

The man said, "Show me."

"Through here." Ellis led him into the cellar and through the smashed wood panel leading to the maze. "Careful, the edges are kinda sharp."

Quinn followed behind both of them. "Was it like this when you moved in?" she asked, noting the broken wood slats.

"No," Ellis replied. "Mom smashed her way through with a sledgehammer."

"I like her already."

"Just a little farther," Ellis said. They continued on, turning right at the final corner and coming face to face with the locked door in the ground. "This is it," they said to the locksmith, who knelt down and immediately got to work, running his hands across the surface of the hatch while unzipping his satchel full of tools.

"You've not found the key for this?" the locksmith asked.

If we had, we wouldn't have called you. "No, but my mom did try to pick the lock."

The locksmith scoffed and got to work examining the hatch. Ellis watched him for a moment before turning around. They saw Quinn standing at the other end of the short passageway with her back to them, having turned left and not right at the fork.

"Quinn?" Ellis went up to her, leaving the locksmith to do his thing. She didn't respond. Through what little daylight streamed through the lone ground-level window there, Ellis saw over her shoulder, as they got closer, something in her hand—something they'd spotted the first time they'd come down here and then forgotten about: a maroon rubber ball, the kind used in elementary school gym class. They were taken aback—they thought they'd only imagined the ball, along with the shadow they'd seen standing over it.

She was shaking, and when she turned her face was wet with tears. She dug her fingers into the ball.

"Quinn?"

"It isn't real," she muttered, teeth clenched.

"What isn't real? The ball?"

"He's here, Ellis. He's still here. He's . . . he's trapped."

"Who? Who's here? What's going on—are you okay?"

But she wasn't listening. She was too busy now staring past them, to the other end of the passageway—to the locksmith there, crouched over the passageway that would lead them deeper into the earth.

"Is he going to do it?" she asked. "Is he going to get inside?"

"Quinn, I . . . I don't know. He's only just begun."

"But what if . . ." She started to hyperventilate. "I need to go. I can't—I don't know—"

"What's wrong? Talk to me, please."

She shook her head vigorously. "No, I need to—I've got to—" And she thrust the ball into Ellis's chest. They clutched it tight as Quinn pressed her way past them and started working her way back through the small but confusing maze.

Ellis looked down at the ball in their hands. They rotated it, stopping at a word—a name scrawled messily in faded black Sharpie:

Trey S.

They dropped the ball and ran after Quinn. They caught her at the front door, just as she was leaving.

"Hey," they said breathlessly. "Talk to me, will you?"

She put a hand to the doorframe but didn't turn around. "I can't," she said. Ellis heard the hitch in her voice, like she was doing all she could to keep from crying. "I'm not ready. I thought I was, but I'm not."

"Not ready for what?"

"For whatever's down there." She paused. "Ellis, your house really is haunted."

"I know," they said, realizing then, for the first time, that they meant it. "But I don't know what that means."

"Neither do I. But I can't stay here . . . I need space."

"I— Okay."

"Okay." She waited a moment longer, perhaps expecting them to come over, to hug her or show her some measure of comfort.

Ellis waited, too, for some sign that it was okay to do just that. That it was desired.

In the end, she left without anything more passing between them.

Ellis watched as, moments later, Robyn's car turned down the street. She passed Quinn on the way.

"Was that . . . ?" she asked a minute later when she arrived at the front door. Ellis just nodded. "She looked upset—everything okay?"

"I think so," Ellis lied. "We were in the cellar together and she sort of freaked out. I think maybe she's claustrophobic or something."

Robyn nodded and headed inside while Ellis remained on the porch, watching as Quinn turned the corner at the end of the street and disappeared from view. Returning inside, their mom was busy talking to the locksmith, who had emerged from the cellar.

"There's not much I can do," the locksmith said. "That's solid steel, several inches thick. And the lock is in a . . . it's a strange configuration."

"You can't bypass it?" Robyn asked.

"I'm not sure if I have the right tools. You might need a specialist."

"Which is . . . what you are, isn't it?"

He shook his head. "I mostly just install and change locks. I'm sorry."

Robyn sighed. "Thank you for coming."

The locksmith shook her hand and left.

"I'm going to bed," Robyn said after another minute. "I'm exhausted. Think you can look after yourself again tonight?"

Ellis nodded. Watched as she dragged herself upstairs. They could sense her disappointment—it was as if this one thing was keeping the house from being truly theirs. She'd hoped this would be the last of it, that they'd get their answers soon, and without having to hire someone to come and dig up half their property.

She paused then, at the top of the stairs. "Oh, and El?" She turned around.

"Yeah?"

"She's very beautiful. Goodnight, kiddo."

That night, Ellis struggled to fall asleep. They couldn't stop thinking about what they'd seen, how Quinn had reacted at the sight of the rubber ball. It wasn't until the middle of the night, when they realized they had to pee, that they rolled over and glanced at the phone next to them on the mattress, its face lit with a string of incoming texts—all from Quinn. They'd texted her earlier, not long after she'd hurried out of their house. They were worried about her and wanted to make sure she was all right. She'd not responded, though—until now.

I'm sorry

I'm okay

I will be okay

Ellis watched the bouncing ellipsis of another incoming message, waiting to see what more she had to say, but nothing came. They considered responding, prying just a little to see what more they could learn, but held back.

Sighing, Ellis climbed out of bed and stumbled down the hall and into the washroom there. They switched on the lights and immediately frowned. In the mirror, their midsection, still too slender for their mom's comfort, appeared hard and protruding. After they finished peeing, they checked their reflection again. Their belly seemed smaller now. They hated how malleable they felt, how quickly their self-perception shifted from totally unacceptable to, well, *fine*. Not great, just . . . fine. And they hated, too, how dialled in they were to literally every shift like this, no matter how large or small. It was in moments like this that they realized, for all the ground they'd regained during the past year, there was still so much yet to cover.

They washed their hands, still staring into the mirror. "Why is this still so fucking hard?" they whispered aloud.

And a woman's voice whispered back: "It's not what you think."

They shut off the tap and spun one-eighty. "Who's there?" They waited. "Mom?"

They heard something else then, a gentle groaning like wood settling but . . . moving. A strange tremor was sliding down the hall on the inside of the walls.

Slowly, Ellis exited the bathroom. They crept down the dark hall, wishing they'd brought their phone with them to use as a light. They paused—quiet whispers then, like the hiss of a leaking gas pipe. They looked up and around—the hissing surrounded them. They swallowed hard, their mouth suddenly desert-dry, and continued on, heart racing, toward the top of the stairs, their hand on the wall to their left to help guide them—

And stopped immediately upon hitting a thick ridge in the wallpaper—beneath it, actually, where it felt as if the wood had ruptured. Hesitating, remembering what happened last time, they placed their palm gently over the hard, asymmetrical ridge, what felt like a tiny mountain range if viewed from above.

The ridge—*the vein*, they said to themself, whatever their mom's objections—was warm. More than warm; it was hot. They felt it pulsing beneath their hand. Slowly. Rhythmically.

They felt it beating.

They shut their eyes then and listened. Stilled their thoughts, the thunder of their own frightened heart as much as possible.

And there. Gentle, like the first drops of rain before the skies open up, they heard it: a pulse.

Slow.

Rhythmic.

Everywhere.

It surrounded them.

CHAPTER
FIFTEEN

I'M GLAD

> *I was definitely worried*
> *You seemed pretty shaken*
> *I'm around if you want or need to talk*

It was just past dawn when Ellis texted Quinn. They'd not slept much—or at all—having spent the night stealthing through the house, running their palms across every bit of wall they could, listening, feeling for further ridges. Beats, inexplicable but there, beneath the wallpaper, in the drywall itself. They'd thought of waking their mom, but they weren't ready to worry her with this, not when she already had so much on her mind. Not until they had evidence. Even a shred would do—they didn't want a repeat of the wallpaper incident. Their own heart had not stopped racing since first hearing the voice. They weren't scared, though; they were curious.

They kept their fear, their concern where it belonged: on Quinn.

Ellis kept a constant eye on their phone, checking for any sign of a response. This went on for several days. Ellis felt the beginnings of a vacuum in their heart, a gaping hole inside of them that had developed far quicker than they'd anticipated. They struggled more and more to sleep.

On Friday, Ellis didn't really feel like painting, so they decided to go for a walk, get some air. Maybe listen to some of the tracks Quinn had added to their phone when they weren't looking. They were standing on the porch and had turned to lock the door behind them when they felt a tap on their shoulder. They spun around to find Quinn there, as if she'd materialized out of nothing. She smiled weakly.

"Hi." She spoke softly.

"Quinn, hey, so . . . if I went in for a hug right now, would that be okay?"

She nodded; they did.

"I'm sorry," she said, pulling away. "For ghosting you all week. I didn't—"

Ellis put up a hand. "You don't need to apologize. But . . . are we okay?"

She was quick to nod. "Can we talk?"

Ten minutes later, Quinn was leading Ellis through the empty, eerie halls of Black Stone High. Ellis followed her through the main concourse and into a nearby art room, where they stopped to note the many large tubs of various acrylic paints, purchased in bulk, that lined the far wall. Next, she took them through a tall black cylindrical doorway that opened on the other side into a very small, very red space filled with sour-smelling basins that had at one time been filled with chemical solutions for developing photographs.

"Huh." Ellis peered around the room, taking it all in. "Been a minute since I've seen a working darkroom. They got rid of the one at my old school. Said they didn't need it after the class went digital."

"Yeah, no one else ever comes in here. I like it, though." She grabbed a small stack of books off the counter there and shoved them in her backpack, along with her camera and some prints she'd made. Ellis caught a quick glimpse of the top image—what looked like the elderly couple they'd seen at the park, hiding beneath the tree there, only they were seated on a bench in front of a small lake with sunlight streaming right through them. So much so that it looked like a double exposure. They were about to inquire about it when Quinn said, "I come here to get away, or sometimes just to talk."

"Who do you talk to in here?" They watched as she continued to pack and repack her bag, making sure her camera was safe and not likely to be damaged by anything else in there.

"Mostly myself. Sometimes I have company, though. I never know when he'll show. He just does. Anyway, I wanted to show you this place. I wanted you to see it. To be here with you. It's like my home away from home."

"Quinn, who do you talk to in here?"

"I'm sorry for the other day," she said at last. "I shouldn't have bolted like that."

Ellis stood behind her as she finished packing. They thought they could hear her sniffling. "What was it?" they asked. "What did you see—whose name was on that ball?"

She faced them. Her cheeks were wet. "Trey's my younger brother. He comes here sometimes. Sits with me. The ball is— was his."

"Was?"

Quinn nodded. "Trey's dead, Ellis. He died five years ago."

A short while later, seated across from one another at Twitch, Quinn sat staring into the drink in front of her while Ellis dumped a packet of sweetener into their espresso.

"What did you say that was again?" they asked.

"A dirty chai." Quinn took a sip. "It's a chai latte with a shot of espresso."

"Sounds good."

"It's the only way I can stand coffee. It's too bitter otherwise."

"Ah, but I like the bitter. I'm here for it."

She raised an eyebrow. "So, should I take that personally, or . . ."

"No— Wait, that's not what I—"

"Ellis, relax. I'm fucking with you."

They sighed. "Between you and my mom you'd think I'd be better at recognizing sarcasm by now."

"You recognize it fine. You're just sensitive. That's a good thing," she added when Ellis appeared suddenly uncomfortable. "Mostly. Providing it doesn't stop you from living your life."

Ellis sipped their espresso, savouring it. "You know, I never used to like this stuff. Even the smell of coffee used to gross me out."

"I think every kid is like that. It's something you get used to. I don't know of anyone who loved the smell or taste of it straight out of the womb. What changed?"

"I started drinking it back when I was sick—when I was still in the thick of it. The thing no one thinks about when getting into it with anorexia is the energy side of things. You learn pretty quickly that oh, hey, when I stop taking in fuel my stores eventually run dry. Hence—" they lifted their tiny espresso cup and took another sip.

"Right. Caffeine."

They finished their drink. "I think," they said, staring down into the now-empty cup, "if I were to trace it back even further, the first signs were there when I was just a kid. Dad had an earlier bout with cancer. You know that old wives' tale about swallowed gum staying in your body for seven years?"

"If by 'old wives' tale' you mean 'hard scientific fact,' then yes."

"Yeah, well, for some reason, six-year-old me thought that rule applied to people too. That if I ate a part of my dad, it would somehow keep him alive or protect him or something. So . . . I started eating his hair—just what bits were falling out. I thought maybe, I don't know . . ." They glanced up and saw Quinn staring at them, part fascinated, part confused. "I know, it makes zero sense, but at the time—"

"I get it," Quinn said. "When you want to save someone, there's nothing you won't try."

Ellis hesitated, knowing what they wanted to ask but unsure how to phrase it.

"Just do it."

Ellis looked up. Quinn was staring intently at them. "Huh?"

Quinn sighed. "You're staring into an empty cup like you expect it to start talking back to you. I know what you want to ask, so go ahead. You won't hurt me," she added. "I swear."

Ellis sighed. "How did he die?"

"A car hit him. Backed over him, actually. He was down near your house—he'd run through the woods out behind our place and ended up on Cherry Lane. He was just chasing after his ball when one of your neighbours was coming out of their driveway and . . ." She wiped her eyes. "He was only six. He was only six, and I should've been watching him and . . ."

"Quinn, I'm—"

"Sorry, I know. Everyone's sorry, so you don't have to fucking say it," she snapped. Sighed. "I didn't mean—"

"I get it," Ellis said. "You've heard it enough."

"It's not that. It's just . . . it doesn't *do* anything. A lot of the time when people tell you how sorry they are for something, it's because they don't know what else to say, but they have to say *something*. Or they think they do."

"What can I say—I come from a long line of fixers. Mom's a nurse. Plus remember five minutes ago, when I said I tried to keep my dad alive by eating his hair?"

Quinn laughed.

"Anyway, sorry for, uh, saying sorry. I guess."

"It's okay, Ellis. Really. I appreciate the sentiment."

Ellis nodded. "All right. Then I suppose the next question is: How did your brother's ball wind up in our cellar?"

"I don't know. I don't even have the first clue. It wasn't there when we got the call—it had already disappeared. Last I saw, he had it in his hands as he was running through the woods. The neighbours, the Chisholm family, said in the police report that it had been on the ground by Trey's— They'd seen it right after, when they realized what had happened. But in the time between going inside to call the police and coming back out again, it had vanished. No one's seen it since."

"Until a few days ago, in a rickety maze beneath our very haunted house."

Her eyes widened. "So, you do believe me."

"It's not just you I believe—this entire town seems to think our home is haunted. Or hunted."

"Hunted?"

"It's a long story. Anyway: yes, I believe you. And . . ."

"Yeah?"

"I've experienced . . . I've seen and heard, uh . . . things."

"What sorts of things?"

"Veins."

"Veins?"

"In the walls. Or something like veins. They're just under the wallpaper, these brownish-reddish webs that I'm willing to bet run through the entire house. They've stained the wood with what looks like blood. Except it's too dark to be blood—fresh blood, anyway. And . . . they beat."

"They beat," she repeated. "Like—"

"A heart. When I put my hand to one, I swear it had a pulse. I could even hear it, if I listened close enough. At least, I think I heard it. I might be losing my mind." Ellis went to take another sip only to be reminded that they'd finished their drink a few minutes earlier. Quinn handed them hers and they had a taste— paused, curious. "Shit, that's not half bad."

"See?"

They slid her drink back across the table. "Also, there's a voice. A woman's voice, I think. It's hard to tell. It sounds, I don't know, thick, I guess. Like there are layers to it. Like it's not just one note but a chord, to get all music nerd on you for a second."

"What does it say?"

"Something like, 'It's not what you think.' Or maybe, 'I'm not what you think.' It was tough to make out." Ellis sat back. "I laughed at those idiots, you know."

"Who?"

"Dominik and his Hardy Boys–slash–Nancy Drew ghost hunter fan club. They told me my house was haunted, and I shrugged them off."

"I wouldn't beat yourself up over that. Dominik *is* an idiot. But stopped clocks and all."

"I don't know what, but something is *definitely* different about this place. Black Stone, I mean. It's so unlike anything around it. On our way here, we passed through Optimism, and let me tell you, *that* place is a ghost town. The cemeteries there are these sprawling things. Even the ground . . . the grass was all dead, and there were barely any trees at all."

Quinn nodded. "But then you hit the border to this place and—"

"—and it was like going from black-and-white to full colour. The world just seemed to come alive."

"And you think your house is responsible?"

"I don't know what to think, but Dominik clearly has some theories of his own."

"Yeah, well Dom's mom also thinks health care is a sin, the trans agenda is real, and that Obama is a secret Kenyan Muslim out to destroy the very notion of freedom *still*. So, you know, grains of salt and all that."

"She sounds like a very fine person."

"I hear they're on both sides now." Quinn shook her head. "I don't know. Maybe your house *is* doing something to this town. It's definitely . . ."

"What?"

"I saw him there. Trey. That day I was standing outside your home . . ." She paused. "Sometimes he visits me in the darkroom. We sit next to one another and talk. Only I've never . . . I'm not sure if he's really there or if I'm just . . . Anyway, that day, I saw him through the trees behind our house, and I followed him. He'd vanish in spurts, whenever he stepped out of the shade and into direct sunlight. That's how I knew he was really there, that I wasn't imagining it. That maybe he wasn't alive anymore but . . . I got to your house then, and I saw him standing on the porch, and then he was—he just vanished. It wasn't like he popped out of existence or anything. He was literally there one second and gone the next. I had my camera with me and everything. I managed to get a picture of him, or I thought I had, but when I checked, the shots were empty. Just your porch, that light, and nothing else. A lot of people in this town have claimed to have seen a ghost or a loved one standing outside your home. Some people go there regularly, just to say hi, I think."

Ellis recalled the older couple they'd seen outside their house. They wondered now who those two had seen. Who it was they themself had seen when they turned to the right and saw the person . . . the actual *ghost*, they now accepted, just standing there in their living room.

"Your photo," they said suddenly.

"Hmm?"

"In the darkroom. I saw one of your prints. An old couple sitting on a bench in the park. Sunlight was passing through them. That . . . that wasn't a double exposure or anything, was it."

She shook her head.

"You'd think by this point I wouldn't still be surprised by any of this."

"It takes time to process," Quinn said. "It's not every day you find out that ghosts are real."

"And potentially your landlords." Ellis rubbed their face with both hands as if to rouse themself from a dream. "So, what's next?"

Quinn stared, confused. "What do you mean?"

"Well, if we know this stuff's going on, do we, I don't know, perform an exorcism or something? Do we try and set the ghosts free?"

"I'm not sure. Do . . . do we know that's what they need? Or even want?"

Ellis stopped themself midreply. That was not something they'd considered. "Okay, so who do we talk to if we want to get to the bottom of this?"

Quinn thought for a moment. "West and Subissati—the occult store owners. Maybe they can help—they know more about this town than anyone."

"I've met them—took your advice. They seemed nice. Weird, but nice."

"Weird and awesome. More importantly, they know their shit. If anyone can help, it's them."

A few minutes later, Ellis and Quinn were standing outside the occult shop, peering in through darkened windows.

"Do they usually close this early?" Ellis checked the time on their phone—it was only ten to five.

"Sometimes. Every now and then they'll shutter for a few days at a time, other times they'll be open at night and stay open 'til morning. They're . . . unpredictable."

"To say the least."

Ellis and Quinn began the walk back home, hand in hand.

"Thank you," Ellis said after a few minutes.

"For what?"

"Trusting me. With, well, everything."

Quinn smiled warmly. "I could say the same for you." She paused. "Hey, are you free tomorrow night?"

"Yeah, why? Gonna subject me to more cinematic agony?"

"Har har. Actually, and feel free to say no if you're not cool with this, but I was wondering if you'd like to have dinner. At my place. Meet my parents. Do that whole 'boyfriend-girlfriend' thing. Or personfriend, I mean. Partner."

Ellis laughed. "It's okay. And yeah, I'd really like that."

Right then, turning out of the town square, they bumped shoulders with someone. Ellis took a step back, but the woman kept her head down, her long dirty blonde hair a shroud over her face. She wore an oversized sweater and jeans, a black carry-on bag slung over one shoulder.

"Excuse me," Ellis said. The woman didn't look up, didn't acknowledge their existence. She continued on, stalking toward the centre of town, eyes to the ground as if following a path only she could see.

Quinn looked back, eyeing the other person curiously.

"Do you know her?" Ellis asked.

"No," Quinn said. "And that's weird."

"What?"

"A place this small doesn't get a ton of visitors, so you get to know or at least recognize everyone real quick. And I've never seen that person before in my life."

"Why is that weird? She might just be passing through."

"She didn't look like she was just passing through." Quinn continued to watch as the other woman walked on, focused only on the ground before her. "She looks like she doesn't want to be seen."

"Well, I can tell you one thing: she's not a ghost." Ellis rubbed their shoulder. "Also, I'm starting to think you've seen too many horror films. She's probably been here before. Or maybe she's a relative of someone in town."

"Maybe. I don't know. It's just . . ."

"Yeah?"

". . . weird."

CHAPTER
SIXTEEN

TESSA SWEET KEPT HER EYES TO THE GROUND AS SHE MADE her way through town. She hadn't been back in Black Stone since she was a teenager, but all the same she didn't want to risk someone recognizing her from afar. She offered no apologies, not even the most basic of acknowledgements as she bumped into the occasional person.

She didn't stop for anything. She couldn't.

She had a mission.

Reece had said as much on their way into town several days earlier, possibly more—it had gotten increasingly difficult for her to keep track of time following the years she'd spent locked away. He'd walked beside her, and she'd watched as the grass on the side of the road withered and died where he—it, she was starting to think, though she did not want to—stepped. And where the decay came to a sudden halt as they crossed into Black Stone; where, it seemed, Reece's presence seemed to lighten suddenly. To lessen. It—no, he, it *had* to be he—told her his spirit was trapped. All he wanted was to move on, but the house had ensnared him. As long as their former home still stood, he and so many like him would remain trapped in Black Stone, prisoners for all eternity.

When Reece first came to her, Tessa had promised to do anything she could to help. She'd promised again, standing amid the bodies left at the motel, telling herself that Reece couldn't help it, couldn't stop himself from lashing out. That he was only doing what was necessary to be liberated, to liberate them all—everyone, he'd explained while breaking her out of the facility, who had died and remained bound to the house.

"But if you're bound to the house," Tessa had said, "how were you able to come for me?"

"I can travel," Reece said. "But I cannot leave this place, this ... world." He stopped and turned his head. "Quick, down here." Tessa followed him down a short embankment just outside of Black Stone while two police cars and an ambulance raced past, heading back toward the motel. They hadn't made it very far in the car Tessa had stolen—she'd swerved to miss a deer and careened right off the road not five kilometres from the scene of their crime. Once the vehicles had passed and it was safe to move again, Tessa scrambled back up to the main road and continued on toward her destination, still several hours away.

Reece filled her in on the mission details as they walked.

"It's not just a house," he said. "You can't set fire to it or blow it up. Maybe at one point in time, when it wasn't so strong. But it's been feeding for years, you see. On the whole town. Feeding, and growing."

"It's bigger now?" Tessa was confused.

"No, not bigger. Its reach has grown."

"What do you mean?"

But Reece ignored her question.

Now, having passed through the centre of town, working to suppress the waves of nostalgia that bubbled up at every sight, sound, and smell, like the past had been bottled just for her, Tessa kept herself on task. She found herself walking along an invisible line—the town's perimeter, angling north, to the very edge of the furthermost circle on her map. She walked this edge for some time, through forest and field, until the sun had set. She stopped only when the grass at her feet dipped and then dropped off at a small cliff face, which she carefully inched her way down, scraping her shins, palms, and one of her knees. She didn't remember the ravine here being so large or cutting so far inland. At the bottom of the short decline, she found the sewer outflow, exactly as Reece had promised. Its chain-link covering was rusted and very easy to cut through with the pair of heavy-duty wire cutters she'd stolen from a hardware store in town two days earlier, after first going to the house—*their* house, hers and Reece's. She'd needed to see it again, for herself. She'd cursed its memory from afar for so long.

"I won't be able to help you in there," Reece said, appearing next to her as she finished cutting a hole wide and tall enough to squeeze through.

"What will I find?" Tessa asked, her body half through the gap she'd cut.

"The limits of her reach. And, hopefully, her weakness."

"Her?" But once more, Reece didn't respond. Tessa finished making her way through the grate. When she reached back for her bag of supplies, Reece was gone.

She entered the tunnel, sticking as close as possible to the sides to avoid the ankle-deep sludge in the centre of the rounded passageway that her brother, when still alive, once told her was made of all the dead babies and animals of the town, which was why there were so few graves in the cemeteries there when compared to those of Optimism or farther east, in Ashwood Barrens. It was just high enough inside for her to stand up straight. She slowly made her way forward, the back of her hand to her nose and mouth to try to stifle the stench—like wet, runny eggs and roadkill. In the distance, she heard the echo of running water. The passage branched to the left and right, narrowing into smaller tunnels through which she'd have to crouch, but Tessa continued forward without pause.

She didn't know what she was looking for—not exactly—but Reece had sworn she'd know it when she saw it.

And then she did.

Ahead of her, the pipe walls seemed different. Textured. She reached into her bag and pulled out a lighter. Sparked it and saw, finally, what Reece had been alluding to.

Dark red vines covered the pipe's interior, top to bottom, spread all over like a root system without earth to slither through. The vines looked strange, Tessa thought—not like anything she'd seen in nature, or on the National Geographic specials they played on a loop in the facility, supposedly to keep the residents from getting too agitated. She got close to a crosshatching of them, held the flame up close. Recoiled sharply when—

One moved.

No, it didn't move; it vibrated.

But.

Yes, that's it. The vine was . . . beating. She swung the flame around to the adjacent wall and saw the same thing—they were all beating as if . . . as if alive. As if they weren't vines at all.

She pulled the wire cutters from her back pocket and held them open. Brushed the top of one of the vines with the blade's edge. Instantly it started to bleed.

And then it beat. Harder.

They all did.

Together, the vines thumped hard against the tunnel's side, causing a localized tremor that nearly knocked Tessa off her feet. She kept her footing, though, and once more brandished the wire cutters against a piece of vine. This time, however, she cut straight through, slicing off a chunk that dropped into her other hand. She rolled it around on her palm.

She looked up and all around her at the vines—the veins, she now thought, seemed to be voicing their hurt, their distaste at what she'd done to them. To it? To her? She had no idea and was becoming concerned. She could feel now how far they stretched—the tremor moving through the sewer system, back toward the centre of town. The *actual* centre of town, that is—what she now knew to be the beating heart of all of Black Stone.

The town wasn't built atop the veins; whatever presence resided within that house had seemingly wormed its way beneath and throughout the entire town.

This was what Reece meant, she thought to herself. *This was how you hurt the house—you had to cut it back to the source, so that it couldn't feed on them any longer.*

She rummaged around in her bag again, depositing the wire cutters in favour of something else—a can of hairspray. With the lighter in her other hand, she popped the lid of the spray canister, gave it a few hard shakes, and then—

"Hey!"

A flashlight beam swept the tunnel. She turned and saw a man in dark blue jeans, an orange work vest, and a bright yellow hard hat trudging toward her.

"What do you think you're doing down here?" the man asked. "We got a call from a nearby resident, said they were out walking their dog when they saw someone cutting through the outflow grating. You know, I could have you arrested just for being down here. This place is off-limits."

Tessa searched her mind for an answer or an excuse, but none came. She raised her hand to show the man the piece of living tissue she'd cut from the walls, as if that would answer everything—or anything at all—but the hunk of vein had turned to ash in her palm.

"What in the— Did you do this?" the man asked. Tessa followed the beam of the man's flashlight as he surveyed the red climbing over all surfaces, growing denser the farther down he shined his light. He went up to a portion of the structure and touched it with his index finger.

And the veins started to thump in concert. They pounded so hard they rocked the tunnel. Tessa managed to keep her footing, putting her hand against a clear portion of the tunnel wall while the maintenance worker stumbled and fell backwards, landing on his back in sewage. She watched then as a vein rose from the water and started to coil itself around the man's left ankle; his waist; his neck. Tessa looked to the left then and saw a vein inching closer to her hand.

Tessa shrieked and ran back toward the tunnel's exit. She didn't stop—not when the beating increased; not when she could hear its dark, otherworldly bass grow as loud as the man's screams—louder now, drowning him out altogether. She kept running until she was outside again.

She slumped against the mouth of the tunnel, listening— for footsteps signalling the worker's escape; for Reece to tell her she'd failed and needed to try again. But there was nothing. She clutched her chest in panic. The beating in the tunnel had stopped, the air fell silent. She didn't know what had happened to the man, and she didn't much care to find out. She pictured him face down in the sewage, held there by a crush of inexplicably living tissue.

She had to catch her breath, figure out a new plan of attack.

She would try again another day.

CHAPTER
SEVENTEEN

SHIT. SHIT SHIT SHIT SHIT SHIT.

The record spinning in Ellis's brain was caught in a groove Saturday night as they stood panicking on Quinn's front step. They'd knocked already; there was no going back now.

"Just be yourself," Robyn said right before they left.

"When has that *ever* been good advice?" Ellis asked.

Their mom made a sound like *I don't know* with the vowels removed. "Probably helps if you're famous or something. With model-quality looks, fistfuls of money . . ."

"I'm confused—is this you trying to help?"

She kissed their forehead. "You're going to be fine. Trust me. Billions of people before you have met their partner's parents."

Trust me, she'd said. If there were a hierarchy of famous last words, trust me was at the very terrible top.

Shiiiiiiii—

The front door opened, and Quinn appeared, standing there in a beautiful maroon maxi dress, her smile a mix of radiance and—yes, terror. Seeing that she was as nervous as they, Ellis suddenly felt more prepared for whatever happened next.

She pulled Ellis inside and shut the door. Whispered, "Are you ready for this?"

"I think so," Ellis whispered back, noting how she fidgeted with her dress. "Are *you*?"

"I don't know. Maybe? I think I am. Did I mention I've never done this before?"

"That makes two of us. You look amazing, by the way."

She beamed.

Ellis stepped forward. They heard music in the background. "That Marvin Gaye?"

A man popped his head out from an adjacent room. "It is indeed. I like a person who knows their Motown." He stepped into the hall and shook Ellis's hand. "Name's William, but call me Bill. I'm this beautiful individual's father." He nodded to Quinn.

"Pleasure to meet you, sir." Ellis took in the tall-but-not-too-tall man: he was bald with a thick, black beard that reminded Ellis of Wooly Willy. He had a dark brown complexion, wore round glasses, and was built solid, like a former college athlete.

"You like a lot of Gaye?" Bill asked.

"I do, but it's gonna get real awkward real fast if you bust out some 'Sexual Healing.'" Ellis cringed internally as soon as they'd finished speaking, meanwhile—thankfully—Bill started to guffaw. It was a deep, joyful sort of laughter Ellis hadn't heard much of, especially not over the past couple of years. It almost took them by surprise.

"What's this I hear about the curative properties of intercourse?" A woman emerged from the kitchen. She had Quinn's face, eyes, and shape, and was busy wiping her hands on a dish towel.

"Oh, god, no," Quinn muttered and hid her face in her hands. Ellis thought they could see her cheeks reddening through the cracks between her fingers.

Bill kissed his wife on the cheek. "Now, honey, we don't want to embarrass the kids."

"Oh, I'm fine." Ellis looked over at Quinn, grinning. "You okay over there?"

"I hate you all," Quinn said through her hands. "I do. I really, really do."

Quinn's mother extended a hand to Ellis. "Cynthia," she said, and drew Ellis in for a hug. "It's so good to meet you! Come in, come in." She motioned for them all to follow her into the kitchen.

Cynthia? As in Mom's friend? Ellis took a moment to absorb their surroundings. Off to one side, from where Bill had appeared, was a den overflowing with books, stacks of paper, reports, and what looked like design schematics; the walls were covered with framed degrees from various universities. In the living room was a tall-back wicker chair, a couch with an army's worth of throw pillows and blankets piled to one side, and a baby grand piano against the south wall. Sheet music cluttered every available inch as if a textbook had exploded.

Mom's a mechanical engineer and Dad's a musician, Quinn had explained to Ellis earlier that day via text. Being there now, at ground zero of all this, Ellis thought to themself: *This is perfect.*

Dinner went off without a hitch. Cynthia, Bill, and Ellis had no trouble getting along. At one point, while Cynthia was pretending to laugh at one of her husband's puns, Quinn leaned over to Ellis and asked, "You okay?"

"Yeah, why?" they replied. She nodded to their plate; they'd barely made a dent in their red beans and brown rice and were busy poking at a piece of Italian sausage with their fork. They put the fork down with more of a clatter than intended. Fortunately, neither Cynthia nor Bill took notice. Or if they did, they pretended not to. Ellis was grateful for that and wondered if Quinn had prepared them for certain things, just in case.

Near the end of the meal, Ellis turned to Cynthia and, sensing an opening, blurted, "So, you know my mom?"

Quinn was taken by surprise. A slight silence descended. Cynthia wiped the edges of her lips with her napkin.

"Sorry, I don't mean to . . . She's mentioned a Cynthia a few times. More than a few times. Said you were childhood friends, back when she used to live here. The first time, I mean. I was wondering if you were—if you are that Cynthia."

Cynthia smiled weakly. "Yes, I know your mother. Robyn and I were actually pretty close at one point."

"She'd love to hear from you sometime."

Cynthia's smile strained. "I'm not so sure about that."

"How come?"

"Oh, you know how it is. People drift. We've stayed in touch, but . . . I'm actually surprised it took her so long to come back."

"She never visited? Not even before I was born?"

Cynthia shook her head. "No, when your mom got out of here, there was no turning back for her. I think she always wanted something more. Something bigger."

"You left, too, didn't you? For school?"

"I did. But I always intended on coming back." She reached to her left and gripped her husband's hand. "My family was here. It was where I felt I belonged."

Ellis felt suddenly shy. "I'm sorry, I shouldn't have put you on the spot like that. It's just, Mom doesn't talk much about her time here. I've never really known why. It's like—"

"Like she's ashamed?"

Ellis nodded.

Cynthia sighed. "I don't know if that's it. It might be part of it, sure. Not everyone likes living in a small town. And to escape it and then have to return . . . She might be having a hard time with that. But things weren't easy for her here. She didn't get along with her parents all that well."

"Yeah, we don't really talk about them."

"And then there was the incident with Reece."

"Reece?"

"Reece Sweet. A boy in our grade. He lived in your house, actually, him and his sister. Your mom was always over there.

Until one day she just . . . stopped. I never knew why, and she didn't say. They just stopped hanging out completely."

"And then Reece died."

"You know then."

"Bits and pieces," Ellis said. "Just."

Cynthia sighed. "Your mom and I . . . I never wanted to lose her like I did. But I think she wanted to lose us. This place. I don't know if she'd want to hear from me."

"Funny, she thinks you probably don't want to hear from her."

"Really? Oh, gosh . . . no, no that's not . . ." She reached out across the table and touched Ellis's hand. "I'll call her. Soon."

"She'd like that." Ellis grinned. "I know she would."

After dinner, Ellis followed Quinn up to her bedroom. "I don't have to tell you to keep the door open, do I?" Cynthia called out to them from downstairs.

"Mom!" Quinn whined. Ellis looked down from the second floor, caught Cynthia walking away, chuckling to herself. And then they heard Bill singing, loudly.

Ellis asked, "Is that—"

"'Sexual Healing,' yes."

Quinn shut the door and fell back against it. "I hate them both so much," she breathed, utterly red-faced.

Ellis had to stifle their laughter. "They're great." They looked around Quinn's room: an open round suitcase on the dresser overflowing with various hats and scarves. On the walls, a map of the New York City subway station with a silhouette of the Flatiron Building artfully spray-painted overtop; photographs of her family—Trey included—and posters from a trip to China some years back; and other black-and-white photos throughout, evidence of a burgeoning passion. On the short bookshelf next to her bed, a plethora of mystery novels and some books on cults. ("They're fascinating to me," she'd said once as they were walking home from their respective shifts, needling each other about their interests. "I just wanna know:

What's missing from a person's life that they think, 'Hey, I'm gonna give up all my worldly possessions and follow some dude out into the desert'?")

"I mean yes, but also just . . . ew." She stepped away from the door. "So, yeah, that's Mom and Dad. I apologize for . . . literally everything."

"Seriously, Quinn, as parents go, they're pretty awesome. I see where you get it from."

She smirked. "You're just trying to butter me up."

"Is it weird that our moms know each other?"

"Should it be?"

"I don't know," Ellis said. "It's just, like, this strange coincidence."

"Is it all that strange? I mean, a place this small . . ." She put her arm around their waist. "Really, though, are you okay?" Her tone shifted to that of concern.

"Yeah, it's just . . . I'm still getting used to eating around other people—especially people I don't know that well. I'm out of practice."

"Anything I can do to help?"

"Honestly? It's one of those 'time' things." They paused. "Your mom, she wasn't offended that I didn't eat more, was she?"

Quinn shook her head. "I . . . sort of gave them a heads-up so they wouldn't mention it. I hope that's okay."

"Totally fine," Ellis said, thinking: *That explains the absence of photos of Trey downstairs.* He'd been missing from all the family photos they'd seen spread throughout the house; and they'd noticed strange gaps on shelves here and there, on the hallway wall, too, where it seemed as if pictures had been removed or taken down only a short time ago. Her parents had probably hoped to avoid certain topics themselves. At least for their first meeting.

"What else do they know about me?" Ellis asked.

"The usual. That you're a good person. That I like you. That you're an *artiste*."

Ellis bristled at the word; it felt too lofty. "So . . . nothing about the house then."

"Not yet. I mean they've experienced things too. Things they couldn't explain. I don't think there's a person in this town who hasn't heard or seen something strange involving that house, even just a rumour, but we haven't talked about it or anything. They don't know . . . you know."

About the ball. Ellis noticed the way she said "that" house and not "your" house, like it was still something she herself was working out. Which was fair—they, too, were still trying to sift through all they'd learned and experienced in the short time they'd lived in Black Stone.

Quinn smiled at them. "You doing okay in there?"

"Huh?"

"You looked like you got lost for a moment."

"Yeah, I think I did."

She moved closer, brought one hand around, and spidered her fingers up their chest. "Anything I can do to help you find your way back?"

"I mean . . ."

She leaned in and kissed them. Pressed herself against them. They stayed like that for several very long seconds before they pulled away.

"Okay seriously," she said, "are you okay?"

Ellis took a beat to catch their breath. "I am. Promise."

"Because . . . I don't know, it's like you're somewhere else right now. Or like maybe you wish you were somewhere else? Whatever it is, you're not here with me. Not really."

Ellis glanced to the carpet. "Sorry."

She touched the side of their face. "Just tell me what's going on."

"It's not you," they were quick to say. "Trust me, you're . . . incredible. I just get that way sometimes. I get too much inside

my own head when it comes to—when things get physical."
They sighed. *Now or never.* "Fuck it. I'm . . . I'm ace, okay?"

She cocked her head, confused. "Ace?"

"Asexual."

"So, like, you can reproduce all on your own? Wow, that's efficient."

"No, it means—"

"I know what it means, Ellis. I'm screwing with you. Again." She gave a comforting grin. "Why didn't you say something earlier?"

"I don't know. It's not a thing I've really talked about with anyone, except my therapist. I've just never had those . . . urges, I guess."

She chuckled. "You sound like a dirty old person when you say it like that."

"At first I thought maybe it was tied to the body stuff. Being able to let go, to just be in the moment like that, physically, it's always seemed so strange to me. Alien. But the more I've sat with it, the more I . . . It's just who I am. I want a great many things in life, but not that. Not with anyone."

"I get that."

"And I thought if I dumped all this on you too soon . . ."

"What?"

"That maybe you'd not want to be with me anymore. That maybe it'd be too much." They bit the inside of their cheek while they waited for Quinn to walk away, to scream—to say or do anything, really.

Finally, she spoke. "I want to ask you a question, but I'm afraid to."

"If I can answer, I will."

"Honestly?"

"Cross my dark and shrivelled heart."

"Okay . . ." She kneaded the fabric of her dress with both hands. "Would it be any different for you if I . . . if I looked—"

They didn't let her finish; they swiftly closed the gap between them, pulled her into a hug from which it felt like there was no escape. "Not a chance. You're perfect as you are. I mean that."

"I believe you. I just had to be sure. And thank you."

"So . . ." They stared into her eyes as if expecting hers to dart away. "None of this is a deal-breaker for you?"

"Not even close. We . . . we just have to figure out what works, for both of us, and go from there. Okay?"

Ellis kissed her again. "Okay." And they remained like that, in each other's arms.

Until they felt a vibration coming up through the floorboards. A rumble, like an earthquake. No, like—

Ellis cocked their head. "Is that—"

Quinn sighed. "'Sexual Healing,' yeah."

Ellis laughed.

"Would you excuse me for a sec?" she said. "I've got some loved ones I need to go murder."

They stayed together another hour and a half, watching a movie on Quinn's iPad while stretched out on her bed.

"*Martyrs* is a classic—you'll love it," she'd said right as she hit play. Afterwards, Ellis glanced at her for upwards of a minute before asking if she actively intended to traumatize them. She brushed their concern aside with a wave of her hand. "You'll be fine. A little gore is good for the soul."

"A little— *She was flayed alive!*"

"It's only a movie," she whispered, kissing their cheek.

They said their goodnights a few minutes later, Cynthia and Bill meeting them at the door. ("Ellis looks a little pale," Cynthia said. "We watched *Martyrs*," Ellis replied. To which Cynthia turned to her daughter and asked, "Are you trying to traumatize them?")

Outside her front door, Quinn hugged Ellis one last time. "See you soon?"

"Absolutely. Do . . . do you want to come over next week and help me look for that key?"

"The locksmith couldn't help?"

"Not without dynamite."

She thought for a moment. "Okay . . . but I'm not going back into that cellar. Not yet. I need more time."

"Not a problem." Ellis smiled and started to walk away.

"Hey."

They turned.

"Thank you. For tonight. For all of it. My parents don't talk about it, but I know . . . They probably needed a night like this as much as we did. Mostly they deal with it by *not* dealing with it. But . . ." She took a deep breath. "I want to get to the bottom of all this."

"We will," Ellis said. "We'll do everything we can to figure this out."

Quinn didn't say anything more. Simply smiled, albeit weakly, and shut the door. It was no surprise to Ellis, though, that she would want to confront and understand what was going on, even if it took time. It was in her nature—that much was already clear. They saw it in how she picked apart the plots of horror films, how much she chided protagonists for not thinking far enough ahead.

"You always hope they're going to be smarter than they are in the end," she'd said in the middle of the film. "You want them to see what you see and figure shit out for themselves."

Which made sense to Ellis. By media and circumstance, Quinn had trained herself to dig deeper, always, and to suspect everything.

The entire short walk home, Ellis felt light. Like they could take off, float through the air if they wanted to. If meeting her parents was a test, they'd passed, and with flying colours.

This lightness continued until they turned onto Cherry Lane. Though dark out, they could make out movement at the end of the street: commotion, shouting, people standing out in front of their house; and Ellis's mom, on the porch, door open behind her, screaming at whoever was there to "Get away, get the hell off our property!"

Next to her, the porch light strobed wildly.

"Get away!" she shouted a second time, voice high, piercing. From afar, Ellis thought, she sounded drunk. Something they hadn't heard since a few weeks after Dad died—the slight slurring of her words, the increased pitch.

Ellis ran to the end of the street. Getting closer, they saw the source of the conflict: two men and a woman, all older—in their sixties at least—supporting a fourth person, another woman, incapable of standing on her own. The fourth person appeared gaunt, sunken cheeks and eyes, pale skin stretched tight over her bones; her clothes were soaked as if she'd sweated right through them.

"Please!" shouted one of the men. "If we don't do this, we'll lose her forever."

"I said no, you . . . you vulture! Leave now, or I'll call the police."

"But—"

"Now!"

By this point, neighbours they'd not yet met were exiting their homes in their pyjamas and robes to see what the hell was going on. One, a woman with her greying hair tumbling out from under a silk sleep cap—Mrs. Hyde, Ellis remembered Robyn saying when they first moved in—asked if she could help, but Robyn seemed not to have heard.

The sickly woman looked up at her friends. "Just leave me on the grass," she said. She struggled to get the words out. Coughed, hard, as if to expel a lung. "She'll take care of me. She always does. She takes care of us all."

"Like hell I will," Robyn said, becoming increasingly irate. She reached behind her and pulled out the sledgehammer. "You've got until the count of three to get off my property. One . . . two . . ."

"You don't own this!" one of the men shouted. "You can't own her—no one can! You can't keep her from us!"

". . . three!"

They relented at the last second, the men hoisting their sick friend back up to her feet and supporting her retreat from the house. The sick woman wailed in response, begging them, pleading to be left behind. "She'll protect me! She protects us all!" she shrieked as they continued back up the street to their car parked on the side of the road. They guided their unwell friend into the back seat after the other woman, leaning her across her friend's lap before climbing in up front and driving off without saying anything further.

Ellis watched through the car's window as they drove away, the sick woman still slumped over, shoulders heaving. Then they looked to their neighbours, who all wordlessly returned to their own homes, quietly shutting their doors as if they'd not witnessed a thing. Off to the side, they caught sight of Travis Hillcox and someone else, someone older—his father, perhaps?—dressed in dark colours. Travis held a rock in one hand as the other man hurled one toward the house but came up short. The older man muttered something under his breath. Ellis caught only a smattering of words: *should, torched, had the chance.*

Ellis faced the house again. There was a man there, between them and the house, standing not two feet away as if he'd walked out of a hole in space. Older, wispy white hair, and even in the dark of night, a face of asphalt and skin like leather. Ellis had never seen him before.

"Why did you let her do that?" he asked. Voice warbly, like marbles across cobblestones. "Why didn't you stop her?"

"I—"

"She could have helped, you know. She's doing important work! It must be done!"

Ellis wanted to ask who this other "she" was, but they were distracted by soft spears of light, from their porchlight, visibly perforating the man—like in the photo of Quinn's they'd assumed was a double exposure. They wondered, if they touched this man's chest, would their hand . . . was he—

"*WHY?*" The man's voice hit like a klaxon. His face was stretched, distorted into a Munch-like terror; his mouth a shrieking dark oblivion. Ellis stumbled, fell backwards in shock.

They shut their eyes, hard.

And when they opened them again, the man had vanished.

Ellis looked around for any trace of him. They spotted Travis and the man they suspected was his father walking away, snickering to themselves. Ellis got up off the ground, their chest tight, eyes darting around, searching for the man. Not seeing him, they hurried to the house, glancing back only once to make sure they weren't being followed. Inside, they found Robyn leaning up against the railing by the stairs, weeping, her face red and blotchy and tear-streaked. They went over to her, gripped her shoulder.

"Mom, what did they—"

"Can you believe these people?" she shouted through snot-filled sobs. "They came to the hospital. They *came to where I work* and asked me if—if their friend could die here. Here! In our fucking house! I tried to see if I could admit them, but they refused. They followed me home after my shift and *begged* me to let them come inside so that their friend could just die! So that she could—so that . . . Can you believe that? It isn't even real! She isn't . . . Who does a thing like that—and to a total stranger! Who . . ."

She trailed off and started sobbing again. Ellis wasn't surprised; working at a hospital was one thing, but having death follow you home like that . . . They'd been through that once already, and, hopefully, it would be a very long time before they ever had to go through it again.

A pop then—a sharp shattering of glass as a stone came through the window to the left of the door. Ellis jumped, and

Robyn let out a scream. By the time Ellis got to the door, there was no one. They suggested calling the police, but Robyn just shook her head and wept.

It was all starting to make a sick sort of sense: the house wasn't devouring people or feeding on their town, but there was still something to it—or the townspeople believed there was. Some of them, anyway—

Ellis paused midthought.

The ball. Trey's ball. The person wanting to be left there—to die, *there*.

Was it collecting *people?*

"Okay, Mom." They reached down and helped Robyn to her feet. "Let's get you upstairs and into bed."

Robyn struggled to stand; she seemed more emotionally wrung out than drunk. Ellis put her arm over their shoulder and they started up the stairs together.

Something caught Ellis's eye, in their periphery. They glanced back, stared out through the broken window by the door. To the porch light.

Solid. Unblinking.

*I*t took several days for Analiese to learn how best to navigate the house, carefully lifting and pulling her heart string around doors and over the banister, learning which parts of the house to avoid—where its floors creaked loudest, its taps leaked, where its walls grew thin from age and the torments of the elements.

By the end of the second week, she was moving around again as quickly as she had before her encounter with Death.

Her insides, though, were another story. With every step, Analiese experienced a sensation of being flayed as her heart unspooled itself. The string pulled taut when she went to check on Isabelle, tighter still when she would go downstairs to fix something to eat, worried whether she'd be able to keep any food down. Analiese's own appetite had dwindled considerably. Isabelle hadn't failed to notice.

"Don't think I don't see it," her daughter said a month after Death came to call. "You barely eat, you don't ever leave the house anymore." She touched her mother's leg, seated on the edge of the bed. "You're skin and bones. What aren't you telling me?"

Analiese reached instinctively for her heart, absent-mindedly playing with the string of muscle as if nervously twirling a curl of hair around her finger. To Isabelle, it appeared as though she was plucking the string of an invisible violin. "It's nothing, sweetie. I'm fine. This," she said, cupping her bone-thin wrist, wrapping her fingers all the way around and then some, "is just stress. You'll see—once you're better, I'll be my old self again. You'll see," she repeated, not sure which one of them she was trying to convince.

But Isabelle saw the strain on Analiese's face, evident in new lines sewn beneath her eyes, down her cheeks, and around her jaw; she knew the toll her illness had taken on her mother, and she vowed to fight harder than ever.

Things continued in this vein for weeks. Where Analiese had previously not liked to leave the house unless absolutely necessary, often paying a neighbour to pick up and deliver their groceries, now she couldn't leave. Most mornings she stood on the porch just outside the front door, heart string cast over her shoulder like a dish towel, observing the quiet of the neighbourhood in the pre-dawn hours. She felt the pulse of her heart string quickening, a soft pumping against her shoulder as the sun warmed the exterior of the house. It wasn't long before the outdoors began to stretch—to drag as if through a tunnel. She'd remain in place for as long as she could tolerate it before it forced her back inside. As soon as she shut the door, the house once more closed off from the world, her heart grew full, the string winding just a little bit back.

This wasn't a serious problem at first. Not until the next time Isabelle couldn't stop coughing.

It was the middle of the night. Another Tuesday. Analiese was awoken again by the awful sound of her daughter hacking fervently into her hands. She rose and went to Isabelle's room, tried desperately to carry her daughter downstairs but couldn't manage her weight. When she tried to lift Isabelle in her arms, her heart string pulsed harder, faster, unravelling her insides quickly. Her legs went out from under her, the house creaking with her, support beams flexing, the floor and ceiling above their heads distending. The groaning tumult stopped only when Analiese collapsed fully to the floor of the bedroom, her daughter's frail body spilling from her arms. Clattering like loose bones on the wood below.

She left Isabelle on the floor and ran back to her room, pausing just long enough to retrieve a loose knot of muscle that had twisted and become wedged beneath the door there. She reached for the phone on the nightstand next to her bed and called for an ambulance.

"Please hurry," she said. "I haven't seen her this bad before." The operator on the other end of the call urged Analiese to remain calm, said the paramedics would be there soon.

Analiese nodded, not caring that the operator couldn't see it. She peered up then, receiver still pressed to her ear, attention fixed on the drooping smile of rapidly beating muscle and the smattering of red stain long gone brown left on the wallpaper behind her bed. For a single, uncanny moment, the rhythm of her heart string perfectly matched Isabelle's coughing, echoing from down the hall.

And then—

—the moment passed, and her heart played alone.

Analiese turned to the entrance of her room, more startled by the sudden silence from down the hall than she'd been at the start of Isabelle's fit.

"Miss? Are you still there?" the operator asked as Analiese lowered, then dropped the receiver. She rose and gripped the heart string in her hands, twisting the house's foundation as if it were a damp cloth to wring dry.

From impossibly far away, tinny, came: "Hello? Miss?"

Her heart string answered for her, a deep, thudding pulse as Analiese saw, trailing out from Isabelle's open door, a long, spider leg-segmented wing of ash and smoke. She sprinted down the hall as the smoke curled inward, the silent storm disappearing inside her daughter's bedroom.

Analiese came around the corner and saw no trace of Death. Just her own daughter, motionless. Lying there as if carved from stone. The only evidence she'd ever lived the still-wet river of blood that had flowed from her mouth and slicked her chin, down her nightdress, and pooled on the floor.

Analiese's scream cracked the night.

CHAPTER
EIGHTEEN

TESSA WAS CONCERNED. WHEN REECE FIRST TOLD HER OF HIS plan, she'd felt so certain: this was what she had to do to make things right. It was how she could make up for what she'd failed to do all those years ago.

"It's time," Reece had said right before they crossed into Black Stone proper. "Help put an end to this so I—so we can *all* rest."

Reece had warned her, though, that he wouldn't be as strong once they entered the town. "Because it's hers now. The entire town belongs to her. It's not just a house—she has woven herself through the fabric of Black Stone. She needs to be stopped before it's too late. Before she spreads beyond its borders."

He'd left her soon after she entered town, telling her she needed to find the limits of the house's reach. Tessa hadn't fully understood what Reece meant until she'd found the red vines— veins—in the sewer. She thought to herself, *If I need to find the edges of its reach, I need to work backwards*. She planned to follow the sewer lines to where they intersected with the house; never did she think she'd find what she was looking for with so much ease, or that the house itself, its influence, could have spread so far.

It was evidence, though, of something she'd long believed; something she'd held to even after the doctors tried to tell her it wasn't real, wasn't possible, it couldn't be: the house, whatever it was, was alive. It bled.

And by that logic, it could be killed.

After the incident in the sewer tunnel, she'd walked only a short distance before coming across the maintenance worker's truck. Wondered to herself just how often anyone came down there, seeing as the house had managed to spread so far without anyone being the wiser. She'd wondered, too, if anyone would come looking for their missing co-worker, if they would get to him in time—or if it was already too late. Had the red on the walls attacked him? Had it bound him there? If she went back in for him, would she have found a thick cord of it still wrapped around his neck, strangling him, or perhaps holding him face-down in the muck until he suffocated?

Feeling guilt at the man's predicament, but too scared to go back into the tunnel herself, Tessa tried the door of the truck. It was unlocked. *Thank god for small town trust*, she thought as she leaned inside and started searching for a phone or walk-ie-talkie or something. She found a CB radio in the dashboard and picked up the microphone. She didn't know what to say— she'd never used anything like it before—so she simply pressed the button on the side and said, "Uh, is anyone there? There's . . . Man down. Send help." Then she dropped the mic to the seat and sprinted away. If anyone did come, she wanted to be long gone before they arrived.

Her curiosity got the best of her, though. She went to the hospital the following day, to check and see if anyone had heard anything about the man. To see what the house—part of it, anyway—had done to him. What it could do to her if she wasn't careful. She stole a grey hoodie from another patient's room and slipped it on, pulling the hood up over her head and keeping her face down as she walked through the hospital.

Immediately she was struck by the intense smell of antiseptic and household cleaning supplies. The emergency room entrance was clean, bright, and far quieter than expected; there were only two others sitting in the waiting area: one person clutching their midsection as if they were about to be sick, the other holding what looked like a small hand towel to their forehead to stem the flow of blood from a large gash. *Probably a car accident*, she thought, staring-but-not at the second person.

She nervously approached the large reception desk, a thick plane of glass separating her from the nurse seated behind it. Tessa awkwardly cleared her throat. The brown-haired, pale-looking woman in scrubs behind the counter looked up from what she was typing and said, "Can I help you?"

Tessa glanced up a bit. "I . . . I'm looking for . . . Was a man brought in here recently? From the sewer? I—" *I called it in*, she wanted to say but didn't for fear of what questions might follow. Questions she couldn't answer, like who she was or why she'd been down there in the first place.

The nurse regarded the woman before her with an uneasy curiosity. "You're asking if a man found in the sewers came through here recently?"

"No, I— Yes."

"All right . . . What's the name? I can take a look for you."

"I don't . . . I'm not sure."

The nurse sighed. "I'm sorry. I can't give out information on patients, except to family."

"He's my . . . uncle."

"Your uncle whose name you don't know."

"I just want to know if he's okay."

The nurse studied Tessa for a moment. She sighed and looked to the screen in front of her. "If you *were* family, I'd be able to tell you that a man was in fact brought in late last night—a town maintenance worker. He had a number of unaccounted-for cuts and scrapes across his face and neck, but nothing life threatening. Those who found him couldn't say what happened, only that they'd received an anonymous call on the man's radio and found him crawling out of an access tunnel." She paused. "I'd also be able to tell you that whomever made that call potentially saved the man's life."

Tessa looked up then. "But you said his injuries weren't life threatening."

"They weren't, but he was screaming uncontrollably when they brought him in. We had to sedate him. Whatever happened to him down there, *something* made him desperately afraid for his life. All of which I could tell you, if only you were family."

Tessa nodded thanks and turned to leave.

"Wait, I'm sorry, but you look so . . . Tessa?"

Tessa halted in place. Immediately started cataloguing possible weapons nearby: a chair, the pens in the jar at the nurse's station, a clipboard to her left.

"It is you, isn't it? Tessa Sweet? Reece's sister? Oh my god, I thought you were— It's me, it's—"

Two older men carrying a sickly woman with them, her arms up over their shoulders, and another woman close behind came quickly up to the front desk right then.

"We need your help," said one of the men.

Tessa used the distraction to slip away before the nurse could probe any further. Though there was something familiar about this nurse, she realized as she made for the exit. Familiar, but just out of reach, like a song heard only once, in another life. She listened in as she hurried away:

"What seems to be the problem?" asked the nurse.

"Our friend, she's dying."

"Okay, let's just—"

"We don't want her admitted," the other man said. "We just need your help—"

Tessa didn't stick around to hear the rest. She did pause, however, upon glancing to the ground just outside the emergency room entrance. Her eyes on a storm drain at the side of the road.

And the little bit of red there she could see poking out at the right corner—like the tiny claw of a baby bird reaching up through the grate.

Tessa returned to the hospital the following night, late—not long past midnight, dressed all in black and lugging the carry-on bag of supplies. She stood at the far end of the parking lot, watched as a doctor and a paramedic lingered out front, smoking cigarettes on their break. She stayed there, beneath a burnt-out streetlight, waiting for the coast to clear. She watched as, eventually, they disappeared back inside. She started forward then, stalking over to where she'd seen the red vein just the day before.

She would try again. She'd find another angle. *Maybe*, she thought, *I could make a bomb*—Reece had told her how to do so with what she'd collected so far. Instead of going down there, putting herself in harm's way, she could attack the house from afar—it had clearly been hurt when she sliced off a piece of it earlier; she couldn't imagine what would happen to the house if she were to blow a portion of it to smithereens.

Had Reece been there with her, he would have told her to do it. To stab at the house with everything she had. But since she'd been in town, he'd only appeared to her periodically, in short bursts here and there that seemed to exhaust him. It was hard for him to be this close to the house—she knew it exerted a terrible control over him, and would continue to do so for as long as it remained standing. It's one reason she'd taken up residence, while in town, in an abandoned, crumbling house right at Black Stone's edge, one she'd heard kids used to drink at on weekends back when she was in school; she figured the farther out she was, the more likely he'd be able to visit her—and the less likely it was that they'd be seen by unwanted eyes.

Had Reece been there, right then, he might've warned her of the security cameras that kept watch over the ER's entrance. He might've told her it wasn't safe, that they could find another time, another strike point.

He might've told her to turn around.

"Freeze!" A woman's voice at her back as she crouched over the grate, trying to knock it in with a large rock she'd picked up off the side of the road. "Get up. Slowly," the voice instructed.

Tessa turned and found herself staring up at a police officer, gun drawn and pointed at Tessa's chest.

"Drop the rock and put your hands behind your head," the officer ordered.

Had Reece been there, he could have done something. He could have distracted the officer, or even killed her—it would have been worth it.

Maybe, had he been there, he could have told Tessa not to run.

CHAPTER
NINETEEN

ON MONDAY, ELLIS MET QUINN OUTSIDE THE RIALTO AFTER her afternoon shift working the ticket booth. It was a cool day—a breeze was coming in off the water. When she appeared, Quinn's hair was wrapped up and she wore a maroon scarf around her neck.

Ellis pointed to the scarf. "A little too July for that, isn't it? It's not *that* cold."

She scoffed. "It's never too early to look F.A.F."

"Say again?"

"Fashionable as fuck. You'll pry my autumn accoutrements out of my cold, dead hands."

"Tell me how you really feel, why don't you."

She took their hand, grinning slyly.

"Are you still okay to do this?" they asked.

Quinn nodded. "As okay as I'm gonna be."

"Then let's go."

They walked mostly in silence as they made their way to Ellis's house. Ellis told her a bit about what happened after dinner on Saturday, and how the next day they'd caught someone trying to break in, a woman who claimed she was only trying to fix the broken window for them. She had supplies with her, and a replacement pane of glass, so Robyn, too exhausted from the previous night, told her to just go, she wouldn't call the cops. It was weird, though, Ellis said, someone just wanting to fix their window like that. Was that what being a good neighbour was like in Black Stone? Quinn responded with a simple "Hmm." Ellis could tell from the way she gripped their hand with increasing severity, from how her breathing seemed to quicken the closer they got to the house, that she was steeling herself.

"You can back out at any time," Ellis said as they unlocked the front door. "You know that, right?"

She nodded. When Quinn took a deep breath, Ellis did the same and opened the front door. They entered together.

The two of them stood there, side by side in the entryway, settled in the moment. The house, thankfully, was quiet, the door to the cellar closed—the sledgehammer leaning against it as if a promise.

Quinn turned to them. "So where do we start?"

They went upstairs—Ellis to their bedroom while Quinn took Robyn's. Each of them took care not to disturb too much as they searched under furniture, knocked on floorboards and walls to check for hollow spaces and hidden passageways, peered into light fixtures and the areas surrounding switch panels to see if they'd been unscrewed.

After fifteen minutes, Quinn shouted from the other room, "So, like, what are we doing exactly?"

"We're looking for a key," Ellis shouted back.

"No, I know that's what we're doing, but what are we *doing*?"

"I . . . don't know. I guess I didn't think about the best way to go about all this." Ellis continued to search their room half-heartedly. In the distance, they heard a sound like metal clanging, followed by a reticent "The fuck?" They turned a moment later at a creaking sound and found Quinn in the doorway, leaning up against the frame with a ragged, weathered-looking leather-bound notebook in one hand.

"Should we maybe discuss this?" she asked. "Figure out some sort of plan, so we're not just banging our heads against— What's that?"

Ellis followed her gaze past their shoulder. They stepped to the left, giving Quinn a clear view of their latest painting, still on the easel.

"Is that—"

"That storm. The night of our first date."

She approached the painting. "That's ... this is ... I mean, it's beautiful, but also so ..."

"Dark?"

"I was going to say terrifying." She glanced to the side then and saw, stacked in the far corner of the bedroom, several more canvases and some sketchbooks piled high right next to them, by the window. She went over to them and, glancing at Ellis to make sure it was okay, started to flip through. On the canvases were self-portraits, mostly, but in pieces: an arm here, a torso there—all identifiably masculine yet soft and slight in spots, and growing slighter as she progressed through them. They started off in pale pinks and various approximations of white skin tones— mixtures of red, green, and brown, with titanium white to lighten when necessary—becoming increasingly vibrant, using a litany of purples, blues, and bright greens that gave them an abstract, almost alien quality. But still, only pieces, never the whole of them. Never a full figure, head to toe, or any identifying marks.

"These are—"

"Me," Ellis said plainly.

Quinn turned and looked. Ellis had stepped back and was making a fist around their left wrist as if they expected their hand to fall off. Their entire body had grown tense, closed off.

"I used to like drawing superheroes, straight from the pages of my comics. That's how I got started. But around the time I was—when I was first running into problems with ... I began drawing myself, to try and ... I don't really know why. I just had to do it. That's how it began, anyway. After a while, I started slicing my body into pieces—visually. It was the only way I could really see myself, not as a whole but piecemeal. Like, I just zeroed in on the things I hated about myself and couldn't see anything else. What's that saying . . . ?"

"When you can't see the forest for the trees?" Quinn supplied.

Ellis snapped their fingers. "That's how it was for me—how it is. Things are getting better, though, slowly."

"Do you still see what it was that you hated so much?"

Ellis thought for a moment. "When I look in a mirror, I don't hate what I see anymore, but I don't love it either. I don't . . . I've accepted I might never see myself how others see me."

Quinn nodded. "I sort of know how that feels. My parents tried to teach me self-love and all that. But every bit of doubt I've ever felt in myself has come from others. I'll never see myself how they see me, either, and I'm fine with that."

Ellis chuckled. "Body-positive activists are always talking about radical self-love, but that's always seemed like this impossible thing. I'll settle for radical self-not-hate."

She smiled appreciatively. "I'll drink to that."

Ellis nodded to the paintings. "If nothing else, these should help with my admissions portfolio. Universities like seeing your process." They regarded Quinn. "Next time I'm over at your place, will you show me more of your photography?"

It was her turn to crumple slightly, as if hit by a sudden attack of shyness. "My stuff's nothing like this."

"Bullshit."

She smiled weakly. "All right."

Ellis took the brief silence that followed as opportunity and nodded to the notebook in her hand. "You found something?"

Quinn held up the book. "I'm not sure. It was stuffed down the heating duct in your mom's room, which was sticking up at an angle—I kicked it when I walked past." She walked over to Ellis. Together they opened the notebook and looked inside.

Most pages were filled edge to edge with a messy, barely legible scrawl. They saw names to the left; and to the right, across from each name, a collection of materials: clothing, toys, trinkets and antiques—all of it going back years.

"It looks like a journal," Ellis said.

"Or a ledger. Look"—Quinn pointed to a name—"you've got names here, and over on this side . . . something . . . that belonged to them?"

"This looks like madness." Ellis continued to flip through, noting as the frantic scrawl slid further into illegibility. "What in the hell is all this? Who left it here?"

Quinn's eyes drifted to the right of Ellis. "What in the world—?"

Ellis tracked Quinn's eyes to the naked patch of wall not yet wallpapered over, and the dark stain there in the shape of a lightning bolt.

"Is that . . . blood?"

"Not according to my mom."

"But you have your doubts."

Ellis exhaled through their nose. "This is what I was telling you about. Shortly after we moved in, I found a vein there. Beneath the wallpaper."

"A vein." She cocked an eyebrow, and moved closer to the wall to investigate.

"Yes, a vein. And I know that's what it was, or something very much like it, because it . . . it was beating. And when I opened up my wall, it was gone and this stain was all that was left."

Quinn noticed something a little farther down, beneath a ragged edge of picked-at wallpaper. She chipped away at some of the paper with the nail of her index finger, revealing a letter. Then another. A whole word—a sentence, faded, in what looked like a child's messy scrawl. She stood back and stared at it.

"*Get well soon, Izzy.* Who's Izzy?" she asked. Ellis merely shrugged.

A low, growing thunder then. An aged roar as every weathered piece of wood in the room started trembling at once, beneath, above, and all around them, as if suddenly expanding and then contracting again. It was a pained sound.

It was pain.

The house moaned.

Quinn and Ellis froze, feeling the floor beneath them rattling.

"What the shit?" Ellis said. "You felt that, right? It wasn't just me?"

Quinn glanced up and around, as if searching for evidence that someone—or something—was listening in on their conversation. "This house really *is* alive, isn't it?"

"A-are you afraid?"

"I'm not sure. Should I be?"

"I don't know. But—"

"What?"

"I . . ." Ellis paused. "At night, when I've heard things, when I've felt . . . Fuck, I don't know what it is I've felt, but I know what it felt *like*."

"What's that?"

"Suffering, I think. Whatever that was just now, it happened when you said that name."

"Izzy."

Another low, tremorous groan. The shaking intensified: lights flickered, windows rattled, and the painting-in-progress tumbled off the easel and clattered to the floor. Ellis gripped the nightstand, Quinn the edge of the bed to keep steady.

"It's all around us," Ellis said.

"Like . . . the house is suffering?" Quinn was glancing up and around the entire room, as if searching for something she could see with her own eyes—a cause to all this commotion.

"Maybe. Or like . . ."

"What?"

"Like it's afraid of something."

"What could a haunted house be afraid of?"

"I don't know. When I first thought I—when I first heard what I think was a person, they sounded sad. The more I hear though, the more I just hear . . ."

"Fear?"

Ellis nodded. "I think it's time we find out as much as we can about this place. I want to know how it got to be this way. And,"—they pointed to the notebook in Quinn's hand—"I want to know what the hell that is and who hid *that* here."

Quinn nodded. "Same." She carefully released her grip on the edge of the bed and straightened up. "Also, we're searching for a key in a haystack here, and we don't even know what it looks like. For all we know, it's been stashed somewhere far away and we're wasting our time looking for it here. We need to find out more about the history of this place."

"And the occult store's still shuttered." They paused. "Is there anyone else in town who might know something?"

Quinn shook her head. "I'm not sure. Everyone here seems to have their own opinions about this house—I can't think of a single kid at school who hasn't helped spread at least one laughable rumour about this place."

"Yeah, that Amara girl was one of the first people I met here, and she wasted not one frigging second before telling me I should be on guard at all times."

Quinn was taken aback. "Who?"

"Amara. Never got a last name. She's our age, I think, maybe a year or two younger. Indian girl, goth, a little high-strung." They clocked the distressed look that swept across Quinn's face. "You know her?"

Quinn cleared her throat. "The Mitras. They live on the east side of town. Quiet, mostly keep to themselves. Years back, their daughter died of a rare form of kidney disease. It happened so fast. They took her to North Ellison for treatment, and we never saw her again—one day she was at school, the next, she wasn't.

Her name was Amara. We were . . . we weren't that close, but we were friends."

"So . . ." Ellis took a deep breath, "you're telling me the literal first person I met in town was—"

"A ghost, yeah." Quinn sat down at the edge of Ellis's bed. They plopped down next to her, and she put her head on their shoulder.

"Every time I think I'm close to processing all this," Ellis said, "things get a little weirder."

"Only a little?"

"Okay, a lot." Ellis glanced to the walls, searching for movement, for anything out of the ordinary. "You're right. We need to learn more about this place before we go poking around its bones."

"I think so," Quinn said. "A haunted house has to have started somewhere, right?"

As if to answer her, the walls of Ellis's room groaned a third time, softly now, with a sound like the wood around them was settling all at once. Quinn shut her eyes and nuzzled into their shoulder.

Right then, Ellis thought they could see the walls moving ever so slightly—in and out in quiet repetition.

Like the house was sighing.

Like it was breathing.

CHAPTER
TWENTY

TESSA STARED BLANKLY AT THE GREY CONCRETE CEILING ABOVE her cot, as she had been doing for the better part of twenty-four hours—when she wasn't staring at the three grey concrete walls that surrounded her or the black iron bars in front. The cell was small, maybe five feet by seven—not that dissimilar to the room she'd occupied for far too many years at Jackson-King—and smelled vaguely of urine.

She'd been in the cell since the deputy who'd found her attempting to vandalize hospital property had opened her bag of supplies and decided she was too dangerous to be let go. The deputy had chased Tessa down and managed to subdue her without having to fire her gun. Then she'd brought Tessa back to the station, processed her, and left her there overnight, thinking the sheriff would deal with her when he came in on Monday.

Tessa was worried. Not so much about the sheriff, but if he were to run her fingerprints . . . The name she'd given to the arresting officer wouldn't hold up under any amount of scrutiny, even she knew that. And she couldn't afford to be sent back to the facility. Not when Reece needed her.

Reece. The other wrinkle in all this. He hadn't appeared to her once since the incident at the sewer outflow. She worried she'd let him down when he needed her most. Again.

The sound of a door opening, keys jangling. Tessa rolled over on the cot. A man was standing on the other side of the bars, keys in one hand and a jumbo-sized coffee tumbler in the other. He was tall and portly, with muscular arms and a rounded mid-section that strained the front of his uniform. The bright gold badge on his chest gleamed under the flickering halogens above.

"So, *Joan Smith*," he said, unlocking the cell. "And here I thought the classics were dead. Come on—let's have a chat."

Tessa sat handcuffed to a metal chair next to the sheriff's desk. It was a small office, used by only a handful of officers, from the looks of it. Made sense. There was only so much crime that went on in places like Black Stone. She scratched at her cuffed wrist, noting with curiosity a name on a nearby desk: Deputy James Tallon. *Jimmy.*

The sheriff reappeared and hefted Tessa's bag onto the desk. He sat down across from her, tented his hands together, and exhaled. "Care to tell me who you really are, and why you were caught attempting to vandalize hospital property with a bag full of potential weapons and common household ingredients all conveniently used in the making of explosives?"

"I wasn't trying to vandalize hospital property." She spoke at a near-whisper. "I . . . I thought I saw something in the sewer, and I wanted to check it out. Besides, it was only a storm drain."

"Which is on hospital property. You see how that works, right?"

Tessa sighed impatiently. "Look, Sheriff . . ."

"Wolf."

"Sheriff Wolf, I wasn't trying to hurt anything or anyone. I simply heard—"

"Heard? I thought you said you saw something."

"I— Yes. I heard something, and then I saw it."

"What?"

"I'm not . . . A cat."

Sheriff Wolf leaned forward. "Let me see if I've got this straight: you were, what, just passing through town on your way to . . ." He left a space for Tessa to speak, but she remained silent. "And then you heard a cat from inside the storm drain and went over there with a big ol' rock and"—he nodded to the bag—"your apocalypse preparedness kit, or whatever, and tried to see if you could help. Being the good Samaritan you are, of course."

"Exactly."

"And you *are* just passing through, right?"

"Absolutely."

"Great, so the multiple reports we've had of a woman fitting your description going into and coming out of the abandoned Sullivan residence at the edge of town are fabrications then."

"I— That is—"

"And the empty food containers and the blanket we found inside, reported stolen just a few days back by Alice down at the market, those definitely aren't yours."

"Yes. I mean no. I mean . . ." Tessa went red in the face. "I think I'd like to speak to . . . to a lawyer."

"Sure thing. You just tell us your real name, and we'll put that through for you."

"I plead the . . . the . . ."

"The fifth?"

Tessa nodded furtively. "That's it. I plead the fifth."

Sheriff Wolf sighed and stood up. Pinched the bridge of his nose. "You're not making this any easier on yourself, you know that, right?" He paused. "There's . . . something real familiar about you," he added, then shook his head and walked away, taking her carry-on bag with him. "Maybe you'll decide you have something more to tell me after another night or two behind—"

"Wait!" she called. He stopped, turned. She tried to stand but was halted after only an inch or two, when the handcuffs went taut. "There's . . . Something's wrong here. In this town. I can't tell you what, but please, you have to believe me: only I can put a stop to it."

He glared at her. "Uh-huh." Eyes narrowed. "God, I swear, I've seen you before . . ."

Tessa cringed. She recognized him, too, and prayed silently that he would not put two and two together. That he would not think back to that night, all those years earlier, when Sheriff Wolf—then Constable Wolf—was first on scene to pull a young Tessa from the house down Cherry Lane, to restrain her, to put her in the back of a squad car, to stop her from burning down her parents' house. She prayed he wouldn't figure out who she was for fear of being sent back there, to that place, the facility, where they told her she wasn't right, where they gave her medicine she knew she didn't need and tried to convince her she'd acted out of grief and not fear.

"You're meddling with forces you can't begin to understand," she said.

The sheriff laughed. "You know, I always wanted someone to say that to me. I thought it'd be this big, grandiose thing, but really . . . it just sounds so small."

"I have a mission, and I can't let you or anyone stand in my way."

"That sounds to me like a threat."

"He told me—" She stopped herself.

Sheriff Wolf stepped closer. "He? Who's *he*? And what exactly did he tell you?"

Tessa shrank inward.

The sheriff's eyes widened suddenly. "Wait . . . Are you . . . Contessa? Contessa Sweet?"

"Don't—"

"Good lord, it is you! I thought— Do your parents know where you are?" He went to his desk and snatched his cell phone. Quickly googled a number, then started to dial.

"Please don't," she said. "I have to . . . I have to finish this."

"Is this the Jackson-King Mental Health Facility?" he said. "Yes, I think I have one of your patients here. My name is Sheriff Wolf, I'm with the Black St—"

"*I said don't!*" Tessa shrieked. She swung out with her free hand. Managed to slap the phone out of the sheriff's hand, in the process striking him across the face.

"Goddamnit," he exclaimed, his phone clattering to the floor. He spun on Tessa. She shielded her face as he uncuffed her, yanked her up off the chair. He led her back to her cell, practically dragging her, and threw her stumbling inside. Slammed the bars behind her and locked them.

She put out her hands to stop from careening into the wall. Turned and faced the sheriff.

He pointed at her while massaging his cheek. "That was strikes one through three, Contessa. I'm going to call the Jackson-King back, and then your parents, and we are going to get whatever this is sorted out." He turned to leave.

"No!" she shouted, but the door to the cells clanked shut behind him. And then Tessa was on her own. Again. "You can't do this! You don't know what you're doing!"

She continued to shout but to no avail. He didn't return. When finally, after several minutes, her throat started to hurt from screaming, she gave up and sat down on the cot with her face in her hands.

After only a few seconds: "That was pathetic."

She glanced up. Reece was standing right in front of her, looking extremely disappointed—and lighter than she'd see him before, partially transparent in direct light.

"Reece, I'm—"

"I should have known this would be too much for you. I thought you were motivated enough. I thought you were determined to right the wrongs done to me. To so many of us. You've failed me. Utterly."

"No. I can still make this right. I can, I swear it. If you could just—"

"Just what? Get you out of here? I have no power here, Tessa. That's what you were supposed to fix. But you didn't." Reece paused. "Do you know how much I despise this? I can't do *anything* here. I should be—I *am* so much more than this. To have to resort to asking such low creatures for help, and all because—"

"There's still time."

Reece hesitated. "Fine," he said at last. "Black Stone will be protected from outside influence—I will make this town an island so as to ensure your safety, but it's up to you to finish what you promised. Or so help me, I'll leave you here for *her*."

Reece disappeared then, blipped out of existence as if a frame cut from a film.

And Tessa was left once more to fend for herself. To make good on her word.

CHAPTER
TWENTY-ONE

QUINN AND ELLIS TRIED THE OCCULT STORE EVERY DAY BOTH before and after their respective shifts, but it remained closed. Friday evening, after yet another unsuccessful attempt, they decided to grab a bite to eat at the deli just across the street. They sat in the front window, where they could still see the entrance to Conundrums and Curiosities, just in case. Ellis took a bite from their turkey and pesto sandwich and sighed contentedly.

"Well . . . shit, this *is* good."

"Told you," Quinn said, biting into her own sandwich—a vegetarian combination of jackfruit and tempeh bacon. "This place is great. My family's been coming here since I was a kid."

"I can see why." They took another bite and closed their eyes, savouring the taste. Slowly, they were getting more comfortable eating in public. They didn't know if it was because they were actually improving, or if perhaps being with Quinn was making them more at ease with, well, everything. The reason didn't matter, though; what mattered was that, ghost house or no, they were, for the first time in a long while, happy.

"All right," Quinn said. "Favourite snack—go."

Ellis thought for a second. "Spicy dill pickle–flavoured roasted almonds."

"Ooh, good choice."

"What about you?"

"Easy: sour candies."

"Bulk or Sour Patch Kids?"

"SPK, baby."

"Ugh, I thought you had standards."

"Oh, I'm sorry, I didn't know I was dating a snack elitist." She took another bite of her sandwich. "Seen any more of that red stuff the past few days?"

They shook their head. "No. No voices or pulsing in the walls either. Been a quiet week, thankfully." They glanced out the window. "You really think they'll be able to help?"

"If those two don't have any answers for us, no one here will." She paused. Tapped Ellis's hand. "Hold up—there." She pointed across the street, to a woman climbing out of a rusted brown hatchback. They watched as she reached into the backseat and hauled out several heavy-looking boxes.

"Is that—?"

"Alex," Quinn said. "Come on." Ellis left their half-eaten sandwich to follow Quinn outside. Together they sprinted across the street, stopping and backing up suddenly when a truck sped by, its driver shouting something at Ellis about living in a devil's shithole of a house. Rattled, they waited until the coast was clear and continued to the other side. They arrived at the door to the occult shop just as Alex was about to close it behind her.

"Wait!" Quinn called out.

"Jesus Christ!" Alex turned, startled, hand on the door for support. "I'm sorry, we're closed right now but— Quinn? What's wrong?"

Quinn and Ellis came to a stop, panting. "We really need to talk to you—you and Andrea," Ellis said.

"Ellis Lang, right?"

Ellis nodded. "We need—we have questions. It's . . . it's about my house."

Alex sighed. "I had a feeling. But I thought you didn't believe in any of that nonsense." She stared Ellis right in the eyes. "Something's happened, hasn't it?"

"Yes."

Alex sighed. "I guess you better come in then."

Ellis was once more taken aback by the smell of the shop—the various candles and mixtures and spices. It was like someone had taken a Renaissance fair and shrunk it down to fit within a space no larger than the inside of a van. They looked at Quinn and wondered how much time she'd spent here over the years, especially following Trey's death. And just how much Alex and Andrea really knew about this place—and their house.

Alex placed the last of the boxes she'd been carrying on the counter by the cash register.

"What's in those?" Quinn asked.

"Talismans," Alex replied.

"Talismans? Like, for warding off evil spirits?" Ellis fought the urge to chuckle.

"Not just evil, but for controlling spirits and other entities, yes."

"Why would you use them if the spirits aren't evil?"

Alex sliced open the first box with a knife she retrieved from behind the counter. "Any number of reasons, really. Sometimes people use a talisman to make sure they're alone. Or to at least make them *feel* like they're alone."

"Do they work?"

"Sometimes. Not these," she said flatly, pulling out a handful of baubles and random bits of jewellery—rings, necklaces, some bracelets too. "Right now, they're just things. What makes a talisman a talisman, what gives a thing its power, is its connection to a spirit. Maybe it belonged to them when they were alive, or perhaps it's a fount for a person's memories. But it must be emotionally imbued in some way for it to work. Every few months I take a trip out of town, hit whatever yard sales I can, and pick up whatever seems worthwhile." She pulled out a pendant from her shirt—

a black dahlia on the end of a silver chain around her neck. "This is mine. It keeps me safe wherever I go. I don't wear it to ward off spirits, though. Not all talismans work that way. It depends on what memories you imbue it with. Sometimes the memories are good. Sometimes," she said, sadly, "you want to keep a spirit close to you instead of driving it away."

She fell silent, clutching the dahlia tightly before slipping it back down her shirt. She cleared her throat. "So, what did you want to talk about?"

Ellis stepped forward. "What you said about my house . . . I need to know more. Look, you were right. It's haunted—occupied. I've heard voices, and there's red in the walls, and we found this hatch or something in the cellar, and—" They took a deep breath. "And I've seen things. People. I believe, okay? I've—we've"—they motioned to Quinn—"experienced things that we can't explain, and we just . . . we want . . ."

"You want to know what you're up against?"

"We just want to understand."

Alex glanced at Quinn, noting how her eyes drifted to the floor. "Oh god, Quinn, did you see . . ." Quinn nodded. Alex heaved out a sigh. "Okay. But if we're going to do this, I need you to be honest. And above all, I need to know I can trust you."

"Whatever you tell us won't leave this store," said Ellis. "I swear." Quinn nodded in agreement.

Alex glanced over her shoulder. "What do you think?" At her words, Andrea drifted out from the shadows behind the counter. Ellis watched then as Andrea went up to her friend and reached for the black dahlia around her neck—and her fingers, her hand, her entire arm passed right through Alex.

Ellis and Quinn stepped back in unison. "Wait," Ellis said, "so your talisman—"

"It was mine," Andrea said. "I gave it to my best friend back when we were teens. Twenty-five years ago, I went hiking north of town and fell and broke my neck when an earthquake hit town and the ravine there turned into a canyon suddenly."

"Oh god," Quinn said, hand to her mouth.

"There's more to this town than either of you realize," Andrea continued. "Black Stone has a great many skeletons in its closets. But not all of them are bad. It's more complicated than that. A lot more."

"I think we need to uncomplicate it," Ellis said. "And fast."

"You mentioned seeing and hearing things," Andrea said. "What kinds of things?"

"A voice, a couple of times. Whispers too. Rumbling in the walls and all around. And . . . blood, I think. Old, though, sort of reddish-brown. It's in the walls, streaked all over."

"And a name," Quinn said. "Scrawled on the wall in Ellis's bedroom—Izzy."

Ellis paused. "Veins too. Pulsing or throbbing or—"

"Beating," Andrea finished.

". . . Yeah."

"Those aren't veins, Ellis."

"What are they?"

"Her heart, pulled into more strings than should ever have been possible. They run throughout the entire house—the entire town, actually."

Alex stamped her foot. "Below us right now. What you've seen in your walls, those heart strings travel beneath every inch of this town. And your home is where it all started."

"Where what started?"

Alex looked to Andrea. "A war," Andrea stated plainly. "A spiteful battle of wills that's been simmering for years—decades now, as a matter of fact."

"What kind of war?" asked Quinn.

"Between a person and an idea. See, it's true that not every haunted house is malevolent. It's equally true that every haunted house was once a human whose spirit or essence has come, through force or happenstance, to embody the very space in which they once lived."

"My house was . . . a person?" Ellis said.

"Your house was just a house until someone refused to leave. It once belonged to a beautiful young woman, her husband, and their daughter. The woman's name was Analiese."

"What happened?"

"Analiese challenged Death," Andrea said, very matter of fact, "and won."

A naliese couldn't leave with the paramedics who came to take her daughter away. Her Izzy, her beautiful, kind girl who was never even given a chance to live.

Analiese sent her neighbours to the hospital in her stead. Begged them to identify the body for her.

The body. She wanted to strangle the paramedic who first used the words—imagined herself garroting him with her heart string.

"You shouldn't be alone right now," Margaret said later that night, once she'd returned from the hospital, having gone there on Analiese's behalf. Margaret was a short, soft mother of three from two doors down. A sweet woman, but a little obtuse. "I read that the first days are always the worst."

A circus procession of neighbours followed over the course of that first week, bringing flowers and cards and various foodstuffs. All saying how sorry they were, how much they wanted to help, that they were just a phone call away.

But Analiese's appetite, for food as well as companionship, was gone. Obliterated. The plethora of pies, casseroles, and domed Jell-O concoctions with marshmallows trapped in some grotesque culinary stasis went uneaten. Abandoned on the front porch—a bounty for ants, racoons, and other local wildlife.

The third week after Analiese's loss, Death appeared again at the foot of her bed. She was awake when It unfolded from emptiness as It had before; awake as she had been every night since her daughter's passing, twisting the heart string around her forearm like latticework. When she made a fist around it, colour drained from the wall behind her.

Analiese rolled onto her back as Death approached her bed, Its razored talons again outstretched in preparation. It didn't say a word to her—It didn't have to.

"Fuck off," she said.

It spoke, Its words a chorus of voices: It is time.

Analiese sat up straight and tightened her grip on the heart string. "Oh, is it time? Was it time for Izzy too? Or was that just to fuck with me, so I wouldn't want to stay?"

Death held Its position, silent as a statue.

"I thought so."

It is time.

But what Analiese thought she heard, beneath the mechanized, otherworldly assault of Death's voices, was . . . resignation. Somewhere in that chorus, there was sadness. She heard amid the tumult the very tenor of Death's nature, separate from wilful action. It was not malevolence or hatred that propelled Death but necessity. Balance. She understood then: Death did not decide who nor when; It was docent, not arbiter.

Analiese shook and asked: "Why?"

Death did not speak. But in the air between them, the ash of Death's aura vibrated in chorus. Had you come with me before, your pain would already be at an end.

Analiese stood then and approached Death. She held up her fist, the pulsing criss-crossed lacing of muscle a chain of her own design. "My pain belongs to me."

Death leaned forward through ash grown quiet; Its maelstrom stilled. Its galaxies directed at Analiese's ghastly, increasingly anemic face. And Analiese flung her arms wide, inviting Death to do Its worst.

In response, the Entity bore another hole through Analiese's chest. It retrieved a second strand from her heart and moved to the opposite end of the room. But before It could affix the tether, Analiese reached out and took hold of the newly excavated string. Death turned to regard her as Analiese gently tugged the string from Its grip. It didn't let go so much as Its razored fingers unbound in loose tendrils and reformed. Analiese took her own string of muscle and walked it to the corner of her room. She climbed atop a low dresser to reach as high as she could, tall enough only to touch the end of the tether to the corner where the ceiling and walls met—the strand of heart muscle did the rest: its end split into hundreds of smaller threads like a piece of yarn unravelling into individual strands too many and too small to quantify. Analiese's breath quickened. As she climbed down from the dresser, her insides stretched like taffy in all directions. She opened her mouth to scream before Death stroked one of Its fingers down her cheek, the spinning razors slicing small canyons there. But no blood fell— Death had stolen that from her as well.

Death looked upon Its work as Analiese writhed in anguish on the floor of her bedroom. Her heart was strung to the ceiling on either side of her bed, twin strands emerging from her chest like ineffectual wings. She looked between them, the life draining from her face as her bifurcated heart pounded in stereo.

Its work completed, Death backed away from Analiese and returned to the nothingness from which It came.

Analiese remained in place, much heavier now than her slender five-foot-nothing frame should have been. Her insides drawn and stretched to their limits, her bones and muscles swollen as the house beat in time with her heart.

The addition of the second heart string made it all but impossible for Analiese to move. With every step an uptick in pain and suffering, knives in her thighs and forearms, twisting with every flex of muscle. By the end of the first night, she'd made it less than halfway to the foot of her bed before collapsing on the ground in a ragdoll heap. She proceeded to crawl, but even that was too heavy a tax on her body.

By dusk on the sixth day, she made it to the entrance of her room. She reached up and grabbed the knobs on either side of the open door and slowly, feeling every tug of the heart strings as if she were being stabbed repeatedly, lifted herself up so she could see down the hall to Isabelle's room.

She started into the hall but staggered when her tethers snapped taut. She tried again and was pulled back, a dog on a leash. Infuriated, she grabbed hold of the new tether and gave it a single hard yank, involuntarily forcing herself to her knees as she was overcome by a hurricane of vertigo.

Analiese steeled herself and pulled again, harder this time. Her forehead pricked with sweat and her wiry arms grew hot with the strain. Still she pulled, until the wall behind her bed heaved outward; a body drawing air into its lungs, and snapped back. Analiese dropped the strings, pulled sharply forward as the wall contracted. Brought to her hands and knees by the house's resistance, as the beams roared and the foundations commanded compliance.

Analiese remained where she'd fallen. The battle with the house had left her dizzy and distracted. While she worked to catch her breath, doing what she could to slow the beating of her peeling heart, she raised her head and stared at the wall behind her bed.

It breathed in sync with Analiese. And as she regained control, the house, too, settled, creaking into stasis.

The following morning, Analiese spent an hour standing in front of the window, staring at her reflection in the glass. She was alarmed; she could make out only a faint pair of shadows like hollowed-out pits where her eyes should have been. She stepped closer, and somehow her skull appeared before the rest of her faded into shape, the white bone visible beneath a thin film of dried-leaf skin. She tore at her ratty black sweater in a flurry. It came apart in her hands, and when she glanced down at herself, she saw her body had lost what little muscle she'd had left.

Before she could contemplate what Death had reduced her to, her attention was drawn to the sound of a key inserting into a lock—followed by the front door opening and shutting, and then footsteps, two pairs, clopping hollow up the stairs.

"What's the story here?" A man, speaking lightly, cautiously.

"A mother and daughter used to live here," said a second voice—a woman. "The daughter died about a year ago—cancer. No one knows what happened to the mother."

A year? Analiese went as close to the door as she could, ignoring to the best of her ability the daggers in her thighs as she moved. She peered out into the hall as the heads of the two intruders came into view. She recognized neither: he was tall, white, and dressed in jeans and a sport coat; she was Black, a head shorter at least, wore a full suit, and carried a clipboard with a realtor's logo at the top in one hand.

"She just vanished?" said the man.

The realtor nodded. "Neighbours never even saw her leave."

"I'm here!" Analiese called out. The intruders reached the top of the stairs, passing directly in front of her without even a glimpse in her direction. "I'm . . . I'm . . ."

I'm right here.

"People in town think maybe she killed herself. Then the place went into foreclosure, and, well, here we are. This used to be the daughter's room," the realtor continued, shifting gears as they lingered in Isabelle's door, regarding a room frozen in time.

"Obviously we'll have to spend the most time here," said the man. He'd wrinkled his nose as if passing a dead animal on the street.

"She died of cancer," the realtor said, disgusted, *"not the plague."*

"Yeah, still. That wallpaper."

Analiese watched as the realtor continued to show the man around, guiding him from room to room until they worked their way back to the main bedroom. Standing now mere inches from Analiese's face, they looked straight through her.

"Which brings me to—"

"The mother's room." The man leaned forward, peered inside. *"What a mess. We'll have to strip out the wallpaper here too. Maybe even the wood—god only knows how much mould is eating away at this place."*

The realtor shook her head and turned away. *"I'll show you the cellar."*

The man lingered a moment longer. Analiese followed his movements as he crossed the threshold into her domain. Watched him assess the mess of her bed, the trail of rot travelling up past the headboard to the wall beyond. She searched his face for some evidence he knew she was there but saw nothing beyond revulsion. As if he couldn't wait to tear away at the remnants of her life, and Isabelle's, and the home she'd hoped to build there with Samir.

She went to the window again, fighting the heart strings with every step—the pain constant now—and wondered how so much time had passed without her knowing. The world outside appeared unchanged, an autumn day identical to the day they came to take Isabelle's body away. Then Analiese turned and was greeted by an empty bedroom, her furniture gone, the walls stripped and repainted around the gnarled roots of her heart strings. As if they weren't there at all.

Footsteps approached quickly. At the top of the stairs appeared two men, one carrying the other across the threshold of her room. They were both trim, close-swept hair, clean-shaven. The first man let go of the second, and they laughed and kissed: a gentle peck on the lips.

"Welcome home," said the first man.

"It's been a long time coming," replied the second, whom Analiese recognized as the man who'd accompanied the realtor there what had been, to her, only moments before.

They kissed again and embraced while Analiese watched. Already her home had been taken from her, gutted and given to another.

The house's new owners disappeared downstairs then. Alarmingly, every time Analiese blinked, the décor in the hallway outside her room shifted and transformed. Every now and then she'd catch a flicker of movement—white static on a television screen. Like switching slides in a projector: blink—an ottoman by the banister; blink—Christmas lights strung across the rotary window at the end of the upstairs hall. She turned and faced her room again—their room—watching as the husbands passed weeks, months together whenever Analiese so much as closed her eyes.

Analiese could not process the passage of time. She would sit in the corner beneath the drapes of her heart strings and listen as they made love, as they argued, as they planned their days and wrote their grocery lists and sometimes just slept, peacefully, without a word passing between them. Living the sort of life she'd imagined living with Samir.

And then years had passed, and the first man sat astride the second in bed. Analiese watched while the men held hands and stared into each other's faces, life sliding gradually from the second man's face—a gentle farewell, the likes of which she never had with Samir. She blinked again—another switch of the slide and one half of the bed was now empty. She saw the first man curled up on his side alone, lying on his side with his knees to his chest. Analiese knelt down beside the bed in front of him, crawling close enough to his face to feel his breath tickle her not-nose. His grey eyes stared straight through her.

She blinked again, and he was gone. But she was not alone.

Death came again then, reappearing behind Analiese. She faced the Entity, her heart strings a curtain across her shoulders. She thought she could see in Death's spiral eyes the faintest glimmer of blue—a shade darker, sadder, then she'd ever seen. It placed a hand on Analiese's shoulders, but already she was shaking her head.

No, she said. And at that moment, she felt the weight the structure had accreted. Not from dirt or grime, nor things purchased and placed, but from bodies and memories. Its exhalations rattled in her.

Her heart strings were more than confinement; they were a support system. To leave now would be to authorize its decay; to remain was to preserve, both the house and herself.

Analiese approached the shadowy figure of Death and took Its razored hand in hers. So cold to the touch, Its wire and void—like how she imagined submerging her hand beneath the Arctic Ocean's waters might have felt. She guided one of Its narrow fingers to her chest and arced her head back as it bore yet another hole in her.

"You can't have them," she whispered, and then, letting go of Death's hand, reached inside and plucked from her heart a third string. She passed it to Death. Watched as It fastened the muscle's tip to the ceiling, this time on the right side of the room, edging that much closer to the centre.

Death did not acknowledge Analiese's decision in any meaningful way. Its task done, It disappeared again, as suddenly as It had first arrived. Analiese, unable to move farther than the foot of the bed, sat on the floor and pulled her knees to her chest, as the widower had done a moment or a year or a decade prior, and slept. And the house slept with her.

When she raised her head again, she found herself staring between dangling black lines as if she were a child crouched in the back of the closet, various articles of clothing hanging in front of her face. There were no lights on in the house, and every surface in the room was fuzzy with dust millimetres thick. She could see furniture in the hall just outside the bedroom door—brown moving boxes piled high.

Another flicker and a young woman stepped into view. Long brown hair to her waist, somewhere in her late thirties—the same age Analiese had been when Isabelle died. The woman hugged her sides as she stared into the empty bedroom, peering in Analiese's general direction.

An older man appeared at the woman's side and put an arm across her shoulders. He hugged her tight.

"Come on," the man said. "There's nothing here for us anymore."

"Something's still here," said the young woman. "I . . . I think it's always been here."

"What is it?"

She shook her head. "I wish I knew. But . . ."

"What?"

"It's sad."

They remained a moment longer before turning to leave. Analiese went to step forward, to go to the door and see what she could glean of those who'd moved through the house—through her. But she quickly discovered, she couldn't move at all. The moment passed, and the two new interlopers—no, residents, she thought, reorienting her perspective—flickered out of existence.

She glanced down then and gasped.

From her chest now extended dozens of heart strands, spread out in a fan. A shield of sorts, of wasted meat and gristle. She looked up and saw the peelings of her most precious muscle tethered from one corner of the bedroom ceiling to the other. From below they resembled gory vines suspended from a canopy, a curtain of entrails before her. When she tried to advance, the wall at her back resisted, support beams digging their heels into the building's foundation.

The walls contracted then, hauling her back, melding what was left of her body to the drywall.

What had Death done to her while she slept?

With the loss of self came a veritable flood of memories: entire lives waterfalling into her, poured from the house through each of her myriad tethers; the memories of every family who'd since passed through what had once been her house—and beyond, too, residents from across Black Stone, people she had not known but now felt, saw, heard as clearly as if they were with her right then. Her heart had wound itself beneath the house and into the town, through its dirt, its sewers, tunnels whose reason and purpose she could not discern. Her torso, seen now from without and within, strapped to the wall in an ornate cat's cradle of viscera, grew solid again. Substantial. As if through the walls, through the paint and support beams, through the foam insulation and cobwebs and nails, the house was feeding her.

In that flood of memory, most present, she felt the grief of those who had lived within her walls. Now, clearly, she could see, could hear that each heart string beat for a separate life—for each soul who'd lost their life in this place. Alongside her.

Alongside Isabelle.

A community, a legacy now lived on inside of her.

Individual voices rising out of the din of her thumping heart, the vibration of each string a memory: an old man who'd moved in after losing his wife of forty years, dead like Samir of a heart attack;

214

a mother of three suffering severe depression who used a blade to take her own life while sitting in the tub; a teenager no older than Isabelle, who'd died in much the same way, with her mother—the women she'd just seen leave—by her side to the very end.

They were there, with her. Analiese wondered how many times the End of All Things had visited her as she sat there on the floor, slipping in and out of dreams. She had missed so much, unaware of how many times she'd extracted another line from inside her chest and passed it off to Death. Not once had It forced oblivion onto her. Instead, the Entity had helped her bind her more fully to this place. This house. Perhaps It thought this to be Analiese's ultimate desire; perhaps It did this as punishment, a lesson for refuting the natural way of things.

Perhaps. Perhaps.

She strummed her hand across a multitude of strands, a bloody harp, and listened for a chord not even Death Itself would be able to hear. She followed the broad strains of breadcrumbed lives back until she found her way to the second strand ever extracted—the first she'd pulled out of her own accord. She hesitated, inhaled, and placed revivified fingers around the muscle—so much drier, so much more taut, than the others.

And Isabelle spoke to her.

Analiese couldn't say how much time passed before Death came to her again. She had been fastened to the wall so long behind her bloody, hundred-pronged star of stripped organ that she was as much the wall as the wood had ever been. When she breathed, the house breathed with her.

Death glided forward on stilled clouds. It is time. You know it is.

Analiese heard the words, finally, as an offer. An invitation. She stared into Death's eyes, to the galaxies swirling therein, and shook her head as much as her confinement would allow.

Never, she said, softly, respectfully.

It bowed then, deeply, and, straightening, extended Its wings to their fullest, to the absolute edges of the room and far beyond, breaking through the geometry of the space. Then Death, too, vanished, swallowed up by the night. It departed the house at the end of Cherry Lane, for it was Death's domain no longer.

In the silence that followed, the house was once more a home, Analiese its steward. And when she caressed and strummed the strands strung from her chest, she felt her family, her new family, beyond even the house and—yes—stretching into the town, join together, their voices raised as if a choir.

PART THREE:

SKELETONS IN EVERY CLOSET

CHAPTER
TWENTY-TWO

REECE SWEET SEARCHED NERVOUSLY FOR ANYTHING THAT MIGHT tell them they were going the right way, but all he could see were trees—dense, dark branches that lacerated the night sky like cracks in almost-shattered glass. He moved deeper into the woods. Stepped on a branch—in the relative silence, it sounded like a gunshot.

"Shh!"

He searched for the voice but still could not see. "Tessa? Where are you?" he whispered.

"I'm right here," she answered.

"Where?"

"Literally two feet in front of you, dumbass."

"I thought you said my eyes would adjust."

"It's not my fault you're deficient. Now hurry up, we're almost there."

"Almost where?" But Tessa didn't answer. Reece followed the sounds of his sister moving just a few feet ahead of him, carefully making her way through the dense brush. He asked her again, swatting at the mosquitos feasting on his neck, now very much regretting having followed his sister out of the house on a Saturday night during the swampiest July on record when there was a perfectly good garbage horror movie marathon on TV right then.

"You know," he said, "we could turn around right now and probably catch the end of *Slumber Party Massacre II* if we hurry, instead of heading wherever you're—"

Reece fell silent then as the trees ahead of them thinned, opening into a clearing lit by what moonlight slipped through the heavy thicket above. He was able to make out five others in the clearing—friends of Tessa's, all standing in a circle: Lucas Hillcox, Betany O'Brien, Connie Wang, James Tallon, Eleanor Paulson.

Reece clenched up. Though they were all in the same grade, he didn't get along with Tessa's friends. Not for lack of trying, just . . . square pegs, round holes. He'd never fit in. Not like he did with Robyn Ridley. Tessa had teased him relentlessly about it—hanging out with a "loser like her"—but it hadn't ever bothered him. But Robyn wouldn't return his calls anymore. He still didn't know why, only that it hurt.

"What's *he* doing here?" Betany demanded, striking Reece's face with a flashlight beam as if it were an interrogation lamp.

Tessa approached the circle. "He caught me sneaking out, okay? I had to bring him along or he'd squeal."

"I wouldn't have said anything," Reece said. "I don't do that."

"Right," Tessa said, "like it wasn't you that ran off and told Mom when you spotted me and Connie smoking a joint behind the bleachers."

"It wasn't!" Reece shouted, defiant as he had been every time she brought this up—which was rather frequent. "I don't know who told, but it wasn't—"

"Narc!" James said, pretending to cough into his fist.

"Fine." Betany clicked her tongue disapprovingly. "You know, when they were giving out twins, you really got the short straw, Tess."

"Don't I know it." Tessa side-eyed her brother with a you-better-not-embarrass-me glare.

Eleanor looked to Reece. "Well? If you're gonna be here, you might as well take part."

Reece slowly approached the small circle. Tessa and Lucas crouched down and flicked a pair of lighters to life. As they did, Reece could see more clearly what was at their feet: a ring of candles to be lit, the perimeter of a circle made of broken twigs and grass. And in the centre of it, a crude pentagram made out of sticks.

"Wait, what the hell are you—" Reece began, but he was cut off by Connie.

"I've got the book," she announced. "Jimmy, did you—"

"Right here." James took off his backpack, reached inside, and pulled out a large mason jar full of something dark and sloshing.

Reece gulped. "Is that—"

"Pig's blood," James said. "Maybe some cow too. Butcher wasn't sure."

"What did you tell him it was for?" Lucas asked.

James shrugged. "He didn't really ask."

"Well, that's . . . comforting."

"Pig's blood, Jimmy? It was supposed to be human." Tessa huffed.

James glared at her while she finished lighting the last few candles. "I'm so sorry, princess," he said snidely. "I wasn't able to find someone willing to bleed out for the hell of it."

"You could've tried the hospital."

"Yeah, and I could've gotten arrested too." He put on a newscaster's voice. "'Local boy asks hospital for blood, won't say why—news at eleven.'"

"We'll make do with what we've got," Lucas said. "Blood is blood."

"Uh, guys," Reece said, timidly, "what's going on here?"

"You want to do the honours?" Lucas said to Tessa.

She finished lighting the last candle and stood back up, faced her brother. "Saṃsāra," she said, as if it were both question and answer.

"What's that?" Reece asked.

"It's Sanskrit." She cleared her throat and spoke with the sort of authority that comes from having memorized a dictionary definition to its last word: "It refers to the never-ending cycle of death and rebirth that connects each and every one of us."

"Okay . . . Is there more to this, or am I going to have to guess?"

Tessa scoffed. "Are you seriously this thick, Reece? Come on, dude, you've heard as much as I have. You know full well how strange this town is. You've heard the whispers in our own walls. The Hydes alone, I mean . . ."

Reece knew what his sister was alluding to. The Hydes were an elderly couple who'd been in Black Stone longer than anyone in the circle, or even their parents, had been alive. They lived in one of the other houses down Cherry Lane, two or three doors from the Sweets. They seemed friendly enough, but there was something fishy about them. Nothing about them ever seemed to change. Literally. No medical problems, no participation in town events. They even looked the same, some in town said, as they had twenty or thirty years prior—down to the very last wrinkle.

They were ghosts.

Or maybe zombies.

Certainly, it was thought—rumoured, discussed in hushed tones at school—they were some flavour of the undead. It was the only thing that made sense.

"It's not just them either," Tessa said. "I've heard talk of others. Tons of people in this town are alive when they shouldn't be."

Reece appeared skeptical. "And this has what to do with, uh . . ."

"Saṃsāra."

"Right. That."

"Connie?"

Connie took off her backpack and pulled out a stack of papers, which she passed to Reece, who stared at them, confused.

They were newspaper printouts. Obituary sections from nearby towns. They were surprisingly busy, Reece thought, considering these other towns were all similar in size to Black Stone.

"What's all this?" he asked.

"Obits from our orbit," Connie answered. "The dead from every town surrounding ours."

"There are so many."

"That's just the past *month*."

Reece whistled. "Shit. What about us?" At that, Connie produced a single sheet of paper. On it were listed all the deaths that had occurred in Black Stone over the same length of time. Reece did not recognize any of the names.

"These ones here," Connie said, tapping the first two names, "they were found just outside of town—less than a kilometre from the border. Both in their twenties, both dead of heart attacks."

"That's weird."

"No," Tessa said, "that's unnatural. And it's only the tip of the iceberg. Whatever's going on in this town, it's disrupted the natural order of things."

Reece stared at his sister as if she had well and truly lost her mind. "So, you read a Sanskrit word in a book that you probably didn't understand and jumped to *this* as your conclusion. You sure that was just weed you smoked?"

"I'm serious!"

"Hey, Bobbsey Twins," Lucas shouted. "We're ready to get this show on the road."

"What are we doing exactly?" Reece asked.

"We need to restart the cycle, of course," Tessa said.

"Saṃsāra," Reece muttered to himself. His sister had always had a lust for the gothic—for a solid year she'd modelled her entire aesthetic on Winona Ryder in *Beetlejuice*—but this seemed absurd and, likely, nonsensical. "Couldn't you, I don't know, start with a Ouija board or something?"

"No!" James said, louder than anyone expected. "No," he said again, calmer, "that won't do it."

"Do what?"

"It won't break her control."

"Whose control? What are you even talking about?"

James sighed. "I saw my sister."

Reece's eyes grew wide. "What do you mean . . . ?"

Chrissie Tallon. James's younger sister. It was the first funeral any of them had ever attended that wasn't for some elderly relative. Chrissie had gotten lost several months earlier while playing with a friend. They found her body just by the highway leading out of town, just outside of its border—mere feet from the *Welcome to Black Stone* sign. No injuries, no trauma that anyone could see. She was just dead.

"She came to me a while ago, as a ghost or . . . something, I don't know. She told me this town was dangerous. That it was cursed. That it was a woman who'd killed her. Who didn't want her to leave. She said the woman's name was Analiese."

Reece started racking his brain, trying to think of anyone in town by that name but coming up empty. "I have no idea who that is."

"Well, you wouldn't have met her at the grocery store. Analiese is dead," Tessa explained. "She's Black Stone's plague, and she lives right under our roof."

"Our . . . as in . . ."

"She's in our house, Reece. There's a ghost living with us, and she owns this town. She's taken the Hydes and others like them, just like she took Chrissie. Just like she's taken so many people who've left or tried to leave this place."

"But people leave and come back all the—"

"And it's only a matter of time before she takes us too."

Reece stared at his sister. "This is nuts. You all know that, right?"

"It's not nuts," said Lucas. "We'll prove it to you. We're going to bring her here ourselves. We're going to expose her for what she is."

"And what's that?"

"Death incarnate."

Reece snorted. "And you're going to do this with some sticks and pig's blood, and a library book on seances?"

"Hey!" Eleanor exclaimed. "That's my mother's book, and she's a very powerful witch, I'll have you know."

"Your mother likes to dance naked in the backyard while listening to Phish. And her skunk weed is as old as she is."

Tessa shrugged. "Sorry, Lea, he's not wrong."

Eleanor waved them off. "Whatever."

"And the Hydes?" Reece went on. "I mean even if what you're saying is . . . they don't seem unhappy. They haven't done anyth—"

"Everyone ready?" Betany asked. "Get in a circle around the candles and hold hands."

"Nu-uh," Reece said. "This is a bad idea." He looked to the tiny flames burning near the forest floor. "And a helluva fire hazard. Come on, Tessa, this is . . . Let's get out of here, okay?"

The six held hands then while Reece stood just outside their circle, away from them and the makeshift pentagram.

"Here we go," Connie said.

"Hear us!" James bellowed. "Spirits who torment this town!"

"Tessa, I want to go," Reece pleaded.

"Just a little longer," she said.

"Demon who stole my sister," James continued, "reveal yourself!"

"You promise?" Reece asked.

Tessa nodded. "Promise."

"*Reveal yourself!*" James screamed, head arched all the way back.

Reece followed his gaze, staring straight up. He could see, clearly, through the tops of the trees as the clouds above them spiralled, a funnel in reverse.

It was as if they were, very suddenly, very impossibly, in the eye of a hurricane.

A maelstrom.

Lightning crackled. It fired down around them in ribbed spires like blades of light penetrating the earth, cutting straight through it like butter.

Reece felt strange. It was as if the world around them had changed, had somehow grown sharp. If he were to move right then, he thought, he might slice his face on the air itself.

"What's happening?" Connie shouted above the wind, the thunder rolling through, around, surrounding them like a war march—a pincer attack.

"Don't let go!" James shouted.

A violent gust of wind whipped through the space and blew out the candles. The ground shook then, a shuddering rumble that knocked every last one of them to the forest floor.

When it seemed as if the chaos had ended, Reece scrambled back to his feet. He was about to go over to his sister, to help her up, when suddenly, on the other side of the clearing, he saw her. Standing there as clear and full as any of the others.

"Chrissie?"

A flash then. Another spear of lightning, inverted somehow— a dagger of pure black, crooked and menacing. A chasm in reality. An absence of everything.

And when, a moment later, Tessa regained her footing, she saw, mere feet away, what remained of her brother.

She screamed.

CHAPTER
TWENTY-THREE

ELLIS AND QUINN LISTENED CAREFULLY TO EVERY WORD OF
Alex and Andrea's story. When it seemed as though they were
finished, Ellis asked, "Is that it?"

Andrea glared at them. "We just finished telling you that
a woman embodies your house and that she has been defying
Death—literally—for decades, and that's all you've got to say?"

"No, I mean—sorry. I just . . . You said my house—Analiese, I
guess—was being hunted. I need to know, with everything we've
seen and heard, if it's the house I should be worried about or
something else. Like, is it Death—actual, honest-to-goodness
Death, cloak and scythe and everything—doing the hunting?
And if that's the case, why? What's Death so upset about?"

"It's upset because Analiese got greedy," Alex said. "Death
was fine with her having her way when it was just her and her
daughter, but the more people that moved in and died inside
that place . . . They became of a part of Analiese. They made her
stronger. They *allowed* her to grow, though Death didn't understand that at the time. Death thought It was punishing her, not
giving her a lesson in power. Now this whole town is a part of
her, and she it. See, when a person dies, Death only takes their
soul; the earth takes their body. And if you think of the soul

as a form of energy . . . energy can't really be destroyed, only transformed. That's Death's function: to shepherd energy from one plane to another. But right now, the house, *your* house, is storing all that energy. It—*she* has made Black Stone into something more than it was, something it should never have been. Something otherworldly. Which also makes this whole town a beacon for weirdness. It's like an outpost of sorts—a lighthouse on an outcropping over an ocean of the impossible. I don't know if Death is angry or jealous or just running on a deficit—" She paused. "Death was trying to hurt Analiese; It never imagined she would thrive. And ever since, It has been like a child starved. With Black Stone, Death lost a piece of Its domain forever."

"That's why places like Optimism are, well, like they are. Death is taking out Its frustrations on them instead. How decidedly human of It."

Alex nodded, touching the talisman around her neck. "It's a risk anytime one of us leaves town. But most people here don't even realize it. Or they just never leave."

"Something about small towns being miniaturized black holes," Ellis said glibly.

"Quinn? How're you holding up over there?" Andrea asked. Ellis turned to Quinn, who was silent as she processed everything they'd just been told.

"So, the ghosts . . ." she began, "they're trapped in the house?"

"Not just the house," Alex said, and Andrea waved jovially as if to remind them she was there and still very much dead. "And they're not trapped either."

Andrea nodded. "Most of us just don't want to leave. We don't know what's on the other side of this existence any more than you do."

Quinn looked up at Andrea. "And Trey, he . . ."

"He's there, I think," Andrea said. "He's with a lot of others. For many of us, your house," she said, turning her attention to Ellis, "is like a city hall of sorts, or a waystation."

"A safehouse," Ellis echoed, thinking to their flickering porch light.

"Bingo."

"Why don't they tell us they're still here?" Quinn asked, tearing up. "Why did he take so long to come back to—" Her voice hitched. She sat down on a small stack of decorative throw pillows and blankets by the door and turned her head away.

Andrea went over to Quinn, crouched down in front of her. "Because we don't know what will happen when we do. We don't know if or when Death will regain control of this town, or what will happen to us when It does. We don't know what will happen to those we loved . . . to those we still love when we return to them. How they will react. Death isn't always the scariest part of dying. Sometimes it's knowing the pain felt by those left behind. Knowing how much you still hurt."

"And sometimes," Alex said, "it's because they know it isn't safe."

"Safe?" Ellis asked.

"There are factions in this town. The house, even some of the ghosts throughout town . . . People are aware of it. Of them. They know something, even if they don't know the full story—Analiese's story. Some of us see the house for the miracle that it is. We want to keep it safe, make sure it isn't harmed. It's like sacred ground. A while back, a handful of families even thought of raising money to buy the property, to preserve it, but most felt it was . . . wrong, I suppose. Garish."

"Because it's a person," Ellis said, thinking back to what had been said to them the night their house was vandalized. "And you can't own a person."

Alex nodded. "Others see, well, what they want to see. For some, there is no such thing as a good miracle. They see the house, they see the ghost of someone they once loved returned to them, and they see a price they will one day have to pay. They see a future they can't understand. And they fear what they don't understand."

"People have tried so many times to hurt or destroy her," Andrea said, returning to her space behind the counter. "Especially when the house has been empty for any length of time. And every time, she—the house—has healed itself. And what can't be healed, others have gone in and fixed. It's like an unspoken war of attrition."

"So, I'm sharing a space with ghosts twenty-four-seven. That's . . . swell. And not in any way an invasion of my privacy." Ellis went over and gripped Quinn's shoulder; she leaned her head against their hand.

Andrea laughed. "Please. We have far better things to do than watch you while you're sleeping."

"Like what?"

"Watching you in the shower, of course."

"That's much worse, actually."

"It's also a joke, Ellis."

"Oh." Ellis paused. "So, the house doesn't want anything from us then?"

Alex shook her head. "Just for you to live in it. And maybe not burn it down."

"Why would I—"

"Twenty-five years ago, a young girl who lived in your house tried to do exactly that. They were the last family to live there, before you and your mom showed up."

"Why would she do that?" Quinn asked, confused.

"Because twenty-five years ago, her brother died, and she blames his death on the house."

"Why?"

"He told her so."

Ellis perked up. "Like . . . before or after he died?"

"After," Andrea said lightly.

"Oh."

"And it wasn't him. Not really."

Alex jumped in, sensing the question forming on Ellis's tongue. "There are two kinds of dead thing in this town, Ellis: ghosts and projections. The ghosts are those who died here, under Analiese's watch. They are who you expect them to be. You see them every time you leave your house on a cloudy day or late at night, when the sun can't give away their secret. They go about their lives—their afterlives, I guess, as simply as any of us. But projections . . . they're something else altogether."

"What?" Quinn asked.

"Masks," said Andrea coolly, as if even thinking about it gave her a chill. "They're Death's property. They're who Death wears when It comes to town. So Death can be anyone—anyone at all, as long as they didn't die within Black Stone's borders."

"But I thought—" Ellis began.

"Death is always here, as It is everywhere. It simply can't do anything to us so long as we stay within the town's borders. Analiese's protection is like a dome around this entire place— her heart strings are Black Stone's root system."

"Then how did that boy die all those years ago?" Ellis asked.

"Same way I did." Andrea pointed straight up, to the sky beyond their tiny shop. "They punched a hole."

"It was a seance," Alex said.

Quinn raised a finger. "Wait—those things actually work?"

Andrea nodded. "Occasionally. When you least want them to. Magic's a lot like that, actually. It's only real when you least want it to be. A group of friends went out into the woods one summer night to try to speak to the dead they thought were trapped inside the house. Except they managed to do something very different, and very, very dangerous. However briefly, they broke through Analiese's protection."

"Just long enough to get one of their own killed," Quinn supplied.

"And about twenty others."

"What?"

Alex nodded. "Most were heart attacks or something that looked like a heart attack. Andrea died when the earthquake that accompanied the ritual took out the northern part of town."

"Turns out," Andrea said, "Death really *is* a force of nature. Also, don't go hiking at night. There're better and less deadly ways to piss off your parents."

"Wait . . . If you died at the same time as that boy and all those others, why didn't Death take you as well?"

"Because they died immediately. I was dying from my injuries, but I remained alive just long enough for Analiese to regain her control. I was lucky."

"After that," Alex continued, "the rumours about the house only seemed to intensify. One of the kids there that night—Betany O'Brien, she's a single mom. Her son is—"

"Dominik," Quinn said.

"That's the one," Alex said. "Anyway, Betany started spreading this idea that it was the house's fault, that it had eaten Reece's soul as it had so many others. Reece was—"

"The boy who died," Ellis said. "He and my mom were friends."

"Yes," said Andrea. "Tessa, Reece's sister, was Betany's closest friend. Betany never got over what happened that night."

"What about Tessa? What happened to her?"

"Her parents had her institutionalized several hours outside of Black Stone. Out in the Meadowlands, I think. She was convinced Reece told her to set fire to the house." Andrea paused. "Word is, she's back. And as long as she's here, you're in danger—we all are."

"Why?" Quinn asked.

"Because if she's back," Andrea said, "odds are she didn't get here on her own."

"Jesus Christ . . ." Ellis said. "So, if the house were to, you know, go up in flames, what would . . . would we all just up and die without its protection?"

"It's hard to say," Alex said. "In a sense, Death is like a lover spurned. Or more like an angry child, someone who's never heard *no*. There's no telling what It will or won't do if given the chance. The more time It's spent bartering with humans, the more human It's become. It has learned to lie and deceive in the years since Analiese's rebellion. It has learned bitterness and vengeance."

"So, Death might just take the lot of you—the ghosts—or It might level this entire town, the living and the dead alike. Like Optimism."

Andrea nodded. "And now you know the whole story."

"Not quite." Ellis looked to Quinn, who nodded. "There's one more thing we need to discuss. In the cellar, there's a—"

"A hatch," Alex finished. "In the middle of a maze. Yes, I know."

"What can you tell us about it?"

"Plenty." Alex sighed. "My dad built it."

"The hell you say," Ellis said.

Alex nodded. "God's honest. We lived there before the Sweets. Dad and I moved out a little while after Mom died. He was never right, though, not after so many years in that space."

"Did you always know it was haunted?"

Alex shook her head. "I'd heard things, and I had my suspicions, but I was only a kid. Who the hell was going to listen to me?" Andrea loudly cleared her throat. "Present company excluded. Anyway, we didn't even know about the cellar at first. Not until we started hearing things at night."

"Voices?" Ellis asked.

"That, and just, you know, sounds and shit. People milling around. The walls beating like they had heart of their very own. Or *were* a heart—which is probably more apt, given the circumstances. Then the damn porch light started to flicker wildly one night, and—"

"The light!" Ellis exclaimed. "What's up with that? We can't even find the switch for it."

"And you won't. It's not yours; it's hers."

"Analiese."

Andrea nodded. "It's how she tells us. How she lets us know."

"What?"

"That Death is near."

"Did she tell you that when she told you the rest of her life story?"

"No," said Alex. "My mom did. She appeared to us that night, when my father was about to take a baseball bat to the porch light to get it to stop strobing. She told us she was okay, that she was safe, but that we had to protect the house at all costs." She paused. "Then she took us into the cellar. We saw then what was at stake."

"What did you find?" Quinn asked. Ellis glanced at her—she was clutching her sides as she spoke.

"A cemetery of sorts. What remained of everyone who'd ever lived and died in or near that house."

"Talismans," Quinn said. "Symbols."

Andrea nodded solemnly. "One person's ghost story is another's legacy."

"What did you and your dad do with it all?" Ellis asked.

"I didn't know what to do," Alex said. "I watched as he ... After Mom came to us, he changed. I'm not much of a religious person, but it was as if he'd had an awakening of sorts. There's really no other way to describe it. At first, he tried documenting everything he found down there."

Ellis looked to Quinn suddenly.

"What is it?" Alex said.

Quinn reached inside her shoulder bag and produced the leather-bound journal, which she passed to Alex. Alex held it in both hands and stared at it. Dug her fingers into it. Her eyes started to water.

"I . . . I remember when I hid this from him. He'd gotten so consumed, he . . . he wanted to tell the story of the house. He thought the world should know, that it would change things—

for everyone—to know there really was more to existence than we thought." She shook her head. "He was right too. It would have changed things. But whenever he tried to tell his story to anyone outside of Black Stone, no matter the ledger of items and lives he'd pieced together, the response was always the same."

"They didn't believe him."

"Worse. They ridiculed him. They tried to put him away as if he were insane." Sorrow was evident in her downturned eyes. "The more people laughed him off as just some lunatic, the more . . . protective he became of what was right beneath our feet. He . . . he felt a responsibility to it."

"He built the door in the ground. The hatch," Ellis said.

"And the maze." Alex sighed. "By the end, he was scrambling for anything he thought might throw Death off or confuse It. As if It weren't some entity beyond comprehension but an easily fooled toddler. He spent weeks not sleeping, just digging out the earth, cutting a cavern into the ground, pouring the concrete . . . he did it all on his own. I only watched. I didn't know what to think about any of it, not until . . ."

"Until the night I fell into the ravine and broke my neck," said Andrea.

Alex nodded. "Dad and I had already moved out by then and were living in a motel near the edge of town. We"—she motioned to Andrea—"had been friends since first grade. When it happened, when she . . . I took a book of Andrea's I'd borrowed weeks earlier and broke into the Sweets' house at night, while they were still grieving over Reece. I slipped in through the ground-level window that drops into the cellar and put her book with the rest. With the heart beneath the heart. I didn't know if it would do anything, but it felt . . . it just felt right. Like it was something I needed to do." At that, she pulled from her pocket a simple, inconspicuous silver key with a looped end. She held it up for Ellis and Quinn to see.

"It was you," Quinn said. "You took Trey's ball down there."

Alex nodded. "The day he died. I thought he'd be safer that way. I didn't have the key with me then, so I couldn't . . . I just thought he'd be safer if he were there."

Quinn fought back tears, nodding *thank you* but not managing the words.

Alex passed the key to Ellis. "I've kept up my dad's work, but it doesn't seem right any longer, having access to a part of your house that you don't."

Ellis hesitated before reaching out and accepting the key. They stared at it a moment before sliding it into their pocket. "It looks so simple."

"You were expecting a skull with glowing emerald eyes or something?"

"Diamond, actually. It's just . . . the locksmith said he couldn't break in. I guess I was expecting something—"

"Mr. Majima's lived here his entire life. His wife, she . . . He was only doing what he thought was right."

"You mean to say he absolutely could've picked that lock."

"Oh, easily." Alex grinned slyly.

"Keep it safe," Andrea said. "Keep *us* safe. We're depending on you now."

"Are you really so afraid of what will happen if Death gets a hold of you?"

Andrea thought for a moment. "I don't know if fear is the right sentiment. We were given a choice few others have ever had. The biggest possible choice you could imagine. That's not a thing to take lightly." She paused. "I don't know if I'll ever move on. I don't know if I want to or will one day have to. That requires something like a leap of faith—that's never been my strong suit."

"Even with all you've learned."

"Which is still impressively little, when you think about it. No matter the hand you're dealt, there are still some things in this life you can't know until you're there. That's just the way of things."

Quinn wiped clear her eyes. "So, this Tessa person, she's back in town?"

"Yes," Alex said.

"And you think she's going to make a play for the house. For Analiese."

"She's already tried twice—at the sewer outflow at the north end of town and at the hospital, where she was arrested."

"And you know this how?"

"Sheriff Wolf is . . . an old friend. He knew my dad. He was there the night Tessa tried to burn down the house. He's also seen— He thought I should know."

"She's out of luck then," said Ellis.

Andrea shook her head. "She's Death's emissary, Ellis. She's not going to be taken out of the game so easily."

"Plus, she's still got friends in town. Friends who think as she does," Alex said.

Andrea nodded. "Precisely."

"Remember: This all started because once, just once, Death made a mistake. An error in judgment. It won't do that again, not if It can help it." She paused. "Analiese was given control over a situation that by all laws of nature she should never have been. Death is fighting to regain said control. That's what all this is about in the end: control."

Without meaning to, Ellis let their hand drift to their midsection. They caught themself feeling self-conscious all of a sudden, wanting to knead, to tug at it, but they stopped themself, dropped their hand again.

"Yeah," they said. "I know a little something about that."

Quinn and Ellis exited the shop several minutes later, their minds awash with new information. Neither spoke for what seemed like an age.

Still attempting to process it all, Ellis ran through what Andrea, a literal, honest-to-goodness ghost had told them only moments earlier.

"How does any of this even work?" Ellis had asked. "How can a person be a house?"

Alex looked at Ellis askew. "If you're asking for a scientific explanation for how this works, I'm afraid, my friend, that you are shit outta luck."

"No, I know, I just . . . What Analiese did, what was done to her, it should be impossible, right? To defy Death like that, it's . . . it's a lot."

"Your capacity for understatement is astounding," Alex joked.

"They're right though." Andrea approached Ellis. "It should have been impossible. It should have been utterly against nature, and it would have been had an aspect of that nature not, for a moment, chosen to do something inexplicably human. For the briefest of moments, Death offered Analiese something outside of a binary right or wrong; It offered—"

"Compassion?" Ellis supplied.

"Punishment, I think, from Its point of view. But for her, hope. That the end wasn't the end. That Analiese could get back what she'd lost—even a fraction of it. A glimmer. Things like love and compassion, they're effective countermeasures in this world. They'll keep you going, keep you warm. But hope . . . hope is the province of the living. Hope in the hands of the dead is a more powerful balm than anything else in this world or, presumably, any other."

"How do we use that?" asked Quinn.

Alex had pointed then to Ellis's pocket, and to the key hidden therein. "It starts with understanding. To keep the house safe, to keep us here, you need to know—*really* know—who you're fighting for. You need to know what it's like to leave a part of yourself in the care of another."

"Earth to Ellis?"

Ellis turned. "Huh?"

Quinn chuckled. "Where did you go just now? I said your name, like, three times."

"Sorry, I just . . ." They glanced back at the occult store, door locked, windows black. "It's just so much. I don't know if I'm up to this. I didn't even know there was going to be a thing to be up against. A haunting. That's all I thought this . . . just a simple haunting, you know? Bring in a priest or two, maybe some bullshit ghost hunters—"

"I will not have you besmirch the very besmirchable names of Ed and Lorraine."

"—and it'd all be taken care of. But this . . ."

"It's—"

"An actual pissing match with Death. Not the *idea* of death, but actual capital *D* Death."

"I was going to say it's a bit of a spiritual quest, but sure, your description works too."

"I'm being serious here, Quinn. Where do we even begin with all this? *How* do we begin?"

"We begin by beginning." She said it as if it were the simplest and most obvious answer in the world. "One foot in front of the other, and all that crap." She smiled, radiant.

"You make it sound so easy."

"It can be. Besides, you won't be doing it alone."

"Oh yeah? How do I know you're not just another ghost like Andrea in there?"

Not one to waste an opportunity, Quinn gripped Ellis's arm and pulled them around. Pulled them in tight. Kissed them. Hard.

"That answer your question?"

Ellis grinned slyly. "Sort of. I mean, I guess. If you like that kind of thing."

Quinn shook her head, and Ellis linked their arm through hers.

"So, we're going to do this," they said. "We're going to go down there."

239

Quinn nodded. "We are."

"Do you think you'll be okay?"

She paused, remembering Trey's ball, all that Alex had revealed. "I will, so long as you're there."

"Then let's do it. Together."

"Together."

CHAPTER
TWENTY-FOUR

"DAMN IT!" BETANY O'BRIEN CURSED, LOUDER THAN SHE'D intended, when she reached into the oven to grab the pan of lasagna, forgetting about the hole in the oven mitt. The hole she'd been meaning to patch now for over six months.

"Why don't you just buy a new one?" Dominik asked her the first time she'd burned herself.

"Oh, and I suppose you're going to give me the money to pay for it, are you?" she snapped back. *That boy. So like his father—that slime couldn't be counted on for anything, much less a dime of child support. And he'd absconded to who-knows-where with what's-her-name who was, at best, half his age. The louse. He didn't know the value of money either.*

She took off the glove and put her hand under the faucet, turned it on as cold as it could go. Cringed and then exhaled as the icy water made contact. She stared at her palm, noticed the new, brighter burn there criss-crossing an older keloid scar she'd had since she was a teenager. Since a week after Tessa's family left town, when she went to the house with Lucas in the middle of the night; to do what, they hadn't figured out, but when she'd tried the front door, the handle had been so hot it singed her hand as though she'd just placed it on an active stovetop.

"Dom," she called out, "can you come give me a ha—"

"Hello, Betany."

Betany's brain careened into a brick wall. She turned, slowly, not actually expecting to see the face tied so utterly to that singsong voice. *It couldn't be*—

It was.

Reece Sweet. Standing there, in her kitchen, looking very much like his sixteen-year-old self.

Except alive.

Or—

"No."

"Betany . . ."

"No!" She stood with her back to the sink, bracing against the counter behind her with both palms. Her heart was racing. Was she having a heart attack? *Oh, god, is this what a heart attack feels like?* "How . . . ? No. It's impossible. Who are you?" she asked in a panic.

The couldn't-be-Reece spread his arms wide. "You know who I am."

"It's not possible. I saw him die. *I saw you die!*"

"You saw a part of me die," the absolutely-had-to-be-an-apparition said to Lucas Hillcox, who was standing on his back porch, pissing his sweatpants in fear while his wife was inside watching television, oblivious to her husband's terror.

"This can't be happening," said Lucas, running short of breath. He held his chest as if he expected his heart to fall from it at any moment.

"It can, and it is."

"But how?" asked Connie Wang, whispering so as not to be heard by her son, who was on his phone two rooms away.

And the not-Reece cocked his—its?—head to one side and said, "Are you really going to ask me that in a town like this? The dead already walk among the living, and you know it."

"What do you want?" asked Eleanor Paulson, standing in the storeroom of her clothing and consignment shop, wishing to god, to anything that would listen, that she was still as alone as she'd thought she'd been only seconds earlier. *Not here, with . . . with this shadow,* she thought to herself.

But—

"I need you," the shadow said. "I need you to do something for me."

"What? What do you need?" James asked, hand on the gun at his side—his police-issue .45. He hadn't once fired it in all his years on the force, but he wanted to now, even though he knew it'd do precisely fuck all.

The thing that called itself Reece, the thing he was beginning to believe *was* Reece, it smiled at him. It smiled like it knew him. Knew what they had done—that it was all their fault. Sure, rumours had spread for years—likely thanks to Lucas and his total inability to keep his mouth shut about anything, especially after he had a few drinks in him—but no one *really* knew. No one.

Except Reece.

This Reece, who'd called James on his crap. Who'd told him, up front, that he and his friends, they owed him, all of them, for what they let happen to him.

They could make it right if they wanted to. There was a way.

Reece spoke, a tremor in James's soul: "I need you to help finish what my sister started: I need you to destroy the house. My old house. It's the only way I'll ever be free."

"Tessa's here?" said Betany. "Where is she? Is she okay?"

"She will be. She's part of this too. But you have to help now. All of you."

"How? Another family lives there now," said Lucas.

"Like last time. I just need you to create an opening. I'll do the rest."

"I don't know," said Connie, growing more afraid by the minute. "I don't think—"

"Nobody asked you what you think, just do it!"

"But—" Eleanor began, and was cut off when Reece, glowering, growing, it seemed, right in front of her, shook the store to its very foundation. The shadow expanded to fill the room.

"Do not deny me this," Reece said. "Do not let me die again!"

"Die *again*?" said James. "What do you mean?"

"I'm growing weak. I need to move on. But I can't. The house, it's as haunted as you've heard. The stories about it are as real as I am to you, right at this very moment." Reece approached, the spectre growing dim, growing dark. "As I was all those years ago when you offered me up for the slaughter. And it's killing me, a death greater than death. It's devouring my very soul. And when it's done with mine, when it's done with your neighbours' souls, and your friends and your families and your children, it will come for you too. It won't stop until it's taken every last one of you."

And Reece stepped forward then, put his hand to James's shoulder.

To Betany's.

To Lucas's.

Connie's.

Eleanor's.

To the five of them, at once, in separate parts of town. Together, they felt nothing physical, no pressure, but the frigid touch of Death all the same. It cut through them, through every part of them. They shuddered as one.

They acquiesced.

"Yes," they said, one after another.

And Death said, "It is time."

CHAPTER
TWENTY-FIVE

THE KEY IN ELLIS'S POCKET MUST HAVE WEIGHED MERE OUNCES at most, but the longer it sat there, through the rest of the weekend and all through their early shift on Monday, the heavier it seemed to grow, as if it were somehow accumulating new metals. By the end of their shift, it took everything they had to not bound out of Twitch and sprint home. Patricia even had to stop them on their way out the door, to hand them their paycheque and remind them to take off their hairnet.

They'd wanted to go straight home and dive into the cellar on Friday night, after Alex and Andrea had given their history lesson; they were energized, ready to see if what they'd learned was true. But Quinn wasn't quite ready—she needed a little time after everything Andrea had said—and the two of them had promised to do it together. And then Robyn spent all weekend at home, working on renovations. Ellis thought of telling her they'd found the key, but they weren't sure they were ready to reveal the rest—not with the Reece connection being what it was. Besides, when they'd tried to ask her about what she'd said that night, to those people outside their house, Robyn had shut down the conversation entirely. She was tired, she said. She didn't remember. She was just rambling.

Whatever more she had to say, she wasn't ready to dig into it. And Ellis knew enough not to push any more than they already had.

They texted Quinn on their way home to see if she was ready. She said she wasn't, not yet; she needed a little more time. Ellis asked where she was, and she replied the darkroom at BSH. Ellis hurried over there—it was only ten minutes away if they jogged. They entered through the side door just south of the art room, which she'd left unlocked for them. When they found her exiting the darkroom, they stopped in place. Tears streamed down her cheeks. There was a glint in her eyes that seemed to shout pain.

Ellis went up to her and took her by the arm. "You okay?" She nodded, wiped her eyes. In one hand she held her SLR camera, and in the other, a folder of recently developed prints. "What're those?"

She passed Ellis the folder. They peeked inside and found several shots of the front of their house. They recognized the angle immediately.

"You took these that day. When I found you. When you were . . ."

She nodded. "Yeah."

"What's wrong?"

She pointed to the top image, to a blank space on the porch. "He's not there."

Ellis paused. "Trey?"

"I was looking right at him, I swear it, but now . . . When I looked at the display on my camera all those weeks ago, the shots were empty. I knew it. I knew what would happen, and so I held off developing these. I don't know if I thought maybe it'd be different somehow, but . . ."

Ellis pulled her in for a hug. "I'm sorry."

"I just wish he'd come back. I wish he'd talk to me again."

"You mean he hasn't?" Ellis nodded toward the darkroom. "I just assumed."

She sniffed. "Do you think he can't? Do you think maybe it's not safe for him with Death out there, trying to get at them? At . . . at her?"

Analiese, Ellis thought. A thing that, despite all they'd experienced, still seemed like something that absolutely shouldn't have been possible but, somehow, impossibly, was.

"I don't know," Ellis said. "But we can do our part to keep them safe. To keep them all safe."

"How?"

And Ellis realized: they had no idea. None. The house was theirs now, on paper, but did that actually mean anything? *You don't own this! You can't own her!* Those words had stuck with them, and now they knew why. What had at first seemed like a threat now felt more like a plea. For them to understand. To recognize what was at stake. What they could do, or couldn't. Could they actually do anything to push back against Death?

"I don't know," Ellis said at last. "Maybe nothing. But I know where to look if we're going to find answers." They patted their pocket, where the key remained safely tucked away. "Whaddya say, you wanna go check out my cellar? Mom's working late tonight—we'll have the whole place to ourselves, and possibly a small legion of ghosts."

Quinn eyed them suspiciously. "So, is 'cellar' a euphemism for something?"

Ellis stepped back, their face neon red. "What? No, that's not—I didn't mean—"

She leaned in, touching her forehead to theirs. "Relax, love machine," she said. "I'm giving you a hard time."

They looked at her askew. "What was that you said about euphemisms?"

She laughed. "At least you didn't give me a 'that's what she said.'"

"Unlike you, I have standards. Some. I think."

"Uh-huh." She kissed them. Took a deep breath. "All right, I'm ready."

"We're going in?"

"Now or never, but always together."

"I like that. Workshop it much?"

"Oh, shut it."

"I mean it rhymes and everything. And without using 'Nantucket.'"

"Are you finished?"

"Now *that's* what she said! In a minute," Ellis added, ignoring Quinn's I-want-to-murder-you glare. "I'm just gonna grab some paint to take home."

She regarded them quizzically. "I'm pretty sure that's called stealing."

"I'm offering it a home where its purpose will be fulfilled."

"Whatever, thief." She smiled wickedly. "Meet you outside?" She left then, and Ellis darted over to where the large cannisters of acrylic paint sat against the wall. They found one that was almost empty and started pouring some purple into it from another mostly full canister so they could finish the painting of the maelstrom. The town's only art supply store was both lacking and far too pricey, they reminded themself, as if to justify their crime.

"Ellis."

That voice.

They turned, already knowing who they would find. "Amara."

She stood there, in the far corner of the room, as if she'd always been there, and looking exactly as she had the day they'd met her. They backed up against the counter, knocking the paint into the sink behind them.

"You're afraid of me," she said. "Why?"

"Are we really gonna do this?" they asked.

"Do what?" Amara replied innocently.

"Ghost or projection?"

She eyed them curiously. "Come again?"

Ellis recalled what Quinn had revealed—how Amara's parents had taken her out of town for treatment, and she'd never

249

returned. Not as herself, anyway. Amara and Ellis hadn't known one another, but Death knew: It could wear her skin around town, and if anyone saw her, they'd think her presence was tied to the house and not something greater. Something sinister.

"Are you a ghost or a projection?" they said again. "You're sure as hell not real—you were, once, but you're not even you, are you." It wasn't a question.

Amara stared. "You've been getting to know your new home, I see."

"Ghost. Or. Projection?" Their heart was racing.

"You think you know what's at stake," Amara said. "You glib little asshole."

"Is this where you tell me my days are numbered if I don't destroy the house?" They paused. "Except you've already enlisted some help in that department, haven't you? That's why Tessa's back in town, right . . . Death?"

Amara laughed. "Is that the limit of your imagination? I guess I shouldn't be surprised. I am so much more than you could even *hope* to understand. Were I to speak my true name, your mind would collapse under the strain, as if torn asunder by an imploding star."

"Gee, that doesn't sound at all like grandstanding, boilerplate horseshit taken from every '80s action-movie villain that ever was."

"If you had any sense of self-preservation, you would line up to help me burn that house and this entire town to its very foundation. You'd leave nothing left."

"That sounds somewhat counterproductive to my continuing to exist, so . . . yeah, hard pass."

"If you truly understood, you'd ravage it and watch with me, celebrate as each strand of that house's heart withers and dies."

"You mean the strands *you* pulled out yourself? The power that you gave her? That's what all this is, right? An attempt to make good on your fuck-up?"

The door to the art room opened then, and in walked Dominik. "Ellis," he said, "I was walking past the school and I saw Quinn waiting outside and— Wait, Amara?"

Ellis glanced back and forth between Dominik and Death-as-Amara. "You can see her?"

"Of course I can see her, but she's—I mean, she—" Dominik stumbled back in fear, pressing his back flat against the wall next to the door.

Ellis returned their attention to Amara. To what *had* been Amara mere seconds earlier and was now a towering, growing transparent shadow with ashen, condor-like wings that stretched and filled the room. The space was suddenly night-dark; the walls shook and desks shifted in place as if the room and only that room had been hit by an earthquake, isolated and severe. The shadow's limbs—or what it had that approximated limbs—were themselves entwined with concertina wire that would have shredded the being's tissue had it not consisted entirely of ash and smoke.

Ellis gulped. "Oh, shit."

"What the fuck!" said Dominik. "Am I on drugs? Ellis, did you give me drugs?"

"*Silence!*" Death swept toward both of them. Instinctively, Dominik reached out and grabbed Ellis by the arm, pulling them back. It was a fruitless gesture, however—or it would have been had Death not stopped in place.

Ellis glanced down. Reaching up through a nearby heating duct, they saw dozens of narrow red veins attaching themselves to the spectre of Death.

Death howled, a sound that was equal parts dying animal and machine factory floor—screeching and clanging and chaos.

"What's happening?" Dominik shrieked. Ellis had no idea. They simply watched as the red pierced and wound its way through Death as if sutures through flesh, stilling Its advance. Whatever the red really was, heart strings or something else, it seemed to weaken Death, to cause It to shrivel and start to fold in on Itself. Gradually, the smoke started to dissipate, the being given human shape once more, albeit still wreathed in shadow.

Ellis stepped out of Dominik's grasp. Slowly, cautiously, they approached the thing still taking shape, becoming something new . . . No. Something old. Something all too familiar.

A single syllable fractured Ellis's voice like a boulder dropped onto plate glass: "Dad?"

The being, Death, shed Its smoke entirely for the figure of a man, white with short brown hair and green eyes that Ellis would remember vividly until the day they died.

"Ellis," he said—*It said*, Ellis reminded themself. *It isn't him. It isn't*— "Help me. Help *us*."

He's not, Ellis told themself. "You're not—"

"Help us!" cried the simulacrum of Michael Lang.

"Ellis!"

They turned and spotted Dominik beckoning them over. Coaxing them, telling them it was okay, it'd all be okay if they just—

But Ellis turned again, just in time to see Death's newest mask slip away, revealing, for only a breath, the terrifying truth of what hunted them. The opposite—the *absence* of life. It was a sight beyond description, one that Ellis realized would haunt them for the rest of their days.

And somewhere, deep beneath the town of Black Stone, Analiese made a fist with her mind, and from some distance away snapped the heart strings taut around Death like the handle of a vice spinning shut. Death let out one final screech then and, as suddenly as It had appeared, vanished into a crack in the air that resealed itself instantaneously.

Dominik slowly approached them from behind. "A-are you okay?"

"You saw all that, right?" Ellis said without turning around.

"I did. But . . ." Dominik trailed off. Ellis glanced back and saw him pointing at the floor, to the many heart strings slowly slithering back underground. "What . . . what are those?"

Ellis, still rocked by the unexpected projection—*that's all it was*, they repeated to themself, over and over again—faced Dominik and said, calmly, "You were right. About the house—my house: it's haunted."

"*I fucking knew it!*" Dominik was practically hopping up and down. He pulled out his phone and started excitedly texting someone.

Ellis put a hand over the phone screen, stopping him. "Will you shut up?" they said sharply. "You were right, but not in the way you thought. There's a lot more going on here than you know."

Right then, Quinn burst into the room. "El, what's taking so—" She stopped upon seeing Dominik, who waved at her awkwardly. "What the shit is he doing here?"

"Come on," Ellis said. "We'll talk on the way."

"On the way where?" Dominik asked, following them out.

"My place," Ellis said. "We've got a tomb to open."

CHAPTER
TWENTY-SIX

FOR ALL HIS TRAINING, FOR ALL THAT HE'D BEEN TAUGHT TO accept only what was irrefutably true, Deputy James Tallon still believed in ghosts. The first he'd seen, when he was just sixteen, was his kid sister, Chrissie, who'd died and then shortly after reappeared one night at the foot of James's bed, dressed in her funeral best. She'd told him there was a way they could speak to one another again, maybe even spend more time together. He and his friends had to gather what had seemed to him like a witch's pantry's worth of supplies and a book owned by one of his friend's parents that sounded like a prop from a bad horror movie but was more powerful than anyone realized.

And things hadn't gone as planned.

James stopped believing, openly, with the help of several therapists and years of antidepressants, but internally he never stopped wondering if she'd been real, if she could one day come back.

If she hated him for how he'd failed her.

Then, last night, he saw, for certain, his second ghost: Reece Sweet. The life he'd unknowingly traded in his attempt to reach Chrissie in the afterlife. To this day, he still didn't know what had gone wrong that night or why, only that it had. Spectacularly. He did know, however, that the sudden and inexplicable rash of deaths that had rocked the town of Black Stone that night twenty-five years ago was as much their fault as Reece's death was.

And now.

Now, there was a chance to undo some of the damage they'd done. To atone, if that were remotely possible.

Reece had laid it out to them—to all of them, James learned earlier that morning in an angry, uncomfortable, accusatory, frightened chain of texts between himself and a group of friends he'd barely spoken to since that night. Since the funeral. Since Tessa tried to—

Since Tessa.

Sure, they'd nodded at one another in the street, acknowledged each other when they had to, but not one of them had openly discussed what had happened until Betany sent out the first tentative message asking if any of them felt like they were, very suddenly, losing their damn minds.

One by one they admitted what they had seen, what had been said.

It's a trick is what it is, Lucas had written between strings of expletives. *Someone knows what happened and they're black-mailing us.*

To what end, James had asked. Reece wasn't demanding anything; he hadn't threatened any of them. No, he was offering them something they couldn't get anywhere else, or from any*one* else. Something they, maybe, never thought possible.

What's that? Connie had asked.

A chance to make it right. A chance to clean up the mess they'd made two decades prior. James thought this to himself all day while seated at his desk at the Black Stone Police Department, slowly plodding his way through paperwork that didn't really need doing. Biding his time until the very last person left for the night.

"You sticking around for a bit, James?" the sheriff asked while putting on his coat.

James nodded. "Sure am, Sheriff Wolf. I got a few things need finishing up before I call it a night."

"Well, don't be too late now or you'll feel like death tomorrow."

James chuckled uncomfortably. "We wouldn't want that." He waved to the sheriff, waited until the coast was clear before getting up from his seat, grabbing the keys to the cell block, and doing what he'd been dreading since first hearing who it was that had been picked up at the hospital.

The cell block was empty save for the person in question, lying on a cot with her back to the iron bars. Her long hair looked thin and ratty, her body frail, underfed. Even from behind, James thought, she seemed at least ten years older than she really was.

He sighed pointedly. "Tess."

A pause.

"I know that voice," she muttered without turning over. "I think I heard it once. In a dream. Or maybe it was a nightmare." She rolled over, faced him. "It's not always so easy to tell the difference these days, is it, Jimmy?"

He swallowed. "You look—"

"If you say 'good,' I'll reach through these bars and snap you in two."

"I was going to say like Linda Hamilton in *T2*. Which . . . yeah, even more now."

She sat up on her cot. "Why are you here, Jimmy? Come to tell me I'm a lunatic? To condemn me like everyone else in this shithole town?"

"I, uh, that is I . . ." He cleared his throat.

She stood up, approached the bars. "You're sweating." She gripped a bar with each hand.

He wiped his brow. "This? No, it's just the AC, it's—"

"Working just fine," she said, staring out at him. Then: "You've seen him."

"What?" James was taken aback.

"He came to you," Tessa continued. "My brother. Reece. He appeared to you, didn't he?"

James took a step closer. Dropped his voice: "He's why you came back."

"What did he tell you to do?"

"He, uh, he said we . . . we need to do it again. The seance. He said we have to do it in order to . . . to weaken the house." He leaned in closer. "Is he telling the truth about that place?"

Tessa pressed herself forward as far as the bars would allow. Whispered, "What do you think?"

"Goddamn." James turned away, started to pace. "What manner of hell have you brought to our doorstep, Tessa?"

"What have *I*—? Oh, screw you, Jimmy. You want to talk about hell? Try being locked away for twenty-five years in places where they tell you that you don't know what you *know* you know. Try being told by every doctor, by your own parents, even, that you're 'not all there.' That what every single part of you is certain you saw with your own two eyes is made up. Imaginary. A figment of your fucked-up mind. Tell me you understand even a shred of that, and I'll share with you my own little corner of hell."

"I didn't mean . . . I saw therapists too. And we all . . . I mean at some point, I think every one of us tried to—"

"Oh, you did? Did you get to go home after every appointment, or did you have someone checking in on you twenty-four-seven? Did you get to hide every empty bottle of pills you downed, or did you have your room tossed and your stomach pumped every time anyone suspected anything? Did you . . . did you get threatened with never seeing your family again if you didn't get your shit together?" Tessa glared. James stared at his feet. "I thought so."

She tightened her grip on the bars, twisting her palms around them as if expecting them to give. "Yes, he's telling the truth," Tessa said. "It's the same truth he's been telling me all this time."

The unease in James's insides roiled worse than any stomach acid he'd ever experienced. He wasn't sure if he wanted to run away or simply throw up right in front of Tessa. The others of their group had told him to get to the bottom of this. They'd practically ordered him, and when that didn't work, they'd begged. *Talk to her*, they'd pleaded. *Figure this out. For us. For all of us.*

He wished he'd imagined this. He wished he'd been able to do nothing, but something in him knew that if he didn't act, Reece would never let him rest.

"What do we do?" he asked, timidly.

"First, get me out of here," Tessa said.

"What then?"

"'What then?'" Tessa glared at him. "Then we burn that fucking house to the ground."

CHAPTER
TWENTY-SEVEN

"... AND THEN IT JUST SORT OF DISSIPATED, AND THAT'S WHEN you came in," Ellis said as the three of them walked down an empty neighbourhood street. They took a quick glance back over their shoulder, as they had every few feet since leaving the school. To make sure they weren't being followed.

"I still don't get it," Quinn said.

"Which part?"

"Why you keep seeing Amara. Why I never have."

"Not Amara—very certainly not even a ... well, a human."

"Whatever. Point remains."

"Maybe you have and didn't realize it," Ellis said.

Quinn halted in place. "Don't."

Ellis faced her. "Oh god, I don't—I didn't mean Trey." They went to put their hand on her shoulder, but she instinctively pulled away, like there was a dagger in there that she didn't want to risk pulling out.

Dominik glanced back and forth between them. "What am I missing here?"

Ellis watched Quinn, to gauge whether it was okay to reveal what she'd told them. She nodded. "Quinn's brother, Trey, died some years back."

"I remember," Dominik said solemnly.

"Yeah, well, not long after we moved in, she saw him again, right outside my house."

Dominik's eyes widened. "Oh."

"Yeah."

"It was him, Ellis. I know it was." Her voice wavered. "It wasn't—"

"I know," Ellis said. "I'm sorry, I didn't think before I spoke."

"Maybe," Dominik interjected, "it's because you're neutral in all this, Ellis. If this *is* Death, It's not wasting Its time on people already in league with the house."

"In league with?" Quinn looked at Dominik like she wanted to throttle him. "This isn't some fucking sport, you little—"

"No, I know, I mean—" Dominik sighed. Looked to Ellis. "You're new. You're fresh meat. It came for you because It thought it might sway you to . . . to Its cause, or whatever."

Ellis and Quinn shared a knowing glance. "I hate to admit it, but he's probably onto something." Then Ellis turned to Dominik and said, "You're still a dick, you know. For how you treated me that first day."

"I was right, though, wasn't I?" Dominik said.

"Only partly."

"Why are you even here?" Quinn asked suddenly. Sharply.

"My mom." Dominik spoke without hesitation. "I overheard her on the phone with someone last night. She was seriously pissed and . . . scared, I think. I don't know what about, but I know it was something to do with the house. And with Reece Sweet."

"You know about Reece?"

"He probably knows as much as Alex and Andrea," Ellis said. "Right? You've been researching our house for years. You know its history. You know what happened there. You just didn't piece it together. Let me guess: your mom raised you thinking it was a death trap."

"Not just her," Dominik said. "A lot of people here don't trust your house. They just don't know why." He paused. "I didn't know why. And . . . I still don't. Not really."

"What's changed?"

"She was talking about making things right. Something they'd done, I think—something bad. I didn't hear much, but at one point she yelled that they should just burn it all down and be done with it. And . . . Look, I don't know what's going on here, not as much as I . . . But actually burning down someone's house? I just . . ." He let out a long breath. "She's always been like, you know, angry. But last night was—"

"Different?"

"Yeah. And a little scary."

"To say the least. And to think, she sold us this fucking place."

"She made her money. She doesn't care what happens after that." Quinn shrugged. "Capitalism's real swell, ain't it?"

Ellis sighed. "Okay, fine. Lesson one: the house isn't evil, but what's trying to get at it . . ." They thought about it a moment. "I guess it's not evil either—not exactly. But it's pissed off, and that puts all of us at risk—the living and the dead of this town."

"Just how many ghosts are there in Black Stone?" Dominik asked.

Quinn shrugged and led the way again. "I guess we'll find out."

They rounded the next corner and their destination came into view.

The house at the end of Cherry Lane.

In the cellar, through the broken slats, Ellis led the three of them deeper into the bowels of their house.

Dominik, bringing up the rear, stopped at the broken wood slats and pressed against a few of them. The slats moved on a hinge. "You know," he said self-satisfyingly, "you didn't need to

261

break your way through like some neanderthal. This thing is supposed to open like a door."

"That would explain how Alex was able to get down here so easily," Quinn whispered to Ellis.

Ellis whispered back, "He's been here five seconds and already I want to punch him."

"Well, you did invite him."

"Really? You want to twist that particular knife right now?"

"I mean it's already in there. What's one more turn?"

"Hey, lovebirds!" Dominik called out. "You want to speak up so I can—"

"*No*," Ellis and Quinn said in unison. Ellis stopped then, right at the mouth of the maze.

Dominik came up behind them. "What in the—"

Ellis touched Quinn's hand. "You ready?"

She nodded. Together, the three of them set off into the ramshackle maze. Ellis felt terrific unease as the trio made their way through, knowing now that it was made in a state of madness, desperation. They tried to imagine how far gone Alex's father must have been to get to such a point—furiously stacking pieces of palettes, crates, broken wood boxes, and slabs of cardboard and drywall, shellacking it all together as fast as possible. Silently, they feared their own capacity for obsessive behaviour. They knew how easily one could fall into a hole so difficult—or impossible—to climb back out of.

After only a few moments, having wound their way through the maze, they arrived at its centre, and the steel hatch there that led deeper into the earth.

"What is this?" Dominik asked.

"That's what we're about to find out," Ellis answered. "Ready?"

"I guess, I mean I don't really—"

"Quinn?" Ellis turned and saw her approaching from the other end of the narrow passage. In her hands, a small red rubber ball, which she clutched tight against her belly.

"Quinn?" Ellis said again, tenderly.

She sucked in a breath. Nodded. "Good to go."

Ellis fished around in their pocket, retrieving the key Alex had given them.

Slid it into the lock. Breathed, and turned.

Ellis grunted and swung the heavy door up. The steel seemed to almost exhale as they heaved it all the way over, the chamber opening up to them as if a sarcophagus. Dry, musty air wafted out.

"Are we about to die?" Dominik asked. "Is this when the house eats me?"

"If we're lucky . . ." Quinn muttered so that only Ellis could hear.

"No one's getting eaten," Ellis said. "Unfortunately."

"How far down does it go?" Quinn asked.

"Not sure."

She pulled out her phone, still clutching the ball with one hand, and tapped the flashlight app. The beam illuminated a vertical tunnel of concrete with a ladder on one side; after ten feet or so, it appeared to open up into a wide earthen chamber.

Ellis put both feet on the second rung of the ladder and started down.

"Careful," Quinn said. Ellis briefly hesitated before continuing, descending all the way to the bottom. It took only a few seconds to reach the last rung, though it felt like a great deal more. Once their feet were on the ground, they pulled out their phone, turned on the flashlight, and started to investigate. The rectangular chamber was only fifteen or twenty feet wide, they estimated, carved poorly, quickly, and filled with stacks of items: clothes, toys, photographs in frames, knick-knacks collected from what looked like all over the world.

And the walls surrounding them, the earth itself to all sides and at their feet as well, was segmented. Divided again and again, too many times to count, by lines, pulsing, throbbing, beating here and throughout all of Black Stone, penetrating the world around them. Suturing it. Holding their town together more than anyone living up above really knew or could know.

Heart strings. Analiese, stretched as far as she could be and too far at once.

It was true. The story, all of it—it was real.

From all around Ellis, a voice echoed through the dirt walls: "It's not what it seems . . ."

"I know," Ellis said, searching for the source of the voice. "I under—I *want* to understand."

"Ellis," Quinn shouted from above. "Is someone else down there? What's going on?"

"Do you?" said another, more isolated voice, from right behind them.

Ellis spun and shone their light in the second voice's direction. They caught only a glimpse—of a boy and a girl, pale skinned, standing in front of a stack of clothes. But as soon as the light hit them, they vanished.

"I do. Really. I know what's coming. I know what hunts you."

"You only think you know."

They turned again, catching part of a young Black woman's calf before the rest of her retreated into the darkness. They could see her, though, clear as day, in the photograph she'd appeared in front of.

"If I don't, then tell me. I want to . . . I have to protect the people I care about," Ellis said.

"You can't. You'll fail. Only she can keep us safe."

Ellis didn't search for this new voice; they were everywhere, it seemed, watching them. Ellis started to feel too exposed. Too visible. They wanted to hide, to make sure their waist wasn't as horrifically obvious as they felt—as they *knew* it was, right then, themself, the one wielding the spotlight yet unable to—

Ellis tapped the flashlight off. Immediately, unexpectedly, they felt more at ease. They walked forward, fumbling in the dark until they touched the wall—warm, hot to the touch—and something there. Something slick and cylindrical, like a thick cord or braid.

A groan then, like a house settling angrily.

"Ellis!" Quinn called. "What's happening? Are you okay?"

"I'm fine," Ellis called up. "I think. Am I fine?" they asked the space around them. Slowly, their eyes started to adjust. Things began to crystallize around them, bodies emerging from the dark like shadows growing solid: legs, several pairs of them; dozens.

"Ellis?"

The space lit up again suddenly. They turned and Quinn and Dominik were both there, standing by the ladder, staring in bafflement at the assortment of odds and ends and lives that surrounded them, crammed into the small space.

"We heard you talking and—"

Ellis motioned for Quinn to put her phone away. She did.

"What are we doing?" she asked.

"Waiting," Ellis replied.

"For what?"

"You'll see."

A few moments passed before Dominik let out a short gasp. Quinn did similarly only seconds later as her eyes adjusted to the dark and she saw, at last, what the others already had:

Analiese's charges. Her family. Everyone, Ellis realized, who'd lived and died in their house, throughout all of Black Stone, over the past few decades, now standing there in front of their memories, their worldly possessions. The pieces of them that were left behind.

"Quinn," Ellis said.

She looked and, through the dark, saw Ellis's hand outstretched, pointing. And at the end of it, a young Black boy, arms open wide.

"Trey . . ."

He nodded. Smiled, a smile bright enough to break the dark in two. She reached for him but her hands passed straight through him. He shrugged as if to say, *it is what it is.* Quinn knew too. She placed the ball on the ground and rolled it to the ghost of her younger brother. It passed through him without pause.

A flash then, and the ghosts phased out of existence all at once.

Dominik checked the picture on his phone. "What the hell," he said. "I don't see them anymore."

"That's . . . because they're not really here," Quinn said. "Just the memory of them." She faced Dominik. "They're no one's to capture. Not really." She turned to Ellis then, saw them staring straight ahead, at something they'd glimpsed through the dark.

"El?"

Ahead of them was a blanket, dried blood speckling it here and there. The fabric was significantly aged and tattered—it looked as if it had been there for decades. *Since the beginning of all this.*

A new figure appeared, materializing between Ellis and the blanket. A young girl with long brown hair. Her face was full and bright—a far cry from what they'd pictured, of a girl slowly having the life siphoned from her far too soon.

She smiled at Ellis.

Isabelle, they thought. *Izzy. Analiese's daughter. The second string plucked from her mother's heart. The name on the wall in their bedroom—her bedroom.*

Betany checked the time on her phone. "He should have been here already. What's keeping him?"

The four of them—Lucas, Betany, Connie, and Eleanor—stood around impatiently, uncomfortably, in a small section of field not one of them had visited in twenty-five years. None of them wanted to be there—Lucas had said no fewer than five times that afternoon how he wished he could be "absolutely anywhere else at that exact shitting moment." But there they were. It's where James had told them to meet, where they could get right what they'd managed to screw up so many years prior.

"Right," Connie had said. "And another one of us will probably bite it in the process."

"I don't think so," James assured her. "We all saw it—him. We all heard the very same thing. We've got a chance to . . . to . . ."

"Die," Eleanor said.

"Do something good," James corrected her.

They still weren't convinced. They had wanted him to talk to her. To Tessa.

"He's probably run off," said Lucas. "Coward that he is. He got us into this mess in the first place all those years ago. If he hadn't tried to contact his dead sister . . ."

Snapping then—twigs breaking underfoot. They glanced north in time to see James, still in uniform, trudging through the thicket. Alone.

"What the fuck, James? Where is she?" Eleanor demanded.

"Tessa isn't right in the head," James replied. "I couldn't risk bringing her."

"Oh, and I suppose the rest of us are all just super stable, doing whatever the hell it is we're about to do."

"You know as well as I do why we're here," James said.

"Screw it. I don't," said Connie. "Why should any of us—"

"Because we fucked up!" James shouted. "Because . . . because we can still help Reece—or what's left of him. You all saw him. Talked to him. You know as well as I do how absurd this seems, how it is, but what choice do we have?"

"We could go home, Jim," said Lucas. "We could just pretend like none of this ever happened."

"Like we've been doing for the past twenty-five years? How's that been working out for you? For any of you? When was the last time one of you slept through the night without a stiff drink, huh? I thought so," he added, looking around at the four uncomfortable faces, weathered by their own personal hells. "Besides, if we don't . . . it could be us next. It could be any one of us."

Betany sighed. "Where do we start?"

"Did you bring the book?" James asked.

Quinn was first out of the chamber. She emerged from the hole in the ground and leaned against the nearest uneasy wall of the maze to catch her breath.

Ellis came up next. They put a hand to her back to comfort her. "Are you okay?"

"I will be," she breathed. "I just—I need a moment." She quickly wound her way back through the maze and up and out of the cellar's entrance and out the front door. She went to the edge of the porch, slammed into the railing, and leaned over it to catch her hitching breath.

It was Trey. It was one hundred and fifty percent Trey.

And he was okay. He'd told her so. He'd told her he loved her and would be with her always. That, like the rest of them, he felt at home here, within the house—within Analiese. He was protected. He said he'd visit more, spend more time up above, with her, if only it were safe; he didn't know what awaited them on the other side, but he—they—knew their guardian would risk everything to ensure their safety.

He promised he would visit her, would never leave her, but he belonged here.

It was almost too much for Quinn to process. When she'd seen him before, there had always been an element of what-if to it all: What if she was imagining it? Losing her grip on reality?

Now, it was real. Trey was there, in Ellis's house. A part of it.

And she knew then that she would protect it, no matter who—

She felt her phone start to buzz—text messages she'd been sent while down in the hole, where apparently there hadn't been any signal.

Six messages, all from her mother, asking if she's okay, when she's coming home, if she's safe from the storm.

Quinn glanced up then. Saw what had her mother so worried: the skies were onyx, a swirling, circular maw like she'd seen only once before—the night she and Ellis went to the movies for their first date.

The clouds cast the town in darkness that should not have been possible at that hour. They were furious. A threat. In the distance, a siren started to wail.

Over her shoulder: A flash. Another—a light, strobing.

She glanced back and saw the porch light flickering, faster and faster. A near constant alarm.

A shadow, a storm given shape, purpose, wandered the streets of Black Stone. It was starting to feel like Itself again. It could sense it—the seance. They were doing it. They were opening a gap—one that, in a matter of moments, would give Death back Its teeth in this place. Would give It the chance to take back that which was rightfully Its. It was a risk, taking physical form. Materializing in, rooting Itself to, however briefly, only one plane when It was supposed to exist across all, always and at all times. It took tremendous amounts of energy to interact with anything in this town, in this pocket of existence.

It was never supposed to be like this—never supposed to be anything more than an idea to the mortals of this world. By being so willing to bend reality to Its own end, to right the wrong of Its one and only act of humanity, It would risk everything. It would make tangible the barriers between realities, threatening to throw the whole of existence into chaos, to overwrite Its error in judgment.

It continued forward, newfound energy coursing through It, a pulsing, surging strength It'd lacked for too long in this town. The energy moved into Its talons, into the whole of Its shape and beyond.

It's working. Death approached Its next target, a plain-looking grey brick building wherein their additional firepower remained under lock and key. She had failed It once already and, Death hoped, had learned her lesson. She would not fail again; It would see to that—It had enlisted enough help from other easily manipulated puppets. It would strike hard, and with terrific ferocity. But It needed help with the tethers, the cursed heart strings that were so many now and extended so far beneath Black Stone that even Death couldn't destroy them on Its own. They were, after all, Its own power reflected back at It. It was a stalemate between two immovable objects. It needed Tessa to accomplish what she'd already attempted—for It would have only a short window during which to attack the house before, It feared, the heart strings would recover and re-wind their way beneath and through the town.

Tessa would do that for It, and It would handle the rest.

It would handle *her.*

The shadow phased through the entrance to the Black Stone Police Department as It felt Its powers return to their fullest.

"C-can I help you?" asked the confused and frightened clerk working the front desk—a short man with wide glasses and even wider eyes.

The dark figure billowing in front of him reached out, Its arm a serpent, and caved in the man's chest. He didn't have time enough to scream, let alone beg for his life.

One life at a time, the shadow, enraptured—Its powers returned after being so long forbidden in this space—cut a swath through the precinct, obliterating anything that moved. It did so swiftly, dispassionately, without hesitation or provocation, simply because they were there. Because It was *owed.*

Upon reaching the cells at the building's rear, It assumed the form of Reece Sweet, one last time, and approached Its not-quite-sister.

It glanced at her, eyes empty, filled not even with malice. Voids, twin and everlasting.

"It is time," It said.

"Holy shit!" Dominik said as he emerged from the house and looked up, to the storm clouds circling high above but not high enough.

Ellis pushed past him and went over to Quinn, caught her just as she was heading down the porch steps. "Wait, where are you going?"

Quinn held up her phone. "Home. I gotta check on my parents, make sure they're okay."

What is this?" Dominik shrieked, still staring skyward. He followed Quinn down off the porch, and the two of them ventured out into the dark.

"I'll be back," he said. "I just . . . I need to see . . . whatever *this* is." He pointed a finger straight up at the sound of another long blast from the warning siren. "Because whatever it is, it's *not* normal!"

"It's not—" Ellis started to say but stopped. Something inside them said to stay where they were, that the storm or whatever it was had everything to do with her. With Analiese.

The porch light was flickering erratically—more than they'd ever seen, like the lights at a rave. They ran back inside and shut the door. Let out the breath they'd been holding. Noticed, as they did, that the walls were doing similarly. The floor, the foundation, every room of the house was groaning, settling, breathing deeply. A centralized earthquake as it came alive, right in front of them—as it revealed to Ellis its true nature.

They saw it then, as the walls shed their skin suddenly, right down to the muscle and veins beneath. A design, an intelligence marked, seared into every surface—a gory latticework. The heart strings, the house's circulatory system, visible in full, rising, pushing through to the surface of every wall. Reacting. Star patterns of viscera too many to count, webbed throughout, wound around every beam; through light fixtures and electrical circuitry, the plumbing and the floorboards.

The house—*their* house, and not. Sentient. Alive.

Awake.

"Hello?" Ellis said, not sure what they thought would happen—if anything.

Only this time, the house answered:

"I'm not what I seem."

A woman's voice. Cool. Stripped bare. Withered.

"Are you . . . Analiese?"

The heart strings moved, all of them in unison. They shifted and stretched along the surfaces across which they were spread like cross-stitching. Ellis spun in place, unsure what was happening, what to do, when—

A hand, on their shoulder.

They turned, slowly, and saw their house—the truth of it—for the first time.

The ghastly spectre of Analiese, neither human nor phantom but something else altogether, floated there in front of them, strung from above, able to raise and lower herself from within the structure like a skeletal marionette. Her eyes were sockets—deep absences of humanity; her skin, if it could be called as such, transparent as cellophane.

Her heart, peeled into thousands upon thousands of tiny and tinier-still strands, strung across her front, suspending in place as if a net. A shield.

A harp, grotesque and impossible.

Ellis felt their insides plummet to their feet, their courage evaporating in an instant. "Analiese," they said again, their voice little more than a frightened whisper.

"I'm not what—"

"I know." Then again, with certainty: "I know."

"It's coming," she said, voice growing full, given weight. A chorus—all of them, every soul within these walls speaking through her at once. "It's coming, and I can't stop It."

"What? What's coming?" Ellis asked, though they already knew.

"Death."

PART FOUR:

HEART STRUNG

*T*here had been a finality to Death's farewell that Analiese found herself unable to quantify. She felt different now. As if something new had been granted to her. Everything was suddenly clear. Vivid. The world seemed to have caught pace with her at long last, or she with it.

With great difficulty, she pulled herself away from the wall to which her heart strings had fastened her. She realized: she didn't know if she were alive or dead. She could still feel her body, frail and stretched, but she felt larger than it too. She felt taller and more in tune with the Earth than any person had ever been, or so she assumed; she could feel, through her toes, the dirt beneath the house's concrete foundation; the soft patter of rain on the tiles above.

When she clutched her fist around a stalk of heart strings, right to their base, she not only heard their twinned souls but also saw them too: the people—the families who'd come and gone in the years of Death's "lesson"; the pieces of themselves they'd left behind in boxes of trinkets and clothes and whatnot, there, in her cellar, because they either couldn't take such details with them or wouldn't. Perhaps they wanted to forget, to move on, to leave behind entire memories, like gravestones in a cemetery no one visits.

She wanted to go there, to the cellar, to see their memories for herself, but she couldn't. As her heart strings multiplied, her body *was increasingly tethered to the structure that surrounded her; the more she tried to move the harder the house seemed to want to keep her in place, stationary, of the house, not separate.*

She felt this when she pulled too forcibly on any one strand—Death hadn't linked her to the house so much as It had linked the house to her: it was no longer a mere piece of property; the house was her and she was it—not one a part of the other but mutual, a whole new entity. A whole new way of being. What that meant, truly . . . well, that was the question most in need of an answer.

An answer, she thought, she would only find if she learned how to move through her new existence. To be whatever she now was.

She tugged on the strings some more. This hurt her heart, or what remained of it, ached like fingernails being yanked free. But she continued to pull, continued to struggle against her confines, not to break the bonds but to perhaps stretch them as one would any muscle. She would stretch them and continue stretching them until she was able to walk forward again, out of her room—her tomb. Then she'd try again, inching farther. She would learn how to navigate this house as she had when it was just a home. A forever house. Their forever house.

She would learn to be herself once more, however that self was to be redefined.

It is time.

It is time.

It is time.

Over and over Death had said this to her, to try to coax her into acquiescence, to convince her she'd had enough of existence. And, repeatedly, she'd denied It. She'd denied Death Itself and remained to tell the tale—though to whom she didn't know. The people currently living in her house? Absolutely not—they were a kind family,

278

devoutly religious. She feared what might happen were she to appear to them out of nowhere.

If she could appear to them, that was. She still hadn't figured out how to accomplish such a thing—she was still working on moving from one room to another without her insides feeling as if they were being forced outside of her, a skeleton stripped of skin.

It's time, she told herself, mocking Death, whenever she tried to reach farther than she had. Time to reclaim her individuality, to retake her space. Her home.

She practised by reminding herself, every time, what it would feel like, how her heart seemed to wind itself up again when she returned to the bedroom and unravel when she left, the sensation similar to a loose flap of skin around a nail bitten too far back.

It hurt, every time; however, she eventually got used to the pain. Grew to dread it less like a wounding and more like a necessary discomfort.

It is time, she said to herself months into this training, when for the first time since Isabelle's death she went downstairs and joined her now family, her current family, for Sunday night dinner. She watched them from the walls. Listened. She could feel them: their love for one another, their feet on her floors, their bodies as they leaned against her walls.

She felt their sorrow too. The change in how they moved when their second child, a son, died in a car accident on his seventeenth birthday. And she felt anger, knowing that he'd died several blocks away but still in town. She wanted to pull out another string of her heart then, to preserve even a piece of him, but she couldn't; she couldn't reach far enough outside her confines to touch even a part of him, beyond what shadows remained in memory, boxed up and abandoned in her cellar.

For months Analiese reached down, deeper and deeper into the earth to just feel; the town, the people in it—everything. She was moving more freely throughout the house now, had learned that she wasn't as confined as she'd previously assumed. She'd had to remind herself: she and the house were one and could move as such. She realized this for the first time when, in a moment of clarity, her hand passed through the wall of her bedroom as if it wasn't even there. She was briefly taken aback but admittedly curious. Unsure what would happen, she slowly moved forward, into the wall, until she'd phased all the way through it to its other side.

She hadn't expected the liminal space between things to allow her the mobility she'd so desired. By phasing through the wall, she discovered she was able to shift from one room to the next with little to no pain or discomfort, simply dropping in from above as if a marionette on a stage. What's more, she was able to see them for what they were: her heart strings, the ends of each tied to the house itself, winding their way through and even into its beams, its support structures, all the way down into the cellar and through the foundation below. She discovered the ends of her strings inching ever forward, continuing through the dirt, extending her presence into the rest of Black Stone. She encouraged this.

She became one with the house to ever-greater extents. To its plumbing, its heating, its electrical systems. She could sense what worked and what didn't, down to the porch light Samir had gone to so much trouble installing but had never gotten around to actually connecting to the rest of the house. It was his "I'll get to it someday, I promise" that he never did get around to—evidence of a life interrupted before its time.

She experienced a jolt then—a shuddering chill she'd not felt in years: Death was in town. It had come for someone—possibly someone she'd known at one time or another.

She wondered who it was, and if they would be all right moving on to whatever was next.

She wondered if Death would treat them well.

She sighed then and felt a charge surge through her that lit up the night outside.

She'd leave a porch light on for them, just in case.

"I'm not what I seem," she said, or tried to say, to everyone who ever lived in the house—in her—but few heard her, and if they did, they did not understand. Those she'd managed to get through to appeared to be those closest to hardship; they'd lost someone close to them or had tried to hurt themselves. They seemed to want to listen the most—they were receptive.

"I had a feeling," said a young mother, relieved to discover her husband was now a part of their house.

"I'm not surprised," said the trans boy who'd lost his father and mother, and was ready to up and leave, to go and stay with his aunt and uncle two towns over.

"I have no idea what's going on," said a young woman putting their house up for sale after her brother's death from an undiagnosed illness. "But I . . . I trust you. I know he's still here, and that you'll take care of him."

He was, and she would, Analiese assured her, assured them all when they took what remained of their lost loves and placed them one after another in the cellar.

As more of her denizens passed on, Analiese felt her heart begin to grow again. To expand and become full. She no longer felt like she was being unwound when she pulled at yet another piece of her. She could move more freely now. Grow. Travel. Stretch past all previous limitations.

She sensed them, the entire town, as she pushed her heart strings far beyond the house, beyond her property, all the way beneath Cherry Lane and farther still.

She got to them, too, before Death. She listened, knowing better than anyone the signs of a spirit failing, its shell withering away. She waited with the dying in their houses and apartments and hospital rooms. She listened to their goodbyes; their confessions; their prayers, possibilities, and promises left unfulfilled, and she brought them into herself without judgment or reservation. Strung herself death by death until she'd reached the town's outermost edges. Until she'd filled her new body to the brim so that when she strummed the harp of her, she heard not a choir but a city. She saw them, too, wandering her halls, passing through and around one another. The dead that wouldn't move on, that no longer had to if they chose not to.

And when she'd reached far enough, when she'd grown too full, she opened her doors and allowed the dead to return to their homes; to continue as though they still lived, leaving neither footprints nor obstacles but there all the same. She saw them, and others did too. Townspeople. The still-living. They didn't even know what it was they were seeing; didn't know, beyond rumours and hearsay, that theirs was a ghost town, arrested in a state of perpetual half-death.

She'd long since lost track of how many in town were now a part of her, or how far the stories of her had spread, but she knew, fully, completely, that Black Stone was hers, and she it.

She was no afterlife—of this she held no illusion.

What she'd become, she realized, was a haven.

A limbo.

It appeared again one day, Death, wishing to treat with Analiese.

She dropped herself down onto her front porch, her heart now a thousand-point star of voices she wore in front of her like a shield.

She flashed the porch light to warn her charges that their would-be jailer had come and to stay away at all costs.

It unfolded in front of her through a chasm in the air, the winged shape she'd found so uncomfortably familiar, like a vicious lover come to beg, to bargain, to plead for a second, fifth, tenth chance.

It stared at Analiese but said nothing.

"Are you going to tell me it's time?" She spoke pointedly.

Death waved a talon, discarding all pretense. "You have had your fun. I gave you this fiefdom so that you might learn respect, but—"

"But what? Have I reached too far for you?"

"Enough!" Death thundered. "There is no place, here or in any realm, that I do not claim as mine." Death swept forward then.

"No," said Analiese.

It started up the steps; the porch light strobed as if a self-contained electrical storm.

"No!" she said again, louder.

"It is time."

"No!"

Death extended an arm toward Analiese, and she shrieked and the force of her cry launched the Entity off her porch. It dissipated into a cloud that quickly reformed and looked to Its limbs. The concertina wire that had kept them bounded in shape was rusting, crumbling where It stood, the limb itself disappearing, dust blowing away in a slight breeze. Quickly, clutching Itself for protection, Death backed away.

"No," she said again, walking forward, descending the steps until her heart strings allowed her to move no farther.

Death watched in resignation; Its countenance, Analiese assumed, the closest to horror Its empty, icy visage could come. It continued to back away as the ground started to tremble, as tiny angel-hair strands of Analiese began to poke up through the earth, rising, seeking of their own volition. The strands created a perimeter surrounding the house; when Death, awash in fury, tried to breach it, the strands pressed back with as much force as to distort Death's shape, shattering, albeit temporarily, the structure that held Death together, that gave It form.

Death reached out once more and felt a wall where there appeared only air. It tried to press beyond, press through, but was met only with resistance.

Frustrated, infuriated, Death glared at Analiese, standing there in front of her porch, heart strings spread above, below, and behind her. And then past Analiese, to the small legion of ghosts who'd assembled on the porch, behind their ward.

"You gave me this," Analiese said, unforgivingly. "You made me this. I don't know if it was a gift or a lesson, or hubris on your part—perhaps all of the above. But this is your doing." She stared at her hand, at daylight passing through her skin, slicing through her spectral self. "I don't know what you've made of me, but I know now what I've made of myself. I'm not what I seem, but I am what I'm supposed to be. I know that now."

"Stop this," Death said. Its voice was narrow, smaller than Analiese had ever heard.

Analiese stared straight ahead. "It is time," she said, flatly.

"Analiese . . ."

"It. Is. Time. Go. Go now, and never return. This town is mine. Its people my charges. They are lost to you."

Death stared her down, but she did not flinch. Briefly, she reached up, clutched a grouping of heart strings for support. Death turned then, and she let loose a sigh of relief.

Very suddenly, Death spun back around, expanded to Its full, terrifying scale—a maelstrom personified—and dove at her like a missile.

Analiese screamed "NO!" in concert with every one of her flock. The sound that erupted from them was enough to obliterate the spectre of Death, leaving only a thin contrail of smoke where It had escaped hurriedly through a fissure into nothingness.

Analiese remained in place, a sentinel, until she felt a grateful hand on her shoulder. Then another. Soon, dozens, wanting to pull her from the moment, from the battle; to return her to the house, her chassis.

She waited, then, for the next family to join her. For their pain to become hers. Their love too.

She waited, watchful for Death, awaiting Its next play.

She waited.

PART FIVE:

MAELSTROM

CHAPTER
TWENTY-EIGHT

"WHAT CAN I DO?" ELLIS ASKED FOR THE THIRD TIME, STARING up as they darted from room to room, following the erratic Analiese as she dropped herself in and out of every room in the house. She moved frantically, unsure where to go, what to do to prevent what she knew was on Its way, what she could feel reverberating throughout her every rafter like terror through a spine.

"No," they heard her mutter from the kitchen, then the hallway, the living room, and main bedroom: "No, no, no, no, no ..."

"Analiese!" Ellis shouted. They turned a corner and were once more face to face with the ghost of Analiese's daughter. She shook her head at Ellis. Her face was stricken with concern, her features long and sallow.

"Izzy," Ellis said. "Isabelle."

"Help us," she said softly.

"How?" Ellis asked. They could still hear Analiese moving about upstairs, travelling between rooms with terrific speed. They wondered if she did this all the time and they simply hadn't—*couldn't have* seen or heard, or if, only now, with Death so close, she'd finally elected to reveal herself. *Why now?* Ellis thought. *Why me?*

"Protect her," came another voice, next to Ellis. They turned to find an older white man there, one of their neighbours from up the street they recalled waving hi to in the evenings and on cloudy days when the sun was—

"Protect the house," said another, appearing to the left of the first young woman. A small Black boy with a very familiar set of eyes.

"Trey . . ." They looked around then, not to the house or to the now-visible plethora of heart strings woven across, through, and around every surface, but to the other ghosts, dozens and more appearing out of thin air, phasing through the walls—approaching the house, Ellis realized, catching sight of a number of familiar faces they'd seen throughout town, people they'd never imagined were dead, from all over Black Stone. They appeared to solidify, all of them, as the skies outside darkened further. As the maelstrom, like an eye wreathed by apocalypse, bore down upon them, intensifying, growing blacker and fiercer with each passing moment.

Soon, Ellis was surrounded by a house teeming with afterlives. The truth of Black Stone—its history laid bare.

"I want to help," Ellis said to the gathering of ghosts, "but I don't know how."

"She can't stop," said Trey, glancing up at the creaking, splintering sounds of Analiese spidering herself from room to room. "She wants to help, but she can't control herself. She's taken on too much."

Izzy nodded in agreement. "She's spread too thin. That's how It will hurt her; It'll cut her back until only this place is left." She paused. "It'll take back what It gave her."

"What will happen to you after that?" Ellis asked. "To the rest of us?"

A collective silence, shaking heads.

"Not one among us knows," said the neighbour whose name Ellis really wished they could remember. "And not one among us is ready to find out for ourselves."

"But isn't that always the case?" Ellis asked. "You're trying to control something that isn't yours to control."

In a flash, Analiese reappeared, dropping down between Ellis and the various apparitions. "What do you know of control?" she shrieked.

"I—"

"I see more than you can imagine," she said. "What you make, how you are, what you want people to see or not see . . . Who are you to judge me? To judge any of us?"

"I'm sorry." Ellis threw their hands up in an attempt at peace. All eyes were upon them—they wanted to crawl out of their skin. "I'm sorry," they said again. "I'm trying to understand."

Analiese glared for a few seconds, and then, very suddenly, her face changed, anger crumbling into sadness. "I'm . . . I didn't . . ."

Tentatively, Ellis reached out and, watching for any sign of resistance or aversion, put a hand to Analiese's cheesecloth skin. They were surprised when they made contact. They'd expected to pass right through. Whatever she was, whatever she'd been reduced to, she was not a ghost. She wasn't like the rest of them; she was something else altogether. Something even Death hadn't imagined.

"Me too," they said.

Analiese stared tenderly, breaking in several places, skin fractured and unreliable. It looked to Ellis as if it might slough off her at any moment.

"I can't . . ." she started to say. "I can't stop this."

"I know," Ellis said.

She smiled sadly, black hole eyes downturned.

A crack of thunder then, lightning not a half second later.

"That was right outside," Ellis said, frightened.

"It's coming," Analiese said gravely. "It's nearly here."

Ellis opened the front door and stared out at the mostly noiseless storm. "Quinn . . ." They tried texting her, but it would not send. *The storm is affecting things*, they thought, trying not to panic. They tried calling her instead, still no response.

They hung up after the third attempt. Stepped out onto the porch.

"I can't protect you out there," Analiese said. "It's found a way through . . . It's coming. It's coming, and I can't save you."

Ellis faced her. "I know," they said, and walked outside. Immediately they were struck by the utter calm of it all. No wind. Nothing, save the occasional flash of lightning. But the air, indeed their whole world seemed . . . cold. Dead-of-winter cold, but it was still the middle of July.

They went anyway. Hurried down off the porch and started jogging, then running, all the way to the far end of Cherry Lane. Thinking if they hurried, they might outrun Death. If only for a time.

CHAPTER
TWENTY-NINE

TESSA STOOD ONCE MORE AT THE MOUTH OF THE SEWER OUT-
flow. Reece at her side.

"You're sure of this?" she asked, feeling a growing chill in the
air. She was surprised to see her breath in front of her face.

"I am," said Reece. "There's little in this world that fire
won't cure."

Tessa hoisted her bag of supplies onto her shoulder and
climbed into the tunnel, to finish the job she'd started. She stood
just inside, at the tunnel's lip, and turned around. "You're not
coming?"

From outside the tunnel, Reece shook his head. "I've things
to do—things I need to prepare. I'll know when you've suc-
ceeded. I'll know when it's time."

Reluctantly, Tessa started forward on her own. She tried to
keep her thoughts on the task at hand and not on Reece's increasingly unsettling tenor, nor on the bodies of the town's police
officers that she'd had to step over on her way out. Who, like
those at the motel, Reece had referred to as "collateral damage."

*After years spent trapped by the house, he's angry, helpless and in
pain.* He'd suffered who knew how much, all because she had
failed to save him the first time.

No more. She would not fail again.

She trudged forward through the ankle-deep waste, stopping where she had last time: at the even-more red vines—veins—scaling all sides of the pipe and spreading along the ground beneath the water. The tissue was pulsing erratically, as if in a panic; it looked like a trellis overgrown—overwhelmed. She wondered how much of it could be found elsewhere, and how easily; how little people paid attention to a visible infection that had been allowed to spread throughout their town. How they'd let it. How they'd seen only what they wanted to see, or perhaps nothing at all. How oblivious they'd been—and were, still.

Tessa touched one of the veins again, felt it shudder beneath her fingertips. She gripped it, made a fist around it as if handling a snake, and heard a scream, a cry, a *"Please, no!"*

She spun, crouched at the ready, as if prepped for an attack. "Who's there? Reece, is that you?"

When no answer came, she touched another strand, clutched it, squeezed until she heard someone else, inside her head. She couldn't tell if it was just one person or many, but he, she, or they begged her, pleaded with her not to do this.

"To do what?" Tessa shouted. "Who's speaking?"

Again: nothing.

"I'm losing my mind." She shut her eyes to still her racing heart. Reece.

She remembered: Reece. What he'd been through. What she—what *they* had lost. She shook her head. *Enough. It's now or never.*

It's time.

And she unzipped her bag and reached inside. Pulled out a lighter and a can of hairspray.

She set the path ahead of her ablaze.

The ground trembled as if a train or subway were rattling underfoot. James steadied himself, as did the others, still standing in a circle around their hastily constructed pentagram of twigs. A thing, he realized, that looked a great deal more ominous back when they were sixteen.

"It's okay," he said unconvincingly. "It's fine."

"Fine?" Connie shouted. "What the hell about any of this feels fine?"

"It's just a little earthquake."

"Yeah?" Lucas pointed directly overhead, at the inverted dark clouds—an eye swirling menacingly above. "What's that then, just a little inclement weather?"

"Are we close?" cried Betany. "Can we go home now?"

"Does anyone else feel that?" asked Eleanor.

"The literal ground moving beneath our feet?" said Lucas, sliding between snide and panicked. "Yeah, we all fucking feel it, Lea."

Eleanor stared at her arm then, at the tiny hairs there sticking up on end, standing straight as if they were about to walk right off her arm. "No, I mean—"

A flash then, in perfect to-the-millisecond synchronicity with its accompanying boom, blinding the lot of them. When their eyes adjusted and they could see again, Eleanor was on the ground, cinched into a fetal position.

Dead.

"Lea!" Betany screamed and ran over to her.

James watched as the rumbling continued. He thought, just maybe, he could hear what sounded like animals screeching underground, beneath their feet—or people, an entire community of them, suffering, crying out.

Another flash of lightning and Betany crumpled to the earth, taken before she could make it to Eleanor's corpse.

"Jesus Chr—" Lucas started before he, too, was cut down.

Connie stared at James, terrified. "I always knew stupid shit like this would get me—"

And then she was gone, on the ground with the rest of them, their bodies and the grass and leaves that surrounded them darkened, singed.

And James watched, nervously, for some indication his end was coming. He didn't know if time would slow, if his life would flash before his eyes.

He certainly didn't know what to make of the fissure that appeared in front of him like stygian lightning, or how quickly a blackness of a degree he'd never imagined—not even in the deepest parts of space—poured out of it, how easily it passed through him, taking from him and from the world everything that ever was or could have been. How simultaneously quick and elongated the moment would be—impossibly so.

And how familiar. Like family. Like Reece.

Like Chrissie.

An open door, at last.

Death experienced a freedom, a sense of fullness It had not experienced for nearly fifty years. What should have been a blip in the enormity of time, in Its awareness, became instead a slow, arduous trial. Death experienced things It never had, never thought It could: anger, rage, and . . . longing of a sort It didn't comprehend. Hadn't. Now, though, Its freedom restored, It finally did. It existed once more in every corner, every molecule of Black Stone. No longer was it relegated to mere observation. So many were past due. So many had been allowed to go on shadow-living for far too long, thinking they were beyond Death's reach. Thinking they were above It.

No more. Had Death the capacity for humour, It would have found delight in how a simple human ritual could be so powerful. But then, if It had learned one thing over the course of eternity, it was this: the single greatest threat to humanity was humans themselves.

And Black Stone was a delicacy Death had been denied for far too long.

Today, It would feast. It would be sated.

It would raze this defiant town to the ground.

Standing in the middle of the street two over from Cherry Lane, Ellis steadied themself as the ground shuddered and rolled beneath them. They glanced to their sides; all around them, houses started to crumble—porches caving in, paint peeling, growth overtaking them suddenly. It wasn't the shaking, they realized, that was causing them to fall apart; it was a glamour in the process of being shed, revealing their true, aged natures—disrepair evident now like death and decomposition. Theirs was a town of ghost houses, Ellis realized. More than they could have imagined. Analiese had done much more than simply keep certain citizens here after death; she'd resurrected a dying town. And whatever was happening here, it seemed as if it was happening all over.

Ellis's phone started to vibrate. They answered without checking caller ID. "Quinn?"

"El, honey, are you all right?"

Shit. "I'm okay, Mom. Where are you?"

"I'm at work." She was speaking loudly—Ellis could hear panic in her voice. "There's something's going on here. There's a horrible storm outside. People are panicking, and I thought . . . I thought I saw someone vanish like they weren't even—"

"I know, Mom. I know what's happening."

"You do?"

"It's the house, Mom. It's *our* house."

"Oh, Ellis, don't start that again. This is not the time to—"

"I'm being serious! I . . . Quinn and I, we found the key. We went into the hatch."

"El, I don't— How did you—"

"Look, just . . . I need you to listen to me, okay? There's a whole lot going on in this town, and it all started with our house—with what's beneath it. With what it is. Our house, I mean. It's . . . it's not what we think."

"Ellis—"

"You know this—I know you know this!"

"Kiddo, you're not making any sense. Are you home?"

"I am. Absolutely." Just then, an ambulance went wailing by. They tried to cup their hand over the mic but were too late.

"You want to try that lie a second time?"

Ellis sighed. "I will be soon. And you should be there too. If what they've said is true, it's maybe the safest place in town right now."

"They? They who?"

"Our ghosts, Mom. Whatever's happening right now, they're at the heart of it. Reece Sweet too. He's involved. And I think it's—"

"El . . . we need to talk," she said, voice laced with a frightened concern. "You're not well. I need you to go home. Now."

"I will, there's just—"

"Now, Ellis!"

"No!" Silence on both ends then as the world continued to rumble. "Mom, I will go home, I swear to you, but there's something I need to do first."

"Ellis, I—" But they ended the call before she could continue. They'd catch hell for it, they knew it, but this couldn't wait. They tried calling Quinn again. Heard her phone ringing nearby and were just about to shout her name when she came running around the corner at the end of the street.

"Quinn!" They ran up to her and hugged her tight. "Are your parents—"

"They're fine," she said, voice trembling. "Ellis, a bolt of lightning hit only a few feet from me, only it wasn't white, it was— *What is going on?*"

Ellis grabbed her hand, and together they hurried back toward the house. "I'm not sure," they said, "but I think . . . I think It's going after Analiese's heart. You know, the veins, or strings, or whatever they are."

"What's *It*?"

And Ellis hesitated, still trying to accept the absurdity, the enormity of what they were about to say. "It's Death. Death is coming for the house. For her."

Quinn jammed on the brakes, yanked her hand free. "And you want to go back there?"

"We've got to help her if we can."

"Right, but . . . do we?"

Ellis stared, confused. "What do you mean?"

Quinn pointed up at the void eye glaring down at them. "All of this, it's because of her. Analiese. Because of what she refused to do."

"No, it's because of Death."

"But Death's just a force of nature. We can't defy It. No one can."

"Analiese was able to."

"No, Death tried to punish her, or . . . maybe It took mercy on her. I don't know. She was only able to *defy* Death because Death fucked up."

"If not for her, you'd never have seen Trey again."

"Yeah, and because of her I might lose the rest of my family!" She wiped tears from her eyes. "We might be about to die, Ellis. Because of her. If she'd gone along with Death when she was supposed to, none of this would be happening right now. We'd be free of this."

"Yeah, well sometimes Death needs to be fucking defied, okay? Sometimes . . ." They realized, as they shouted, they'd been clutching their stomach, kneading it nervously. They stopped. "Sometimes you think you're ready for it, or maybe you don't but you know it's there, this . . . possibility in the back of your brain like the absolute shittiest, most BS option on a multiple-choice exam. And maybe you just need to tell it to go fuck itself."

Quinn put one hand to Ellis's cheek; her eyes were large and wet as she fought back tears. "You don't think I want that? You don't think I'd give literally anything to wind the clock back and give myself, my parents, even one more day with Trey?"

Ellis turned out of her hand, ashamed. "I didn't—"

"Maybe in the beginning this was some beautiful, powerful stance she was taking; maybe Analiese thought she was only hurting herself. But it's a war now. It's like some messed-up, devastating lover's quarrel, and all of us are caught in the crossfire."

"I know." Ellis sighed. "And you're right. But . . . I can't just let her die. Let them all disappear like that."

"But that's what the dead are supposed to do. Aren't they?"

Ellis shook their head. "Not if there's something I can do to help."

"But Ellis . . . she's already dead."

"She's not. Not entirely."

"How do you know?"

Deep breath. "I saw her. I spoke with her."

Quinn's eyes widened. "What? When?"

"Just after you left. She's like a puppet held in place by her heart strings. Some part of her is still holding on to this . . . this plane, or place, or whatever. She said she could protect us if we stayed in the house."

"I don't know that I feel safe there right now, not with everything that's—"

A flash of lightning then—a strike only ten feet away. Singed grass just to the side of the road.

Ellis stared at her. "As opposed to being out here?"

"Good point." She took their hand and they hurried back together.

———

Tessa was dripping with sweat; it stung her eyes, soaked through the collar of the too-large shirt she'd stolen from a dead woman at a motel what felt like a lifetime ago now. It was singed in spots, on the sleeves and down by the hem, where she'd been less-than-accurate with her torching.

She backed away from the flames, dropped the now-empty spray can in the water at her feet. The tunnel ahead of her was yellow and orange and red, a flickering, overwhelmingly hot burn travelling through the sewers, the fire tracing a line all the way back to its point of origin. Above her, all around her, Black Stone was shuddering.

Tessa breathed a sigh of relief. Whatever was happening needed to happen. He'd be free now. All of them—anyone taken by that house would soon be free.

"It's done," she whispered to herself.

"It's not," said a voice.

"It doesn't have to be," said another.

"You can stop this," said a third.

"Who's there?" Tessa shouted. She spun around. In the dark of the tunnel, she could just see . . . body parts. Torsos and arms and legs, but no heads. Then, as the fire behind her started to recede, as it travelled farther down the tunnel, away from them, and the world ahead of Tessa began to dim, she started to see more clearly what was there with her.

In front of her, twelve, maybe fifteen people, young and old and all points between. Some she thought she recognized but wasn't sure—her memories from so long ago seemed a dream to her now, something only partially recalled, lost soon after waking. Though they seemed solid, real, bits of them flitted away here and there with the continued flickering of flames—a piece of a cheek here, an eye, an ear there. Only when the tunnel was at its darkest did Tessa see them in their entirety. She flicked on her lighter and held it an inch from the nearest person, a young boy who looked about Reece's age. The flame seemed to slice a streak right through him. She stepped back and put her lighter away, and the apparition appeared to solidify.

"Who are you?" she asked.

"You can stop this. You can still save us."

"Save you? Who are you?" she asked again, louder this time.

The group responded in unison:

"We're your friends."

"We're your family."

"We're Black Stone."

"This is our home."

"You're *killing* our home."

"*You're damning us.*"

Tessa shook her head. "No . . . no, I'm freeing you. All of you. You don't have to stay here any longer."

"We want to."

"We've been given a second chance."

"No!" Tessa shouted, clutched the sides of her head. "Reece! Reece, where are you? I need you!"

"He's not coming."

"He never will."

"He's moved on."

"He was never—"

"Stop it!" Tessa screamed. "Show me my brother. Reece, help me!"

"He can't," said the boy at the very front. "He was never here. She never had him."

"Who never had him?"

"The house. Analiese. He was never hers."

"No. He was mine." A thunderous echo from farther down the tunnel. The people—the ghosts, Tessa now realized, were swept away by a column of night that suddenly filled the space, blocking off its exit, the world beyond. Its voice was sonorous, ghastly. But beneath the swirl of aural chaos, a familiar note:

". . . Reece?"

"Is gone," Death said from within the dark. "He was always gone."

Over her shoulder, Tessa watched the consuming fire. "Then, all this . . ."

Death approached her, moving like smoke. "All this was necessary. This place was stolen from me. You've helped me restore things." It extended from Its largely shapeless mass a single column resembling an arm bounded by razor wire. "I'll remember this."

"No." Tessa started to cry. "Please don't." She shut her eyes.

"You can't know what you know. I can't let you live. It'll be over before you know it. I swear it." Death lunged forward then, engulfing Tessa in Its contrails, and—

Nothing happened.

She opened her eyes again in the centre of the storm cloud that should have taken her from this world but couldn't. She felt it swirling around her, frigid air, like how she imagined Antarctica might be, but . . . nothing.

It took shape again, a black, angry vortex confined to the narrow passageway, and screamed—bellowed—shook the entire world, it seemed to Tessa, with a voice like symphonic cannon fire. And for a split second, before it dissipated altogether, she thought she could see him.

Reece, at the centre of the cloud. A part of it but never a part of her. Never with her. She knew this now. She'd been lied to. Yet . . . she wasn't dead. She should be, so why—

She noticed it then, a small, slick something tugging at her leg. She glanced down and saw a single charred red vine wrapped around her ankle. She felt it . . . beating, through her—through all of her. A warmth like summer. Like protection.

She heard them then. Those who'd been there with her in the tunnels. Those up above, in the house, throughout the entire town. She heard them: their lives, their loves, their deaths, and their fears of what lay beyond. She heard them and knew, in that moment, her soul swan diving into the deepest pit of her stomach, that she'd betrayed them.

She watched then as the vine that had saved her life slowly uncoiled itself from around her leg and fell into the water, where it dissolved into ash. She peered down the tunnels heading toward the true centre of town and could see, barely, the fire still racing along the vines, devouring them, erasing them from beneath all of Black Stone.

And she asked herself, "What have I done?"

CHAPTER
THIRTY

ELLIS RISKED A GLANCE SKYWARD AS THE TWO OF THEM hurtled toward the house. The maelstrom was centred directly overhead, a funnel cloud ready to strike down upon Analiese with the fury of nature unbounded.

"Oh god," Quinn said. "Are we— Is it going to come down on us?"

"The house or the storm?"

"Take your pick."

Ellis kept running, pulling Quinn across the lawn, which was rapidly turning brown, from its outer edge in. They raced up the front steps, which aged and crumbled beneath their feet, stopping only when they were on the porch. They opened the door then and—

Quinn let go of Ellis's hand, skidded to a stop. In front of them, just inside the front door, appeared the alarming upside-down harp of heart strings suspending a dead-but-not-really Analiese.

"Ellis . . ."

"It's okay," Ellis said, gently taking her hand again and leading her across the threshold. Quinn's eyes were on Analiese the entire time, as if the house's caregiver—persona?—were an oversized spider who might leap forward at the slightest provocation.

Analiese watched her, too, or so Quinn thought while staring into the twin absences of light where Analiese's eyes should have been but most definitely were not.

Ellis stared up at Analiese. "It's happening," they said as the ground shook again. "It's coming right now, isn't it?"

Analiese's face twisted in pain. She screamed and a series of heart strings crumbled, right in front of them, flaking away like ash off the end of a cigarette. Her body fell with a jolt, dropping several inches. Both Ellis and Quinn jumped back.

"What's going on?" Quinn asked.

Analiese raised one arm through some of her many still-intact heart strings, watched then as they faded, became charred. They fell apart in her hands, turned to dust before they even made it to the ground. She made a fist around several others, shut her eyes, and listened to them, clung to them until they, too, were gone, and she slipped down farther, dropping even closer to the ground.

"I can't . . ." she said. "I'm losing . . . they're being ripped from me."

"What can we do?" asked Ellis.

"Uh, El? You should take a look at this."

Ellis left Analiese to obsess over her fading heart strings. They went over to Quinn, who was standing by the window, staring out into the street. Ellis opened the door and went out onto the porch.

Coming down Cherry Lane, they saw Dominik with maybe twenty others, all people—kids and teens, mostly—that Ellis recognized from around town. They looked as if they were following the clouds above Ellis's house, the vicious eye centred so perfectly overhead that it looked like one might have spawned the other.

"People were getting scared," Dominik announced as the group got closer. "I told them I thought it'd be safe here. That . . . that your house wasn't what we thought it was."

"The fuck is going on?" Travis Hillcox yelled.

"Has anyone seen my mom?" a boy called out to no one in particular.

"Everyone, inside!" Ellis yelled.

Robyn's car careened around the corner then. She sped toward the end of the street, veering wildly around the approaching group of kids. She pulled into the driveway and had barely cut the engine before she jumped out and ran toward the house.

"El!" she shouted, sprinting up onto the porch and hugging them. She was frantic. "Don't you *ever* hang up on me like that again, do you under—" She stopped then. Stared straight up, past Ellis and through the open door.

To the woman-that-shouldn't-be, the slaughterhouse of a person, an almost-skeleton, suspended in her foyer and pawing at pieces that strung out from her chest, a canopy of gore.

Robyn swept in front of Ellis suddenly, arm out to protect them as she stared down the creature directly in front of her. "You! You're real, you're— You were there when—I was hiding in that closest when you touched me. You touched my shoulder and you said—"

"I'm not what I seem," Analiese muttered sadly.

"I tried to tell. My parents said I was . . . that I didn't know what I . . . *You stay away from my kid!*"

Ellis gripped their mother's outstretched arm. "It's all right, Mom."

"Ellis, you don't know what she—"

"*No!*" Ellis stepped around their mother, positioned themself between Robyn and Analiese. They faced their mother. "I do know. I do, and I promise I'll explain everything. But right now, I need you to just come inside. *Please*," they added, glimpsing the fear in Robyn's eyes at even the idea of getting close to Analiese.

"Ellis, she . . . this *thing*, it . . ." She regarded Analiese again. Cautiously. A sense of awe beneath the dread of it all. "I didn't imagine you. I didn't. They told me I—I thought I was facing my fears by coming back here. I thought . . ."

"Ellis, look!" Quinn was pointing to the porch light, which had grown even more erratic—strobing now with the intensity of a panic attack.

"It's almost here," Analiese wailed.

"What? What's almost here?" Robyn asked. She was shocked, unnerved by Analiese's ability to speak. By the simultaneous depth and frailty of her voice.

"Death," Ellis said, plainly. "Death is almost here."

"Ellis, what are you . . . you're not making any sense." Robyn went silent then, watching past her child's shoulder as a new face appeared rather suddenly—a young boy she didn't know but whose features she saw reflected in Quinn's. "Who . . . ?"

Ellis turned. "Trey."

Quinn looked back. "Trey?"

Trey smiled grimly at Quinn. "She's dying," he said.

"Who?" Quinn asked. Trey pointed to Analiese, who appeared despondent, afraid, slipping farther down from the ceiling with the dissolving and scattering of each and every one of her heart strings.

"Ellis!" Robyn cried.

Ellis turned to their mother again. She sank to the floor as she stared up and all around her in confusion at the filigree of Analiese's heart adorning every available surface.

Ellis knelt in front of her. "Mom, our house is . . . it's haunted. It's been this way for years, decades. But . . ." They paused, glancing to Trey; to Quinn, standing by her brother, wanting to embrace him but knowing she couldn't; to Analiese, watching expectantly. "Not all hauntings are bad. Sometimes . . . sometimes you think a thing's a threat, a danger, like it's got you trapped. Like it's not what you want, not exactly, but . . . you're wrong to treat it like it's your enemy. You're wrong, because it's . . . it's actually protecting you. It's keeping you strong, it's . . . keeping you alive." They ignored the many sets of eyes they felt boring into them at that moment. They wanted, desperately, to be able to tug off the pieces of their body that they hated most, that were too visible, too apparent, they assumed, to anyone paying them even the smallest amount of attention. They wanted to hide. To control what others saw. But they couldn't, and they knew it—and they knew, too, that it was okay. Even if it didn't feel okay. They exhaled deeply and stood up. Reached down and helped Robyn to her feet again.

"Sometimes," they said, "you think something's a prison when really it's . . . it's all you've got. It's your home."

They turned then, glanced over their shoulder and all around them, at Quinn, at Trey; at the people from across town who'd gathered on the porch, many of them watching in stunned silence the strange and disconcerting sight before them.

At the legion of ghosts appearing all around them, pouring out of walls, climbing up from the cellar, approaching from outside and around the house.

As many of Analiese's heart strings continued to contract, to fade, to die small deaths of their very own—as she continued to lose her tethers to the rest of Black Stone, Black Stone had come to her.

The porch light grew brighter, luminous, their very own star—a diamond shining in the dark that swelled and billowed around and above them.

"It's here," Quinn said. She shivered then, a rush of freezing air knifing through the open door.

Ellis peered outside. They could no longer see beyond the edge of their property; it was as if the impossible night had become a wall that cut them off from the rest of the world.

The dark appeared to open down the centre, a vertical incision. And from it poured the Entity, the being Ellis had seen in Its true form only once before. It was twice the size of Its former self and still growing; soon, Ellis thought, It would be taller than the house. It barely bothered with taking a recognizable form, what had previously been wings now vast curtains of absolute nothing, absent all possibility of colour, light, life.

Quinn stood next to Ellis, aghast. She pulled out her phone and turned on the flashlight app. Pointed it directly at the formless thing in front of them; however, instead of sweeping through the Entity the light merely landed on it, disappeared into it. Was swallowed up entirely as if it didn't exist. Death had torn reality asunder. Black Stone would never be the same.

"It's not like a ghost," Ellis said. "It's not something that's there one second and gone the next. Death's here, always, whether we see It or not."

"What do we do?" Quinn asked.

"I don't know." They stood side by side in the doorway, too scared to move. Suddenly, Ellis felt Quinn's fingers interlace with theirs. She squeezed as hard as she could.

They looked directly into her eyes and said, "I love you."

"I love you, too," she said.

From the other end of Cherry Lane, Tessa Sweet stared at the wall of black that appeared to sever the far end of the street from the rest of the town. It was as if she were looking at the literal end of the world, and on the other side of it, a sheer cliff over the edge of which all reason, all sense of reality had plummeted.

But she knew now what existed on the other side of that wall, impossible though it seemed. She knew what a fool she'd been. She'd heard it herself, in her head, when the piece of it had wrapped itself around her—when it had saved her from the same end that had befallen her brother.

Reece.

His name, the very idea of him was an ice pick in her brain. It was clarity—horrible, naked reality. She knew then for certain the thing her parents, her doctors had wanted her to know for twenty-five years:

Her brother was gone. Reece Sweet was no more.

She'd been lied to. She'd done horrible things.

She'd invited Hell itself into Black Stone and had even opened the door for it.

She stared into the dark a moment longer. There wasn't anything more she could do here. There was only a moment—this moment—in which she could escape. Make her way out of town. Out of the area, the entire country if need be. She knew Death would remember her, would come for her when It wasn't so consumed. For now, leaving was all she could do.

There was nothing here for her—she knew that. Not now. Not ever again. But out there ... maybe she could find something.

Maybe she could find a life. A semblance of one, even. A shred. Anything would do. Mercy from Death, at least for a time.

Tessa turned from the darkness and walked away from Cherry Lane. From Black Stone.

Forever.

"Look!" Quinn pointed to the sky. To the maelstrom swirling, segmenting into pieces, forming tendrils—no, *talons*, dagger-like fingers that arced down and toward them. Toward the house. The shapeless Entity in front of them appeared to rise in triumph and expectation, Its tornado-like claws descending as if to grasp each and every one of the townspeople standing there in its county-sized palm. The talons met with the ground, tore vast tracts into the earth and concrete with a grinding, deathly crunch before upending the grass and dirt of their front lawn and closing in around the house, a storm of a cage slowly slamming shut all around them.

Quinn shuddered, squeezed harder. She shut her eyes. "Ellis ..."

"I know." There was so much more they wanted to say to her, so much they feared they wouldn't ever get the cha—

"ENOUGH!"

They both turned and looked behind them. They parted, making space for Analiese, who slowly lowered herself the rest of the way to the floor by what strings remained. She touched her toes to the hardwood with a dancer's grace, hung there a moment before setting down hard and stumbling to her knees, as if she'd forgotten the true weight of gravity.

Both Ellis and Quinn reached down and, setting aside their fears, took her by the arms, mindful of the tender pieces of her heart still stretched taut. With their help, Analiese regained her footing then started forward on her own. Each step was fragile, tentative, as if she were unsure she'd be able to keep herself upright. But she continued forward, one step at a time. Through the open door, down the front steps. Every inch a wince, every step a strain on her already-stretched and tormented insides.

Ellis watched from behind, remaining atop the porch with Quinn and Robyn as Analiese continued out into the dark. As one after another, step by step, the remaining heart strings started to snap free of the house. Still, Analiese kept going, pieces of her trailing behind, a limp and gory curtain fanning the ground like the train of a wedding dress.

She made it to the grass; she felt her body weakening, her transparent skin fading almost entirely, only bits of flesh and tissue left on her skeleton. She reached up, held her remaining heart strings aloft, and listened. She said her goodbyes as her choir left her, one voice after another. *Snap, snap, snap*—and soon only one string remained. She clutched it tighter, as if it were life itself.

"Stay with me," Robyn whispered at Ellis's back. She wrapped her hand around their forearm.

"Stay with me," Analiese said. "Please."

"To the very end," came a voice from behind. Ellis and Quinn turned at the same time and saw the spectre of Isabelle, watching tearfully as Analiese made her way toward the storm.

The three of them—Ellis, Quinn, and Robyn—parted ways as the ghost of Isabelle stepped between them and went out onto the porch to view her mother's final stand against Death.

Analiese, still gripping the final heart string, the second pulled from her all those many years ago—the first now lost to the voices already leached from her memory—came within a foot of the undulating maelstrom and said, dispassionately and with resignation, "You win."

The maelstrom continued to billow angrily, but the talons halted in place. From the darkest depths of the storm, Death appeared, smaller now, familiar, emerging from within as if passing through a shroud lighter than air.

Death stared at Analiese, Its galaxies unmoving, cold.

"You win," she said again as she, at long last, released the very last of her heart. The final string held in place, strained but intact.

Death glared at her. In Its cosmic visage, Ellis wasn't sure if they saw fury or hurt or simply emptiness. The Entity swelled suddenly as if to strike Analiese down. It paused then. Pulled Itself inward ever so slightly. It approached Analiese and, unexpectedly, knelt in front of her.

"It was never about winning." Death's true voice was sonorous, confounding. Robyn clutched the sides of her head while Ellis and Quinn cringed in unison.

"Then what?" Analiese asked. "Punishment? *Compassion?*"

Death said nothing.

"Right."

"You were never meant to be me."

"I never wanted to be. I just . . ."

"I know. But you took something that didn't belong to you."

"You *gave* something you didn't intend."

Death appeared to bristle at that, a fierce, sudden bulge in Its form that faded as quickly as it had occurred. Analiese didn't react; she continued to glare, unfazed, as if to challenge It further. The two stared silently until finally, Death reached out and placed a palm-like thing on the side of her face.

Not punishment, not any longer. This Ellis realized but did not say. No, what they were witnessing in that moment was something else entirely.

"Will . . . will I see her there? Where we're going?"

"I can't tell you that," Death said. "You'll have to find out for yourself."

Analiese turned to the house again. To the family she'd amassed over decades, collected there on the porch, on the lawn, interspersed with the still-living from all around town. Suspended between planes as two forces of nature bartered for clarity, reason. She could hear them no more.

"You'll spare them? If I go with you?" she said. But Death didn't respond. "Please. I never wanted this to be anything more than a home," she said then to all of Black Stone. "I never wanted to be your death." She faced the Entity again. "I'm ready," she announced, and reached up one last time.

"I love you, Mom," whispered the ghost of Isabelle, in front of Ellis. "We'll see each other again. We will."

And Analiese ripped the final heart string from her chest.

She collapsed suddenly, sapped of all remaining strength, and fell into Death's waiting embrace.

The winged being that had first visited her all those many years ago. It stroked her cheek and spoke to her with a tenderness that surprised Ellis:

"It is time."

Ellis watched, a sense of awe as the talons shrank and, instead of closing in around the house, instead of taking them all, circled the twin forms of Death and Analiese. They narrowed in around them, becoming a single spire that was then enveloped by the wall of pure darkness that had blocked them off from the rest of the town.

At long last, Analiese had moved on.

The wall of night dissolved then, revealing to them the rest of Black Stone and beyond, and the collection of townspeople from all around who'd made their way to Cherry Lane to see what was happening for themselves.

They were alive, all of them. Death had taken Analiese but spared the rest. Their war had ended.

Quinn saw her parents coming down the street, holding one another. When the last of the veil had lifted, they sprang toward the house, hand in hand. They stopped suddenly, frightened and apprehensive at the sight of Analiese's ghosts, together on the porch, a chorus line of things—people—that should not have been.

And at the centre of them, to Quinn's right, the son they thought they would never see again.

Quinn instinctively reached for Trey's hand, but she couldn't touch him, couldn't take him with her. She looked down at him as he stared back up at her, and she knew: this was it. This was the very end of the road.

Ellis noticed it, too, how as the darkness evaporated and daylight once more filtered down onto their tiny corner of the world; how the ghosts, Analiese's flock, started to vanish. This time, they suspected, for good. Ellis held Quinn tight in their arms as she shuddered, whispering goodbyes to Trey that were meant for the two of them and only them.

Trey told her it was okay, he'd be okay, he'd see her again someday. He believed it.

And then he was gone.

Quinn buried her face in Ellis's shoulder and wept. They comforted her until her parents reached the porch and took over for Ellis, told her it would be all right. They had questions, so many, but they could wait.

Ellis, too, felt a hand on their shoulder. They turned into a hug and let out every last bit of emotion they'd managed to keep to themself until exactly that moment.

"Shh," Robyn said as Ellis cried. "It's okay, kiddo. It'll all be okay." She glanced up then; she and Cynthia caught sight of each other and shared a knowing nod.

Ellis lifted their head from Robyn's shoulder. They stared into the house, and then out toward the empty space on the porch where Isabelle had watched her mother's final moments. "I have so much I want to tell you." They pulled the small silver key from their pocket and handed it to her. "There's so much you need to see. It's not just a house," they said. "It's a story."

Behind them, the porch light went out.

EPILOGUE

"I GUESS . . . I DON'T KNOW WHAT'S NEXT," ELLIS SAID, STARING AT the open laptop in front of them.

Dr. Webb sat up straight. "How do you feel about that lack of knowing?"

Ellis thought for a moment. "Good, I think. It's a change."

"It's a lot more than a change, Ellis. Giving up control to that degree, it's a risk. What's more, it's growth. I'm proud of you."

"Thanks, Doc. Couldn't have made it this far without you."

"But you did, Ellis. *You* made it this far. All I did was help light the way."

"I know, but still, thanks."

"You're very welcome." She offered a warm, assuring grin.

"So . . . how does it work now?"

"Now? We play it by ear. We've done the work, and now it's up to you to apply it. Not just here and there but in your daily life. Do you think you're ready?"

Ellis nodded. "I do."

"And if you need me—"

"I know. You're just a phone call away."

Dr. Webb nodded. "Good luck, Ellis. I'll be thinking of you."

"Bye, Dr. Webb."

In the hours and days following Analiese's departure, fear and panic spread as people learned the full truth of Black Stone. What had made it so special. Many houses thought well-kept, iconic of their community, turned out to be mere shells of their former selves, having, in the wake of their owner's deaths and belated disappearances, fallen into disrepair and decrepitude. Many citizens, too, previously thought of as quiet, upstanding residents, were themselves revealed to be a fiction rooted in the memory of what once was. Analiese, it was now known, had done a lot more than provide a safehouse for the dead; she'd fed their town, unwilling to let it die even a little bit. She'd provided a canvas onto which her flock had painted their desired reality. Many had known pieces of her story, and had believed here and there, when it made sense to them, but there were few in town who weren't, to some degree, shocked as to the extent of her influence.

And then there were those who'd always feared the house. Those for whom their terror, their mistrust felt suddenly, intensely, justified. The rumours had been true, they'd realized, or parts of them had; the dread they'd whispered among themselves was reasonable, their worst fears realized. They didn't care that Analiese had never been a threat to them or their loved ones. For them, it was a simple equation: there were things in their town they could not comprehend, and what they could not comprehend, they could not trust.

For them, Analiese's house, the Lang residence they now called it, was a thing to watch with some measure of concern. To observe from afar. Dominik—living now with his aunt and uncle on the other side of town—and others now worked to push against this fear, and would continue to do so, but it was clear that many in town, like Travis Hillcox and others who'd lost family during Analiese's final stand, would not, could not be swayed from their convictions, no matter how ill-founded. That they had discovered such chaos on their doorstep—bodies dead in two police cars and in an ambulance with *Jackson-King* on the side found just outside of town; Death's work, to keep Tessa on task—had only added fuel to their fears.

In the weeks to come, after the shock of what happened had worn off and people had said their goodbyes to friends and family they'd not known they had to say farewell to in the first place, Black Stone started to rebuild. It would recover, the mayor promised to a small crowd gathered at City Hall, because theirs was a town that had defied Death Itself—surely, they could keep themselves alive and limping along if only they pulled together.

"It probably wasn't a good idea to lean on that whole 'defying Death' angle," Robyn said the day following the mayor's speech, when an op-ed in the *Black Stone Examiner* called it a grave error in judgment and suggested the town keep an exorcist on retainer at all times, "just in case."

Ellis sat across from her, two plates of pad Thai between them at the same restaurant they'd eaten at upon their arrival in town. "Yeah, well, being the mayor of a modern-day ghost town has got to be a weird kind of novelty." Which was, they'd learned, the message that had spread to the world beyond. In little time, Black Stone was simultaneously a laughingstock and a curiosity—a brand-new entry on haunted travel itineraries nationwide: an actual ghost town. A corpse community. A treatise on the death of the working class. Robyn joked about turning the house into an Airbnb when Ellis moved out: "It's a lot of space for just me, and besides, who wouldn't want to stay in a haunted house?"

"*Formerly* haunted," Ellis reminded her.

However things were described in the paper or by others, Ellis was grateful for one thing: what happened at the house had helped Robyn process a great many things she'd repressed for far too long. That night, after the chaos of it all, when the town had cleared out and it was just Robyn and Ellis, she'd sat with them on the living room floor of their house and revealed what had happened the last day she'd spent with Reece. They'd been playing backgammon in the house, and rather than lose, Robyn had stolen Reece's dice and hidden herself in the hall closet upstairs. While there, laughing to herself and listening for Reece, she'd heard something. She didn't know for sure, but she thought she'd heard a voice. That it had tried to tell her something.

"I'm not what I seem," Ellis supplied.

Robyn nodded and continued with her story. "That's when I felt it—a hand on my shoulder. Except when I looked, there was no one there. But I knew it, I knew that's what it was."

"It was Analiese. She was reaching out."

"God, I ran out of there so fast. Reece had no idea what had happened. I wanted to tell him but I . . . I couldn't. I was afraid he'd think I was crazy or something."

"Why?"

"Because my parents did. I tried to tell them. They said . . . they told me I had too active an imagination. That I shouldn't make things up. That no one liked a girl with an active imagination." She shook her head. "They were always like that. Whenever I needed them to believe me, they . . ."

She didn't finish, but she didn't have to. Ellis had known from an early age not to ask about their grandparents. Some things were left unsaid for a reason.

She'd not gone back to the house, not as a child anyway. Not before the day they moved in. When Ellis asked why she felt so pulled to purchase it if it had been the source of so much pain, she said she wasn't entirely sure. Maybe she wanted to prove to herself that what she'd experienced was real. Or wasn't. Or maybe she just felt she needed to be there.

"Or maybe," she said in a moment of introspection, "it's because it took something from me. After that day, I didn't speak to Reece again. Not really. I was too afraid. And then . . . It wasn't long after that, he died." She paused. "I lost the last days with my friend because I was afraid of this place. And now, maybe a piece of him is here with us."

Ellis noticed then, staring across the table as their mom read the paper in the restaurant, a small story on the back of a page: a manhunt called off for a woman who'd escaped from a mental health facility several weeks back. They sighed. They hadn't met Tessa Sweet, not officially, but she'd clearly suffered as much as anyone in this battle. They hoped that wherever she was, she was okay. That Death would be kind to her.

Ellis heard as much when they came home, a week to the day after Analiese's disappearance, and found Robyn and Quinn's mother, Cynthia, sitting out on the porch with a couple of glasses of bourbon. Ellis didn't stick around long—the two of them deserved the chance to reconnect in private—but they did overhear them discussing past times and old friends, names like Ollie and Theo and Spencer. And Tessa too. They knew her. Had known her. They spoke about her with some measure of sorrow; they knew what she'd been through.

And they knew as well as Ellis that Tessa deserved the same chance as they did, as their town. She deserved a fresh start.

And then it was January. Six months after the standoff with Death, Black Stone seemed almost *normal*, Ellis thought, dressed in a heavy wool coat and standing on the new porch they'd helped to build. It wasn't a sensation they were particularly used to—they weren't even sure they trusted it, not fully—but it was nice. After all they'd been through, the lives Death had taken that day in anger, "nice" was a balm as worthwhile as any currency. It was the stock they would trade in for as long as they possibly could.

"Hey!"

Ellis watched as Quinn got out of her car, which she'd parked behind Robyn's in the driveway. It was a vomit-green two-door crime against the environment she'd picked up for a song with the money she'd made over the summer working at the Rialto. It wasn't much, but it got her to and from school, and that's all she needed. She waved as she approached. She wore a long dark purple maxi dress with a pink and black jacket. Her nails were the same shade of pewter as Ellis's. She hopped up the stairs and they kissed.

"How'd it go?" she asked.

Ellis grinned. "Clean bill of health. Periodic check-ins if and when I need them, but for now we're done."

"That's fantastic!"

"Portfolio's coming along too. Still need to figure out what I want to put in it, though. Wanna help?" Together, they went upstairs.

While Quinn had started at Haraway in the fall, Ellis had decided to take a gap year. To save up, to help rebuild the house. And most importantly, to get better. Or to work on it, anyway. And during that time, when they weren't helping with renovations or picking up whatever extra shifts they could at Twitch, they had painted as much and as often as they could.

The interior of Ellis's room was beyond cluttered—every bit of non-sleeping space was filled with canvases. Many were portraits, but not of Ellis.

Quinn sifted through a handful of canvases piled against the closet door. "These are . . ."

"Yeah, a few of them. What I can remember of them, anyway," Ellis said, watching as Quinn flipped through the images they'd painted of the ghosts they'd seen that day. Analiese's charges. At first, they'd only painted Trey, which they gave to Quinn as a present on their three-month anniversary. Since then, however, Ellis had painted or sketched every face they could remember from that day, and others they'd met but not known at the time were ghosts.

They saw then as Quinn flipped past one of their more recent works: one of Andrea Subissati, based on a headshot they'd stumbled across in the yearbook archives at BSH.

"Have you been back to their store?" they asked.

Quinn nodded. "Last week. Alex is doing okay. Mostly, she misses her friend. But she also misses the novelty of it all, running an occult store with an honest-to-god ghost at her side."

"That feels like the plot of some B-tier trash you've yet to force me to watch."

"How dare you—I only subject you to the highest of art."

"Key words there: *subject me to*."

"You love me, and you know it."

"Maybe." Ellis hesitated. "I wonder about it sometimes."

"About what I make you watch?"

"No, about quote-unquote high art. What is and isn't. I don't know . . . Do you think any of these stand a chance?"

She faced them. "If you're asking me whether or not these will get you into art school, I think so. I have faith in you. But whether or not they're high art . . . What does that even mean? Does something have to be capital *A* Art for it to be any good? I don't know, and I don't know who decides that, anyway, or if it even matters." She walked over to them. "Art doesn't have to change the world, El. It just has to speak its piece. Whatever else happens, where it goes from there, that's not up to you." She gently placed a hand on their side. "You just have to let yourself be seen."

Ellis smiled weakly. "If I didn't know any better, I'd think you were trying to comfort me."

"You take that back right now."

Ellis held her then—they held each other.

"You know," she said, "if you do get in, we can drive there together. Maybe even get lost along the way. I can take you on a road trip and not tell you a thing—you'd just have to surrender control to me, fully."

"I'd like that," Ellis said.

"Really? That's a big step for you. You sure you're ready for something like that?"

"With you? Absolutely."

It was then that Quinn noticed an old, weathered-looking sketchbook on Ellis's nightstand. "What else are you working on?" she asked, reaching for it.

"Oh, no, that's not—"

But Quinn had already picked up the book and opened it. She flipped through page after page of quick, furious pencil and ink drawings of Ellis's body from years back—and some that were dated recently, done within the past few weeks. The newer images, she noticed, were cleaner, done with considerably more care and attention to detail.

"What's this?" she asked.

Ellis took the book from her. "I tried to throw it out. I wanted to make a fresh start of my own. I thought that I had to . . . But then I realized: no, I couldn't expect to start new if I ignored who I was or where I'd been." They paused. "You can't cut off a piece of your soul like that and still be you. I couldn't, anyway. It . . . it's my process. It's me—all of me."

"It's your story," she added. Ellis nodded and closed the book.

The two of them left Ellis's room then and walked slowly through the upstairs hallway, mentally documenting the work that remained: the paint and plaster still needing repairs so many months after Analiese had revealed herself to them; had pulled herself, forcefully, from their ceiling, and from the house as a whole.

Ellis told Quinn that for weeks now, since stripping the wallpaper in the main bedroom, Robyn had been sleeping on the living room couch.

"Why?" Quinn asked, and then she saw for herself when Ellis led her into what had been Robyn's room, and Analiese's many years before that, and countless others' in the time between.

What they found there, when they pulled the paper down off the walls to get ready to paint, was an impression: of a body, a woman, pressed against—pressed *into* the wall; and radiating out from her chest, the shadows of what looked like cords or strings arcing out and up, arranged like a harp.

"Analiese," said Quinn.

"Analiese," Ellis echoed.

"What will you do?" she asked.

"Paint it, I suppose. When the moment's right. Maybe after we've had a little more time."

"To do what?"

Ellis reached out and put their palm to the wall. Pressed against its rather cool surface, expecting to feel . . . anything. A flash at best. A pulse—something. They thought of taking a knife then, carving out a chunk of the wall they could fill in later with plaster. To have with them wherever they went after this. A piece of home—theirs and Analiese's.

A talisman.

"To remember."

ACKNOWLEDGEMENTS

BOOKS ARE WEIRD. MAKING THEM IS EVEN WEIRDER.

Initially, it's all fun and excitement—the thrill of a new sandbox in which to play!—but then you start actually writing "the thing" and not just taking notes on an idea, and suddenly you're yanking off one poorly applied mental health bandage after another. Maybe some wounds have managed to heal over the years, so you pick at them a bit, get them to open up and spill out some things you'd rather not deal with again. Except you know you have to. You know it's going to hurt. It's going to be messy, and you're going to be a mess in turn, but you have to do it still. You just do. Because that's where the good shit resides.

And then you do it all over again the next time.

Withered's path to publication has been an unexpected one. It started life over a decade ago as a short story titled "Heart Strung"—the entirety of which is contained within this book, as Analiese's tale. Over time, however, as I dealt with more of my eating disordered past, a larger story started to form around the idea that an object or domicile—or in this case one's body— might feel, to someone struggling with anorexia, bulimia, or any other form of eating disorder or body dysmorphia, as a prison, a thing you wish you could escape at all costs. But your body isn't your enemy; it's keeping you going, keeping you alive, even when you think you're locked in battle with it.

And so, writing this involved addressing a great many past traumas. And the thing is, trauma's a bit like venturing into a haunted house at night: you shouldn't go alone. Fortunately, publishing is a communal experience. No book—no story exists without a small army of people at your side. Yeah, sure, the author's name goes on the cover, but not one of us is an island. We don't get from "idea" to "printed, bound, and sold in stores" without an incredible amount of help, support, and, yes, love.

Starting from the beginning, I need to thank Michael Matheson for being a generous sounding board, and for their sharp eye and care in helping to edit the earliest version of "Heart Strung."

My beta readers Rai Venne, Cary Webb, Alexis Kienlen, Monica Miller, Jenn Weisner, Kinsey Skye, Michelle Bourbonniere, Christina Robins, and Cait Gordon—each and every one of you has helped shape this book, and I am beyond grateful for your assistance.

To Alex West and Andrea Subissati, co-hosts of the *Faculty of Horror* podcast, thank you so much for allowing me to include you in this weird little world of mine.

To Jen Albert and Terese Mason Pierre, who selected this book for publication, I owe a debt of gratitude I will never be able to repay.

To my agent, Kelvin Kong, I am thankful for your support in all things writing and in helping me navigate the absolutely baffling world of contracts—a nightmarish hell for which I will always want and need a guide.

To Jen Albert, Rachel Ironstone, and Lindsay Hobbs, I thank you for your candour, your brilliance, and your attention to detail— together you made the editorial process a joy.

To Ian Sullivan Cant, thank you so much for your brilliant work on the cover—you managed to capture the essence of this book beautifully.

To the ECW crew: Jessica Albert, Sammy Chin, Emily Ferko, David Caron, and Jack David, thanks for all your support.

And to my partner in life, my real-life Quinn, Jaime Patterson, I owe you everything. It was a privilege to imagine what might have been had we known each other back when we were kids. This book would not be what it is without your support, your ideas, and your love.

A.G.A. Wilmot (BFA, MPub) is a writer, editor, and painter based out of Toronto, Ontario. They have won awards for fiction, short fiction, and screenwriting, including the Friends of Merril Short Story Contest and ECW Press's Best New Speculative Novel Contest. For seven years they served as co-publisher and co-EIC of the Ignyte- and British Fantasy Award-nominated *Anathema: Spec from the Margins*. Their credits include myriad online and in-print publications and anthologies. They are also on the editorial advisory board for Poplar Press, the speculative fiction imprint of Wolsak & Wynn. Books of A.G.A.'s include *The Death Scene Artist* (Buckrider Books, 2018) and *Withered* (ECW Press, 2024). They are represented by Kelvin Kong of K2 Literary (k2literary.com). Find them online at agawilmot.ca.

This book is also available as a Global Certified Accessible™ (GCA) ebook. ECW Press's ebooks are screen reader friendly and are built to meet the needs of those who are unable to read standard print due to blindness, low vision, dyslexia, or a physical disability.

At ECW Press, we want you to enjoy our books in whatever format you like. If you've bought a print copy just send an email to ebook@ecwpress.com and include:

- the book title
- the name of the store where you purchased it
- a screenshot or picture of your order/receipt number and your name

A real person will respond to your email with your ePub attached. If you prefer to receive the ebook in PDF format, please let us know in your email.

Some restrictions apply. This offer is only valid for books already available in the ePub format. Some ECW Press books do not have an ePub format for us to send you. In those cases, we will let you know if a PDF format is available as an alternative. This offer is only valid for books purchased for personal use. At this time, this program is not offered on school or library copies.

Thank you for supporting an independently owned Canadian publisher with your purchase!